hatever they were, they were definitely not human.

Revna watched for another half minute. What were they doing here? What *were* they? A hundred questions formed and tried to rise all at once. Incredible.

He licked his lips and focused on one of the alien faces. Some kind of mask it wore, like the others. Breathing gear?

He would go back to town, get some of the ranchers, some photo equipment—

Revna blinked. One of the creatures turned and looked at him. It threw back its head; its long, odd braids fell back. A long, crazy howl filled the canyon, echoed off the cliffs and beat at his ears, joined by others.

Impossible; he was mostly hidden from view, and he could hardly see them with the scope. They couldn't see him.

But they did. He knew for sure in a second:

When they ran toward him, waving those spears, screaming.

Also available from Millennium

Aliens: Earth Hive
Aliens: Nightmare Asylum
Aliens: The Female War
Aliens: Genocide

ALIENS™
VS.
PREDATOR™
P R E Y

STEVE PERRY
STEPHANI PERRY

Based on the Twentieth Century Fox motion pictures,
the designs of H. R. Giger
and the Dark Horse graphic story
by Randy Stradley and Chris Warner.

MILLENNIUM

First published in Great Britain in 1994 by
Millennium
The Orion Publishing Group
5 Upper St Martin's Lane
London WC2H 9EA

Millennium Paperback
Number Twenty-four

ISBN: 1 85798 227 4

For Dianne, and for
the unsung campaign crew who did the work,
from bulk mail stamps to the phones:
Dennis, Ann, Bobbye, Bob,
Gina, Diane, Rosie, Ingrid.
SCP

For six women who saved my life,
my sanity, or a bit of both:
Leslie, Tamara, Dianne,
Gwen, Charlene and Cheryl. Thanks, y'all.
SDP

Thanks this time go to Kij Johnson, for giving us the work—despite all that ugly money stuff that came later. Or didn't come later . . .

Fiend behind the fiend behind the fiend behind the
fiend.
Mastodon with mastery, monster
with an ache at the tooth of the ego,
the dead drunk judge:
Wheresoever Thou art our agony will find Thee
enthroned on the darkest altar of our heartbreak
perfect.
Beast, brute, bastard. O dog my God!

George Barker

1

ell, not to put too fine a point on it, I still think you're full of crap."

Scott smiled to take a little of the sting out, but not that much. They'd dropped out of hyperspace a week back, were running on the new and improved gravity drives, and the old argument had been lit and burning almost since the crew left the sleep chambers. The others were working the plant or attending to ship routine and the two pilots were alone in the control module, staring into the blackness of the Big Deep. Still a few weeks out from their next port, but it was starting to look like a few years.

Tom, whose still-short dark hair had been cropped to his skull before he'd gone into the sleep chamber, was up on his soapbox again, looking kind of like a military-college freshman in free-speak alley.

Scott stroked his blond beard and waited for the reply he knew was coming. Around them, the stale ship air smelled like a gym locker.

Tom didn't miss a beat. "Sure, I'm full of crap. Me and everybody else. But I'm telling you, the bill is gonna come due sooner or later. You can't just keep raping virgin planets, stripping them of everything valuable, and leaving the hulks behind."

"I don't recall that I stuck my dick into the dirt anywhere lately," Scott said.

"You know what I mean."

"No, I don't. *The Lector*, in case you fell asleep during the orientation session, is a tug. We're towing a half-full barge with about fifteen million tons of rendered fish and animal products and the processor that did it to collect *more* meat on the hoof from the poor suckers on Ryushi, a bunch of shit-kicker cowboys—no, not even cows, they're *rhynth*boys—living on a middle-of-nowhere planet."

"Scott—"

"And," he continued, ignoring Tom, "*and* the barge, this ship, the cowboys, *and* you and me are all owned body and soul by the Corp. Talk to old man Chigusa with your raping-the-environment complaints."

"Jesus, you are so damned close-minded—whoa!"

Scott waved his hands over the controls, trying to get a fix on the blip. Here in the middle of the Big Deep, where there was nothing but their vessel and occasional hydrogen atoms to bounce off it, something had just shot past them so fast it wasn't even a blur. And gaining speed like a bitch, too. Okay, yeah, it was a couple hundred klicks away, but out here, that was almost a sideswipe.

"Goddamned cheap fucking doppler!" Tom said,

trying to get the computer to adjust its scan. "What the hell was that? A ship?"

"Not hardly. That acceleration would probably turn people into seat pancakes. Nova debris, maybe, old rock spat out by a real big planet-buster blast."

"Yeah? Maybe it's God on His way to the Final Reckoning. Better scrub your conscience clean, Scotty."

"I'm just a grunt, pal, don't blame me for the way the universe gets run."

"Fucking spectrograph missed it altogether." He slammed the heel of his hand against the console. Nobody wasted any money on these ships for such things as decent hardware.

"Like we were going to chase and catch it even if it was solid platinum, right?" Scott smiled. "It's not our job, buddy. One more rock in the dark, who cares?"

Seated in front of the sensor array on *Ne'dtesei*, Yeyinde watched the alien ship dwindle in their wake. He was Leader; his very name meant "brave one" but he knew the warriors called him "Dachande" when they thought his ears too dull to hear them. That name meant "different knife," and it referred to his left lower tusk, broken in a bare-handed fight against the Hard Meat, the *kainde amedha*, they of the black armored exoskeletons and acid blood. He smiled inwardly at the name. It could be considered an insult, but he was proud of it. The Hard Meat, save for the queens, were no smarter than dogs, but they were fierce and deadly game. Good prey upon which to train the young warriors. He could have had the tusk capped and reground, but he had left the broken fang a dull stump to remind himself—and any warriors who felt brave or particularly stupid—that only one yautja of all had ever faced the Hard Meat unarmed and walked away. As befitted a true warrior, Dachande himself never spoke of the battle, but let others tell the tale, holding a serious mandible at the embellishments they added in the singing of it. He was Leader of the *Ne'dtesei*, son and grandson of ship leaders and warrior trainers, and he bowed to no one in his skill with blade or burner. He had taken hundreds of young males out to learn the Hunt and had lost but a dozen, most of whom would still be among the living had they obeyed his orders.

But he sighed at the ship now so far behind him as to be invisible to even the sensors' keen eyes. Oomans flew in that vessel. He knew of them, the oomans, though he himself had never Hunted them. They were toolfolk, had weapons equal to those of the yautja, and were, if the stories could be believed, the ultimate *pyode amedha*. Soft Meat. But with deadly stingers, the oomans. A true test of skill. What were they doing out here? Where were they bound? A pity he was locked into this Hunt, responsible for a score of itchy would-be warriors full of themselves and ready to show off their prowess.

Well. Someday he would Hunt them, the oomans.

For now, he had a ship to fly, Hunts to prepare.

He switched to the electronic eyes that watched the Hard Meat queen in the nest they had made for her deep in the belly of the ship.

The image blossomed on the plate in front of him.

Tall she was, the queen, twice his own height, massive even in the reduced gen-pull of the ship, probably four times his weight. Black as a nestcleaner's hands, gleaming dully under the lights, the queen looked like a giant *zabin* bug, with the addition of a long segmented tail and smaller supplemental arms jutting from her torso. Her comb rose high like antlers, flat and flaring, and she had two sets of needle-toothed jaws, one nesting inside the other and able to extrude a span from her mouth to grab like pincers. Freed, she would be a formidable opponent, fast, powerful, intelligent. But she was not free, the queen. She was bound in bands of dlex, wound in restraints that could resist the sharpest blades, the hottest fires, the strongest acids. Bound and made into nothing more than an egg-laying captive, subject to the will of the ship's Leader. A conveyer ran beneath her massive ovipositor, catching the precious eggs and carrying them to the packing compartment. There, they were fed into the robot crawler in the sucker ships connected to the *Ne'dtesei* like leeches on either side. Inside the suckers the robots—treaded machines designed for one purpose—prepared themselves to transport and place the eggs on fertile ground. Like a mechanical mother, the robots would leave the eggs where they could open and the crablike first-stage Hard Meat could find game to infect with the next stage. Those embryos would eventually chew their way free of the hapless host to become drones, the final stage for most of the Hard Meat. Prey, to the warriors he had brought to learn the rules of the Hunt. Stupid but deadly, the Hard Meat would teach the main lesson the young ones needed to know: move well or die. There was no room for error in the Hunt.

Dachande looked at the fettered queen, the fleshy eggs she laid. His own trophy wall on the homeworld held half a dozen of the Hard Meat skulls, bleached and clean, including the one he had killed with his bare hands, as well as a queen, taken during a hellish hunt in which nine already-Blooded warriors had died. He had killed fifty others, but had kept, as was proper, only those he had thought worthy of his wall. They were fierce, but usually no challenge to one such as himself. If he had occasion to face one on these Hunts, he would limit himself to spear or wrist knife. After all, any yautja could *burn* the Hard Meat; a Leader had to handicap himself. The females smiled upon a brave male more often than they did others; Dachande had never lacked for female attention before, nor did he intend to begin now. He had sired seventy-three suckers over the years since first he had become a Blooded warrior and he was planning on reaching eighty by the end of the next breeding season. A yautja did what a yautja had to do to bolster his line and when his Final Hunt took place, he intended to leave behind a legion of younglings.

He grinned. Any Hunt could be the Final Hunt, that was the Path, but he did not think this would be the one. This was routine; he had led a score of missions such as this one, and he could do it blindfolded, with dull blades and a dead burner in his sleep. An easy run, *gkei'moun* simple.

He switched off the eyes watching the queen. He should go and release some of the pressure that had built up among the young males. A couple of them in particular were showing signs of preparing to do something stupid, such as challenging a Blooded warrior or even the Leader himself. Young males were not a whole lot brighter than the Hard Meat, Dachande sometimes thought. He could still recall his prewarrior days when he had known everything, was the bravest yautja ever born and ready to prove it at the slightest provocation. Ah, the days of his invincible youth. Surely there could have been no male who had swaggered more, thought more highly of himself; acted as if he were the linchpin around which the galaxy would someday turn. A creature of destiny, he had thought, different from the other obnoxious would-be heroes who strutted and stood ready to be offended at the hint of disrespect.

He recalled an instance when a younger male had glanced at him with what he thought an inappropriate demeanor, had allowed his gaze to linger a quarter second longer than the galaxy's would-be linchpin had deemed respectful. How he had puffed up like a poison-toad and stepped forward to issue a claw-challenge, and that only because death-challenges were forbidden to the un-Blooded. How when crossing the empty space between himself and the insolent pup who had offended him, he had been knocked sprawling by a female going about her business. By the time he had recovered, the disrespectful one had gone and the female, if she had even noticed, had also continued on her way.

He grinned, tusks going wide. Such a long time ago that had been, before most of the current class of pups had been sap in their fathers' rods. They would learn, just as he had learned. They were not the gods' gift to the universe. He would see to it. Or he would see them dead. Either way was the Path.

2

achande walked slowly
down the dim corridor toward the *kehrite*, the room
where the training yautja learned blade and simple
unarmed combat. Many Leaders focused on the importance of shiftsuit mechanics and burners in the
teaching of the Hunt, but not he; from long experience Dachande knew that sometimes there was nothing to rely on outside of one's own prowess. To teach
anything else would be to risk the death of future
warriors, and a good Leader had many students still
Hunting.

The measure of a teacher was the life span of those
he taught. The longer they lived, the better the in-
structor.

Dachande inhaled deeply as he neared the *kehrite*.
The musk of aggression was strong in the air, an oily,

bitter smell that promised confrontation, but he did not hurry. Being the eldest Blooded on a Hunt had its privileges; no fight would begin without the Leader to witness it.

The winding passageway narrowed to an arched entry in front of Dachande, the walls lined with Hard Meat armor. Already he could hear the clatter of taloned feet and the mumblings of expectation. He stepped through the arch and waited for acknowledgment. Quickly, he located the few students he had picked to cause trouble early on and marked them; Mahnde, the short one; Ghardeh, with the long tress; and Tichinde, who talked louder than any other. Of the three, Ghardeh would be the least trouble; he was but a follower. But the other two . . .

Within a short span, all yautja had turned their attention to him. There were fourteen in all who wore the plain dlex headband of student, plus two Blooded warriors who helped supervise; these two, Skemte and Warkha, were also the navigator and flyer. The ship was fully automated, a single trained yautja could handle it—but it did not hurt to take precautions. Both warriors carried Dachande's signature mark upon their foreheads like a third eye, the etch of Hard Meat blood from their first kill, and they watched him carefully for direction; each sought their own Leaderships; both were wise enough to know such achievement would not be through Challenge against him.

One by one, all heads bowed to him. Dachande nodded curtly, never taking his sharp yellow gaze from the group—Tichinde in particular. What he saw did not surprise him. Tichinde had lowered his head but kept his own gaze on Dachande. When he saw that his Leader watched in return, he flared his lower

mandibles and raised his head to face him—a sure
sign of aggression. It was insolent, but forgivable,
were his Leader a patient one; had Tichinde begun the
low growl of confrontation, it would not be so easy to
allow him to remain unmolested. As it stood, this was
a prime opportunity to let the cooped-up young males
practice.

"Tichinde!" Dachande made his voice angrier than
he was. The yautja surrounding the arrogant youth
stepped away from him, tusks opened wide.

"You may show your 'skills,'" Dachande continued,
his voice threaded with sarcasm, "by a *jehdin/jehdin*
spar with ... Mahnde. First fall determines the win-
ner."

There were rumblings of disappointment as the
young males moved from the match area to line the
scarred *kehrite* walls; with no weapons to be used,
both combatants would probably still be alive after
the match. Still, the energy was high. Several yautja
had seen the look between Tichinde and the Leader,
and all could see the disrespectful face of the student
now. What would the Leader do about this? How
would he respond? Was he weak enough to allow a
Challenge to pass, even one so veiled?

Dachande paused until all were in place before giving the command.

"Begin!"

As one, the yautja began to howl and chant as the
two young males circled. Dachande watched carefully
as Mahnde lunged forward for the first blow, arms
raised.

Tichinde blocked easily and countered with a jab
to the throat.

Mahnde moved aside, not fast enough to avoid the
shot completely. A chorus of guttural hisses filled the

room as he stumbled and pulled back. A clumsy response. No one was impressed.

Tichinde shrieked and ran at Mahnde, talons extended for a stab to the abdomen.

The defender, already off-balance, blocked too high. Tichinde hit full on and knocked Mahnde to the padded floor. The victorious youth threw back his head and screamed in triumph. The *kehrite* pounded with the cries of the agitated students. The match was over.

Too soon. Blood was still too warm; none would be satisfied with such a quick bout.

Dachande looked for a challenger amidst the yowls and clicks of the clamoring spectators, displeased with Mahnde's performance. Perhaps Chulonte, he showed promise ...

A score of new sounds filled the room as the yautja began to scream in surprise and renewed excitement. Dachande's gaze flickered back to the match area—and he watched in amazement as Tichinde kicked his fallen opponent in the head.

"Ki'cte!" Dachande had to shriek to be heard. "Enough!"

Tichinde kicked again. Mahnde rolled over, tried to cover his face and grab at Tichinde's foot at the same time. The yautja were going wild. Blood was molten; spittle flew as they shook their heads in excitement.

"Tichinde!" Rarely had Dachande seen such disobedience. He stalked onto the match floor and shouted again.

Tichinde turned to face the Leader. He snarled. The young male extended one hand and shoved at Dachande's left shoulder.

Dachande avoided the push automatically.

The clawed hand fell short.

The watching yautja suddenly fell silent, only a few dying clicks and cries of wonder. Tichinde's movement was unmistakable, and since Dachande had attained Leadership, a move that he had not seen. The sign of direct challenge.

Dachande sighed to himself silently. What an idiot this one was. How had he survived this long?

The baked dirt that covered the valley floor appeared nearly lifeless under the searing heat of the dual suns. What vegetation there was appeared stunted, twisted, cooked. The twin stars were hardly an exact match; the secondary's shadows were barely visible, a frail blur next to the deeper charcoal hues cast by the primary. The towering plateaus of dirty tan rock—there had once been water here to cut them so—ran in corridors throughout the basin and offered no comfort unless you crawled among the stones—which no sane human would want to do for all of the venomous forms of hidden life there. Besides the stinging flies and poisonous snakes, there was a particularly lethal form of scorpion that nested amidst the boulders during Ryushi's nineteen-hour day. Even after sundown, the heat rarely fell below body temperature, and without the relief of the cool breezes that sometimes came with desert climate after dark. The air was always bone-dry and the feverish winds that occasionally blew were sharp and unpleasant, the crack of a hot whip. Maybe it was somebody's idea of paradise—

But not mine.

Machiko Noguchi ran a delicate hand through her short black hair and punched the scan button. The portable eye panned across the barren wasteland, showing her more of the same. It was identical to almost everywhere else on Ryushi. Besides the few artificial watering holes and the settlement itself, the whole planet looked like a desert prospector's version of hell—rocks, dirt and heat, and no precious metals hidden there, either.

Noguchi sighed and tapped a few keys. As the small screen faded to black, she leaned back in her form-chair and closed her eyes. She took a deep breath and growled softly through clenched teeth. When the opportunity had presented itself, she had not hesitated. Only twenty-nine years old and already offered an overseer's post for the Chigusa Corporation. Prosperity Wells, at the far edge of the Beta Cygni system, very quiet; "Sounds exhilarating," she'd said.

Right. Only her six months of phase-in was almost up and she was so sick of this rock she could vomit. A necessary career move, she kept telling herself.

Well, at least there's air-conditioning . . .

Noguchi stretched her arms over her head and arched her back. Her lunch break was almost over, time to get back to the office. She usually ate with Hiroki, but he'd had a meeting with a few of the ranchers and she had decided to slip back to her apartment and go over a stat report for the company. Might as well let him keep the reins for the last few weeks of his stay. Besides, only in her private chamber did she feel free to relax; to let her feelings show anywhere else was—it was not an option. There was too much at stake for her to be anything but completely professional.

She glanced at the holomirror by her door on the way out' and nodded at what she saw—cool, composed, detached. Attractive in a typical Japanese way, although that was not important to her. She looked

... *authoritative*. The ranchers didn't seem to like her very much, but they *would* respect her—her honor would accept nothing less.

Dachande felt his anger flare and then, almost regretfully, he let it pass. Half a lifetime ago, such a display of brash audacity would have meant a quick death for the young male; the yautja who would dare to challenge him? Certain *thei-de*. And grinning all the while he delivered it, too.

But he was Leader now. Not a kind Leader, but a just one. There were others who would kill for such an offense—but these days, he would teach. There was no point in a match you knew you would win. Doubt was necessary or it was but an exercise.

All of this flitted through his mind in less than a second.

Tichinde pushed at him again.

Again Dachande slipped the move unthinkingly. He saw the surprise on the young one's face. And perhaps, too late, a touch of realization that he had made an error. A very bad error.

The juvenile yautja gave up their stunned hush at this new transgression and roared for blood. It did not matter whose.

Dachande reflected no longer. He grabbed Tichinde's hands and held them high with his own.

Tichinde screamed into his face, the shrill sound blended with the cries of the spectators.

Dachande did not pause.

The Leader jerked his head forward. Their skulls met with a dull *crack* that sent a peal of renewed clatterings and hisses through the assemblage.

Tichinde pulled his hands loose and staggered back, arms still held high, but dazed.

They circled.

A tiny trickle of pale blood ran down Tichinde's face from beneath his dlex band. Without taking his gaze from Dachande, the student reached up and touched the flow, rubbed it between his fingers for confirmation; he did not seem to like the feel.

Too bad.

Tichinde spread his arms wide, back hunched, and screamed. The sounds were garbled with fury, but the inflections unmistakable—*Nan-deThan-gaun*. The Kiss of Midnight.

Tichinde's intentions were crystal: he would kill his Leader, if he could.

Enough was enough. Dachande locked his fingers together and leapt. He landed beside the impudent yautja and brought his double-fist down, hard, into the small of the still-screaming Tichinde's back. Tichinde fell to the floor. His lower jaw smacked the mat quite audibly.

Dachande jumped back quickly as Tichinde slowly regained his feet. Aware of his audience, the Leader moved with all the grace and skill he could muster. The motion was nearly perfect and any of the watchers who could recall even a bit of training would be impressed by the flow of it. Which was the point.

New blood oozed from the young male's lower mandibles. The watching students sang out calls of victory for their Leader as Tichinde turned to face Dachande. The cries of derision from his peers were perhaps what spurred the young male into action. With a strangled hiss, the bleeding yautja ran at Dachande, fists extended.

Give him credit for spirit. Credit for brains, no. For skill, hardly. But he was no coward.

Still, it was poor form. Dachande fell to his knees before Tichinde reached him and grasped the student's overstretched upper body with one hand, his nearer leg with the other. Suppressing a grunt, he strove to make the move appear effortless.

As if the youth weighed no more than a suckling, Dachande stood and thrust Tichinde high over his head.

The howling yautja tried to escape and regain the floor, but his writhings were to no avail. Dachande held the young male high, let out a growl of conquest—then threw Tichinde across the room.

The mob of howling young males split, narrowly avoided the flung body before it smacked into the wall. They chanted triumph for Dachande, harsh sounds of *nain-desintje-de*; pure win.

Dachande made no chant himself and none was needed. The fallen Tichinde spoke for him.

For a short time, nobody moved.

Finally, Tichinde staggered upright and walked slowly toward his Leader, head bowed. The outcome was obvious, and a further display of aggression would be dishonorable, not to mention stupid. Tichinde stopped in front of him and raised only his eyes to see what Dachande would decide; in such a Challenge, death was not an unreasonable punishment.

Dachande pretended to consider his options as the chants fell to a breath-held stillness and overstretched tension. There was really no question for him; a good Leader did not have to kill one of his own to prove anything—and to embarrass the young male would

tell later in Tichinde's Hunts. He waited because all
eyes watched and the hesitation was penalty enough.

After a few breaths-time Dachande tilted his head
to one side and spoke. *"Payas leitjin-de."* He paused.
"Hma'mi-de."

Tichinde hung his head lower and stepped back,
his relief visible. Several young males came forward
to touch Tichinde's hair in appreciation of the Leader's compliment. The precise tip of Dachande's head
combined with the words indicated both acknowledgment of the student's submission and a respect for his
bravery—"Remember God's practice." Tichinde was
allowed his life and his name, but with the ritual
warning a slap to his embarrassed face. Still, there
was no real shame in losing to one who had faced the
Hard Meat with nothing but talons and blade.

Dachande almost allowed himself a grin, but did
not want to lighten the effect of his pronouncement;
he raised his hand and gestured for the students to
fall in line for training. Tichinde knew who was
Leader, and would not forget it. And if another yautja
strayed from obedience . . . ?

After this, it would not likely happen. If it did,
there would be more than one "dachande" on ship.
His honor would accept nothing less.

3

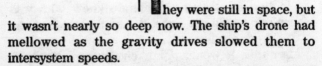hey were still in space, but it wasn't nearly so deep now. The ship's drone had mellowed as the gravity drives slowed them to intersystem speeds.

"Eleven days, buddy boy, and then no more of your dick in my ear for what, seventy-two hours?"

Tom grinned and shook his head. "You wish."

Scott raised his coffee cup in a mock toast. "Here's to pretty girls and sunny days, Tommy." He sipped the watery liquid and grimaced. "Nothing like a nice mug of shit to put a shine on the morning, hey?"

"It's ..." Tom glanced at his terminal. "Four in the afternoon, you pig. Happy hour."

"Right," said Scott. "Whatever."

They sat in silence for a few moments. Tom worked studiously at one of his crosswords, tapping

in words and erasing them at the same rate. Scott
gazed into the darkness and tried to remember the
words of a poem he used to know. He could probably
just look it up in the ship's library, same as Tom and
his puzzle, but learning how to kill time was a good
trick in their line of work. Nothing to do and plenty of
hours to do it.

*'Twas brillig and the slithy toves, did gyre and—
something-something wabe—all mimsy were the
borogoves and the something-hath outgrabe—*

"Six-letter word for 'saint'?"

Scott thought for a second and then smiled.
"Thomas."

"Funny. Like not wanting to fuck over all things
great and small makes me some kinda prince. I mean,
really—" Tom paused. "Hey, that's it. Prince. You're
good for something after all, you pagan asshole."

"You still pissed about last night?" Scott shook his
head. It seemed that this debate would never die—but
eleven days *was* eleven days. "Like I said, survival of
the fittest. The fact remains that if the human race
needs to do something to survive—and the lower orders don't have the power to stop us—we'll prevail.
It's not right or wrong, it's just the way things are."

Tom looked up from the monitor, jaw set. "So it's
all right to do whatever we want, exploit any eco-
system, as long as we don't run into anything big
enough to kick our butts—that's basically it, right?"

"Couldn't have put it better myself."

"That's opportunistic rationalization, Scott. Where's
your sense of social responsibility? Didn't your mama
raise you right?"

"I was a tube child, thank you very much."

"That must be it." Tom hit the store button on his
keyboard and stood. "Now, if you'll excuse me a mo-

ment, I have this sudden overwhelming urge to take a dump."

Scott chuckled. "I'm not even gonna *touch* that one."

Tom slapped him on the shoulder and exited the control module. Tom was all right, he didn't take himself too seriously at least. Scott had been paired up with worse. He felt his grin slowly melt as he turned his gaze back to the deep. Killing time, that was all.

Beware the jabberwock, my son, the jaws that bite the claws that catch—beware the jub-jub bird and shun the frumious bandersnatch.

Yeah, that was it. What, he wondered, did it mean? And why was he thinking about it now?

Hiroki's face remained expressionless as Noguchi lit a cigarette at her desk and exhaled a haze of gray smoke. She knew he disapproved, but she also knew that it was not appropriate for him to speak of it; it was, after all, her office now. It was not even a habit that she was particularly attached to—

But wouldn't your father *be displeased, Machiko?*

Noguchi inhaled deeply.

Hiroki uncrossed his legs on the couch and smoothed his small mustache carefully with one finger. "As I was saying, Ackland expressed some concerns with the agreement. He says that he has the support of the other ranchers, or at least Harrison and Marianetti."

"Well, that's three of the big four," Noguchi began. "Perhaps we should contact the company—"

A small green light flashed from the control panel set into her desk, accompanied by a low tone.

"Excuse me, Hiroki."

"Of course." He picked up a sheaf of hard copy and settled back into a plush cushion.

Noguchi punched up visual and hit receive.

"Mr. Shimura, we have an unidentified incoming at—oh, Ms. Noguchi."

Noguchi smiled slightly at the young man's visible discomfort and waited. He was one of the scan watchers, a low-level company worker.

"I, uh, I have a message for Mr. Shimura. Is he there?"

Noguchi frowned. "Yes, he's here. But you can give *me* the message, Mason." She glanced at Hiroki, who made a point of being deeply engrossed in the rhynth count report he was reading.

Mason swallowed. "Uh, yes, ma'am. Long range is showing a UFO. It's probably just a meteor, but it's not breaking up, it is going to hit—if it stays on its present course, it'll make planetfall about thirty klicks north of here—open pasture. Make a boom when it lands."

"Any damage likely?"

"No, it's not that big."

"Then don't worry about it." Noguchi stubbed her cigarette out into the pewter tray on the desk. "We can investigate after the roundup. Noguchi out."

The screen went blank. She took a deep breath and then looked at Hiroki. He had set down the file and was watching her, face impassive as usual. At least there was no sympathy. She opened her mouth, uncertain as to what she was going to say; their relationship had progressed to a first-name basis, but that didn't make them friends.

"I—" She forced herself not to look away. "I've been here nearly six months, Hiroki—and still they report to you. The ranchers, even the staff treat me like a stranger. I have done all I can think of to make this job mine—"

Noguchi fell silent and waited. Hiroki watched her for a few seconds and then stood and faced her, hands clasped behind his back.

"Maybe that is your problem, Machiko. You're trying to adapt the job to you, rather than adapting yourself to it. You can't run an operation like this and hide from it at the same time, no matter how nice the office."

Noguchi nodded slightly, thoughtful. This sounded like something he had been waiting to say until asked, which made her wonder how long he had been holding his tongue. Still, she needed an informed opinion. The ranchers respected Shimura—no, even further, they *trusted* him. She had not thought to find out how he had achieved their loyalty.

"There are only one hundred and thirteen civilians on Ryushi," he continued, "and besides the thirty or so company staff, we are dealing with freelancers here—not men and women who jump when the voice of the corporation speaks. They are not drones looking for advancement; they are people with children and homes. Quoting regulations will not get you very far."

Noguchi felt a flash of anger, but she fought to keep it under control. "What would you suggest, Hiroki? That I bake cookies and invite them on picnics?"

"I suggest that when you ask for an opinion, you should consider the advice you receive." Hiroki picked up his sun helmet from the synth-marble coffee table and walked to the door. He paused with his hand on the entry controls and looked back at her.

"Look, I'll be around for another two weeks, and

then you're on your own. I will do what I can to help in the meantime." He smiled a little. "I think you will do fine, Machiko."

She stood and nodded at him. "Thank you for your ... assistance, Hiroki."

"It is nothing. Get out of the office once in a while, get your hands dirty." He opened the door and then grinned easily. "Get some rhynth shit between your toes."

Noguchi sat back down and rested her hands lightly on the black-lacquered surface of her desk. Hiroki's words had stung a bit, but perhaps because there was some truth there; it deserved consideration. Hiroki was, after all, being promoted off of Ryushi. The ones who went up the ladder were generally not those that kept a low profile, as she had been doing.

Perhaps it's time to make some of my own moves ... Noguchi took another cigarette from the small silver case in her desk drawer and rolled it thoughtfully between her thumb and forefinger. What was the saying?

The journey of a thousand kilometers begins with one step ...

At first there was only the vision of dark, cracked matter all around, seen through a thick cloud of oily smoke. The electronic eye scanned the pit and then looked up. With a sudden lurch, the *lou-dte kalei* moved forward, using its segmented pincers to pull itself out of the crater.

It was a large, armored mechanism, the *lou-dte kalei*, designed to withstand almost any type of environment so far encountered; it was actually modeled after a kind of predator discovered on Thän, a world of dense metals and poisonous weather. Something like the Hard Meat, but more efficiently built—it could climb, walk, run, or dive into liquid. And while the robot crawler did not Hunt as the real creature could, it served a purpose that was more important than simple survival; it was the bearer of life.

Dachande switched to the rear *gkinmara*, another of the rounded eyes that transmitted sensory information. "*Lou-dte kalei*" was a joke, really, a derogatory term that was sometimes used for a female—literally, "child-maker." Not that Dachande had ever heard the name spoken to a female's face. A warrior who would dare such would not be wise, for an insulted and angry yautja female was not something even a not-too-wise male wanted to create. Assuming the warrior was armed and expert, it might almost be an even match, but Dachande would put his wager on the female. His most recent partner had tossed him across a room during the heat of their mating and that had been an accident.

Mating. Ah, now there was a pleasant thought.

As if in accordance with Dachande's thoughts, the heavy dlex ramp in the tail of the crawler lowered and the machine began its function. An egg, the beginning of the Hunt, made its way gently down the plated ramp to be deposited on the dusty ground.

The crawler moved slowly forward to lay another.

Dachande rolled the control bar on the table in his private chamber. The front view appeared again in the oval monitor's screen; the crawler went toward a high mountain of some unknown material, perhaps the cliff was of *tjau'ke* or compressed dust. This world was a warm place, but not as humid as some. Twin suns and no freestanding liquid in sensory range. The read on the crawler showed that there were still dozens of eggs to be set; the red lines and smudges of the counter changed with each placement. Each egg was coded and tuned to a reader that would maintain the connection even after the egg hatched and became Hard Meat. They would not leave the Hunt until all the prey had been taken. To leave even a single one behind was criminal.

Dachande had not visited this place before, although the records showed that there had been Hunts here, many seasons earlier. It was listed as wide and spacious, with no antagonists and many hiding places; large, four legged creatures dwelled there naturally, ideal hosts—perfect for training. They would go in fast and dark, that was standard, but there could hardly be anything on the planet to cause them problems. It was but another dry world with little to offer save a place to Hunt. The galaxy was full of such places.

A small *tarei'hsan* ran in front of the egg-layer, dark in color and spined like an insect of some sort. Its tail curved over its body and ended in a point, and its arms were much like the arms of the *lou-dte kalei*. The crawler rolled over it, the treads crushing the tiny bug into the mottled ground. Dachande shook his head. Better it should die thus, for stupidity did not further any race and running under tank treads was not high up the scale of cleverness.

He watched as the counter ran slowly backward. They were close to this place, this dust world, but there was still plenty of time for the Hard Meat children to find hosts. The tagged babes should be drones by the ship's arrival, but there was not so much slack that they would have time to colonize. Timing was all.

Dachande smiled. Part of being a Leader was not to seem excited by the prospect of a training Hunt, but in the privacy of his chamber, he allowed himself to feel the warmth of things to come. And somehow, this one felt different—there was an air of . . . something.

He switched the monitor off and stroked his broken tusk absently. He was too old to muddle himself with cosmic questions, but he knew the words of his ancestors: *Thin-de le'hsaun 'aloun'myin-de/bpi-de gka-de hsou-depaya*—Learn the gift of all sights or finish in the dance of fallen gods.

Dachande cackled and stood up. Philosophy was not his bent. He was a warrior. Let the old ones worry about such things. He was a doer, not a thinker. It was better that way. Almost always.

4

achiko Noguchi couldn't find the green crayon. There was the jade one and the blue-green, but the emerald-green was missing, and it was the only color that would work for the dragon's eyes.

She sighed and carefully dumped out the crayon pack. Things had been going so *well* until now, it wasn't fair. It was her day off from school and she had received permission to play quietly in her room for two whole hours before dinnertime. The picture of the dragon was going to be a gift for her father; she knew that he had been talking about a promotion for a long time, and that today he had an important meeting with his supervisor.

And the green was misplaced: Her parents had taught her to put things in their place because order was a very important rule; knowing where things were was a crucial ingredient to a successful life. She felt vaguely anxious as she sorted through the different shades—what if it wasn't there? What then?

Machiko spotted the crayon and nodded to herself. She had put it in with the blues by mistake, that was all. It was understandable; she would just have to be more careful ...

She heard the front door open and close downstairs as she meticulously shaded in the dragon's eyes—emerald with gold rims. A cool spring breeze wafted in through her open window with the sounds of small children playing down the street. A good day. And it was going to be a beautiful picture, a long-tailed, proud dragon with green and lavender scales and red taloned feet—

Machiko frowned and looked up. Her mother had not called out to her. Mother had gone to the store to buy things for a special dinner, her father's favorite dishes. But Mother *always* called to her when she returned from an errand. Perhaps she had gone back outside to carry in more things ...

Machiko stood and walked to the door of her tidy room where she paused and listened. Maybe she had not heard her mother come in after all; the house was very still. She was about to go back to her picture when she heard a noise.

"Mother?" Nothing.

It had been like a heavy sigh, that noise. From down the hall—her father's study or perhaps her parents' room. Machiko was suddenly not sure if it was a good day at all. The silent house was not peaceful anymore, it was—empty.

Bad.

She walked very slowly down the hallway, staying

close to one wall. Her feet seemed like lead; with each step, her fear increased. Her mother would have surely answered, wouldn't she? Who was in their house? Should she leave?

Yes. Machiko decided that it would be good to wait outside for her mother to return. She would say that she had heard a noise and her mother would know what to do.

Except the front door . . .

Was past the study. Past her parents' room.

Machiko felt her legs trembling. The back of her neck was damp and sticky, and her stomach felt as if it were made of stone. She took another tentative step and hesitated. And she heard another noise.

All at once, Machiko relaxed. It was her father! That was the sound of his chair creaking back, as familiar a sound as his voice or the clatter of his key cards. She straightened up and started toward his door, smiling in relief. He had come home early, that was all.

"Father," she began, and reached out to knock. "I thought—"

Her words faltered as the door to his study swung inward. She had time to register surprise that he had left it unlatched before she saw him. Before she saw the knife.

And the blood.

Machiko screamed and ran to her father's side, where she pleaded and cried for him to get up, to speak, to stop pretending. She pulled at him for a long time. When he finally fell to the floor, she was drenched in his blood. He opened his eyes and sat up, smiling gently at her, arms spread.

"This is for you, Machiko," he said, and embraced her. Except that now his arms were claws and his head was a dragon's. His forked tongue flickered out as his gold-rimmed eyes began to bleed emerald tears. He pulled back to look at her as she began to wail in terror.

"You are my child," the words rasped from his dragon-face. "Redeem me . . ."

Noguchi sat up quickly, her breath coming in short gasps. She almost screamed before she realized where she was.

"Lights," she called out shakily. Her room glowed gently to life. Noguchi hugged her knees to her chest and tried to breathe deeply. Always the same dream—except she had not had it for a long time.

She *had* been covered in her father's blood when her mother had found her. There had been no note, only the Death Poem that her mother would not let her read until years later, but the reason had come to light that same night: the esteemed Akira Noguchi, an accountant for the Yashido Company, had been fired for embezzlement. The same man who had scolded her when she had lied about stealing a piece of candy at the age of five, the man who had taught her the value of order. The father who had taught her honor . . .

"Bastard," she murmured, angry. Except her voice didn't sound angry at all. The memories came back so easily when she let them, and now she was helpless to stop them. She had ripped up the dragon picture after the funeral; it had never been finished. The stain on their family's name had eventually faded, and when she was in college, her mother had remarried. She had met her stepfather once. He had seemed like a pleasant man, but she never got past the feeling that her mother had married him so that she would no longer be a Noguchi.

She and her mother spoke occasionally, but any closeness they had once shared was gone. Keiko Noguchi Ueda had never understood how her daughter had really felt. When she had called her mother with the news of her move to Ryushi, her mother had been so proud. "Your father would have been pleased," she had said. Her father.

Noguchi took in a deep breath and closed her eyes. None of that mattered anymore, she did not need to think of it. She was a corporate overseer for a major corporation on a planet far from Earth, and she was good at her job. She would become better in time; she would earn the ranchers' trust and would carry out her position with—with—

"Honor," she whispered. And try as she might, she could not hold back the single tear that coursed down her cheek.

The Lector had made it to Ryushi a little before local nightfall. Scott knew there would be some hard workdays ahead for the ranchers and *The Lector* crew, but as pilot, he had minimal responsibilities for a few days. About damned time for a break.

He and Tom stepped off the ramp and into the deepening twilight of the desert world. They were at the edge of a small, dingy town that smelled like manure, straight out of an old Western vid. There was no one to greet them. In fact, the place looked uninhabited.

Scott grinned. "Looks like somebody forgot to organize the parade," he said. He turned to look at Tom—and Tom wasn't there.

Scott spun and looked around. *The Lector*, too, was gone. Behind him lay only a vast, dusty plain, with mountains far in the distance.

"Tom!" he shouted. No reply.

Scott turned to look at the deserted town. It was almost full dark now, but there were no lights in any of the empty windows. There were only a few faded, almost nondescript buildings, their doors latched against the hot, sandy winds that blew mournfully through the lonely settlement.

Scott cupped his hands around his mouth and shouted.

"Hello! Is anyone here?"

Nothing. In spite of the weather, Scott was suddenly cold. He took a few steps toward the nearest structure and then stopped.

A high, piercing cry came from inside the building. It had the same shrill tone of an animal in pain— except it was angry. The keening wail rose to a fevered pitch, the sound of insanity and hatred. There was nothing human about it.

Scott stumbled backward and fell. He scrambled at the ground, tried desperately to pull himself back to his feet, but he couldn't seem to manage it. He tried to crawl away from the horrible sound but it filled his ears and surrounded him. From behind, he heard the door swing open and the shriek of the creature got impossibly louder.

There was no escape. Scott began to scream. He screamed because he knew what it was, the thing, and he knew that to look at it meant death.

—the Jabberwocky—!

* * *

Scott woke up in a cold sweat in a dark room on *The Lector*, still over a week out from Ryushi. He did not get back to sleep that night.

Under the pouring rain, Yeyinde aimed at the Hard Meat drone with his burner and depressed the control. The running bug howled and fell back in a gout of *thwei*, limbs clattering.

Behind him the Leader shouted commands to the other students as the hot, harsh liquid splashed down from the sky, obscuring suit vision.

Another drone ran toward him and Yeyinde fired again, excited and anxious all at once. He felt fear clench his bowels briefly, but the cold twist was quickly overriden by heat. The beast in him snarled and grew proud: *Two!* His first Hunt and there were *two* in his name!

The threat seemed to fall away as the bugs stopped their assault. Yeyinde spun around, looked for more to kill. Between the burning rain and the hanging trees of the *dto*, it was hard to see.

The Leader, 'A'ni-de, called out. The Hunt was completed. The yautja cheered and hissed their triumph, Yeyinde's voice among them. He looked through the dancing young warriors for Nei'hman-de, whose blood he shared by the same father. Nei'hman-de was a strong yautja and fast fighter, but he surely did not kill *two*. Nei'hma-de and he had grown together, play-Hunting as growing suckers—and now they would share their first kill, share the victory of the Blooding. How could life get any better than this?

"Nei'hman-de!" Yeyinde moved through the rain and called for his *mei'hswei*. "Nei'hman-de!"

A talon fell hard on his shoulder. 'A'ni-de.

"Nei'hman-de is dead," the Leader said coldly. "He did not move properly. Now go stand at your kill for approval."

Yeyinde widened his eyes. "But Nei'hman-de is—"

'A'ni-de backhanded him roughly, sent Yeyinde to his knees in the mud. "You question?" The Leader glowered over him, tusks flared.

Yeyinde bowed his head in submission. After a tense moment, 'A'ni-de stalked away.

The young warrior stood and trudged through the downpour back to the fallen drones. That a warrior's life was hard, he knew. That yautja sometimes died, he knew as well. Nei'hman-de, gone. It did not seem real that it could be.

Unbidden came a memory. Of a time when he and his brother had sat drinking *c'ntlip*, the fiery brew that fogged mind and body with pleasure. Someday they would be Leaders, not only of ships but of other Leaders. Great would be their fame. Stories would be sung of their Hunts for a thousand years, each of them was certain. It had been as clear as the high mountain air to them. Warriors together, they would Hunt, they would make the females howl in ecstasy, they would father each two hundred sucklings. Much could be laid to the liquor, of course, but he and his brother had truly believed the core of their fantasy. They would be the ones to survive and rise; it would be the other un-Blooded who would fall. Of that there had been no doubt, none.

Only now, it was his brother who had fallen and his own head was hung low after his first Hunt . . .

Yeyinde raised his eyes and saw the results of his prowess. Two bugs lay on the watery ground because of him. And at that moment, he saw the Path; there would no longer be a place for the dreams of youth in him. Nei'hman-de was gone, but *he* was alive—and now a warrior. And a warrior did not waste his time looking over his shoulder at the past. Done was done. Regret would not bring back the dead.

Yeyinde held his head high as 'A'ni-de traced a claw wet with Hard Meat *thwei* in the space between his eyes. He ignored the sharp sting as the acid *thwei* cut into his flesh to mingle with his own blood, blood that neutralized much of the Hard Meat's power. The burning mark was proof of his skill and his adulthood, a jagged etched badge for all to see. Of all the yautja on this Hunt, only *he* had killed two. Never again would he bow to the kinship of other males; aligning oneself with a loser was not the Path, and any yautja could lose . . .

Dachande awoke warm with pride of the memory. It was long ago and there had been many Hunts since, many of them harder and bloodier than the first. But the first had been where he discovered the truth of the warrior; it was a truth that had served him well. Now it was his turn to pass the knowledge on, to teach it to the young ones who had yet to feel the power of the Hunt, to know the joy of the first kill. It had been a long time since he had felt that newness but the dream brought it back as if it had been only moments past. The Hunt was what a warrior lived for; all else was nothing compared to it. Honor. Skill. Victory. Those were the things of life.

5

oguchi left her apartment early so she could catch Hiroki before he made rounds. The corporation employees' living quarters were all in the same building as the offices and mess hall, along with the community center and central operations; narrow passageways connected this building to the equipment storage and the main garage. To the east and south was open range; the north, mountains, and west was Iwa Gorge, a canyon too deep and long to herd the rhynth—although it certainly kept them from wandering too far in that direction. One less fence to build.

Noguchi walked through the connecting hall and saw one of the geotechs headed toward her, a thin older man with brown skin and very little hair. His name was ... Hein? Hinn?

As they passed she made a conscious effort to smile and nod at the man. He seemed vaguely surprised, but returned the courtesy, his teeth a sharp contrast to his dark face.

A condescending voice spoke in her head. *That wasn't too hard, now was it?*

Noguchi made a mental note to check the personnel files that evening. She felt almost embarrassed; six months and she didn't even know the people she was supposed to be working with.

All of that was going to change. Noguchi had started to realize just how little she had seen of Prosperity Wells. She had, of course, spent time learning the layout of the complex when she'd first arrived; it was an efficient setup. A med center with helipad; there were quarantine and holding pens for the rhynth, a transmitter/communications control shack, and a school connected to a rec center. There was also a fairly decent, if very small, shopping mall, complete with two tiny restaurants and a bar. Not that any of these got much use. Only the company people lived in the Wells, although most of the ranchers were in walking distance—if you didn't mind a long and hot hike. If it wasn't Earth, at least an attempt had been made to try to make it look like a town. There were hardly enough people in the gene pool to turn the planet into anything civilized, and even with more settlers, it wasn't likely to ever be a major population center; still, the company had made a token effort to make it look like home.

But besides seeing an occasional holovid at the rec's theater, she hadn't really been a member of the community. It wasn't her home and she wasn't going to stay here any longer than it took to show a profit and shine in the company's eyes enough to earn a transfer to the next rung on the ladder. But Hiroki was right, she would have to do what was necessary to earn the spot and so far she had remained as insulated as a thermetic bottle.

And *The Lector* would be arriving in less than seventy-two hours ...

So I imagine everyone will welcome me with open arms and songs of greeting now that I'm finally ready, hai?

Right.

As she walked between shelves piled high with bike and copter parts, she heard voices from the direction of the open entryway into the yard. She could make out the distinct soft tone of Hiroki's voice among the others; he sounded irritated.

Noguchi slowed her pace to catch the gist of the conversation she was about to walk into.

"... not the point, Hiroki! The company's making a killing from our sweat and we're getting screwed— right, Ackland?"

"That's the way the Ranchers Association sees it."

Noguchi waited just inside the door to listen for another moment; several ranchers and Hiroki stood in a loose circle several meters away. She could just see the edge of Ackland's heavy rhynth-hide coat, which he wore even on the hottest day. He was a large, opinionated man who had an amazing ability to cause friction.

"I don't even know why I'm discussing this with you," said Hiroki. "Ms. Noguchi is in charge now. You should be talking to her."

A perfect cue. Noguchi stepped forward and through the entry.

"That bitch? She doesn't give a shit about us," said Ackland.

"Maybe if she got laid once in a while—" started one of the other ranchers. Rick Harrison.

"Anybody who tried would freeze his dick off," said one of Ackland's men.

The group chuckled, all except for Hiroki.

Harrison broke off abruptly when he spotted her striding toward them. He coughed suddenly into his hand.

"Ms. Noguchi," he said. His voice was loud.

She held her head high and stared at him. He dropped his gaze, as did the other men. Only Ackland had the nerve to meet her eyes.

"I thought we were in the middle of a roundup, gentlemen," she said, voice cool.

Hiroki stepped in. "We were just discussing the agreement their association has already signed."

Ackland tapped his pipe with the heel of one hand. "That was before we saw what the market was doing back on Earth. If we'd known the price of meat was going to jump like this, we'd have asked for more."

"And if the bottom had fallen out of the market, would you have offered to take less?" said Hiroki.

All eyes turned to Noguchi. She faced Ackland, obviously the man to negotiate with.

"I'll talk to the company and see if I can swing a larger cut for your ranchers," she said. "We want to be fair."

Ackland nodded and tugged at his dirty red beard. He opened his mouth to speak, but Noguchi cut him off.

"But there won't be anything for anyone if your rhynth aren't ready for shipment when *The Lector* arrives." She noted his flash of annoyance with smug satisfaction. No matter what she changed, Ackland was never going to be a man she enjoyed working with. "I suggest you get back to your jobs."

She smiled at the others as they followed Ackland across the yard.

Hiroki raised his eyebrows at her after the ranchers had reached a safe distance.

"Pleasant man, Ackland," he said blandly.

"Perhaps someday we'll marry," she said, keeping a straight face.

Hiroki grinned.

"Let's saddle up," said Noguchi. She shaded her eyes against the suns and looked out at the open plain. "I'm ready to get some rhynth shit between my toes."

"Words of wisdom," said Hiroki.

Noguchi nodded and then walked with Hiroki toward the hover bikes. Already she felt as if she'd set wheels in motion; and once started, there would be no turning back.

The young males stood in standard formation and watched Dachande expectantly. The *kehrite* stank of musk and the air was alive with tension. He had made them wait long enough; it was time.

Dachande looked at the heaps of armor and weaponry that Skemte and Warkha had lined up against the wall. "You may collect your *'awu'asa'*," he said, waving at the armor. "Now."

With passionate cries of excitement, the yautja ran to the piles of equipment and Hard Meat shell, shoving and kicking to get there first. There was enough to suit all of them, of course, but they would fight for the better trappings; the stronger males would get the prime supplies. That was always the way.

Dachande watched as the yautja strapped on the scarred platings and struggled for arm sheaths and masks. Shafted knives were weighed and measured, burners' sights checked. Med kits and multiple eyes weren't standard for young males' armor, nor were *tarei'hsan* loops; only the warriors used such additions. There was shift capacity in a few of the suits, but the young males would not need such things anyway; the first Hunt was more a matter of point-and-kill than tracking and hiding. Invisibility was generally reserved for prey that shot back. You had to earn the right to use the better gear, and the prey for which it was necessary.

It was still two nights until landing on the seeded world, but the yautja would need to become accustomed to their *'awu'asa'*, to feel comfortable with movement and weight. Dachande himself had slept in his armor the first night he had donned it. They had worn the gear only briefly during their training and under strict supervision. For this there were reasons—the main being that a young male given too much power too early was a hazard to himself and others. Turn some of the wet-behind-the-knees younglings loose with a burner even a few weeks ago and there would have been the risk of holes in the ship's hull or bodies piled in the corridors. The ceiling of the firing range had more scars than a ceremonial blood-pig.

Dachande watched Tichinde backhand a smaller male for the mask he held and hiss triumphantly at the gain. The Leader nodded thoughtfully; Tichinde was strong but reckless. Such recklessness could get him killed. Did he survive, however, he could be a great warrior and a credit to his teacher. It was far better to be brave and die than to be cowardly and survive by hiding from the Black Warrior. Songs were not sung about those who showed their back to an attack.

One by one, the dressed yautja held up their shafted knives and howled to each other, pointing their burners to the floor and pretending to fire in mock battle. Skemte caught Dachande's gaze and growled amusement at their fervor. Dachande nodded and echoed the growl. Doubtless each of the would-be warriors thought himself the bravest to have ever picked up a spear and waved it.

The young males were as ready as he could make them. He hoped they were ready enough. If they were not, it was too late. And too bad—their successes or failures would start soon on the planet now speeding toward them.

Dtai'kai'-dte sa-de nau'gkon dtain'aun bpi-de. The fight begun would not end until the end; a tired saying but a true one.

The Hunt was about to begin.

6

oguchi rode slightly behind Hiroki through the midafternoon light, their hover bikes setting up whirls of baked tan dust and hot pebbles in their wake. Earlier they had skimmed the inner ridges of the gorge and then circled back to town for a light lunch. Now they were headed out again, toward Beriki canyon, one of the primary runs for the majority of the herds.

Noguchi had spent most of the morning getting used to the flier's controls; fortunately, they weren't too hard to figure out—stop, go, height and speed adjustments. The trick was to watch for obstacles that might cause problems; jump a big rock too fast and you could find yourself on your back, your scooter flying merrily along without you, at least until the deadhand control shut it down. Besides basic instruc-

tions and a few landscape remarks through the
comsets, Hiroki had kept quiet during their ride.

It was the longest she'd spent outdoors since arriving on Ryushi. The heat was incredible, the rays from
two suns slapping at them with tangible force. Fiery
winds ruffled the tips of her black hair at the base of
her visor, and particles of sandy dirt kicked up by
Hiroki's bike pelted her goggles and dusted her
cheeks. Ahead and all around, huge cliffs encircled
them.

Initially, it had all looked the same, harsh and un-
forgiving. But she had to admit there was a sparse
beauty to the plains as well. It recalled images of sand
gardens that Noguchi had visited in her youth at
Kyoto. Here the sand was unchanneled and pocked
with planets and rocks. Knee-high stands of beige
reeds grew randomly near the edges of the valleys.
Stones jutted from the earth in layers of shaded
browns and grays. The fractured topsoil was a huge
jigsaw puzzle with no end. There was plenty of sand,
to be sure, but no order here, no simple zen lines. It
was raw chaos. Billions of years in the making, this
world, and she and a handful of men and women now
held sway over it, masters of all the dry land. It was
not hard to believe in manifest destiny out here in the
far reaches of the galaxy, that mankind's true role was
to minister to and control all things.

Their revving motors had surprised a goodly
number of small animals out of hiding. A family of
jack-lizards hopped in front of Noguchi's bike near the
gorge, headed for cover in the grasses. And Hiroki
had pointed out an armored fire-walker and her mate
as they slipped through a pile of rocks earlier in the
morning. The female was a rosy brown, her smaller
mate a faded gray. They had been poking at gravel

with their short, pointed snouts, probably searching for snake eggs or beetles.

Noguchi could understand, at least intellectually, why the ranchers had left Earth to make Ryushi their home. There was a kind of freedom to the prairies, a calm serenity to the stark lands. A certain beauty in it all. On Earth, a single living plex could house fifty thousand people in tight, tiny cubicles. On Earth, open land still existed but under so many regulations that just to walk upon it without a proper license might be worth a year in prison. Nowhere on the homeworld was there such vast *emptiness* as was all around her here. She found herself even enjoying the weather as they neared the southern end of Beriki canyon, the simplicity of a dry wind in her face. She wondered if it was too late for this new understanding to change her standing with the ranchers. Perhaps with time . . .

"We're coming up on one of Ackland's camps," Hiroki crackled in her ear.

"Right." She slowed as they rounded a bend in the gully. There were several dozen rhynth grazing on weeds a couple of hundred meters ahead, and beyond, the large treaded vehicle that Ackland used to check on his herds. The crawler could hold twenty people comfortably and was equipped with a full kitchen and sleeping accommodations for at least six; most of the ranchers had automatic vehicles—AVs— but Ackland's was the biggest.

Of course.

The rhynth themselves seemed to be unlikely meat animals. They looked to Noguchi much like a beast she had seen in a zoo as a child, a rhinoceros. The rhynth were slightly bigger than her memory of the gray-brown Terran creature, and they had a mottled purple and ochre skin. They walked on stumpy, oddly jointed legs that ended in nailed pads, and they had a hooked, beaklike mouth above which were a pair of in-line horns, the greater horn a wrist-thick and sharp cone that jutted straight up in front, the lesser horn smaller and angled slightly backward toward the animal's rear. Ugly brutes, no brighter than cattle, but very tasty when cooked properly.

Noguchi came to a stop next to Hiroki's bike and dismounted, legs still throbbing with the feel of the engine. Ackland and several of his people stood grouped near the AV and watched them approach. Noguchi set her eye protectors up on her cap and patted dust from her clothing as they neared Ackland.

The big man gazed at them with a sneer. "What's the problem, Hiroki? You and the boss lady get lost?"

"We're just making the rounds—" began Hiroki.

"Yeah, right." Ackland grinned without humor. "What's the real reason? The company shoot down the price increase?"

Noguchi cleared her throat. "You know we can't get through the magnetic interference during the day. I'll contact them this evening."

Ackland scoffed and started to turn away.

"And," she continued, "I'll do all I can to get you a bigger cut."

She wouldn't be talking to Earth, of course, the newly invented subspace radio wouldn't stretch that far, but she could get a response from the corporate sub HQ on Kijita's World. Even though it was light-years away, the new equipment could shrink that to a few light-hours, effectively only a few billion kilometers. They could get an answer by morning and the sub HQ was empowered to make such niggling decisions.

Ackland raised an eyebrow. "So what are you doing here?" He made no effort to keep irritation out of his voice.

Hiroki remained silent. "We're checking on everyone's progress—seeing if there's anything we can do to help," she said.

The late-afternoon light glinted off of the AV's pitted hull behind him as Ackland looked her up and down. Finally, he nodded.

"Yeah, you can help. You can stay out of our way. The last thing we need is 'help' from corporate paper-pushers."

He faced the young woman next to him and pointed to the shaded monitor built into the AV. "Roth, take some of the boys and run these three gullies. Drive 'em down into the canyon and hook up with Cho's group."

Roth nodded and motioned to two of the men in Ackland's company. Ackland presented his back to Noguchi and Hiroki and punched at the controls set into the monitor's rim. Apparently, they had been dismissed.

They walked back to their bikes slowly. Hiroki placed a hand on her forearm gently as they reached the flyers.

"I'm sorry about the way Ackland treated you," he said.

Noguchi shrugged. "Actually, it's okay. I know how—" she paused, searched for the right word. "I know what kind of an uncaring bitch I've been. I would have been surprised if he had had any other reaction. It is as if I have been in some kind of suspended animation for the last few months. I cannot explain it."

She pulled her visor down firmly and looked to-

ward Prosperity Wells, about to say something else—
except all thoughts disappeared.

"Wow," she whispered.

"What—?" Hiroki looked past her. "Oh, yes. You
haven't gotten out much since you arrived, have you?"

Noguchi barely heard him. The suns were setting,
the desert was bathed now in golds and reds. Long
shadows stretched from the mountains toward them,
and in the cloudless sky, the arrangement of shade
and light left her breathless. It was actually the first
time she had ever seen the sunset outside.

Her mind couldn't pair the stunning sight with the
thoughts she'd had of Ryushi for the past six months;
she would have to let one or the other go.

Ryushi was, in its way, a beautiful place, at least
here and in this moment it was. Noguchi sighed and
watched the sunset, Hiroki quiet beside her. When
they finally mounted their bikes to head home, she
felt as if a heavy weight had been lifted from her
shoulders, one she had not been aware of until it was
gone.

Tom scanned the console and spoke without looking
up.

"Geosynch orbit in twenty hours, and check on tur-
bulence."

Scott's hands fluttered over the controls. "Some
fluctuation, but we can compensate no prob—we can
decouple anytime after orbit is achieved, then it's—"

The magnified Ryushi holo had appeared on the
screen.

"Hel-lo Ryushi! Jesus, what a dust ball!"

Tom looked up and nodded. "So it's a tad dry, big
deal."

Scott leaned back in his form-chair and cracked his knuckles behind his head. "Yeah, but we're not talking vague thirst here—this is just one big parched hell-hole." He watched the vid as it panned the ranges and cliffs of Ryushi. "What kind of mouth-breather would want to move way the fuck out here? Especially when there's still plenty of land available on Nova Terra?"

Tom glanced at the screen and then went back to plugging in data. "Who the hell knows? One man's poison and all like that."

"Yeah, but lookit the reads on the native life. This place *is* poison."

"Ah, I'm sure Ryushi is the perfect home for some-body *somewhere*."

"Not me," Scott mumbled under his breath. Great place for a nice vacation from the tug, sure. If you were a fucking lizard. Oh, well. He could spend his time in the local bar talking to the women, he didn't have to go hiking around in the sunshine now, did he?

Dachande studied the file picture of the desert world less than a half cycle away. Behind him, the yautja sparred under Skemte's supervision and screamed in blood lust. Soon they would have real targets.

He watched the *gkinmara* record and hissed in anticipation.

Perfect.

7

At a quarter past three in the morning, Jame Roth leaned against her flyer and watched for Ackland's headlights. The night was hot and free of wind, and stars twinkled faintly over the mountains. Her dog, Creep, lay panting at her feet, occasionally whining at the bulging sack hooked to the scooter's seat. Behind her a hundred meters or so, Travis and Adam watched over a small herd of rhynth, most of them on the ground asleep.

"Except rhynth sleep standing, eh, Creep?'

The mutt raised his head and whined again.

Roth considered herself a practical woman, but something about all of this gave her the shivers. The things she had found in the canyon were, well, odd. Unnatural to say the least. And now the rhynth were acting funny and Ackland's vet had found no

cause for the symptoms. She didn't like it, not one
bit.

She heard Ackland's AV long before it came into
view. The desert was like that at night; it was one of
the reasons that she and her spouse, Cathie Dowes,
had moved to Ryushi. Calm and quiet, far away from
crowds and the tame ugliness of Earth. Out here was
freedom, and for almost three years, she and Cathie
had been happy working for the ranchers. They were
even discussing having a child together ...

She cast an uneasy glance at the bundle and waited
for Ackland. He was an asshole, sure, but he was the
biggest herd-runner on the planet and it was his
money that was going to set her and Cathie up after
the sale. This was his responsibility.

The AV came rumbling around the bend up ahead
and squealed to a halt in front of her, the headlights
almost blinding to her dark-adjusted eyes. Ackland
climbed down from the cab almost before the transport had stopped moving. Roth unhooked the sack
and started toward him, Creep at her heels. He looked
at the rhynth beyond her and walked quickly to meet
them halfway.

"I got your message, Roth." He sounded out of
breath. "What's the problem?"

"Take a look," she said, and crouched down to
empty her find onto the dusty ground. Creep growled
at the lifeless things and backed away. Roth speared
one of the three creatures with a rhynth-stick and
held it up for Ackland to see.

It looked like nothing so much as a huge spider
with a spiny tail, a little smaller than a male fire-
walker, perhaps two hand-spans. Its long, segmented
legs curved under its plated body and its half-meter
tail looked prehensile. There were no eyes as far as

Roth could tell, but there was a short fleshy tube that perhaps served as a mouth; it hung limply at the head of the creature. The thing was a mottled slate-gray all over.

Ackland took the stick from her and studied it carefully. "What the hell *is* it?" His voice was thick with disgust.

"Besides uglier than shit? I was hoping you could tell me," she said.

Ackland frowned and set the spider down next to the other two. "I've never seen anything like these things. Where'd you find them?"

"Up at the head of Beriki canyon. There were a couple dozen of them lying around dead." She brushed a long strand of sun-bleached hair out of her eyes and looked over at the rhynth. A few of them lowed mournfully, the sounds quiet in the still air. "That's where we scared up these poke-snoots. They were stumbling around and bumping into each other like they were half-asleep." She rose to her feet and faced Ackland, who had also stood.

"I think maybe they're sick, Mr. Ackland. I thought you should know."

"What did T. Stone say?"

"Tests all clean so far."

Ackland tipped his wide-brimmed hat back on his head and then nodded at her. "You did the right thing, Roth." He looked at the herd and then down at the alien things thoughtfully. Roth waited.

"We don't *know* that there's anything wrong with the rhynth," he said carefully. "And we wouldn't want some dickhead from the company to panic and set up a quarantine, right?" Ackland's speculative gaze turned to her face. "I mean, we've invested a lot of time here—and something like that, well, that would mean that some of us wouldn't get the payoffs that we deserve ..."

He trailed off, leaving the obvious unstated. Roth chewed at her lower lip and nudged one of the creatures with one boot. Ackland was a greedy man, but he would be a *rich* greedy man within the week. And she had checked the main herd before she had called him; the only affected rhynth were the thirty-plus head behind her. Something like this could ruin all that she and Cathie had worked for ...

Roth shrugged mentally, her decision made. This was Ackland's problem now. "I understand."

Ackland grinned and rocked back on his heels, nodding.

"But what do I do with these things?" she said.

"Take 'em to Dr. Revna—but tell him you found them in Iwa Gorge, okay?" He put one hand on her shoulder and squeezed lightly. "You're doing a great job, Roth. There will be a bonus for you when this roundup is over."

As he walked back to the AV, Roth brushed at the place his hand had touched her shoulder. Asshole.

She shoved the creatures back into the bag with the rhynth-stick and loaded it onto the bike for the trip into town. "C'mon Creep." She patted her thigh and the herd dog followed her back to the watch; the rhynth that weren't asleep lay on their sides, panting heavily. Wet ropes of mucus hung from their mouths and trembled with each gasp. Poke-snoots were stupid beasts, but she didn't like to see them this way— like they had swallowed something poison ...

Noguchi sat *seiza* on the rounded mat in her apartment and breathed deeply, head down. It was just after dawn, and today *The Lector* came. She had awakened nervous and wanted to try to relax before starting the final roundup—but it had been almost a month since her last real practice and she could feel the muscles in her legs groaning from the stretch.

She had gotten her brown belt in karate before she'd left Earth for Ryushi, and had not been far away from black. While there were holo teaching devices that she could train to at the rec center, she had decided to put her lessons aside for a while—at least until she had found a human sparring partner. Holos weren't a bad way to go, but they lacked something. Dignity, perhaps.

But she hadn't made any close enough friends to work out with . . .

No friends, Machiko, close or otherwise. Don't kid yourself.

Right. Most ranchers probably weren't into martial arts anyway.

Her thighs trembled when she stood to form riding-horse stance; her old sensei, Master Ko, would have put her on the floor for letting herself go like this. She ran through blocks and kicks to loosen up a little, and was surprised at the vague sadness she felt at the familiarity of the moves. Homesickness? No, she had left little behind on Earth worth missing. It was . . .

Loneliness. The thought struck a chord within her that she hadn't felt for a very long time. It was the sense of—not belonging. At least on Earth she had worked in an office building with thousands of other employees, had walked through streets full of people; she had been in a karate class. Noguchi hadn't been very close to anyone, but at least there had been that option. And here there was only Hiroki, who seemed to disapprove of her somehow in spite of his smiling facade. Hiroki and a group of ranchers who didn't give a shit if she came or went.

She stopped midway through the fourth form and frowned, sweat light on her brow. What was next? Block-claw or drop to her right knee and clutch—?

She started the form over and went slowly, concentrating this time.

Chop to throat, that was it. For some reason, she felt near tears for having forgotten. Had it been so long?

She ran through the rest of her workout quickly and then kneeled into *seiza* again, bangs plastered to her forehead. Today would be a nonstop panic, supervising roundup and then preparations for the arrival of *The Lector*. There were responsibilities to delegate and papers to shuffle. She wished there was someone to talk to, someone to commiserate with over the busy day to come ...

Well. There was no time to regret her choices now, there was too much to be done. She had practiced smiling and nodding and tonight would be her first gesture of goodwill toward the ranchers, the company approved price increase. She hoped that it would be the start of a new relationship of mutual respect.

It has to be; Hiroki leaves in a few days with the rhynth shipment.

Right. Time to get ready.

Noguchi tripped on the step into the bathroom and knocked her head solidly into the door frame. She cursed and placed a hand on the swelling lump, eyes squeezed shut. Great. The bruise would match her lavender blouse for the party. A terrific start to the day, O master martial artist.

She hoped any other disasters would wait until tomorrow.

* * *

Kesar Revna was fascinated. Alien biology was supposedly his forte, but he hadn't seen anything quite like it. He tried to keep up with the UMA reports from Earth, and Chigusa had a monthly online biomed journal that was one of the best; new species were being discovered every day, it seemed. But besides a mutant form of crab that had turned up on Terra Nova a few years back after a radioactive waste mishap, he found nothing in the literature that looked quite like this . . .

"I have to get back to work, Dr. Revna, if that's okay—"

He reluctantly looked up from the examination table at the young woman who had brought in the amazing creatures. She seemed nervous, anxious to be gone; she certainly looked out of place in the lab. Her dusty range clothes and darkly tanned skin didn't seem to agree with indoor lighting.

"Of course," he said. "It's the big day, isn't it?"

"Yeah."

"And you say you found these in Iwa Gorge?"

"Uh, yeah. Right." She dropped her gaze to the table and shuddered slightly. "Mr. Ackland said you might want to take a look at them."

"Give Mr. Ackland my thanks. And I appreciate you coming in, I know how busy you must be."

"Sure, no problem. Let us know how things turn out when you get a chance." She turned to walk out and nearly collided with Miriam, the town's human doctor and Kesar's wife, which made her Dr. Revna, too.

"Excuse me, Dr. Revna."

Miriam smiled. Her tanned skin crinkled at the corners of her eyes. She had her long and dark hair pulled back into a ponytail and she always seemed so tiny and petite she made Roth feel like a rhynth. "Hello, Jame. How's Cathie's knee?"

"Great. Good as new. I'm sorry, I really have to run—"

"That's all right. We'll hopefully see you both tonight."

Kesar had already turned his attention back to the specimen. "What do you make of this, Doc?"

Miriam laughed. "Oh, thank you. No 'good morning, my love, how did you sleep'?"

Kesar looked at his wife and grinned. "Good morning, my love, how did you sleep? Now take a look at what Roth brought in. I could use a second opinion."

Miriam bent over the table and raised her eyebrows. "She found this on *Ryushi*?"

"Iwa Gorge, she says. And she also said that there were at least twenty more, dead. I've already tried to cut one of the legs with the Killian, and nothing. Not a scratch."

"You're kidding." Miriam searched his face for the joke. "Any carbon-based animal ..." she trailed off. "Silicon? Couldn't be and even if it was, that would at least have been marked—" She gazed at the specimen in wonder. "What is it, Kesar? You're the DVM."

He shook his head. "I don't know. There was that Terra Nova mutation, and I heard some rumors about a weird life form found in a mining colony somewhere, but somebody clamped down on that, nothing substantiated. We're going to need to run some tests; and I think afterward, I'm going to take a little ride up to the gorge and poke around."

Miriam frowned. "Alone?"

Kesar nodded. He felt wired. This was a totally new species . . .

"One of us should stay in case of any problems with the herding. Anyway, like you just said, I'm the vet, right? If I can find one of these alive—"

"—it could bite you, Kesar. Perhaps you should wait for a few days. Until someone can come with you."

"Right. I need a guard to protect me from this little fist-sized spider. Don't worry, I'll be fine, Miriam." He patted her hand and smiled. "I'll take a net and watch where I put my feet."

He turned his attention back to the specimen even though he was aware she was hovering there, concerned.

"Hmm. The belly looks a lot softer than the legs. I bet I can incise along this plate line. Could you please fetch me the scalpel kit? Oh, and the Menashe saw? I'll peel this critter, one way or another."

She pursed her lips doubtfully but went to get the equipment from storage. He stooped over the alien again, already lost in thought. Miriam was a good doctor and a good spouse, but she worried too much. This creature was the most intriguing thing he'd come across on this planet so far. Hell, that's why he'd gotten into offworld medicine, stuff like this. To have some new and fascinating creature with his own Latinized name hung on it and then studied in biology classes at prestigious universities was perhaps an egotistical wish, but not an immoral one, was it? *Why, yes, this is the first of the many unique life forms discovered by the galactically famous Dr. Kesar Revna. A minor find compared to his later work, of course, but even great men must*

*have beginnings. Let him stand as an example to
you all . . .*

He smiled at the fantasy.

How could anyone fear such a unique find?

Besides, the creature was probably as harmless as
his fantasy of academic greatness.

8

They landed on the parched world in the bottom of a vast ravine, far from where the *lou-dte kalei* had sown the Hard Meat eggs; they came in cloaked and during light hours, although the Hunt would not begin until after dark. It was all standard procedure; there were some worlds upon which the natives had developed weaponry and would fight for their skins, infected or not. Dachande had not lived long by being careless on strange terrain, and the planet had not been used for a Hunt so recently that precautions could be discarded. Especially now, because since the yautja's last visit to Hunt here, others had come.

The Soft Meat, bleeding all over the radio bands for all to hear.

It was a shock to find them here. Given his choice,

he would hunt the Soft Meat, a thing he had long desired. They were cunning and they shot back. Soft Meat skulls were highly prized, the centerpiece of a warrior's trophy wall. He would challenge them, were it at all possible. But not with a handful of raw and unseasoned would-be warriors. Not only would it be foolish, it was also against the rules of the Hunt. Dachande could almost smell them, the Soft Meat, and he would like nothing better than to test his mettle against them, but he would not, not this time. He had responsibilities, duties, and to cast them aside for his personal satisfaction would be to dishonor his name. So the ship would remain cloaked, any of his party who might venture even remotely close to the oomans would do so in a shiftsuit, and the Soft Meat would never now how lucky they had been. Reluctantly and without explanation, Dachande caused shiftsuit electronics to be issued to the students. Let them wonder what his motivations were—they knew enough not to ask. He would tell the other Blooded of the danger, but there would be no contact with the oomans on this trip. Was an ooman sighted, the Blooded would order the students to shift into camouflage and to avoid contact. A pity, but that was the way of it. After he finished this training Hunt, his dues would be paid and his application to a Blooded Warrior Only ship would be accepted. Then he would at last get his chance at the oomans. Not here, not now.

In the staging area, the younglings were so *ch'hkt-a* that they would burn each other if they didn't calm down.

Dachande watched the young males hurriedly don their suits. He stood in the entry and felt the thick anticipation that radiated from them in their frenzied

movements. It never failed to please him, to see the
young so eager to spill first *thwei*.

There would be a short practice outside of the ship
to test the world's gravity while Warkha scanned for
anything unexpected—it was killing nothing other
than time, a chance to wear the edge off of the young
males' hyper-enthusiasm. Too, the Hard Meat would
also be more active after the suns dropped. It was
hardly sport to shoot a target curled up asleep.

Dachande turned and walked through the corridor
toward the front of the ship. As Leader, he would be
the first to set foot on the Hunting grounds, a pleasure that rumbled deep in his gut.

This would be a good Hunt, oomans notwithstanding.

Noguchi took her second shower of the day in the
early evening, as twilight fell over Prosperity Wells. It
had been a hard day but a good one; all of the herds
had been penned except for one of Cho's and that one
was on its way.

She stood in front of the holomirror in the green
linen suit she had worn on her first day in Ryushi and
smiled at her wind-burned complexion. After only a
few days outside, her face had begun to take on the
look of a rancher's. She liked it; it was the appearance
of a person who didn't mind hard work, even though
she had to innoculate herself against skin cancers and
had run a small fever from the vaccine for most of a
day.

The Chigusa staff had been setting up tables and
portable roasting pits near the shield wall when she
had gone to shower and change, but she was surprised at the crowd that had gathered in her short ab-

sence. She stepped out of her building and was nearly run over by a group of giggling children. Not many of those here, children, but some.

The scent of grilled rhynth steaks carried to her along with the sounds of people talking and laughing. Ranchers and their spouses walked past, hand in hand, all headed toward the landing pad. Noguchi joined them.

Hiroki was easy to spot amid the ranchers in his dark dress suit; he stood near the loading ramp, drink in hand. He returned her wave and wove his way through the crowd to meet her.

"You look lovely, Machiko-*san*."

"Thank you. You look very nice yourself." She gazed wonderingly at the mass of people all around. "Is every person on the planet here?"

"Just about. A few of the staff are watching screens in ops, but other than that . . ."

Noguchi smiled. "A hundred people in one place is now a mob to me. Funny, how perspectives change."

Hiroki nodded. "It is. And I'm glad to see them enjoying themselves. This is their first roundup, everything they've worked for, for three years."

Noguchi looked around at the ranchers, relaxed and mingling in the open compound. It was impossible not to pick up on the mood of excitement and accomplishment. Someone had even fed music over the public address system; couples danced in the deepening dusk while their children ran and played through the streets.

"Come on, let's go greet the ship," said Hiroki. "It's due any minute."

She followed him through the dancing crowd toward the antenna tower. "The home office called," she said mildly. "They've approved the price hike for the ranchers."

Hiroki raised his eyebrows and smiled at her. "Good work, boss."

"Where are we headed, anyway? Wouldn't the best place be—"

"The tower is the only place to watch a landing." Hiroki stopped in front of the runged ladder that ran up one side of the transmitting structure and rested one hand on the lowest step.

"Can that thing support both of us?" Noguchi looked at the ladder doubtfully.

"Let's find out, shall we?"

They scaled one story and hit the first landing, then slowly climbed the stairs to the top, five floors up. There was a moderate, warm breeze blowing, and Noguchi looked down to see the miniature people milling about in the night air.

It was easy to forget the pressures of work on such an occasion. Pleasant memories from long ago ran through her head, Nakama festivals with her parents, walks through bonsai forests that made her feel like a giant.

A low rumbling began, somewhere in the sky. The people below watched the clouds for movement.

Noguchi looked up to see the ship, and even so far away, she could tell it was big. Huge. It was hard for her mind to grasp such a gigantic object in the air. She had seen craft like it before, of course—but this one was bigger than the entire rec center and op building combined. It had pusher vents easily twenty meters long and half as wide on either side; there were three loading docks in front, each big enough to admit four rhynth side by side; giant air-pushers

swept a benign wind over the crowd as the ship rumbled toward the landing pad.

With a roar that drowned out all other sound, *The
Lector* settled gently. It was quite a trick to land such
a tub in atmosphere; the aerodynamics were hardly
conducive to such things. The shield wall protected
the complex from most of the engine wash, but the
sudden gale that hit all of them was enough to whip
up dresses and hair and a considerable haze of dust.
As the thunder dwindled slowly, Noguchi heard a chorus of laughter and hand clapping.

It was a magnificent spectacle, *The Lector* come to
roost. Well, part of the ship anyway. The rest was still
in orbit.

A hand landed on her shoulder. Hiroki. He grinned
at her.

"Down to the final klick, eh? Let's go introduce ourselves to the crew."

They started toward the stairs, Hiroki leading.
Noguchi cast one last look at the ship and thought
about what he had said, the final kilometer. In spite of
the mood of the evening, she had felt a chill at his
words. Odd.

She brushed the ominous speculation aside and
went to join the party.

Scott and Tom stepped off the ramp together into
Prosperity Wells. For some reason, the mass of people
assembled to greet them was a relief to Scott, although he wasn't sure why. Other crew members filed
out past them to shake hands and chat with the
ranchers and their families.

"Hey, we're celebrities, man, check it out," Tom
mumbled.

Scott smirked. It was true; the locals had gathered around each of *The Lector*'s crew with smiles and backslaps.

"Guess they don't get out much," Scott whispered.

A tall, husky man, about forty TS, with a red beard and a grin stepped toward them. He held out two cups of beer to the pilots. "Ackland's the name," he said, extending his large hand. Tom shook it, then Scott. "I'm head of the local ranchers association. How was your trip, Captains—?"

"Strandberg," said Tom. "But just call me Tom. This is my copilot, Scott Conover. The trip was fine."

"Nice to meet you, sirs. Hope you and your crew are ready to party; we got some nice steaks on the grill—" Ackland leaned closer and lowered his voice. "And we got some fine young ladies looking for dance partners, I'll bet. That is, if you're inclined that way—"

Scott grinned. "You bet. Tom here was starting to look pretty good near the last leg of the trip, if you know what I mean."

Ackland chuckled, a forced and overly jovial sound, and clapped Scott on the back. "I thought so," he started. "You know, I was—"

"Can I have your attention, please?" A short Japanese woman in a green suit stood on a chair a few meters away, a dinner tray in hand. "Can I have everyone's attention, please?"

She was pretty, that one. Scott looked her up and down. Nice legs, nice butt. A little shy in the breast department, but Scott had seen worse.

"Who's the babe?" he said quietly to Ackland. Tom elbowed him in the gut. Damn feminist.

"You mean bitch," Ackland replied. "Nitrogen queen. That's the boss."

"I know you're all anxious for the festivities to begin, but first I have an important announcement." The crowd calmed as everyone turned to look at her.

"Loading will proceed as follows—Ackland, you're first on deck. Harrison's next, followed by Luccini and Marianetti. The rest of the assignments will be handed out tomorrow at dusk." She paused, then smiled.

"One more thing. The company gave their answer on the price adjustment—you'll be getting the increase you requested. Enjoy the party, everyone."

She stepped off the chair to the sounds of scattered clapping and hoots of excitement.

"Go figure," said Ackland. "Maybe she's good for something after all."

Scott took a long gulp of beer and then laughed. "I could think of a few other things she might be good at."

Tom rolled his eyes, and Ackland shook his head. "I wouldn't try it. Noguchi probably doesn't uncross her legs to take a shit, you know?"

"Too bad," mumbled Tom. He wandered off.

Scott took another slug and belched softly. "Takes all kinds, right?" he said, and looked into his cup. Not bad for a local brew. He picked out the Japanese woman again and studied her smile as she talked to some rancher woman. Ackland was babbling something about the weather, but Scott watched Noguchi.

Dust ball it was, but the place wasn't a lost cause. He swigged more beer and turned his attention back to Ackland. Anything could happen in three days, no matter what the rancher said. Hell, nitrogen was his specialty ...

Noguchi walked toward the ops center, the party in full swing behind her. It was definitely a success, in

more ways than one. A few of the ranchers had
warmed toward her after the announcement, and she
had kept up a steady patter of innocuous conversation for at least two hours. Nice people. And she had
been doing a good job of nodding and smiling—

*Although one day doesn't undo six months of stu-
pidity, Machiko.*

Right. But it was a start. It had finally hit home that
Hiroki would be leaving with *The Lector*. A vague sadness had come over her, along with a desire to be
alone for a little while. He was perhaps her only
friend . . .

She walked into operations to see only one person
manning the screens.

"Collins, right?" she said hopefully.

The young man nodded and stood up.

"Go join the party, okay? I'll watch things here for
a while."

Collins's eyes widened. "Really? Thanks, Ms.
Noguchi."

"It's just Machiko from now on." She smiled at him
and moved by so that he could pass.

"Uh, okay," he said. "Machiko." He sounded uncomfortable with her first name but he smiled back. He
started to walk out and then turned.

"Oh, listen—when Doc Revna gets back, tell him
the home office received his report. It's in the tray
with his notes."

Noguchi frowned. She had seen Fem Doc at the
party, but Revna hadn't been around, had he?

"Gets back from where?" she said.

"Said he was going up to Iwa Gorge to look for
something," he said. "He signed out a hover bike a
couple of hours ago."

"Today? Bad timing," she said.

"Yeah, that's what *I* said." Collins shrugged. "But he said it was important. Listen, thanks again."

After he had left, Noguchi sat at the console and gazed at the radar, lost in thought. She hadn't expected much from Hiroki at the beginning, but he had been unfailingly patient with her. His professionalism was top-notch; it would be sad to see him leave . . .

She shook her head and glanced around for something to take her mind off of Hiroki. Doc Revna's report lay in a basket nearby, but she hesitated picking it up. What if it were private information—?

Then he wouldn't have let Collins send it, he would've done it himself.

Brilliant. She picked up the stack of hard copy and leaned back in her chair. What the hell was in Iwa Gorge, anyway? She liked the doc, he was a smart man. She leafed through the papers and settled down to read, with a silent wish for Revna to find whatever it was he was looking for . . .

Kesar trained his binoculars on the sight at the bottom of the gorge and inhaled sharply. His heart hammered in his chest and his hands shook. It was incredible. It was unbelievable.

A dozen or so humanoids stood surrounding a large craft, the likes of which he had never seen. The ship looked like a cross between a fish and a huge engine tube, it was tinted a strange greenish hue, with a broad ramp set into the ground.

The humanoids were tall; he couldn't be sure because of nothing to show relative size, and the scaler in his scope was malfunctioning, but he would guess two and a half meters, maybe a little more. More amazing, they appeared to be carrying ... spears.

Revna had stopped halfway down into the gorge, had parked his bike near some rocks twenty meters behind him or so. The adrenaline in his system was screaming at him to go back to the flyer, now. Big aliens with spears did not seem like the kind of folks you wanted to meet by yourself in the middle of the desert. But he couldn't stop looking at the amazing sight.

He hit the full magnification button and the creatures zoomed closer. Tall, muscular, definitely armed. Still too far away to get a good view and it was also too bad the scope's scaler was out of whack, he wanted to get a size on them.

Whatever they were, they were definitely not human. Now here was a discovery that would get his name in the books. Not just a new species of spider or crab, but sentient aliens!

He watched for another half minute. What were they doing here? What *were* they? A hundred questions formed and tried to rise all at once. Incredible.

He licked his lips and focused on one of the alien faces. Some kind of mask it wore, like the others. Breathing gear?

He would go back to town, get some of the ranchers, some photo equipment—

Kesar blinked. One of the creatures turned and looked at him. It threw back its head, its long, odd braids fell back. A long, crazy howl filled the canyon, echoed off of the cliffs, and beat at his ears, joined by others.

Impossible, he was mostly hidden from view, and he could hardly see them with the scope. They *couldn't* see him.

But they did. He knew for sure in a second.

When they ran toward him, waving their spears, screaming.

9

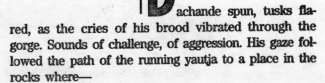

achande spun, tusks flared, as the cries of his brood vibrated through the gorge. Sounds of challenge, of aggression. His gaze followed the path of the running yautja to a place in the rocks where—

Ooman!

Warkha spoke behind him, but the words were swallowed in the frenzy.

Dachande gave orders without looking.

"Tell Skemte to prepare flight and gather those you can! *Ki'cte!*"

He ran, blade in hand. The Hunt would have to be aborted, but the ooman would die first. There was no other way. Dachande cursed mentally and ran faster.

He was almost to the rocks when the noise of a craft starting hit him.

Damn! If the ooman got away, it would bring others!

He saw that at least two of the students had already made it to the place he was headed, Chulonte and another, he couldn't tell—

The small flying craft came over the rise and struck Chulonte at chest level.

A single ooman manned the ship, was balanced clumsily at the controls, hair swept back from an ugly, pale face.

Chulonte scrabbled at the craft to hold on, but the ooman ran the flyer close to a rock face. Chulonte's skull cracked against the cliff and he fell suddenly boneless to the ground, the mint gray-green of his brain tissue mixed with the darker phosphor-green of his blood splattered on the stone.

Cjit! The Hunt had not even begun and already he had lost a student. Damn!

The ooman's craft was turned by the collision. It roared and swerved past Dachande and headed straight for their ship, the ooman's intentions unknown.

The Leader ran back toward the ship. He screamed the death cry to all: kill the ooman!

It would pay with its life for the death of Chulonte.

Revna ran to his bike, his stomach an empty hole. Stark terror made him fumble the starter. His hands shook uncontrollably.

"Start, please, oh, please, start, start—" He heard his own voice and for a moment it sounded as if it belonged to someone else.

The cycle roared to life. Relief rushed through him,

cool and welcome. He stepped on the accelerator, hard, thinking only of escape.

And he flew directly into them. He topped the rock formation, his thoughts clouded with panic; turn, turn, *turn*, fool—

One of the creatures leapt up in front of him. He tried to swerve, but it was too late. The impact jarred him from his seat; he would have fallen except for the reflexive grab at the handles. The alien was huge; Revna caught a whiff of some musky, bitter oil. Its screech was one of pain and fury. It grabbed for him.

Without thinking, Revna veered toward a cliff wall. The screaming thing smacked into the rocks, hard, and then was gone. He tried to regain control of the scooter but the impact had thrown him into a turn. And the controls were damaged, he couldn't turn, the flier responded sluggishly.

All right, don't panic, it's okay. He would have to use speed to get past them, have to go so fast they couldn't catch him, couldn't *spear* him—

Another of the creatures reached for him, but he passed it. Revna smashed on the accelerator all the way forward as a blast of incredible heat blew by him. He ducked, felt his facial hair singe.

The craft didn't want to alter its course. He was going to pass right next to the ship.

Altitude, he had to get high enough so they couldn't grab him!

The repellors still worked, he managed to trim the elevators and start to climb. Five meters, seven, still heading right at the ship but he would clear it—

Another blast of heat, this one splashed the underside of the flier, cooked plastic and metal. The repellors coughed and the craft dropped a meter, sputtered.

That was no spear! They've got guns! Lasers, plasma rifles, Jesus!

He raised his watering eyes just in time to see that he was headed for the alien craft at high speed and that he wasn't going to clear it.

He was going to hit it dead center—

Miriam—

It was his last thought before the world turned to fire.

Dachande saw the ooman fly at the ship and he ran faster. Most of the students were clear, but at that speed, an impact could cause damage, big damage—

The tiny flier smashed into the ship and blew apart in a fireball that shattered both craft. A second later came another blast, bigger than the first. Flame and debris sprayed, scorched rocks, moved boulders, knocked over delicate formations that had stood undisturbed for millions of years. Huge chunks of burning ship flew through the gully as the hunters were blown to the ground by the blast.

After a moment Tichinde stood and looked around at his fallen peers. He waited to hear direction from the Leader, but there were no instructive cries.

Other yautja rose to their feet, dazed. Small pools of *mi* burned, their flickerings reaching into the dusk, carrying in their fumes the smells of ash and soil and oily death.

The Leader had fallen not far from Tichinde. Several of the others stumbled with him to where Dachande lay.

The Leader was barely alive, his mandibles caked

with *thwei*. Wreckage had hit him, knocked him into *dhi'ki-de*, the sleep near death.

A quick survey showed them that Warkha, too, was dead, and the other Blooded had been on the ship that still burned and smoked and looked now like nothing so much as a gutted crab. No one would be leaving this world on that vessel. And it would be weeks, months, years perhaps, before anybody came to look for them. Not good.

When all of the students alive had gathered around Dachande, Tichinde counted. Ten of them. No transport and no elder to tell them what would happen—

"What will we do?" From 'Aseigan.

"Dachande still breathes," said Gkyaun. "We could—"

"You are a medic?" Tichinde snorted. "He is beyond the aid kits, look at him. Let him die honorably of his wounds, wounds sustained in battle." He waved at the smoking ship. "The ooman deliberately attacked us and killed our ship. Therefore, we will kill the oomans, that is what we will do. Dachande lives but his time is short."

'Aseigan growled. "Who proclaimed you Leader?" His voice was thick with contempt. "You will not lead me. And Hunting Soft Meat is forbidden to un-Blooded, even a fool such as you knows this."

Tichinde grinned and pointed his burner at the yautja. 'Aseigan took a step toward him, arms high.

Tichinde fired.

The blast blew 'Aseigan against a pile of smoking rock. The others leapt back in surprise.

"Others dispute?" Tichinde swung the burner in a circle. "I will spill your *thwei* as easily as I do that of the ooman dogs later! This is not a Hunt, as that dead slave-to-rules thought, but self-defense. We are al-

lowed to defend ourselves from attack, are we not?"
Once again he waved at the ruins of their ship.

None of the nine disagreed. They watched him war-
ily, hands close to their own burners. There was a
long moment when a Challenge might have come,
when one of the nine might have taken it upon himself to raise his burner and try him, but that moment
passed. If another would be Leader, he would have
made his move and none did.

Tichinde smiled. They would follow him, reluctantly or not.

He raised his staff to the sky and screamed of revenge. When Gkyaun returned from the wreck and
handed him the smoldering ooman skull a moment
later, Tichinde crushed it with bare claw to the ap-
proving hisses of the others. It had killed itself and
bravely in the doing, so it could not be a proper trophy. But there would be others to be earned.

The yautja chanted and howled their approval into
the night. Tichinde sent them to scavenge for whole
weapons and armor.

They were stuck here. So be it. The oomans would
be sorry they dared attack the yautja. Sorry they
dared to cross blades with Tichinde.

Very sorry.

10

he disparity in ratio between the smooth-backed specimens and the single carcass with dorsal spines notwithstanding, I believe the differences between the two types represent sexual indicators—not of the specimens themselves, but of the zygote or "egg" that each carries. As stated above, none of the specimens is equipped for independent life, their sole purpose seems to be nothing more than that of a living delivery vehicle—an ambulatory penis, if you will.

Noguchi tapped her cigarette without looking at the tray and skimmed back to the top of the page, totally absorbed. *This* is what Revna had gone after? Why hadn't he told anyone? Why hadn't he told *her?*

While it is risky to postulate so much from such a tiny sample, we need to know as much as possible

*about these specimens as quickly as possible. If my
assumptions are correct, or even near the mark,
we're dealing with only one stage of this organism.
The hybrid silicon-carbon cell construction would
lead—*

" 'Ambulatory penis,' huh? Conjures quite an image,
don't it?"

Noguchi jumped in her chair and turned quickly,
heart pounding. A tall man with blond hair and beard
stood there, grinning. He swayed slightly on his feet;
from the smell of him, he had been drinking. A lot.

She stood and backed away a step. "You're from
The Lector, right?"

The stranger took a step closer. "Hell, I *fly* that
bucket!" He belched softly. " 'Scuse me. Scott Conover
atcher service."

Noguchi smiled but inched back a little more. His
intentions weren't exactly clear but one thing was . . .

"You're drunk, Mr. Conover."

"Yeah, but not *too* drunk, if you know what I mean.
You're Ms. Nogooshi. I've been watching you—"

"It's Noguchi," she said coolly. "And you can call
me ma'am."

Conover laughed and reached out to take her hand.
Noguchi tried to pull away, but the pilot gripped her
wrist tightly. He leaned close, his alcohol breath moist
and pungent. "I heard about what a tough lady you
were, the company ramrod, right?" His words slurred
together slightly.

The drunken pilot tried to pull her hand down to
his crotch. "I got your ramrod right here, ma'am," he
stage-whispered.

Noguchi narrowed her eyes and took a deep
breath.

* * *

Scott couldn't find the Jap girl anywhere; he wandered around for a while and eventually he heard some guy say that she was watching screens.

"Operations," he said to no one in particular, and stumbled in that direction.

The door was open. He was torn between the desire to march right in and woo the woman and the desire to piss—which had gotten pretty overwhelming. He compromised and peed on the entry frame before his imminent conquest.

She was reading some kind of porn hard copy, he could see that much. Damn, but she was fine! He imagined that small mouth all over him, on his dick; and she wanted it, too, he could tell.

They did the small talk thing for a minute or two, and she told him she was into being dominant—'call me ma'am'—and the little vixen played chase, backing up, her cheeks flushed with desire.

And he reached out to touch her, to put her hand on his ready-and-willing equipment—and then he wasn't sure what happened.

He must have tripped—

Noguchi grabbed his arm above the elbow with her free hand and hooked one foot behind his. She twisted, pushing up and over at the same time, and the pilot went down. She jumped back and struck a ready pose, left foot forward, fists made. It had happened so fast, she was barely aware that she had done it.

The drunk groaned loudly; he didn't get up. Noguchi relaxed slightly, but kept her distance.

Another man stepped into the room, dark-haired, wearing glasses.

"Scott?" He looked down and moved immediately to the fallen man. "Jesus, what happened?" He stared up at Noguchi, at her fighting stance; realization dawned on his face.

"You next?" Adrenaline still pumped through her system.

The drunk's friend stood, hands in the air. "No, no, I was just coming to tell you that the ship is loaded and that we'll be making our first shuttle run as soon as the inspectors give the rhynth a clean bill of health—" He spoke all at once, in a rush, but seemed to catch himself.

Noguchi nodded. "You'd better have them check out this pilot, too." She looked down at Conover and frowned. "Especially his judgment."

"I'm Tom Strandberg, ma'am. I'm sorry about this, he's the designated drinker on this run." As the man spoke, he bent down and tried to help Conover to his feet. He grinned sheepishly. "Tomorrow it'll be my turn."

With a grunt of effort, Strandberg stood up, Conover half over one shoulder.

"Your turn to drink or your turn to get some of what I gave him?" Noguchi spoke sharply; she knew that none of this was Strandberg's fault, but damn him for excusing his friend so lightly; attempted rape wasn't particularly funny.

Strandberg edged toward the door with his heavy load. "Look, I'll make sure he doesn't bother you again, okay?"

It seemed to be the perfect cue. Conover raised his head slightly. "Damn bitch," he mumbled, and nodded back out.

Strandberg carried the other pilot out without another word.

Noguchi sat back in her chair and felt her heart slow down little by little. If she didn't receive a formal apology the next morning, she would file a complaint with the company.

Maybe I'll do that anyway. Conover certainly didn't deserve anything less, ol' I-got-your-ramrod-right-here.

She surprised herself by laughing out loud. How classically dumb *male*. Did they teach lines like that in Neanderthal 101?

Noguchi picked up the papers she had been reading, a smile still on her face. Well, it had broken the tension she'd been feeling.

After she'd read the same paragraph three times, she sighed and put the report down. This was important stuff, but she couldn't seem to regain her concentration after the rush of adrenaline that idiot's advances had created. Besides, it was late. Revna must have gone to the party or just gone home.

She stood, stretched, and yawned. Maybe she wasn't so very out of martial arts' practice after all. She had tossed him without thinking about it. It came back quick enough when she'd needed it.

She made sure that the recorders were all on and pulled her jacket off the back of the chair. She would talk to Revna tomorrow about these "specimens"; from the sound of it, there might be some crucial things going on out at Iwa Gorge—and it was her job to know about it.

It was dark and hot. The smell of burned materials worked its way into that darkness, and with the scent came pain.

Dachande opened his mouth to scream at the young males to fall in line, but nothing happened. He sensed no movement, no sound of the students came to him. He tried to lift one arm to clear his vision, but nothing happened. Only heat and blackness and far-away pain.

And then only dark.

Scott hurt. He rolled his head and opened his eyes, but closed them again immediately. The whole fuckin' *planet* was spinning. And there was an earthquake or something.

What planet?

"Wha' the fuck?" he mumbled. He opened his eyes again.

"Back to the land of the living?" Tom's face swam into view next to him. They were riding a small cart outside, back to the ship—the earthquake was the rumbling motor. On Ryushi. *The Lector.* Cowboys.

Japanese babe—

Scott focused on Tom's face. "Nogooshi," he said. It was coming back.

Tom grinned. "Scott, you're plowed. Apparently you tried to have sex with the head of the company here, a very capable woman who knocked the shit out of you before you got around to figuring out she wasn't interested." He paused for a second and then added, "And if you ask me, you're lucky she didn't rip your dick off and feed it to you."

"Great," said Scott. He closed his eyes, exhausted. "Nice to have you on my side, ol' buddy ol' pal."

Scott was almost asleep when the cart stopped. He growled and pulled himself upright. They were back at *The Lector.*

"Need help?"

"*No.* Fucking Judas." He got out of the cart okay, but discovered that his legs weren't particularly interested in staying straight. Tom grabbed one of his arms and pulled it over his own shoulder. Scott leaned on him heavily.

"Yeah, okay." He shuffled along next to Tom as they walked onto the second loading ramp. "She can't treat me like that, you know."

"Maybe you want to go back and tell her that," Tom said. "What's with the lights? Prindle's team is getting sloppy, maintenance is going to hell—"

Scott sighed. "Fuck the lights. But you know what I mean, right? I mean, I'm a goddamned *star*-pilot, you know?" On top of the humiliation of it all, he was getting a *huge* headache.

Tom leaned him up against a wall. "Hang on a sec, let me get a light."

Scott went on. "Who the fuck does she think she is, you know?" He stared at the floor. Goddamn rhynth all over the place, looked like one of them had thrown up on the floor. He toed the puddle of wet, mucusy goo with one foot and then looked away quickly; that was enough to make his stomach pretty damn unhappy.

"She's corporate," said Tom. "She pulled rank on you." He reappeared holding a flashlight and reached out to steady Scott with his free arm.

"That's not all she pulled," said Scott glumly. "I think my back is broken or something."

"Who in the hell left this hatch open?" Tom stepped forward and shined the light into the dark rhynth pen.

"You're not listening to me." Scott leaned back on the wall. Fuck the hatch.

"Hey, Ackland warned you, right?" Tom's voice had

taken on an echolike quality. He had walked into the pen.

With the last of his coordination, Scott followed him, narrowly missing a renegade doorway. Rhynth puke *everywhere*.

Tom continued. "But you wouldn't listen, *no*. You just had to go mess with the queen—"

Tom stopped short. The flashlight hit the floor and a low hiss filled the room, coming from all around.

Scott shook his head and followed Tom's gaze. There were four. Or seven. Or twenty. A flurry of horrible images: long, dark skulls and dripping razor teeth. Gigantic, black, all arms and legs and spiny tails, hissing. Moving forward.

Reaching toward them—

11

There was darkness. Not with the cold that she had once associated with the black hours, not with a sense of night or time. It was a stifling darkness that echoed with soft, wet sounds of rhythmic movement—the insistent pulse of body against body, but far from any act of love. It was the black of a huge machine, steadily devouring light, continually working, thrumming. Eating. Building toward the inevitable scream. The darkness was the dragon, calling her name, calling its prey, and there was no escape . . .

"Machiko?"

Light blared, loud and unwanted. Noguchi started, sat up. She rubbed her eyes. "What—?"

Hiroki stood in her doorway, his hand on the control panel.

The darkness machine, insatiable—

She shook her head. "I had a dream ... Hiroki. What time is it?"

"Almost noon." Hiroki smiled apologetically. "I know you were up late last night, sorry to disturb you—"

"What is it?" Noguchi felt the last of the dream slip away as her eyes adjusted to the brightness. She was suddenly aware that she wore only an undershirt, and a tight one at that.

"Doc Revna still hasn't returned, and Mrs. Doc is starting to worry. I've sent out a crew in the copter to search for him, but I thought it would be best if the staff saw that you were in on this, too."

Noguchi nodded. "Thank you, Hiroki. You're right. Give me two minutes to get dressed."

Hiroki averted his eyes politely as she walked to the 'fresher to splash water on her face. Revna wasn't back? He'd been gone—fifteen or sixteen hours, at least. Too long.

She dressed quickly and rinsed her mouth with water. In spite of the cool liquid, she felt hot, her eyes sticky and full of sand. Not enough sleep. Noguchi combed through her hair with her fingers and stepped out to meet Hiroki. She glanced longingly at her bed; a nap later, perhaps.

Doc had probably just had some engine trouble; he would know to stay put and wait for help. Hell, the copter was most likely on its way back with Revna already; nothing to worry about.

Except for the darkness.

She shuddered as they reached the door to the building; her dream—

"You okay?"

Noguchi smiled and gave up on the half-remembered image. "Fine. I just—I dreamed it was hot."

Hiroki laughed. "Pure fantasy."

Noguchi smiled again, but felt the shudder deep inside. She hoped the dark feelings were just that, fantasy. She donned her sunglasses and followed Hiroki into the blazing day.

David Spanner had one fuck of a nasty headache. The pressers on the goddamn copter were incredibly noisy—no, more than that, they were *deadly*, that was it. He had been sent out because of all of his sins to die by slow torture. *Loud* torture.

"How about after this we go to the cafe and get some sushi, Spanner? Nice and fresh, maybe the abalone, all squishy and raw, or the octopus—"

"Fuck you very much, Ikeda." Great. Only big party of the year, everyone in town is sleeping it off, and *he* gets sent to pick up the doc. With the only person in town who wasn't suffering a severe hangover.

His copilot grinned, her smile relaxed and easy. "Or we could have a few cold ones. What do you say? Couple of big frosty quarts of beer, to wash down the snake-roll?"

Spanner scowled. "I could just throw up on you now, save you the trouble of making me."

"No time," she said. "We're almost there."

Ikeda pulled up on the stick as they rounded a cliff and flew into the gorge. Spanner's stomach protested at the sudden dip. He wrapped his arms around his chest and closed his eyes, taking deep breaths.

"You did that on purpose, Ikeda."

"Maybe. Help me look, lush."

Spanner shook his head, eyes still closed. "Uh-uh. You look. I'm just here for the fresh air."

They flew without talking for a few minutes, but it was far from silent. The pressers. It was the goddamn age of science, and no one had invented a decent muffler; what were the techs thinking? Spanner considered jumping. At least it would be quiet . . .

"What the *fuck*?"

Spanner sat up quickly. They had just come over a low cliff, and on the floor of the gorge—

There had been an explosion, a big one.

Huge metallic arches like the rib cage of a giant stretched up from still-smoldering wreckage. The charred ground around the arches were strewn with large chunks of blackened debris—of what, Spanner couldn't tell.

His hangover was forgotten.

As Ikeda started to set down at the edge of the site, he wished he had thought to bring a weapon more powerful than a rhynth-stick.

"It's a ship, isn't it?" Spanner scanned the gorge side to side. Lots of places to hide . . .

"Yeah, I think so." Ikeda's eye were wide. "*Was* a ship. But not any human design I recognize."

She shut off the pressers. The sudden silence wasn't so welcome anymore. Spanner gripped his rhynth-stick tightly.

They got out of the copter carefully and walked toward the burnt-out shell. It was very quiet. Spanner's fear dissolved into awe as they neared the towering arcs. It was—

"Incredible," Ikeda said softly.

Spanner nodded. And from the smell of it, the fire had been recent. Like yesterday, maybe.

"This thing—you ever heard of *anything* like this?"

Spanner looked at her. Ikeda kicked at a chunk of the odd substance.

"Never." She turned and started to poke through the rubble.

"Think of what this *means*, Ikeda! We're talking intelligent life here, not just some new strain of amoeba! This could be the first real proof, you know?" His brain kicked in to overdrive. Fucking *wow*!

"Think of the new information! If we could figure out who made this ship, could figure out some way to test this material—" He trailed off, mind alive with the possibilities.

"Why don't you just ask him?"

Spanner twisted around to see Ikeda crouched down by a fallen figure. He stepped closer. "Doc—?" And stopped short.

It wasn't human. Some sort of armored animal, but humanoid form—except this thing was *big*. Spanner himself stood a little under two meters, and he was probably the tallest man in Prosperity Wells. This guy had half a meter on him, easy. Jesus fucking Buddha.

"Careful, Ikeda."

"I think it's dead," she said, and then watched the figure for a second.

Spanner joined her.

"No, it's breathing," said Spanner. "What the fuck?"

Ikeda shaded her eyes and looked up at him. "You tell me," she said quietly. Her words sounded flat in the hot, dry air.

The initial anxiety he had felt surged back. They were an open target down here. And maybe this guy's friends were nearby . . .

He looked at the steep walls of rock on either side

of them and suddenly felt claustrophobic. "Let's get outta here, what say?"

Ikeda nodded and dropped her gaze back to the creature. "Yeah. But help me get him into the copter, first. We'll have to come back to look for Revna later."

They loaded the thing into the copter as quickly as possible considering he weighed about a ton. They did their best to strap him to the stretcher with the human-sized bonds. It was a tight fit. When they finally lifted, Spanner felt relieved. No way was he coming back later unless everybody in town came with him.

On the trip home he kept his eyes open and aimed at their passenger; his headache had crept back, and it pulsed sharply at his temples as the suns beat down hard in piercing shafts of brightness.

Dr. Miriam Revna was an attractive woman even when she was worried. Which she was—in spite of her calm composure, the lines on her brow and the concern in her smile gave her away. Noguchi felt an instant sympathy for the woman; her attempt to maintain cool and continue functioning in spite of her emotions was a state Noguchi was quite familiar with.

"Is there anything you can think of that might help us locate your spouse?" Hiroki said.

Revna walked over to an examination table and motioned for them to join her. "He went to Iwa Gorge to find more of these," she said, and lifted a plastic sheet to expose some kind of spider. Hiroki frowned and stepped closer.

"They're unclassifiable," the doctor continued.

"Their structure bears characteristics of both carbon-based and silicon-based life forms."

Noguchi nodded. "Yes, I read the report. But what made him decide to look all the way up in Iwa Gorge?"

Revna smiled weakly. "That's where she said she'd found them."

" 'She'?" Noguchi and Hiroki almost spoke in unison.

The doctor nodded. "Jame Roth. The young woman who works for Ackland."

"Thank you for your time," Noguchi said. "We will contact you as soon as we know anything, Dr. Revna." She smiled warmly and touched the older woman's hand. "I'm sure everything will be fine."

They walked into the searing heat together and started toward the garage.

"What would Roth be doing at Iwa Gorge?" Hiroki said. "Ackland doesn't have any herds within twenty klicks of there."

"Those things weren't found in Iwa Gorge, Hiroki." Of course! It was obvious once she thought about it.

"What?" Hiroki stopped to look at her.

"Think about it. If you were Ackland and you found some new life form the night before the roundup, would you risk having three years' profit tied up in quarantine? No. You'd say the creature was discovered far from where your herd was pastured."

"But why would he report it at all? The things we saw might not be any threat to rhynth. I mean, if they were like ticks or something, they'd be easy to spot."

Noguchi felt a spark of anger deep in her gut. "To cover his ass. Say his rhynth *do* come down with some disease. Maybe the crab things are carriers, they bite an animal and infect it. He's done his duty, right? He reported it, even though they were found a long way from his animals."

Hiroki nodded thoughtfully. "So do we talk to Ackland first, or Roth?"

"Roth. She'd be more likely to admit to something like this than Ackland. Besides, if we go to Ackland first, he might bribe her to stay quiet before we can get to her."

Hiroki smiled appreciatively. "Good thinking, Machiko."

Noguchi barely heard him. "If anything has happened to Kesar Revna, Ackland will be sorry," she said softly. "He sent the doc to chase dust up there. He could have had an accident, hurt himself, and that's a long way from help."

After the ooman craft left, Tichinde and the others moved back to the smashed and burned wreckage to see what they had done.

M'icli-de had wanted to kill them, but Tichinde had held them back; he had a better idea.

Dachande was gone. He'd been dead already, of course, but the oomans were *h'ulij-bpe*, crazy. In a way, it was fitting. The oomans had taken the old Leader, had left him to be the new one. He was a warrior now, 'Aseigan had been his first kill. And so he would Lead them to their first Hunt. Later, he would Blood himself, design his own mark, and etch it in place with Hard Meat *thwei;* and he would also mark the other students as his own.

The ooman craft had surely gone in the direction of

their dwellings; and if not, it did not matter. They would go and find the ugly small ones wherever they might be. It was only a matter of how long it would take, and that was not a concern.

They had nothing if not plenty of time.

12

ath sucked, and it sucked *hard*; if Bobby Sheldon had children someday, he would see to it that they never had to do fractions if they didn't feel like it. Because fractions sucked worse than anything. In fact, they sucked *shit*.

"Bobby?"

He jerked around in his chair and flushed slightly at the sound of his mother's voice. The s-word was totally unallowed, even if he'd only thought about it.

"Yeah?"

"Finish what you're on and go wash up for lunch. You can do the rest later, okay?"

Bobby nodded at his mom. " 'Kay."

He looked back at the screen and sighed. One-tenth of ten was one. So three-sevenths of twenty was—

Stupid. Why the hell did he have to know this anyway? He tapped the save control and went to wash his hands. He was going to be a rancher, and what rancher needed to know fractions? His dad said that they came in handy for counting heads, but his dad was a rancher and so far as Bobby could tell, Dad had *never* used that shit.

Bobby walked back into the living room of their small house and looked out the window for Dad. Tomorrow was school day, which he looked forward to as usual; not that class was so great, but it was the only time of the week he got to hang out with the guys. They lived too far out of town for him to go every day, like some of the other kids. Although he'd gone to see the ship come in last night, that'd been cool. He had played spy-tag with Dal and Alan and Hung and eaten about a ton of banana popsicles.

Bobby heard his dad before he saw him. Actually, he heard Dax first; the terrier always sounded like a bike out of fuel after a morning's work. Dax padded into view a few seconds before his father and headed straight for the water dish at the side of the house.

"Hey, how's the best eleven-year-old in the world?" Bob Senior opened the door in a blast of hot air and smiled at Bobby. The joke was old, but Bobby grinned; he *was* the only eleven-year-old on the whole planet, at least for another month. And then Hung's sister, Ri, would have a birthday. Stupid *girl*.

"What's for lunch, hon?" Dad stood in the doorway and patted his thigh. "C'mon, Daxter, we don't have all day." Dax hurried inside and Dad shut the door against the simmering heat.

Mom walked into the room and smoothed her short blond hair down. She was pretty for a mom, although she was old, at least thirty-six or so. She smiled at Dad and kissed him on his cheek.

"Tuna casserole."

"Tuna! Where'd you get tuna?"

"I traded some of our jerky for three cans of it from one of *The Lector*'s crew." She sounded pleased with herself.

"Good deal. Maybe tomorrow when you take Bobby in, you can see what else you can get."

Bobby followed them into the dining room and listened to them talk about their days. Dad's boss, Mr. Cho, was going to give him a raise; Mom still wanted to build another room onto their small house, a reading room. And there was a rumor that some of the rhynth had contracted a virus of some kind, although none of Cho's got sick.

"It's probably just talk," his father said. "Like that thing about the flies last year. That had everyone going crazy, until the doc declared the whole thing a farce."

"I heard the doc was missing," Mom called from the kitchen. "One of Chigusa's people called this morning to tell us to keep our eyes open. He may have been near the gorge ..."

She carried a steaming dish into the room and set it on the table. Bobby felt his mouth water; they mostly ate meat and canned vegetables.

"This looks great. Yeah, I heard the same thing, but they've already sent out a copter, probably found him by now. I'll check later, but I doubt they'll need any more help."

Mom spooned the casserole onto their plates. Dax ran into the room and started to whine.

"Hey, no chance, Daxter! You'll get yours later." Dad reached for the water pitcher.

Dax whined louder and went to the front door. Dad

sighed and pushed back from the table. "Good timing, Dax; why couldn't—"

He stopped short as Dax growled at the door, teeth bared.

Bobby stood. "What is it, boy? What's the matter?"

Dax continued to growl, and then barked, the sound deep and fierce.

"Bob?" Bobby's mother wore a look of concern. Bobby started around the table, but his dad motioned him back. Dax barked again.

"One of those damned briar-wolves again," his father said, and went to the door. "I thought we'd gotten 'em all." He picked up the carbine that they kept by the coat rack and checked it. And then opened the door.

"Sic 'em, Dax!"

Dax ran outside full speed, his barking a continuous war cry.

Dad stepped onto the porch, Bobby and his mother behind him.

Dax stopped in the middle of the yard and circled, growling. He acted like there was something there—but there wasn't. The dog backed away and edged forward, all the time barking and growling at nothing.

Bobby's eyes widened. There *was* something! A ripple of—dust and light. Dax flickered like he had gone into some kind of magnifier as he circled again.

Bobby felt his mom's hands grip his shoulders.

"Dad? What—?"

"Both of you, in the house, now!"

His mother pulled him backward, but he still watched. And saw as Dax was lifted off of the ground in a gout of blood. A huge beast—a monster!— appeared from out of nowhere, he held the spear stuck into Daxter!

Bobby heard a dull sound like an ax hitting meat. Dax made one short howl of pain and then went quiet.

"Good God—!" his father whispered.

The monster was tall, masked, inhuman. It shook the dead dog on its spear, sent a rain of red to the ground.

"Be careful, Bob!" His mother almost screamed it.

Bobby was petrified, unable to look away.

"Dax?" He watched as the monster tossed the dog over its shoulder and turned to face his father.

Dad brought the carbine up and aimed. There was a sudden shift and creak from the roof, like when Dad had patched the tiling, like somebody was *up* there—

—and a ripple of light and dust plunged into his father's skull. Bobby screamed. Dad reached up to clutch at the now-visible metal claws that had worked into his face—

Mom spun him to face the kitchen. Her breath came in short gasps.

"Run, Bobby!"

"Mommy? Is—"

"Run! We have to get to the truck! Out the back!"

He tripped and sprawled on the floor. His mother pulled him up and shoved him toward the rear door.

There was a giant, splintering crunch from the front porch. Bobby and his mother both turned.

The monster crouched in the doorway.

Impossibly fast, it reached for Mom, grabbed her—

And ripped her throat open.

Once again, the sound of meat being cut.

Warmth dotted Bobby's face, turned his vision to red.

He screamed, "Mom!"

He ran. There was no time to think, only move. The

flier outside his parents' room, Daddy had shown him
how—

Bobby ducked across the hall and into their bed-
room. Without a pause, he ran and jumped through
the thin plastic window. There was another scream—
his—as the window shattered, and there was the bike,
within reach—

He hit the ignition button as if he had ridden a
thousand times. The machine roared to life, raised up
from the ground—

—and behind him was the sound of some evil bird,
screeching, hoarse and piercing. Something touched
his shoe, still inside the house—

—and the bike lurched forward, pulled him away.
There was another, and another of the murdering
creatures, all claws and hate. They came out of nowhere, appearing like magic.

They reached for him—

—and he took off, tilted wildly. He aimed the bike
east, toward town.

He kept his sweaty hand jammed to the accelerator. Behind him the things howled and screamed, horrible, horrible, Mom, Dad—

There was a noise like gunfire, but hollow—and the
wall of rock in front of him to the left exploded, sharp
pieces hammered the bike, stuck into his skin, but it
didn't matter, it didn't hurt. And beyond that, Bobby
knew nothing.

Tichinde was pleased. True, they had lost one—but
they had faced the deadly oomans and come away unscathed, with two kills. The escaped one would die
soon enough, with the rest. It had surely gone to alert
the others; they would have to be prepared . . .

Tichinde watched as the other yautja danced and cried over the victory. He himself had killed the second ooman; it had been without weapon, but as dangerous as he had heard oomans to be, that was allowable. Hunt or be Hunted . . .

Dachande would have disapproved. Tichinde flared his tusks in amusement at the thought. Dachande was *thei-de*; his opinion no longer held meaning. Besides, with no one to hold judgment over their actions, they would take what they wanted; from what he had seen so far, the oomans were not so dangerous as the yautja had been led to believe.

13

Roth cleaned the dirt from under her nails with her teeth. It was a nervous and dirty habit; Cathie was always getting on her case about it. But considering the circumstances at the moment, she didn't really give a flying fuck about biting her nails.

The two heads of Chigusa onworld stood over her small table in the rec center and glowered at her. Creep snuffled blissfully by her feet, probably thrilled to get out of the sun; she wished she felt the same.

"Do you know what charges you could face if Ackland's rhynth turn up infected with dangerous bacteria or a virus?" Hiroki had always been an amiable sort, but his eyes flashed with anger. At her. "And you were responsible for sending them to Earth?"

Roth opened her mouth to speak, but was cut off by the Noguchi woman.

"Ms. Roth—if anything has happened to Kesar Revna, you will be held accountable." She leaned toward Roth, expression cold. "How do you feel about that? He's been missing for almost a day now. He might be injured. Or dead."

Roth nodded slowly. She had lied for Ackland, had put her reputation at stake for him—after all, he was the boss. But she wasn't about to get caught holding *this* bag; it was just a little bit too heavy.

"Ackland told me to," she said quietly. "I realize that doesn't excuse my actions, but I just work for the man, you know?"

Hiroki and Noguchi exchanged glances.

"So Ackland told you to tell Revna that the spider creatures were in Iwa Gorge?" Noguchi leaned forward again, but her eyes weren't as angry as before.

"Right."

"What the hell is going on here?"

Roth looked up, surprised.

Ackland marched across the room, his face sweaty and red.

"Roth? What have you done?" Ackland stopped at their table and glared down at her accusingly. "What's this I hear about you lying to Doc Revna?"

Roth felt raw anger hit her system. He was going to let her take the fall, after she'd worked her ass off for him for three years!

What a surprise.

She stood abruptly. "Mr. Ackland, I've already explained the situation. And I quit. I'll expect to be paid within the month." Roth nodded at Noguchi and Hiroki.

"Please let me know if I can help in any way, and

contact me about charges as soon as you've decided."
She whistled softly; Creep jumped up to follow her to
the exit. Already she could hear Ackland's voice
raised in a huff.

". . . I thought a man had a right to be present when
his accusers were testifying against him!"

She was glad to get out. Ackland talked big, there
would be quite a scene—but he had enough sense to
know when he was caught. Hiroki was a fair man . . .
but Noguchi? Something about her was pure steel.

Roth would hate to cross that one; nitrogen queen
was right.

"So you were planning to try me in absentia? Don't
you need a judge to hold trial? Or is that some old-
fashioned notion—"

"Shut up, Ackland."

Stunned, he did.

"You've violated company policy and jeopardized
the security of this complex and its personnel,
Ackland. I figure that's all the legal authority I need."
Noguchi was royally pissed, but she kept her voice
low. This overblown rancher had the *gall* to try to
screw things for everyone and then cover it up?

"You really think you've got the backing to make
charges stick? In case you haven't noticed, you aren't
exactly the most popular person in this settlement."
Ackland was shaken, she could tell, but he smirked at
her.

"You're right, I'm just the new boss." She had to
make a conscious effort not to shout. "But Doc Revna
has been here since the beginning, treating the ranchers' stock, treating their families—delivering their ba-
bies. So far, he's just missing. But if he turns up dead,

who do you think folks are going to side with, you? Or his grieving widow?"

Ackland seemed to shrink a little in front of her. He dropped his gaze to the unlit cigar he held and spoke uneasily.

"Look, I didn't expect the doc to go out looking for more of those things—"

Hiroki stepped in. "But if he did, you wanted to make sure he looked in the wrong place."

Ackland flared again, but his anger seemed weak. "We had no way of knowing whether those rhynth were infected or not! I didn't want to delay the whole operation—"

Hiroki frowned angrily and pointed his finger at the rancher's chest. "Didn't it occur to you that trouble with your herd could be the reason *The Lector* is still parked out front?"

Noguchi raised her eyebrows. *"What?"*

"I meant to tell you—" Hiroki started, but she was already headed to one of the wall screens. She punched up a southern compound view and looked in disbelief.

"Those rhynth are going to be hell to manage after standing in the sun all day!" She turned to glare accusingly at Ackland. He looked away.

Noguchi tapped into operations. Collins appeared in front of her.

"Collins—why hasn't *The Lector* taken its first load back to its orbiter?"

"I couldn't say—ah, Machiko. We've been trying to contact them all day, but they haven't responded . . ."

"Send someone in person."

Collins nodded. "I'll go myself."

"Good. And don't waste your time with Conover,

talk to Strandberg. Remind him we're on a tight schedule. Report back immediately, okay?"

"Gotcha."

The screen went blank. At least *that* was taken care of. She walked back to the table where Ackland had sat down, his face blank.

"If this has anything to do with your little lie, Ackland," she said smoothly, calmly, "I'll see to it that you are put away for it. Until hell freezes solid."

The look in his eyes, defeated and guilty, was exactly what she wanted.

Scott ached all over. It was the hangover, and that Japanese woman, she was responsible—

Except he couldn't move his arms. And he was standing up—?

He opened his heavy eyelids and blinked several times. It was dark, but he was inside; there was weak light coming from somewhere . . .

"Tom?" His voice was a raspy croak. God, he was thirsty! He cleared his throat and tried again.

"Tom. Can you hear me?"

No answer. Was he in a med center, maybe? There might have been some kind of accident . . .

He took a deep breath and spoke as loud as he could. "Hello! Where am I? Tom!" His throat protested; it felt like he'd swallowed a bucket of sand.

A slow hissing filled the room. The shadows in the room moved, unfurled themselves from the walls and the dark corners. He could make out—

Teeth.

Jesus!

He tried to move, but his arms were pinned.

"Oh, God, no—" His voice was barely a whisper.

The room swam with darkness, and then once again, there was nothing.

"... the company has billions invested in this project," she continued. "Where the hell do you get off fucking with us? Not to mention possibly endangering the lives of millions, maybe billions of people? You think the quarantine laws are there just for the fun of it?" She was still on a roll and unwilling to doppler down.

Ackland hadn't spoken for several minutes. Neither had Hiroki.

"Well?"

Ackland looked up at her and said nothing.

The tension was broken by an incoming message over Noguchi's com. "Ms. Noguchi, report to the med center immediately. Ms. Noguchi to the med center." Miriam Revna. She sounded agitated.

Noguchi tapped the received button and looked at the rancher. "You'd better pray they've found Revna, Ackland."

"I didn't make him go out there! And if he hurt himself, it's his own fault!"

She hurried out of the rec center and was blasted by the afternoon heat.

Ackland and Hiroki followed; she deliberately walked ahead of them to avoid further conversation for the moment; by the sound of it, Ackland was trying to reason with Hiroki, his deep voice apologetic and contrite.

Asshole.

Noguchi waited at the entry to the lab for them to catch up; if Revna was dead, she wouldn't want to walk into it alone.

The three of them stepped into the lab together. Noguchi saw what was strapped to an examination table, and took in a deep breath, to scream or faint she didn't know.

Dragon!

14

o much for your precious quarantine," said Ackland softly.

Noguchi closed her mouth. Miriam Revna and two local pilots were looking at a readout on a small screen across the lab.

One of the pilots, Spanner, turned and grinned. "Hey, look what we found!" He pointed at the creature unnecessarily.

Hiroki took a step toward it and then paused. "Is it—alive?"

Miriam Revna stood and walked over. "Yes. It's injured, but not in any danger. At least, I don't *think* so. Four cracked ribs and extensive contusions in the dorsal region. And it's male, I'm fairly certain."

Noguchi saw what she meant about the maleness. She couldn't miss it.

The thing was a giant, maybe two and a half meters tall. Humanoid, but its head like some sort of mutated crab. It wore armor, and was bound to the exam table by several thick straps of rhynth hide—its long, taloned arms were speckled, reptilian, but not scaled. Noguchi saw the slight rise and fall of its chest. There was a mask over its face. What was it breathing? she wondered.

After the initial shock, she tried to remember what the company's off-planet manual contained on the subject of possible XT encounters; something like "Avoid direct contact until trained personnel arrive!"

Looks like we're going to write a whole new chapter . . .

"We found a ship, too," Spanner said. "It's mostly blown to shit, but we should get a salvage team up there!"

Noguchi found her tongue. "Any idea what it is, Doctor?"

Revna looked at her blankly. "Hmm? I'm sorry, I'm not thinking clearly today."

Noguchi nodded. "Of course. We are still looking for Kesar. I just wondered if there was any connection between this and those unclassifieds that Roth brought in."

The doctor shook her head. "This creature has a completely different cell structure. No relationship at all. He"—she nodded at the monster—"is more like us than the little crablike things."

Hiroki walked over to a table covered with pieces of the alien's armor. He held up a broken staff tipped with a vicious-looking blade. "Quite an arsenal."

Noguchi joined him and picked up a large chunk of dark metal with a strap. She could barely lift it. At closer inspection, it was apparently some kind of weapon, a rifle or a flamethrower. It was damaged.

She set it down and picked up a mask.

"This is stuff you'd pack for a hunting trip. Or an invasion," she said. "This guy's no peaceful explorer."

Hiroki fingered the strap on the odd weapon. "I don't think this is his first trip to Ryushi, either. I can't place the rest of it, but this strap is definitely rhynth-hide."

"Any sign of the Doc?" Ackland nodded at the pilots.

The slender young woman, Ikeda, sighed. "Negatory. But Iwa Gorge connects with a maze of canyons and arroyos; it'd be easy to get lost. We'll go back out pretty soon."

There was a small shield of some kind with the other weaponry, a plate-sized disk with a strange-looking creature etched on it. Noguchi ran a finger over the blackened metallic substance. The drawing was the head of an unknown animal or bug, an elongated skull with sharp teeth and no eyes; she traced the outline thoughtfully. There was something familiar about it.

Was it a dream? It was dark and hot . . .

She looked again at the unconscious alien and shuddered. Maybe Doc Revna hadn't gotten lost—

There was a scream from outside, followed by a crash. Noguchi started; what now? She and Hiroki ran to the door together with Ackland behind them.

A flier had slammed into the transmitter building directly across from the med center. There was no fire but a lot of oily smoke; a small body lay on the hot pavement next to the accident. Several others had come out of the op center and were also running toward the scene. Hiroki got there first.

"What happened?" Noguchi called out.

Hiroki knelt by the victim and carefully touched its face. "It's the Sheldon boy," he said.

Noguchi looked down at the child's still, tear-streaked face and felt her heart tighten. So young . . .

The boy opened his eyes and started to scream.

Bobby woke up with a scream. It was hot, the air smelled burnt, and his parents—

He sat up quickly and looked around. He was in Prosperity Wells, there were a bunch of people gathered around him and the flier lay nearby, broken.

"Bobby," said a calm voice. Mr. Shimura was next to him. "Are you hurt—?"

"Monsters," he whispered. And he started to cry.

Ms. Noguchi was there, too. She leaned down next to Mr. Shimura and smiled at him. "It's okay, Bobby. You're safe now. What happened?"

He closed his eyes, unable to stop the tears. "Mu—monsters killed my dad and then my mommy and then before that they kuh—kuh—killed Dax and we couldn't *see* them, but then I got away—"

He couldn't say anything else; he wanted to tell them how scared he had been, how there were so many of them, and how Dax had seen them first—but all that came out were loud sobs of terror and sadness.

"Let's get him to the med center," someone said. Gentle hands lifted him off of the burning ground and carried him away. One of his legs hurt really bad and he cried harder.

Cool air washed over him as they went inside, the world dimmed.

"We've got an emergency here, Doc!" the person holding him shouted. Mr. Shimura.

Bobby opened his eyes and looked past Dr. Revna at the medical room. And he started to scream again; just like the tears, he was unable to stop. Fear and hatred and sadness and anger for the thing that they had lying on a table.

"Monsters! Monsters! Monsters!"

Dachande remembered movement after the loneliness of pain, the new pain. Once, he had opened his eyes and seen that he was indoors, in a moving ship. There had been heat and then cool, and strange, animal sounds—

He realized he could see a little, but could not focus. Dark and light shapes folded and formed in front of him. But now his gaze sharpened, just for a second, at the horrible cries of some creature in front of him. It screamed and howled its nonsense language, the thing. It was pale and little, like—

Like an ooman?

Dachande sank back into the quiet darkness. Fear fought to rise in him.

He was caught by monsters.

15

Noguchi and Hiroki walked into a room filled with low, nervous chatter and grim faces. The gathered ranchers and Chigusa staff fell silent and looked at them, their expressions fearful and expectant. The rec center was packed, but suddenly a hundred-plus people didn't seem like so many.

Noguchi cleared her throat. "Before we start, is everyone here?"

Mason stood from his seat near the door and read from a piece of paper. "Everyone except Ikeda, both Revnas, three ops people, two of Marianetti's people who are on their way—and the Sheldons. Oh, and the Barkers haven't answered yet."

Noguchi nodded. "Ikeda will be here shortly, and Miriam Revna is tending to Bobby Sheldon—"

A slender blond woman called out from a back corner of the room, her voice tinged with worry. "Is it true? About the Sheldons?" Noguchi recognized her as one of the garage maintenance workers, a mechanic.

Noguchi took a deep breath; she and Hiroki had discussed how to handle the situation after Ikeda had called in, but it wasn't going to be easy—the Sheldons had apparently been well liked on Ryushi.

"I'm not sure what you've heard, but I'll tell you what we know," she said. She consciously kept her voice low and firm; panic in the crowd would help no one.

"Approximately two hours ago Bobby Sheldon came into town on a flier, alone. He said that his parents had been killed by a group of XT life forms. Just before he arrived, Spanner and Ikeda found an injured . . . being in Iwa Gorge that is currently unconscious in the med center. Bobby Sheldon identified this being as similar to the life forms that killed his parents." Noguchi took another deep breath. "When we were unable to reach Mr. and Mrs. Sheldon by radio, we sent Ashley Ikeda on a flyby. I am sad to report that she just called in with the news that the Sheldon house is in flames, and their breeding stock has been slaughtered.

"We must assume that an attack is imminent."

There was a slight murmur through the crowd. A few people coughed, a few children started to cry softly.

Loren Gaunt, one of the ops screen-watchers, stood and raised his voice to be heard above the uneasy group. "So what are we going to do with the thing in the med center? And what is it, exactly?"

Several others nodded.

Hiroki stepped forward. "At this time, we know

very little about the creature currently in Miriam Revna's care. It is a large, humanoid being, unlike anything previously registered in the EXT guide. It is under restraint, and has shown no signs of recovering so far—although Revna doesn't seem to think it's in critical condition—"

"You mean you haven't *killed* it?" Gaunt sounded incredulous. "After it murdered Bob and Sylvan?" A couple of others called out agreement.

Noguchi raised a hand for silence. "The creature in the med center was not involved in their deaths; the time frame—"

"*Fuck* the time frame," said Gaunt. "For all we know, that thing was responsible for sending its buddies out to murder them!"

The calls of agreement were shouts now.

Noguchi felt that spark of anger she'd had for Ackland. She clapped her hands sharply above her head and yelled.

"*Be quiet!*"

The room quieted. An infant howled loudly in the back and was soothed by its mother.

"Perhaps if we all panic and turn ourselves into mindless animals, we'll get out of this situation! Who else wants to add to the problem?"

Her voice carried well. She could feel her cheeks flushed with anger, and was gratified to see that Gaunt's were also red—he dropped his gaze to the floor and didn't speak again.

Noguchi nodded. She had everyone's attention.

A young boy raised his hand.

"Yes?"

"Is Bobby okay?" The boy was no more than twelve; his voice was high and shaky, obviously upset by the situation. His father placed a hand on the child's shoulder.

She nodded and attempted to smile. "He has a sprained ankle and is in shock, but he'll be all right. Squires has agreed to watch him for a while."

Noguchi motioned at the young teacher who chewed nervously at her lip.

She scanned the room, watched the fearful crowd with a calm eye.

This is bad, but we will handle it. She felt in control; for once, the people of Ryushi looked to her to tell them what to do. She wouldn't let them down.

"If we could hold other questions for a few moments, I'll tell you what we propose. Mr. Shimura is in charge of security. All ablebodied personnel will be expected to take a shift on watch, and anyone not on duty will remain within the main complex. First, we'll do what we can to barricade the town with the cargo crates from the move here—" She nodded at Mason. "Mason here will head up that maneuver. Anyone trained on lift equipment will report to him after the meeting. There is a thirty-three-hour curfew in effect as of now; no one will go anywhere alone unless they've cleared it with me or Hiroki, and it will have to be a good reason. Those of you with weapons, please list them with Spanner ASAP. Ben Davidson and Jess Jonson have volunteered to show our younger members holovid graphics at the school this afternoon, so meet with them afterward for specific times."

People nodded; she could almost feel the fear in the room become less tangible. It was a good thing to remember that most crises just needed some organization and clear thinking to be handled efficiently.

Hiroki read from a list the first watch team and

then suggested another meeting later, at dusk or when the work was finished, whichever came first. As the gathering drew to its close, Noguchi was pleased to see that order and confidence had been restored quickly after Gaunt's outburst.

Except—

Except only a few people had heard what Bobby Sheldon had said. Or seen what the thing in the lab looked like . . .

Noguchi shook her head. It didn't matter. Wishing for other circumstances was pointless.

She took a deep breath and went outside to do what she could.

Twilight was almost there when it occurred to Noguchi that she hadn't heard back from Collins.

Under Hiroki's capable direction, they had set up an admirable line of defense; the house-sized moving crates had been lined up around the perimeter of the compound quickly; with the willing aid of both the ranchers and the staff, the work had been neatly done.

A copter crew had made runs to fetch all of the weapons listed by the ranchers; Noguchi had felt her heart sink at the inventory. Twenty-seven scatter guns, ten pistols earmarked for a police force that had never been needed, and six old-fashioned flare guns. There were also a few hunting rifles and handguns. Not much.

She sat in the ops center hunched over a cup of black coffee that was barely tepid. Her body ached from all of the work; Hiroki had insisted that she take five, and she was only too glad to comply. Hiroki was going to take a team to walk the compound and se-

cure any place they had missed. Around her, four
staffers watched screens. Noguchi was exhausted,
and there was still too much to do, too many vari-
ables to consider—

Like *The Lector*.

Noguchi straightened. The crew outside was just
finishing up, and another meeting was coming up
within the hour—but had she seen anyone from the
ship? That obnoxious Conover—?

"Weaver, have you seen Collins anywhere?"

The tall, dark-haired staff woman looked up from
her console. "No. *I* haven't at least—Downey, have
you seen Collins?"

Sid Downey shrugged. "No one's seen him since he
went to talk to *The Lector*'s people."

Noguchi sighed and stood up reluctantly. "Any
progress?"

Downey shook his head. "The Barkers still don't
answer. And Dr. Revna refuses to be moved to the
main building—other than that, everyone is accounted
for."

Noguchi patted him on the shoulder as she walked
toward the door. "Keep up the good work. I'm going
to go talk to *The Lector* folks, see if they've kidnapped
Collins."

She almost collided with Hiroki in the doorway.

"Where are you going?" Hiroki looked like she felt.
Dark smears of dust painted his face, and his eyes
looked weary and old.

"Collins still hasn't come back from the ship; I'm
going to find out what's going on with them. But first,
I'm going to see if I can talk some sense into Dr.
Revna."

Hiroki frowned. "It's not safe, Machiko." His tone
was gentle.

She felt oddly touched by his concern, but she was also tired of not knowing what the hell that ship was up to. "Someone has to go; may as well be me."

Hiroki looked at her seriously for a beat and then unhooked his holster strap. He handed the revolver to her, butt first.

"I see you've made up your mind—but take this. It's a 12.5 mm Smith. It belonged to my grandfather. It is loaded with jacketed bullets, for hunting big game."

She stared at the weapon.

He pushed it into her hands. "If you have to shoot something, make sure it has a thick wall behind it— these bullets will go right through a rhynth. I'll call the sentries and let them know you're on your way."

Noguchi accepted the weapon gingerly and nodded. She knew how to shoot, of course, it was SOP for offworld execs to take a course. Never knew what you'd run into out on the frontier. For once, the company was right.

"Fine. Have Weaver set up the sat-link as soon as the suns set, and ask them to cut a deal for Marine support." She smiled tiredly. "And thanks, Hiroki. Be careful."

He smiled in return. "You're doing a good job, Machiko."

She walked into the late-afternoon heat and headed for the med center, her thoughts jumbled with exhaustion. There was still a crew of a dozen or so outside, setting the final walls into place. Amazing, that in the space of one day, they'd gone from peaceful town to armed camp. The gun was heavy in her hands. She paused long enough to strap the holster on and settle it on her hip. Still heavy but comforting. She wanted desperately to believe that their measures were needless, but her gut told her otherwise; tired though she was, there was a chilling certainty in her bones that tonight would be a long one, and come morning, things might be very different . . .

Miriam watched the stats on the screen with something like awe; she was glad to have something to do besides worry over Kesar, and the alien was distracting, to say the least, now that Bobby was gone.

Her stomach tightened at the thought of her husband; she had always thought that she would know if he was gone—that deep knowing that two people shared if enough years had passed. But there was nothing; she just missed him; she kept thinking of what he would say about the incredible reads that flashed across the console . . .

"Doctor . . ."

Revna turned in her chair, heart pounding. "Ms. Noguchi?"

The attractive Japanese woman smiled gently. "I'm sorry, we haven't heard anything—"

The doctor took a deep breath. "Then you've come to check on our patient." She tilted her head toward the prone form on the exam table nearby. "He's still not awake, but he's making remarkable progress; his respiration has deepened, and I believe that two of his ribs have begun to heal."

The gentle smile never left Noguchi's face. The obvious sympathy there made Revna want to cry, so she turned back to the screen.

"I'll let you know if he regains consciousness," she said.

"Doctor, I'd like to move you and our 'visitor' to the main complex; the security is better there, and—"

"Thank you, no," said Revna. "I prefer to remain

here. I have everything I need to look after my patient . . ." She hoped she sounded collected and normal, but she heard her voice crack slightly on the truth. "Besides, this is where Kesar will come when he returns."

She didn't turn around, but she sensed the Noguchi woman's hesitation. Before, they could have hoped for an accident, with her husband lying injured, waiting for help. But now? Revna could almost hear her thoughts—that she was fooling herself. Kesar Revna had undoubtedly met the same fate as Bobby's parents. He had gone right to where the wrecked ship lay.

Miriam spoke again, her voice firmer this time. "I'm fine, Ms. Noguchi. Really."

"Very well, Doctor," she said. "I'll check back on you later."

"Thank you, Ms. Noguchi. Machiko."

When she heard the door close, Revna finally relaxed a bit. A lone tear trickled down her cheek; she wiped at it absently and concentrated on the task at hand. He would be back soon; and if he wasn't, she would find him somehow . . .

Mason rolled his head and yawned; he and Riley had run out of things to say about twenty minutes ago. The initial adrenaline of the situation was long gone, and their nervous small talk had disintegrated into a watchful silence. At least it wouldn't get any hotter today; the suns were headed down. And in another hour or so, he and Riley would be inside drinking beer and shooting the shit; he pitied the next watch; being out here after dark would be a bitch.

"Hi, Riley. Hi, Mason." The boss lady walked toward them smoothly, a smile of greeting on her lips. *Speak of the devil.*

Riley nodded back and Mason stepped forward. He dropped his cigarette on the dusty ground and squashed it with one boot.

"Ms. Noguchi," he said politely. "Mr. Shimura said you were coming. I'm to escort you to *The Lector.*"

"Let me guess, Mason—Hiroki ordered you to follow me even if I declined your escort?"

"Yes, ma'am."

She nodded and sighed. "Well, come on then." She stepped ahead of him and headed toward the ship.

Mason glanced over his shoulder to see Riley grinning at him and shot him the finger; smarmy bastard. He jogged to catch up to Noguchi and walked in front of her. This would be a prime opportunity to tell the management what he had been thinking.

"You know, I think we're worrying too much. I mean, look at the size of the complex. You'd need an army to attack, right?" He looked back at Noguchi and stopped at the base of the ramp for her to catch up. She didn't answer, didn't even look at him, really. He might as well be talking to a block of plastecrete.

"I think those XTs are gonna take one look at Prosperity Wells and go back home," he continued. Fuck her, anyway. He stepped into the open door at the top of the ramp and pointed his scatter gun at nothing in particular; it was dark in there. He took another step inside and then turned his head to call back to the ice queen.

"Just give me a second to get the lights." He edged to the left and groped blindly with one hand. Something wet dripped on his hand.

"Hey," he said under his breath. Another drop of warm liquid splashed the top of his head. Fucking disgusting! Where was the goddamn light switch anyway?

He got the impression of sudden movement overhead—and then there was only pain.

Noguchi stood at the top of the ramp and listened to Mason babble mindlessly. Mason was something of a jerk, that was certain. He stepped into the dark and fumbled for the lights, still chattering away. She turned to look at him—

—just in time to see him lifted straight up into the darkness. There was a strangled, wet cry—

—and the darkness rushed forward to greet her, a dozen arms and a thousand teeth, all screaming, all hungry.

16

Noguchi grabbed for the revolver in slow motion. The single patch of darkness separated into many forms; she fell backward as the dozen or so nightmares came at her.

What—?

She fired four times and stumbled down the ramp without looking. The deafening shots echoed from the walls and in her head and two of the things dropped.

She backed up against the shield wall, revolver extended toward the huge bugs, Jesus, they were half again her size! They came, but slower, their short, twisted limbs reached for her. They hissed and cried out like demented banshees. Double rows of teeth snapped and dripped a clear, slimy mucus.

Noguchi didn't take her gaze off them, even as she heard more of the things come down the ramp.

She was going to die—

She panted shallowly and backed farther up the incline, revolver heavy in her trembling hands.

Another of the bugs rushed forward with a scream. She jerked the trigger again and again. The thing howled in fury and pain and fell—

She fired again, only—the shots were quiet, dull clicks. The gun was empty.

Was there more ammunition on the belt? Did she have time to reload?

Yes. No.

The nightmares advanced; she backed up, her last moment of life. Nothing flashed before her eyes save the horror coming for her; no memories, fond or otherwise, came to haunt or comfort her. She was in the moment and in this moment, the leading bug cried out and jumped—

—and a hollow thump sounded behind her, as if something had imploded. A rush of heat stirred her hair, and the creature closest flew backward in a rain of hissing liquid, its head gone.

The horde screamed in unison but stayed at the bottom of the wall, their dark limbs clattering on the ground in—anger?

Noguchi risked a glance behind her.

The dragon—?

It was the monster, masked and armored. It held the spear with the broken shaft—except it was whole now, the long pole mended; the heavy dark weapon it held was slightly different—

It wasn't the creature from the med lab. It was one of the others, the killers.

It aimed the weapon at her and fired.

Noguchi felt a cry escape her throat—

—and another of the bugs exploded behind her.

She looked back down at the advancing army and felt a rush of air again behind her.

The monster warrior leapt *over* her and landed on the pack of seething black bugs.

Noguchi could do nothing but stare.

The dragon fell into battle, its movements so swift she could barely follow them. The savage spear sliced and cut another bug in pieces. Another shot from the strange weapon and dismembered limbs clattered to the ground.

The blood of the dark spidery bugs hissed and melted into the plastecrete; some kind of acid—?

She couldn't tell from the screams which was which. As the warrior spun and hacked two of the bugs at once, a flash of Noguchi's childhood came to her—

—*Samurai*—!

More of the bugs came down the ramp, scrabbled wildly to get at the warrior.

Noguchi, still unable to move, looked on at the storm of death and battle.

Gkyaun had been sent in to scout, but the Hunting he had found was too good to walk away from. Here was a sickly, pale ooman—with *no defense*! He had watched as the cowering ooman's small burner died, then as the *kainde amedha* swarm approached the ooman. It did not seem able to defend itself. Where was its spear? Its wrist knives? This terrified creature was the monster of which he had been frightened as a suckling? It was a joke.

The ooman was *thei-de* without him; he would save the ugly creature for later.

First, the Hard Meat—

Gkyaun's heart hammered with glory as he caught the ooman's attention by burning the first drone. The drone exploded.

The others cringed, drew back, looked upon him with the respect befitting a Blooded warrior. On some deep cellular level, they knew his kind. Knew the danger he presented.

This *dtai'kai'-dte* was nothing! He could have won in infancy! Yautja would cry his name this night, victor of drone and ooman alike. He would bring the ooman's blackened skull to drink from—

He fired again, and was again rewarded with a shower of acidic *thwei*. The Hard Meat screamed in loss.

Gkyaun howled the war cry and jumped. He landed amid the hissing drones and moved among them like the *setg'-in*, deadly and quick. So easy! He spun and slashed, burned and cut at the same time.

Two bugs fell with one slice of his spear.

A drone from behind lost its head; he gutted yet another.

He was *Paya*, the conquering warrior! *Thwei* ran at his feet, the Hard Meat shrank in terror—!

More came at him, a relentless flow of fury and sound. He pivoted, Hunted, his every movement was an arc of doom and pain.

Noguchi gulped air and pushed herself backward, toward the top of the shield wall. The warrior was a dervish of wild energy and prowess—the nightmare creatures fell all around him.

But more monsters flooded toward him. And despite the fighter's speed and strength, he fought poorly; he hadn't allowed for any outcome other than victory. It was as if he were a *karateka* who had mastered *kata*, but had never faced an opponent in actual combat . . .

The clamoring dark animals surrounded him, pulled him down. The warrior struggled, but to no avail; one of the giant bugs ripped off his mask with one spidery clawed arm and plunged its razor teeth forward—

Noguchi scrambled backward and to her feet, atop the wall. She ran back toward the complex and didn't look back. The cries of hunger and triumph followed her, told her the warrior was no more.

What *were* these things? What new disaster had come to visit them?

17

he noise came from a million klicks to his right. It was a familiar sound, one he had known for a very long time—back on Earth, from before he knew what it meant.

He felt his consciousness as it rose upward, swam to the surface of a depthless abyss—the knowing part of him, the tomes of understanding. He fought to keep it from happening, but was helpless to stop it. There was something that he didn't want to know, was terrified of knowing ...

The sound again. *Scott? Scott, are you?*

Scott?

Scott was him. The blissful nothing dwindled away as the aches in his body stepped in to greet him, coupled with a horrible, consuming hunger.

"Scott?"

Scott opened his swollen eyes to blackness and took a deep breath. He almost choked on the cloying, wet air.

"Scott, are you awake? Can you hear me?"

He coughed, the minor movement sparking a thousand pains. "Yeah." He swallowed gummy spittle and turned his head toward the voice. "Tom?"

"I think I can get my arm free," the other pilot said.

Scott couldn't see him, but his friend was only a few meters away from the sounds of hurried struggle.

The rest of the nightmare clicked in to place. "Where did they go?" Scott strained to see in the dark room, memories of hissing motion and giant teeth adding sharp panic to his dull and clouded mind. "Tom, did you see them? Where did they all go?"

"Shh! I'm almost out—" A grunt of exertion and Tom's welcome face appeared in front of him, grimy, fearful, pale.

"Hurry! Jesus, where did they go? Get me out of this, hurry, please!"

"Be *quiet!*" Tom spoke in a harsh whisper and reached for Scott's immobilized hands. The ropes of resinous dark material holding him in place snapped and crumbled to the floor.

Tom glanced over his shoulder every other second, eyes wide.

As soon as one of his arms was free, Scott tore at the weird matter at his midriff and leg—and tumbled to the floor.

He had been suspended a half meter in the air.

Tom slipped an arm around his waist and helped him up, speaking quickly and quietly.

"They were all around us, and something happened outside, I guess; they swarmed out of here like mad bees, and I didn't know if you were here—" Tom seemed to realize he was babbling and cut himself off.

"It's okay, man. Let's just get the hell out of here, okay?"

Leaning on each other heavily, they stumbled toward the emergency hatch. It was hard to see anything, but Scott could make out areas of the dock where the shadows were denser, more solid.

A raspy breath came from one of the darker corners of the room. Scott stopped and turned toward the noise. At first he couldn't see what was the cause—and then he was unable to believe what he saw.

It was one of the creatures.

It was bigger than the others. Its huge, flattened skull was curved downward, its limbs drawn up in front of its dripping jaws. The thing was curled up, a horrible caricature of the human fetal position.

"I think it's asleep," Tom said softly. "It hasn't moved since before all the other ones left."

Scott couldn't pull his gaze away from the dormant monster, the slow rise and fall of the thing's furled body with each slow breath. It was the most frightening thing he had ever seen, like a giant spider-lizard with knives for teeth, deadly, insectile. Strings of sticky goo fell from its jaws, the dim light from the partly opened dock door reflected in the glistening slime.

"Let's go before she wakes up," Tom whispered urgently.

"She—?" Scott shook his head and looked at the pilot, but Tom was already pulling him toward the hatch.

"Yeah," Scott whispered back. He wanted nothing more than to get the fuck out of there. Get help, get weapons; just see another human *face*. But as they hurried to their escape, Scott glanced over his shoulder to look at the thing once again. Where had they come from? What were they capable of? There was something strangely familiar about them . . .

He did a double take. His heart pounded. The angle of the creature's head seemed to have changed slightly . . .

"Come *on!*" Tom pulled at his arm.

Scott nodded mutely and followed. There would be time to think about *why* later, not now, not fucking now . . .

Scott shuddered as they reached the emergency hatch. The thing was frighteningly similar to the picture in his head of the jabberwock, from that old poem.

He had the sudden, certain feeling that this was far from being over with.

Noguchi ran through the deserted streets of Prosperity Wells. There was distant thunder, harsh and unreal—

Thunder? She grabbed for the comset around her neck, feeling like an idiot for not having thought of it before; everything had happened so *fast*.

"Hiroki, this is Machiko! Do you read?"

A hiss of static, and then thunder assaulted her ears. She twisted the volume switch in a panic. Not thunder. Gunfire.

"Hiroki! Come in, please!"

". . . achiko?" The reception was bad, but it was him. The sound of his voice was music.

"Listen, I'm approaching the south lock. We're in real trouble, you're not going to believe this!"

"At this point, I'd believe anything," Hiroki said. His usual calm was gone, replaced by tension and worry. The sounds of weaponfire clattered loudly through the com, blocking out whatever he said next.

"Hiroki? Where are you?" Her thoughts buzzed and clamored loudly as she stopped in the street and listened. Nothing. "Hiroki? Are you there?" Her voice cracked in tension.

". . . welding the inner doors of the west lock. We'll hold them off as long as . . ." Static. ". . . wish we could see what the hell we're . . ."

Noguchi slapped the receiver, hard. "I can't *hear* you!"

His next words came through clearly. "Get everyone to *The Lector,*" he said. And the com fuzzed out.

"*No!*" she breathed. "Hiroki?"

He was gone. There had to be another way! *The Lector* wasn't an option anymore, there was nowhere to go—

Noguchi ran toward the main well, where Riley and Mason had been only a few moments before. Riley would still have his weapon, they could—

Riley lay facedown in the dust, the late sun shining on the pool of red that had formed around him. The dry soil drank deeply; even as she watched, the blood drained into the earth, leaving a wet stain of crimson mud. A large hole had been punched through Riley's back, the ragged edges raw and meaty. His rifle lay nearby.

She ran to the fallen form and crouched next to it. She pressed numb fingers to Riley's throat and gagged on the thick, metallic scent of fresh blood. No pulse.

"Shit," she whispered. She looked around, eyes wide. The warriors, like the one that had saved her life—

She reached for Riley's rifle quickly, stood. And heard a sound right behind her, nothing so much like a sharp intake of breath. It wasn't Riley, that was certain. She turned in slow motion—

—and saw nothing. She let out a sigh of relief. There was a lot to be worried about, but no immediate threat, at least.

That was when the earth rose up, the dust wavering in the dimming light, to knock her to the ground.

18

Tichinde led the willing yautja into battle as the light grew shallow on the arid world. The *kwei* oomans had barricaded themselves behind a heavy door, their stingers on the outside but controlled from within. Their weapons were hot and deadly, their fire had already taken two of the warriors before Tichinde had decided to pull back and organize a stronger attack. Tricky devils, to hide behind the door and kill from a distance.

There were now only six other students left. They crouched behind one of the ooman structures and looked to him for command. Any doubt Tichinde had felt after watching two of his yautja fall evaporated as he saw the eager Hunters before him; Mahnde and Da-ec'te had been slow and foolish, but these warriors would go on to the victory Hunt.

"Skl'da'-si, you will be *hult'ah* and stand behind."
Skl'da'-si had the best eyes; they would need sharp vision to watch for any ooman who might be waiting to ambush.

The yautja tilted his head and stepped away from the rest.

"It is time for the Hunt of *nain-de*," the new Leader growled. He raised his voice steadily as he spoke the truth aloud to the others. "Time to kill until the *pyode amedha* trophies sit on our spears, until their *thwei* flows in our honor and the fight is done. A thousand stories will be sung in our names, for we will conquer!"

Tichinde flared his mandibles in pleasure at the low hisses that came from his warriors. They were ready.

It was Etah'-dte who began the chant of the Midnight Kiss. One by one, the yautja raised their spears and voices to the sky, the screams true and harsh in the dry dead air of the ooman world. Tichinde howled loud and long with his warrior brood; the Soft Meat would die in scores this night, and he would Lead the slaughter.

The Hunt was all.

Noguchi scrabbled backward on her elbows from her bizarre attacker.

There's nothing there—!

Even as the thought popped into her head, the magnified dust rippled and changed. One of the warriors suddenly towered over her, its thick arms high over its head. The spear it held was pointed at her.

Earlier, in the ship, she had forgotten in her panic

that she'd had a rifle strapped on her back. She remembered now.

She swung the heavy rifle up.

Too slow. Time expanded, flowed like thick oil. It took a millennium to thrust the weapon against her shoulder and aim—

Darkness sprang and covered the dragon.

From the main well structure behind the creature, the metallic black bugs shrieked and swarmed and fell on him, their talons fast and sharp.

Noguchi had not seen them there, hadn't heard them come. It didn't matter. She jumped to her feet and stumbled backward, watched as the warrior hit the ground and screamed horribly. The nightmare insects cried and tore at their prey. A pale green fluid, the dragon's blood, sprayed the dark animals. They threw back their obscenely long heads and screamed.

Fuck this!

Noguchi turned and ran.

Roth stood behind Cathie at the ops panel near the south lock when Ackland shouted from his position near the heavily fortified entry.

"Get ready! Something's coming!"

Roth gave Cathie's shoulders a light, reassuring squeeze before she picked up her carbine and joined the other armed men and women at the door, Creep at her heels.

Her heart thudded dully in her chest as she ran the dozen meters or so. Hiroki's broadcasts had been coming in from the ops console for the last twenty minutes or so. His team was doing their best to ward off the attackers, but they had wasted a lot of their ammo on thin air; the going belief was that the alien creatures had some kind of invisibility cloak. The camera angle was such that only a few of the team could be seen—not what they were fighting.

Roth took a position toward the front of the group and trained her weapon on the reinforced plexi door, arms steady. The tension around her was heavy; they didn't know enough about the aliens, what they were after or what they could do. Maybe they wouldn't be so easy to kill . . .

Reuben Hein, one of the geotechs, was on watch. His face was pressed closely to the loophole in the wall. He held up one of his dark hands for silence as the seconds ticked by.

Roth felt a trickle of sweat run down the nape of her neck; she closed one eye, finger rested lightly on the trigger.

"It's okay, don't shoot!" Hein called. "It's Noguchi!"

Roth hadn't realized how nervous she had been until his words flooded her with cool relief. She and the others lowered their weapons and stepped back from the door.

Noguchi had obviously been in a fight; her clothes were rumpled and dusty, her normally sleek hair was plastered to her head in strings, her face flushed. She walked in quickly and surveyed the situation.

"Did you see them? What the hell are they? How many were there?" Ackland half blocked her entrance, his red face betraying the fear he was hiding.

"Too many," said Noguchi. She turned to the assembled group of ranchers and company people and spoke clearly, her voice one of authority. "Fall back to the inner doors and get someone with a welding torch over here. Seal all of the doors—upper level, too— except the east lock. And no one goes in or out without my authorization."

She looked at Hein. "Are we organized enough to get this done without tripping over each other?"

He nodded. "I'll make sure of it."

"Are the children here?"

Loren Gaunt spoke up. "Yeah, they're eating back in the conference room with Davidson and Jonson."

Noguchi exhaled slightly, and some of the tension left her shoulders. She picked out Spanner in the crowd and walked over to him, her revolver extended butt first. "Please load this for me. And get me some extra rounds for it. More of the armor-piercing hunting rounds like it had before."

He took the weapon carefully. "How much extra ammo you think you'll need?"

"Ten speedloaders. And seal those doors ASAP."

She walked back toward the ops panel, not noticing the effect her words had on the group. *Ten speedloaders?* A low murmur rippled through the room.

Roth followed Noguchi to the back to tell Cathie what was going on.

The Japanese woman stopped near the board and spoke calmly to one of the staffers.

"Downey, do you have that sat-link hooked up yet?"

"Little Cygni's still interfering—but it'll be below the horizon in the next hour."

Noguchi nodded at that and turned to Weaver. "What do you have on the cameras? Can you get me a fix on Hiroki and his team?"

Cathie stepped up behind Roth and grabbed her hand, both of them watching the conversation. Weaver looked up at Noguchi slowly and said nothing; her brimming eyes said enough.

Noguchi threw her comset on the panel and took

the one that Weaver held out. She stood behind Weaver's chair and looked at the scant visual.

"Hiroki! This is Machiko, do you read?" Her voice held an edge of panic.

From their position, both Cathie and Roth could see what little there was to see on the small screen. A med kit lay open on the floor, its contents scattered. There was a white cable in one corner of the visual—which Roth realized, with dawning horror, was a human arm. The body of the fallen person was offscreen. Cathie's grip tightened in hers. Muted sounds of gunfire rattled through the com.

"Hiroki, this is Machiko! Do you—"

"Ma . . . iko?" The reception was terrible, but Roth felt her spirits lift slightly; he wasn't dead . . . bzzt. "—you in the tower? Friedman, get down!"

More static.

Noguchi grasped the com tightly, as if doing so would help somehow. She spoke in a rush; it was maybe the first time Roth had seen her with her cool exterior completely blown. The nitrogen queen was terrified.

"Listen, Horiki! Tell your team to stand by, we're going to open the doors and pull you in, do you read me? Tell your team to *stand by*!"

Hiroki had backed up so that part of his profile was visible in the screen. He held a rifle aimed offscreen and pulled the trigger uselessly.

"No time," he spoke in a half shout. Onscreen, Hiroki held the rifle up by its barrel, like a club. Static. ". . . team left, anyway! Just . . . and Friedman." Static. "I don't think we've hit any . . . them! Ammo's gone, us, too, I . . ."

He said something else, but his words were

drowned out by the sound of breaking plexi. Hiroki held his empty rifle higher.

Someone, Friedman, shouted offscreen. "... they come!"

"Stay safe, Machi ..." Static.

Roth watched as huge, dark shapes, the alien warriors, swarmed onto the screen. Hiroki brought the rifle down, hard—to no effect. The attacker he had tried to fend off knocked him to the floor easily, as if he were a child. Mercifully, he fell out of the camera's range. But the pool of red that flowed sluggishly into view must have come from Hiroki.

Noguchi made a strangled sound deep in her throat and looked away. And then Cathie was crying, and Roth turned to comfort her as best she could.

The mighty yautja burst through the shoddy ooman defenses with no further losses. There were only two of the Soft Meat still upright, and they fell in the span of a breath. Tichinde himself took out the smaller of the two. The ooman tried to stop him with a dead burner, like a staff—there was no contest.

The new Leader relished the decapitation of the small creature; it had put up a fight, however meager. Its skull would look fine on Tichinde's trophy wall, once it was polished clean of the sickly pale flesh.

Tichinde howled, the head of the ooman dripping *thwei* from his spear. Perhaps the Soft Meat were not as deadly as the yautja had been told. If this was the best they could do, he and his warriors would have many trophies to take home.

19

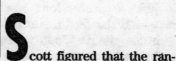

cott figured that the ranchers and staff were probably holed up in the main operations building; there was no one in sight as they stumbled through the empty streets toward the structure. Twilight had fallen over the town with no respite from the heat.

Scott felt a sense of déjà vu as they walked. Deserted town, lights low, unknown dangers—he looked over his shoulder several times to see if *The Lector* was still there. He was aware that there was no reason it wouldn't be, but he couldn't shake the feeling that he was in deadly danger and that there was no escape from it.

They were near the first set of holding pens when they heard the shriek.

From behind them somewhere, a long, shrill squeal

that seemed to echo in the still air rose in pitch and then dwindled into nothing.

Not human, whatever it was. Those things in the ship?

Scott glanced at Tom. He had gone a deathly white, his eyes huge in his face.

"What the fuck—?"

Before Tom could finish, the horrible cry came again. Closer.

Gaining.

Scott grabbed Tom's arm and they ran for the nearest holding pen. His gut had twisted at the alien scream; this whole thing was some kind of bad dream, one he didn't want to be in anymore.

I'd like to wake up now, please.

The entry to the pen stood open. They scrambled in just as another long howl came—louder, closer still—and slammed the heavy door shut.

Inside, the dark, stuffy room stank of perspiration and rhynth shit. At least they seemed to be alone.

"What are we gonna do?" Tom managed, his voice nearly a gasp.

Scott shook his head, tried to catch his own breath.

The only light in the large room came through a row of small, dirty windows set high on one wall. Other than the door they both leaned against, the only other way in was through the loading hatch—which was closed and locked.

"We're going to stay here," Scott said finally.

"But the other people must be—"

"Fuck the other people. The other people have guns, you heard the shooting. We don't. Do you want to go back out without a weapon?"

Another scream from outside. Tom's silence was answer enough. They would wait. If somebody wanted in, they could knock and ask politely and if the voice wasn't human, they sure as shit weren't gonna get an open door.

Noguchi sat on her bed and stared at the floor, one shaky hand on her forehead. She didn't feel much of anything; at first there had been a huge sadness, but it had been replaced with a kind of dull acceptance.

Hiroki was dead. He and the others had sacrificed themselves for the rest of the colony, and she had failed to use the time he had bought for them; she had failed at everything.

Part of her mind kept shouting at her: *Organize! Get this under control! Get yourself together!*

It was the same voice that had pushed her through most of her life, the driver of the strong Machiko who allowed her to hold her head up. It clamored in her thoughts now, directed her to get up, get up now! and get going—but she let it run itself in circles.

Where was there to go?

Noguchi felt as if she had been sitting there for hours, but she knew it had been only a few minutes. Funny; all she really wanted to do was lie down and sleep until she woke up at home. On Earth, back in the tiny apartment she'd left a million years before . . .

Would that be so bad? Just to give up and wait there until help came, until the damn company sent someone to pick them up? They could probably hold out, just do some heavy reinforcing of the locks and then sit tight. Maybe she could even stay here, in her room. The people downstairs could make do without her. They would figure out something. Hide away, do nothing, wait. Yes, that felt right—

"Ms. Noguchi?" A soft voice crackled over her com.

Noguchi felt her stomach tighten at the sound. Why did they need *her*, it wasn't fair! She couldn't run a battle, she was an *overseer* for Christ's sake!

"Ms. Noguchi, this is Weaver." The hesitant voice called again.

Noguchi sighed. "Yes, what is it?" It didn't matter, none of it did.

"I'm sorry to interrupt or anything. I thought—I mean, I know you and Mr. Shimura were friends, and I'm sorry to bother—"

"What?" She wanted to feel angry, but there was still nothing.

"There's something you should see. I could transfer it to your screen, it's the feed from the security cam on the southwest side of the tower. It's dark, though I've boosted the gain—I guess there are a lot of lights out over there—"

Noguchi turned wearily and looked at the console on her wall, already sorry she'd admitted to being there. Fuck these people. They didn't even *like* her. What did they expect? Why did she have to take care of them? Why her?

The screen snapped on.

It was a bonfire. At first, Noguchi didn't recognize that it was a picture from anywhere on Ryushi; she was reminded of old holos she had seen on Earth, of tribal dancing, ritual stuff.

But the dancers were the warriors. The dragons. Well, no, not really dragons, aliens.

There were five or six of them, the creatures who had killed Hiroki and the others. They ran and stumbled and jumped high in the air all around the fire, which was probably built with debris from the west lock. Sparks flew, flame cracked and rose into the early evening sky as the aliens danced and circled. And they carried spears . . .

There was no audio, but Noguchi could imagine the howls of victory. For the spears they held high in the air were decorated with their conquests. As she watched, one of the warriors danced past the cam with one of the black nightmare-bug skulls jammed onto the point of his spear.

And the next warrior—

She quickly looked away, then returned her gaze to the screen. She didn't want to believe what she had seen, but it was true. Fuzzy and distorted by the heat and bad lighting, but there.

Hiroki's decapitated head on the tip of the creature's spear, the sharp, bladed end running through his neck and out of his mouth.

For just a moment, she thought she might vomit.

The alien danced from view, but Noguchi had seen what she had needed to see. The nausea passed. Something new, some new feeling was filling her up. It wasn't sorrow or sickness, although she felt both of those things. No, it was dark and solid and throbbing, like a huge, black machine had started running deep inside, at the core of her being. It was a physical sensation, this feeling, a rumble of newness.

It was many things, but the easiest to understand was the anger. She watched the celebrating warriors and felt the apathy get eaten by the new machine, chewed and burned away, fuel for the thing at her center. It cleared her mind for what she would need to do.

She was going to kill them. All of them. Not just for Hiroki's death or the lives of the ranchers or her career—she felt almost selfish about her reasons, but in the end, it wouldn't matter. They would die because they dared to try her. She was a woman of honor and they stood against her.

Roth and Cathie stood near the table where Spanner sat, Noguchi's gun in front of him. A lot of the others watched also, although there really wasn't much to see. Spanner had already filled eight speedloaders, and was working on his ninth. He fed the rounds in slowly and the metallic clicks were loud in the quiet room when he closed the latch knob. It had been pretty silent here since Hiroki's last transmission.

Noguchi had been gone for twenty minutes or so, which was just as well. Roth hadn't liked seeing the new overseer choke up. Tears would have been okay, but Noguchi had just—swallowed it and gone inside of herself. It was too bad; Roth had seen an iron thread in Noguchi during the setup of the barricades, and had hoped they would all see more of it. Bitch or no, she was competent under stress. Or so they had thought. They were gonna need that, given what they were up against.

Ackland had made a short speech after Noguchi had walked out, about how they were all going to have to pull together and decide what their next move would be. But he was dry-mouthed and scared, he didn't have any suggestions after that, and finally he sat back down. He didn't know what to do, either.

Cathie kept a firm grip on her arm as the silent tension grew. Roth knew her spouse didn't want her to step forward, although she was as qualified as anyone else, maybe more so. She didn't want to lead the colony, but someone would have to. Much as she wished it would have been Noguchi, Roth didn't think she was going to come back.

Spanner continued to load the bullet holders methodically. High velocity hunting rounds, jacketed slugs that would punch through a wall. Someone would need them.

Noguchi stepped into the room quietly.

"Ms. Noguchi—" Ackland looked and sounded confused.

She had pulled her hair back and knotted it tightly at the base of her neck. She wore a fully padded coverall, the kind that the rhynth workers wore during gelding time; the suit was designed to dull impact from stray kicks, and had saved Roth herself from a lot of injuries. She had strapped a carbine to her back and wore knee and elbow leathers, as well as gloves. A comset hung loosely around her neck, and her eyes were cold and hard.

Roth grinned nervously, and felt Cathie's arm slip around her waist. Noguchi was back—and looked like a woman to reckon with.

"Who owns the fastest hover bike?" she said, her voice cool. Cool, strong, authoritative.

Roth said, "I guess that would be me."

Noguchi nodded at her. "Where is it?"

"East lock. Keycard's in it."

Noguchi smiled briefly at her, the expression calm and yet somehow chilling. The nitrogen queen was back, only this time, there was something else under the icy facade.

Ackland laid a hand on Noguchi's shoulder and turned her roughly to face him. "That's it? You're taking off? What about the rest of us?" His voice was heavy with anger, his composure blustery. "I thought you were supposed to be in charge! Where's your sense of responsibility?"

Noguchi took a deep breath. And then she punched Ackland low in the gut, hard.

20

The anger rested in her like a dormant but wild animal, waiting to be awakened and used. Noguchi knew she had bigger things to deal with than this overblown rancher who stood fuming, his fat finger pointed at her chest. But she had had more than enough from him. She took a breath and jabbed. It was a reaction more than a decision.

Ackland folded, gasped, and fell to the floor.

She heard the people all around step back; two or three applauded.

"Responsibility?" Her voice sounded strange to her ears, cold and furious. "Hiroki is dead, Ackland! And a big part of this shit sandwich is on your plate! *If* we live through this, you're going to find out what happens to people who are *responsible*!"

Ackland was still on the floor, face red, trying to catch his breath. The anger suddenly coiled back to a resting state, left her exhilarated and exhausted all at once. Ackland was an annoyance, but nothing to slow down for.

Like a headache.

She raised her gaze and looked around at the watching crowd. The faces she saw weren't angry, just somber. Maybe Ackland wasn't quite as popular as he thought. The only important thing now was getting the job done, the job she *was* responsible for— hunting down the things that had disturbed Prosperity Wells. But not simply for vengeance.

For honor.

Noguchi raised her voice so that everyone could hear. "Weaver, you're in charge until I get back! The rest of you will follow her orders to the letter, is that clear?"

A few of the ranchers nodded. It would have to do.

Spanner had holstered Hiroki's revolver to a rhynth-hide belt with pouches for the extra ammunition carriers. Noguchi smiled briefly at him and strapped it on without another word. No one spoke.

Several of the ranchers and employees followed her down the long hall to the east lock, but she didn't have anything else to tell them. She had an idea, but the details weren't quite worked out yet; she had told Weaver the basics over the com, so help on this end was covered. But judging from how fast Hiroki and his team had been taken out, time couldn't be wasted on planning; she'd have to play it mostly by ear.

Noguchi reached the lock and peered out of the loophole window; the bike was only a few meters from the entry. The deepening dusk was deceptively peaceful-looking, quiet.

Roth stepped up behind her, expression set. "I could come with you," she said softly.

Noguchi considered it, then shook her head. "No. If I don't come back, someone will have to come up with other plans. You'll help most by staying here. Talk to Weaver, she'll fill you in."

Roth nodded. "Let me cover you, then."

"Okay. I'll signal here in approximately twenty minutes; if I haven't called, weld this lock and keep a CDS going to the corporation's sub-HQ. If you keep backing up and sealing the doors as you go, you might be able to hold out until they give up, or until my idea pans out."

Or they get in . . .

It didn't need to be said. Roth nodded again and shouldered her rifle.

Noguchi opened the door and broke into a run in the hot night air.

The pain had been flowing away for a long time, how long he didn't know. Or where he was, or what exactly had happened. More than once, he had risen from the dark to feel that he was still alive, still *nan'ku*. There were straps on his body, which conjured images of a snarling dark creature in bands of dlex.

Queen. *Kainde amedha.*

He surfaced briefly with the familiar image and then decided to sleep a little more. He must still be unwell, although he felt that his strength had somewhat returned. The sickness was sensory; the smells in consciousness were alien, strange. The air was wrong. And he sensed no yautja nearby . . .

Dachande slept, but left his inner eye open and

watchful. He would investigate the situation later. Soon.

Noguchi jumped on the bike and stabbed at the key at the same time. Her adrenaline was in overload, her breath shallow. Everything around her had slowed down, but she was at light-speed.

She jammed the accelerator down and flew toward *The Lector*, free from fear. Death wasn't so scary once decided on; Noguchi didn't want to die, but the odds weren't in her favor. After seeing Hiroki's head on a spear, she had accepted the futility of the situation. She would probably die—but not without company.

There was an overpass ahead, the second-story walkway between the sewage treatment plant and the main well. Noguchi floored the pedal; the shadows there were thick and secretive.

She was halfway through when the dark exploded to life.

The attack came from her left. A high shriek, then something big and heavy hit. The bike tipped, veered toward a wall in the dark, claws ripped, the bike righted—

—and she was back in the open. The creature had fallen off of the unbalanced bike. There was another shriek behind her. She got the impression of great speed from behind, as the thing ran—

Noguchi grabbed for the rifle on her back and circled wide. It was one of the bugs. Because everything had slowed, she saw it in perfect detail as it ran. Long black skull with razor teeth, an impossible body, segmented, black, metallic. There was only the one.

She flew straight at it, a part of her mind screaming at her to get away, fast.

She aimed the rifle ...

The creature's head blew apart in a spray of blood.

Another jumped out from the heavy shadows, ran at her—

—she hit it, heard the cry of pain and rage. It clutched at the cycle, scrabbled up, loomed above her.

There was a meter-thick beam under the walkway, barely visible in the dark. Noguchi ducked low and flew straight at it.

The bug's howl was cut short and the bike lifted again.

Noguchi circled back and headed again for the ship, heart pounding. In spite of the physical reaction, she felt calm. Very awake, but not panicked; she felt in complete control, she knew exactly what she was doing ...

She slammed on the brakes suddenly and cried out, enraged by her own stupidity.

"Shit, shit, *shit!*"

Miriam Revna. She had forgotten.

The coms had been out for several hours before Miriam heard the shots echo through the compound. There had been gunfire before, but it hadn't been so close. Several times, she had heard weird screams, alien sounds.

Miriam held the bonecutter tightly and tried to breathe deeply. She had stood by the door for what seemed like days, and she was exhausted. The patient had not regained consciousness, although his readings had jumped several times, indicating a raise of bodily functions—increased heart rate, blood pressure, temperature. The readings could be wrong, though, probably were; she had never seen a creature quite like it. Neither had Kesar . . .

Kesar.

Miriam closed her eyes and breathed deeper. She didn't want to think about him, not yet. She wasn't ready to admit that he . . . she wasn't ready to grieve.

The two coms in the lab were notorious for fuzzing out, sometimes for days at a time. They had never bothered getting them fixed—the lab was only a few dozen meters from the main transmitting antenna, not a hassle to walk. No one had tried to contact her— although she wouldn't know, of course. She was scared, and she missed Kesar more with every second.

A hover bike pulled up outside, and Miriam heard running footsteps. Perhaps it was Kesar—

She knew it wasn't somewhere inside even before she heard Machiko Noguchi's voice.

"Dr. Revna! It's me, Machiko!"

Miriam gripped the bonesaw closer and went to the door. She punched the entry button and looked outside, cautiously.

It *was* the overseer. She wore a padded coverall and held a rifle. Her gaze scanned from left to right as she edged into the lab, facing out.

As soon as she was inside, Miriam hit the control and the door slid shut.

"Machiko, I heard shooting! What happened?"

The younger woman turned to face her. Miriam was struck by the changes she saw in Noguchi's cool expression. Something huge had occurred, something that had made everything different. It was in her eyes, in the set of her mouth—

"Things are bad, and they're about to get worse." In

spite of the circumstances, Machiko Noguchi sounded calm. "Can you handle a hover bike?"

Miriam shook her head and set the cutter on a table. "No. I never learned. Kesar was going to teach me, but we never—"

"Do you know how to use one of these?" Machiko cut her off, held up the rifle she carried. "I don't have time to get you back to ops."

Miriam shook her head again.

Machiko handed it to her anyway and spoke quickly. "It's a semiautomatic, so it does all the work for you. Just point it at what you want to shoot and squeeze this trigger." She motioned at the crook of the rifle. "You only have six rounds, so don't waste any on warning shots."

Miriam took the rifle hesitantly and frowned. "Ms. Noguchi, I'm a doctor, not a soldier . . ."

"This isn't war," Noguchi said softly. "This is survival."

Miriam felt tears in her eyes, but wasn't sure why. "Who might I be—shooting at?" The words were strange in her mouth.

"Your patient's brothers. Or something that looks like a two-meter-tall black insect with a banana-shaped head full of teeth." Machiko said. She walked over to the patient and the table of artifacts and picked up the odd shield she and Hiroki had studied before. She held it up toward Miriam.

"The unclassifieds that Roth brought in—Kesar's report said he thought they might transport eggs, or spores, to host bodies. Is it possible that when those spores grew up, they'd look like this?" She pointed at the strange animal etched into the surface.

"It's impossible to say," Miriam said slowly. She felt horribly confused. "Why?"

"Because I've seen some of these things tonight. There were dozens, maybe hundreds of them in *The Lector*. And I think Ackland's rhynth were infected"— she paused—"or *impregnated* by these things. And they've spread it to all of the herds on the ship. I think our two unclassifieds are connected somehow."

Miriam looked at the etching and then over to the specimen strapped to the table. "Not biologically. They're quite different in chemical makeup."

Machiko nodded. "There's no time to worry about it now, anyway." She looked at the injured alien. "We ought to shoot that thing," she said. "But maybe we'll need it as a hostage later." She walked toward the door.

"What are you going to do?"

Noguchi turned. "I have an idea or two. Listen, I want you to *stay here*, okay? Outside is not safe. Keep the door locked. I'll come back for you as soon as I can, but if you haven't seen me within the next hour, start thinking about how you can get to ops. Wait until daylight, and take the rifle when you go. I'll tell the ranchers to watch for you."

And she was gone, just like that.

Miriam set the heavy weapon on the table and stood with her eyes closed for a moment. It was all like a dream, surreal and frightening. None of this could be happening. She looked at the alien creature on the exam table and tried to get her thoughts in order.

Kesar was dead. Thinking anything else was folly. Perhaps the broken-tusked alien had something to do with it, but there was no anger in her heart, only a soft, wishful ache.

"It's so wasteful," she said quietly. "We could learn so much from one another ..."

There was a sudden scratching sound at the door, a sliding knock.

"Dr. Revna! It's me, Machiko!"

Why had she come back?

Miriam hurried to the door. "Machiko? What happened?"

She hit the entry control and stepped back. "Did—"

Words escaped. The patient—no, it was a creature like the one on the table—

Miriam turned and ran, even as the armored monster clutched for her.

The weapon, table, trigger—!

She ran, but the thing screamed behind her, too close.

She was going to die.

21

After the initial conquest, Tichinde left the yautja to circle the ooman dwellings and get a feel for where the others might be. There were many in the same structure as the first group, but he wanted to be certain that there weren't more, perhaps waiting to ambush them.

He walked. And heard the sound of machinery behind him, coming closer. Tichinde blended with the shadows as they had all been taught and waited to see what would come. He patted the mesh sack on his belt; there were already three ooman trophies in it; there would be more.

A single ooman drove a small aircraft into view, landed it, then ran to one of the dwellings, a short burner in its hand.

Tichinde pressed the loop control on his shiftsuit,

one that he had salvaged from the wreck, to record the language spoken. The tiny ooman shouted and then entered the building at the beck of another ooman inside.

A short span passed and the flyer ooman came out and went away. He thought it was the same one—they looked much alike to him.

Tichinde waited a few breaths and then walked to the same door from which the creature had come. He pushed the loop control on the arm of his suit and listened to the odd language spill from the copier.

There was movement inside. And the door opened to reveal a lone ooman, defenseless. The creature's face distorted in reaction and it howled.

Tichinde ran forward and screamed for blood.

The ooman stumbled back, turned, and ran for a table. A table with a strange burner on it.

Tichinde raised his bladed staff high, ready for the final cut—

—and there was something familiar here, a scent he knew, but it didn't matter because the ooman must die—

—the ooman raised the burner slowly and fired at nothing, the shot far and wide, then another—

—and Tichinde brought the blade down, prowess and certainty in the fatal cut—

Noguchi heard a shot, then another. It came from the lab, or somewhere near it.

She had stopped at the main control hatch for the front six buildings of the compound and studied the numbers, not certain of the proper codes for what she needed to do. She'd punched buttons, pretty sure that she had gotten it right, and checked her chronograph.

The shots made her jump; they were accompanied by a shrill and primal scream.

Noguchi jumped on the bike, turned it back toward the lab, and hoped she would get there in time.

Dachande opened his eyes at the sound of the yautja death cry and growled softly.

Tichinde. And he pursued the creature, the ooman whose smell had become familiar.

The desperate ooman ran to the table in front of Dachande's resting place and snatched at a burner clumsily. Tichinde towered over it in classic pose, ready to deliver the death blow to the panicked ooman. The ooman who had nurtured him through the dark, what could have been his final moments until *dhi'ki-de*.

Dachande lifted one of his arms. The strap holding it snapped. He thrust his talon forward and caught the staff right below the blade.

Tichinde's head jerked up in surprise. The ooman fell to the ground.

With a quick shove, Dachande rammed the staff upward and knocked Tichinde backward.

Tichinde jumped up and popped his wrist forward, extended the double bladed *ki'cti-pa* toward Dachande.

The Leader growled in fury. Tichinde would raise a weapon against *him*? Had he lost his memory?

Dachande freed his other arm easily and struggled, tried to leap. His lower body was still bound—

Tichinde jumped to meet him, *ki'cti-pa* raised to slash.

And the world exploded into a million flying pieces.

The sounds of battle were unmistakable. So was Miriam Revna's scream.

Noguchi stamped the pedal and ducked.

Miriam cried out and fell to the floor as the wall cracked open in a roar of thunder and shattered around her. A chunk of something sharp and heavy gouged her right calf. The pain was horrible. The terror was worse.

The thunder ceased. Miriam pulled herself around a table leg and turned to see what had happened.

Noguchi had come through the wall. The bike was turned on its side and Machiko was propped on her elbows, pistol aimed behind Miriam.

The doctor snapped her head around and saw that the attacking creature was sprawled facedown on the floor. It didn't move, but she could hear its labored breathing.

The patient was still on the exam table, pinned there by one remaining bond across its abdomen. He fumbled with the strap frantically.

"Lay down flat, Miriam!"

Noguchi had her gun pointed at the struggling patient. Her finger tightened on the trigger.

The doctor stood up, right in the line of fire.

"Jesus, get *down*!" Noguchi's heart pounded.

Miriam didn't even look back at her. She held both

of her hands up and walked slowly toward the tethered warrior.

Dachande redoubled his futile attempts at freedom as the ooman came at him. The creature held its odd, clawless hands open and moved slowly. The other, dressed as a warrior, had a weapon on him—but the approaching ooman blocked the small warrior's efforts.

It could be a trick, a ploy to calm him before the Soft Meat ripped him open . . .

But the slow-moving creature was the one that had tended to him; the *ki'cti-pa* was unmistakable. If it had wanted him dead, wouldn't it have struck when he was injured and unaware? There was a thick bandage of some kind around his chest—not the work of a Hunter. A healer, then.

Dachande stopped his labors and held still, but kept his body tensed and ready. He hissed a warning to the ooman.

And it leaned toward him, very slowly, and unlatched the restraint.

Miriam unhooked the bond and stepped back, careful not to move suddenly. The creature had growled at her, a foreboding gurgling sound, but didn't attack when she was in reach.

"What are you *doing*?!"

Miriam kept her eyes on the patient. "I think it's okay," she said softly.

The creature studied her for several long seconds. Miriam held still, not wanting to frighten it.

"Are you insane?" Noguchi was furious. "They killed Hiroki and six others!"

She didn't move. "*They* did. He didn't."

Miriam was scared, in spite of her intuitive feeling that the creature wouldn't harm her. Intuition wasn't a lot in the face of death.

The patient moved fast. It slammed one clawed hand down on her shoulder.

Dachande inspected the ooman thoughtfully. *This* was what he had wanted to Hunt all of his life? It was ugly, but certainly not dangerous-looking. It was stupid, too. Approaching a warrior with no weapon didn't indicate a particularly high intelligence. Or it was incredibly brave and ready to do battle. Small as it was, if it wanted to fight, perhaps it was also mad?

The armed one babbled at the ooman next to him. Dachande got the impression that the defenseless creature had kept him from being killed. The ooman with the hand-held burner lowered the weapon slowly.

Overcoming a lifetime of yautja lore was not a thing he wanted to do—but good warriors stayed open to new information. Perhaps the Soft Meat on this world were different.

Dachande decided. He placed one of his claws on the ooman's shoulder and shook, the symbol of greeting.

The ooman shrank slightly, and the other raised its weapon again. Dachande took his claw away and waited.

After a pause, the tiny ooman stretched itself high and returned the gesture.

Dachande tilted his head at her. Fascinating!

Then it was that Tichinde clattered his mandibles and slowly got to his feet.

Dachande's anger flared. The *s'yuit-de*! He would die!

Dachande jumped past the ooman and whacked Tichinde's skull. The blow knocked the student to the ground.

Tichinde said nothing, but scrabbled at the pouch on his belt.

Dachande snatched the sack from the idiot yautja and held it up. Trophies.

Ooman trophies.

His rage was blinding. Tichinde had Hunted with no supervision—and had Hunted ooman!

Dachande lifted the yautja by his tresses, the fury boosting his strength. He could smell his own musk, hot and heavy with the desire to kill. He raised one fist and smashed Tichinde in the mouth.

Tichinde tried to pull away, responded with a weak blow to Dachande's gut.

Dachande howled in his face, a shriek of pure disgust and outrage. He struck again.

Tichinde was his student, once. He had broken the rules of the Hunt. There was only so much slack Dachande could give him, even as a Leader. Now the rope must be pulled taut. Now, Tichinde must be destroyed.

It was the law.

It was a matter of honor.

22

oguchi watched in amazement as the two huge warriors fought. The broken-tusked "patient" was the more skillful—and was winning easily.

Myriad half thoughts ran through her mind. The patient was grateful, the other was with the killers, the broken tusk was better, older, brighter perhaps, the doctor was insane, they had to *get out*—

Miriam stood a few meters from the battle, just stood there and watched.

Noguchi ran forward, pistol ready, and grabbed the doctor by the arm.

"Come on!"

The monsters could slug it out to the death for all she cared; they had work to do.

She and Miriam ducked through the shattered wall

and ran across the compound. Noguchi steered them toward the main garage, to the east. The med center was closer to the holding pens, but they would need a flyer for what she had in mind and the hover bike was totaled; there would be other bikes at the garage—

Except Miriam can't fly one and they won't carry two people.

Noguchi wanted to scream. *Fuck, fuck, fuck!*

And on the heels of the panic, she remembered the copter.

The copter!

She ran faster.

Miriam had trouble keeping up; blood ran down one of her legs. The compound was completely dark now. Many of the building lights had been broken at some point, and the few remaining only seemed to add to the shadows. A faint breeze had sprung up, hot and fetid. A death wind, full of carrion stench.

Behind them and ahead, shapes moved and shrieked. It was hard to see what was happening. Noguchi guessed that the two alien races were fighting.

Maybe they won't even notice us—

A giant black bug leapt in front of them from a shadow and raised its strange arms to attack.

Miriam screamed.

Noguchi pointed and fired twice. The first shot was too high. The second tore out the bug's throat. Blood sprayed.

A drop of the fluid spattered against one of Noguchi's padded suit arms and hissed, ate through the fabric and burned her skin.

Acid, some kind of acid—

The noxious substance ate deep into her flesh. As

they ran forward the garage, Noguchi felt her own blood soak into the coverall. She ignored it as best she could; they were almost there.

They reached the garage, Miriam now stumbling badly. Noguchi half dragged her toward the back of the building. The copter was usually kept at the med center, on the roof's helipad; the doctors used it to get to emergencies. But Noguchi remembered that it needed some minor adjustment after the weapons-collecting run.

I just hope it wasn't engine trouble—

Noguchi laughed sharply as the rounded the corner, a short bark of relief. It was there! She looked around for trouble, but the yard seemed clean.

Miriam stumbled behind her and fell.

"Oh, *shit*, I can't get up, I'm sorry, Kesar, I'm sorry, I can't—" The doctor tried to hold it together, but she looked close to a breakdown. Her face was the color of dust, her eyes rolled upward.

Noguchi pulled Miriam to her feet and dragged her to the copter.

"It's okay, Miriam, you're going to be fine, okay?" She hoped she sounded soothing. "Everything will be fine, really, okay?"

They reached the vehicle. She opened the door and hustled Miriam in, still talking. "Don't worry, we're going to get out of here, okay? I'll help you fly this thing, just tell me what to do and we'll be fine."

That seemed to cut through the doctor's hysteria. Revna raised her tear-streaked face to Noguchi, eyes wide.

"Kesar always flew. I don't know *how*."

* * *

Dachande didn't want to spend too much time on Tichinde, much as he felt the idiot deserved to die slowly. He had to find the other yautja, if there were any. Find out what was going on, how he had come to this state. It did not feel good, what had happened.

Tichinde fell again. His tresses were matted with *thwei*, two of his mandibles broken and crushed against his worthless, dying skin.

Any fight the student had in him had fled. He tried to crawl away.

The sight of the yautja slowly inching from his Leader was infuriating. The *kwei* would die as an animal, a coward, rather than go out like a warrior.

Dachande waited no longer. He snatched Tichinde's bladed staff from the floor and raised it over his head, aimed it at the base of his student's upper spine.

Brought the sharp blade down—

Shiiink!

Dachande jerked the blade from the body in a patter of blood and then spit on the corpse. The Leader donned the *kwei*'s armor and took his weapons; he left the bandage on his chest. There was some pain there, perhaps the dressing would help. After a second's hesitation, he pulled the recording loop from Tichinde's chest; there might be a use for it later.

Armed and ready, with a fire in his gut that screamed for justice, Dachande stepped into the dark night to find his other students. Perhaps Tichinde had been alone, but he doubted it. Hunting alone was not common behavior to the young.

And if they were here, in the ooman camp, on a Hunt—nothing would stop him from the lessons he would teach them.

* * *

"What?"

Revna nodded. "He was going to teach me—"

Noguchi tuned her out for a second.

Okay, she can't do it, we're fucked—

She searched the myriad of buttons and switches on the console and found one that said MAIN. She flipped it.

The copter's engine hummed to life.

She tapped her comset. "This is Noguchi in copter"—she looked over the board quickly—"copter one. Do you read me, tower?"

A hiss of static.

And then Weaver's welcome voice.

"We copy. What's happening?"

"Miriam Revna and I are at the garage and neither of us are checked out in a copter. We could use some help here."

Weaver sounded calm. "Okay, we got you. Hit the switch that says MAIN."

"Did it."

"Do you see the button that says COMP? Punch that."

Noguchi spotted it and did what she was told. A small screen flickered on with program questions. She and Revna both sighed at once.

"Okay, we're on a roll," Noguchi said quietly.

"David, get over here." Weaver's voice was distant, then came back through the com. "I'm going to let Spanner talk you up, okay?"

"Fine. What's the situation there?" Noguchi touched her arm lightly and grimaced at the pain. At least the bleeding seemed to have stopped.

"We're all set for your signal. Everything's locked up, for a while at least. But you should see what's happening in the southwest quad; looks like an all-out war."

"Consider the signal given. Wait until we get off the ground, and then go as soon as you hear it. Good luck."

"Copy that, boss."

There was a pause; Noguchi waited for Spanner to come on and tapped the comset, anxious to get out of there. She turned to look at Miriam—

—a dark shape popped up in front of the copter, a nightmare bug. Its teeth dripped and gnashed as it plunged one claw through the windshield.

Scott and Tom had stayed quiet for a long time. The sounds outside of weapons fire and death cries were incentive not to move around much. The monsters were out there and maybe if they stayed under their rock here long enough, they'd eat each other and go away.

Scott figured out that they were in the southwest quadrant of the compound, in one of the two empty holding pens. There were six others, full of bellowing rhynth; their cries mingled with the alien screams.

Harmony à la hell.

"I'm starting to think we were better off in the ship," Tom whispered.

"Yeah, right. Stuck in the spider's web waiting around for dinner. Their dinner."

Scott cracked the door slightly to see if anyone was coming to help. So far, they had seen nothing. Well, no *people.*

Strange humanoid creatures were at war with the bizarre animals that had taken over the ship. It was too dark to make anything out clearly, but the situation was obvious; between the screams and the weapons, there was one *fuck* of a battle going on out there. They couldn't tell who was doing what to whom and for what reasons, but it was bad.

Scott was exhausted and he felt like shit. They had been stuck there for what felt like days. He wanted a shower, a steak, a few beers, and a soft bed. No way he was going out there to get it, but it helped to take his mind off of the situation at hand. Which looked like Armageddon. It was all so ... unreal.

Tom groaned softly and shifted to sit on the dirty floor. He was sick, had been coughing and having cramps for over an hour, but he was trying to keep it to himself; the look on his face expressed enough. Scott looked at his friend, worried, then back out at the bloody combat.

Something screamed piercingly and then was silenced.

"Hang on, Tommy," Scott whispered. "We're going to be okay."

Yeah. Maybe we'll sprout wings and just fly back to Earth.

Noguchi jabbed her leg forward and up and pushed as hard as she could. The bug barely moved, but it was enough. Maybe.

She pulled the trigger four times, fast. The animal's head exploded, sent a spray of deadly blood across the windshield and onto the console. The noise of the gun hit her ears like hard slaps. The plexi material began to smoke immediately and the small compartment filled with a foul and acrid stink.

Noguchi whipped her head around. Nothing else coming at the moment.

"You okay?"

Revna held up one shaky hand and nodded.

Noguchi took a deep breath and strapped herself into the chair. "Buckle up, Miriam."

She ejected the spent shells and slammed another speedloader in before she looked down at the controls and took a deep breath.

"Let's do it, Spanner. What's first?"

The copter rose in a series of sharp jerks before Noguchi turned it toward the south end of the complex. Miriam still wasn't sure what the plan was, but she was glad to get off of the ground.

She felt her injured leg carefully and winced. It was a bad wound. Each second that passed left her weaker, dizzier; she had lost a lot of blood, maybe too much—

Miriam applied pressure to the wound with part of her jacket and prayed silently that she and Kesar would be together soon.

Dachande ran through the oddly structured system of ooman buildings toward the sounds of battle. He ached all over and at least two of his ribs were broken, but he put the pain aside for now.

Shattered buildings and other rubble littered the grounds. Dachande hopped over the torso of a fallen drone; its life fluid still hissed on the soil.

He heard burners and screams in the distance, to the left. He cursed mentally and ran in that direction.

The *s'yuit-de*! They Hunted oomans, worse, they did so without proper surveillance. It was bad enough to have broken the law; to use poor strategy and tactics only compounded the error.

The other two Blooded must certainly be dead; they would not have allowed this. As sketchily trained as these yautja were, the bugs would be more than just a minor challenge. Armed oomans would be worse.

A small torrent of the Hard Meat appeared suddenly, leapt from the dark shadows to scream at him. Dachande pulled his burner. He was in too much of a hurry for prowess feats.

There were four. They circled him.

The first darted forward, teeth chittering. The outer jaws spread wide, the smaller teeth on the inner rod gaped.

Dachande burned it, the hollow thump of the weapon exploding the drone's gut into bloody bits. Without turning, Dachande took out the second and the third. He shot one, and used the spear in *hiju* position to disembowel the other.

The final drone screeched, turned, and ran. Unusual behavior, but they sometimes did that when there was a queen nearby. It was not fear, for they had none, but instinct to warn the nest.

Dachande sped on. Perhaps a few of the students would be salvageable. If not, he would have to kill them. Whatever they had stepped into on this world, they had sunk up to their necks in it and the stink was bad. Real bad.

Roth loaded food and water packs into the AVs with the others. With any luck they'd be back the next day, but they had taken almost everything. Most of the ranchers were seated and ready; just a final check and they could move.

Weaver had outlined Noguchi's plan briefly; it was shaky, but there was a chance it could work. Only a few people had protested—Ackland's voice above the rest, of course—but Weaver had shut them up with a few well-chosen words. Roth had liked "or we'll kick your fucking ass" in particular.

Roth stood cover outside the east lock as Weaver directed the last few people to either an AV or a ship loader. The largest piece of machinery, one of the carts that had carried most of the building supplies for the shield wall, now held thirty-seven people. Most of the transmitting equipment was also loaded—they would continue the CDS from the desert.

If they got that far.

Creep whined softly at the sound of one of the children crying. He kept saying that it was too hot outside. Roth silently agreed; she was reminded of the thunderstorms in southern Texas, where she had grown up. The stifling summer air would get even hotter as the clouds pressed down; as a child, she had waited eagerly for the first drops to fall, filled with the joy of expectation. There was a wild feeling in the air that had always made her think of carnivals in the dark, although she didn't know why. And then the rain, heavy and warm—

Weaver interrupted her thoughts. "We're ready."

Roth nodded and whistled for Creep to get on the bike. Cathie was watching some of the children in one of Harrison's AV; they would hook up later.

. A low rumble shook the ground with no warning and then grew louder. Roth hopped on a bike and started it up, the sound quickly lost in the rising tremors that beat through the soil. Goddamn if that didn't sound like thunder; Roth hit the accelerator and headed east, the AVs and loaders behind.

Miriam opened her eyes and looked down when the noise rolled over them. There was an ocean of life directly below them; the entire compound was moving, undulating in a quake of heaving bodies and animal cries.

Noguchi had stampeded the rhynth.

23

Dachande heard the rumble and immediately ran for the nearest structure he could climb.

Directly after he had attained Leader, he had taken a group on a Hunt and he had heard the same rumble; it was the sound of many animals running in mindless *gry'sui-bpe*. The yautja had clambered onto a low rise and watched as a herd of four-legged hosts had stampeded past in front of them. Had they stayed on the low ground, they would have been trampled.

He spotted a ladder bolted to a tall structure and ran for it.

He had not found the students yet, but before he could do so, he needed to avoid being crushed by the stampede. He hoped the students would understand what the sound meant and seek high ground or protection.

He growled in irritation as he climbed the rungs of the ladder. If they paid attention to his lessons, maybe they wouldn't die. If they had not listened, then they *deserved* to die. That was the way of it. His hope was not all that good.

Considering how well they've learned so far ...

Dachande climbed as the rumble thickened into an all-encompassing roar.

Noguchi buzzed the pens as low as she dared and hoped the locks had opened according to the codes she'd set.

The rhynth had been in the hot sunlight all day without food and a minimum of water. The sound of the copter must have echoed loudly in the pens. It only took one spooked animal to get it going. And as soon as one rhynth jumped forward, the rest followed.

The animals tore through the doors she had unlocked.

Within a few seconds, all of the rhynth joined the stampede, headed straight through Prosperity Wells. Anything small enough to get in their way was trampled, crushed, kicked aside.

The searchlight on the copter illuminated the scene dimly. Noguchi only glanced at the panicked herds; she had her hands full piloting. Miriam Revna cried out in delight.

"They just ran over about two dozen of the unclassifieds!" It was hard to hear over the clatter of hooves and the bellows of the frightened rhynth.

Noguchi smiled tightly and pulled up on the control

stick. She wanted to check and see if the ranchers had gotten out—

She veered east. All she needed to see were the lights of the AVs—

Noguchi allowed herself a short rush of relief. The low red and white lights were visible. The ranchers and staff were headed away from town into open desert.

It was working! Her plan was working!

She circled the copter back toward *The Lector* to make another run on the animals. The colonists were headed to relative safety, and the rhynth were stomping everything in sight. Maybe she wouldn't have to sacrifice anything else.

Of course, there were still the creatures on the ship to deal with—and it was probable that a few of the other kind had survived. But to take out the majority ...

As they neared the transmitting tower, Miriam sat up straighter and pointed. Noguchi shot a sideways glance at what the doctor motioned at—it was one of the warriors. It had climbed the ladder and was almost to the top—and there were three or four of the huge black bugs clambering up after him.

Miriam saw the broken-tusked warrior nearing the top of the transmitter and pointed. He still wore the cast she had strapped him in for his damaged ribs.

"Machiko, look!"

"*What?!*" The stampede was deafening.

Miriam shouted louder. "It's my patient! We have to save him!"

Noguchi whipped her head around. "No fucking

way! Those things are the reason we're in this mess!" She looked back at the controls.

Miriam chewed at her lip in frustration. How could she make Noguchi understand? It was important, the most important thing in the world right now. She could not have said why.

"He saved my life, Machiko!"

Noguchi opened her mouth and then closed it. "Look, I don't—"

"*Please!* Machiko, he risked his life to save mine!"

The doctor looked at her patient, getting closer to the top now. The dark, segmented creatures were also getting closer.

"*Please!*"

Noguchi didn't say anything. She veered toward the tower.

I must be out of my mind, that's it, I finally went insane—

Noguchi steered the copter toward the tower in disbelief. What the hell was she thinking? Dr. Revna was a nice lady, ordinarily she wouldn't mind doing her a favor, but this—?

She watched as Broken Tusk kicked at one of his pursuers and then stabbed the closest one; the bug screamed and fell. He refused to give up fighting, she'd credit him that much.

But she could barely fly! Even a trained pilot would have doubts about trying to hover next to a *tower*. And to save an alien that they knew almost nothing about.

Except it had saved Miriam's life.

Right.

It would break every rule in her book, to risk their lives on this. And she had about a second to decide.

Below them, the rhynth ran on.

Dachande kicked at one of the drones and then used the spear to take out the gut of another. It fell, still kicking—but there were two others.

He heard a ship over the sound of the running hosts but he ignored it. He had enough to worry about. On the ground, the bugs were no match. But fighting while hanging one-handed and almost upside down—

The metal he gripped let out a high groan; he could feel the structure shift under the combined weight of himself and the drones.

Again the weak substance creaked—and started to separate from the building.

If he didn't think of something, he would be on the ground in a few breaths.

Fighting the Hard Meat and in the path of the stampeding hosts.

The Black Warrior must wish for Dachande's immediate company.

And the Black Warrior eventually won all battles.

Noguchi lowered the copter toward the tower. Which had started to quake dangerously. It was collapsing under all the weight.

"Shit—"

Miriam fumbled around the console for a second and then hit a button. Her next words blared incredibly loud.

"Grab the strut! We'll take you to safety!"

Noguchi winced. The doctor had found the PA.

She lowered the ship a little more. It was hard, but not as hard as she had expected. On the other hand, a series of red lights had lit up on the control panel. She was too intent on the task at hand to figure out what they meant, but she also didn't want to find out the hard way.

"Grab on!"

Noguchi screamed to be heard. "I can't do this forever, Miriam! He doesn't *understand*—"

The copter dipped, and then pulled up again. He had grabbed on to the strut.

Noguchi let out a cry of disbelief. It had worked! Broken Tusk had jumped to the copter!

Now what the fuck are we going to do with him?

And then everything happened at once. A dark shape lunged at them. Noguchi just had time to register that it was one of the bugs before it landed on top of one of the compressors, on the same side as Broken Tusk. It scrabbled to hold on, screamed.

The copter tilted alarmingly and Noguchi jerked the controls instinctively upward—

—there was a rending screech of metal as the tower collapsed—

—and everything turned the wrong way as—

—the copter went down.

24

They were both sleeping when the stampede hit.

Scott hadn't thought it was possible for him to nod out, but he was exhausted, hung over, and probably coming down with whatever Tom had. There was still fighting outside, but the pen they had holed up in seemed safe. The sounds of battle had almost become a background drone, and had moved away after a while.

Scott had been dreaming that he and Tom were explaining what had happened to them to a doubtful audience of company people back on Earth. They were all sitting around a huge wooden table in a dim conference room. At first, the suits had seemed interested as Tom spoke. Except Tom kept saying all of the wrong things, and every time Scott opened his mouth, nothing would come out.

And all at once, the people started slamming their fists down on the table. One of them, a very tall man in a black shirt, kept yelling, "Liar! Liar!" And the sounds of their knuckles hitting wood get louder, more insistent, deafening.

Scott snapped awake as the table broke.

"Oh, shit—" Tom jumped up and lurched to the door. Even in the dark pen, Scott could see that Tom didn't look too good, pale and strained.

Scott pulled his aching body off the floor and joined him. By now, the noise had drowned out all else. He looked out the crack in the door and felt his mouth gape.

The rhynth weren't running past the pen, at least not the front. But they could see the dust kicked up by the animals to their right, maybe six or seven meters away. The whole building shook as the thick stream of animals tore past, headed north. Tom said something that Scott couldn't catch.

"What?!" Scott couldn't hear his own scream.

Tom shook his head and pointed.

At first, Scott wasn't sure what he was looking for. Tom was motioning at a transmitting tower, two structures away.

Tom finally pointed straight up, and then back at the tower.

Scott looked at the top and felt his heart jump. A copter hovered there shakily. It was involved in some kind of rescue mission; there was a person trapped on the tower, being pursued by—

Scott peered closer. The alien creatures from *The Lector*.

They watched as the person on the tower—who seemed to be some kind of giant—reached for the strut of the copter and made it. Scott grinned widely as the stranded person made it to the copter in a breathtaking leap and looked at Tom. Tom laughed without sound and clapped Scott on the back.

The excitement on Tom's face melted suddenly into horror.

Scott looked back at the copter just in time to see it spin down toward the ground, toward them. Something had gone very wrong; one of the creatures had jumped on the roof of the copter and the pilot had panicked. They watched as the flyer spun out of control to crash, a few dozen meters past them to the left.

The explosion was loud enough to be audible above the stampede; it was getting quieter, the majority of the animals already gone.

By silent assent, he and Tom opened the door and ran toward the crash, the stench of burning fuel and cooked dirt heavy in the air.

The hot night had just gotten hotter.

Noguchi opened her eyes as the thunder fell to the sound and heat of a bonfire. Above her, the Ryushi night sparkled with stars. She had a sunburn and there was something wrong, she couldn't move—

"Miriam?" Her voice was barely audible.

A face appeared over hers, familiar, bearded.

"Conover."

"I should've guessed it'd be you!" The pilot had to shout to be heard over the final remnants of the stampede. "You're lucky to be alive, lady!"

Noguchi remembered all of it at once as Conover unbelted her and half lifted her out of the wreckage.

Broken Tusk, the rhynth are stampeding and the people went to the desert and Miriam—

"Who the hell taught you to fly?" Behind Conover stood the other one, Strandberg. He looked sick.

"Nobody, yet," Noguchi said. She sounded weak, hated that she did. All around them were bits of burning wreckage; the main part of the copter was behind them, still on fire. The flames crackled and danced.

She leaned heavily on the pilot as they stumbled away from the smashed cockpit.

"Where's Miriam?" she said. The doctor hadn't been next to her when she had come to. It was an effort to look around; her neck didn't seem to want to hold her head up.

Strandberg stepped forward and grabbed her other arm.

"Listen, we gotta get out of here! The bugs will be back soon!"

On closer inspection, she could see that Strandberg *was* sick. He looked like she felt; shaky, pale, nauseous.

The last of the rhynth had gone. Besides a fading rumble, the only noise was the hiss of fire—and somewhere close by, the piercing trill of a nightmare creature.

"Miriam," she said again. "Broken Tusk, Miriam had to save him—"

The pilots ignored her and started pulling her toward one of the holding pens.

Noguchi pushed them away and turned back to the remains of the copter.

"Dr. Revna, the woman who was in the copter with me! I'm not leaving without her!"

Conover's voice was both apologetic and irritated at once. "I didn't see anyone else," he began. And then stopped.

"Oh, Jesus—"

Noguchi glanced at both of the pilots, who stood with looks of awe and terror on their faces.

She spun back around and felt her heart sink.

It was Broken Tusk, surrounded by flames.

He carried Miriam Revna in his arms.

Dachande hit the ground, hard, but shouldered the impact well. It helped that he had the time to jump before the ooman flyer had crashed.

He stood and winced at the tight feeling in his chest; he had probably rebroken what had started mending.

But the host stampede had passed, and the drones were nowhere around, at least for the moment.

Dachande looked around at the burning pieces of material and walked around them slowly. The oomans had been trying to save him; there was no question. And they had probably died for their efforts.

He saw a fallen form on the ground, thrown clear of the wreck. Dachande approached it carefully. It did not move.

The small figure was turned on its stomach, but he knew what it was before he turned it over. It was the ooman who had tended him, then released him. It was the ooman who had tried to save him from the drones and had lost its life trying. There was no question that it was *thei-de*; thick *thwei* dripped sluggishly from deep gashes in its face and neck, and its position suggested a snapped spine.

Dachande scooped the tiny body up and paused for a moment, uncertain of what to do with it. Now that the animals were gone, he heard sounds of ooman language from somewhere near; past the largest part of the burning flyer, just a few paces away.

The other oomans would want it. For such a brave being, they would want to properly care for it before it's *u'sl-kwe*, final rest. It was no warrior, but it had a sensitivity that Dachande had never seen before, except in the smallest of children.

He carried the ooman to the others. There were three. One he recognized as the armed ooman from before. The other two were bigger, but unarmed. They held very still as he approached.

The small warrior held no weapon against him now; it ran toward him, the hold of its body frantic.

Dachande could see that it was not an attack. The warrior reached him and then gently stroked the face of the dead one that he carried, its composure one of sorrow.

It repeated something over and over as it touched the dead face. Dachande suddenly remembered the animal loop on his forearm, and tapped it quickly.

The ooman's language babbled back at it. The warrior looked up at him and then motioned for him to set the corpse down.

Dachande did it gently; the ooman had shown him respect. He would do no less for it in its death.

Noguchi stared in shock as she heard her own voice spill out from behind the creature's mask.

"I'm sorry, Miriam."

She pointed to the ground and then back to Miriam's body. Broken Tusk carefully set the doctor's body down and then stepped back.

Noguchi knelt over Miriam, could already see that it was too late.

That's okay, Machiko. Someone else you cared

about, someone who depended on you, dead. No big deal.

Just because it's your fault.

She allowed herself one second of pure grief. Her head dropped into her hands, and she let out a soft moan of despair and sorrow. The pain was sharp and cruel, the guilt tremendous and stabbing. And she didn't have time for it.

Noguchi stood slowly and took a deep breath. The pilots kept their silence, in respect or embarrassment she didn't know. She turned to look at the warrior, who also gazed at Revna's broken body; his odd mask flickered with strange shadows.

"It's time to put an end to this," she said quietly.

Broken Tusk stepped toward her and put one clawed hand on her shoulder. Noguchi did her best to return the gesture, although she couldn't quite reach.

It looked like she had an ally, at least for a while.

25

Scott and Tom followed the Noguchi woman through a deserted alley in the dark town. Scott wasn't sure where they were headed, but Noguchi moved with certainty.

He glanced over his shoulder from time to time, wary of the huge alien that brought up the rear. They had left the dead woman behind, soaked her corpse with fuel, and set it ablaze.

After listening to Noguchi's summary of what had happened in the last twenty-eight hours, Scott hurried to talk to her.

"Are you saying that *they*"—he tilted his head back at the giant—"let those bugs loose on a populated planet so they could *hunt* them?" He kept his voice low.

Noguchi nodded. "Just a theory, but it fits. Except

I don't think his kind knew there were humans on Ryushi. And from his actions, they weren't supposed to be shooting at us. We haven't been here that long, and it looks pretty certain that they were here before."

Her voice was edged with dry sarcasm when next she spoke: "I imagine we would have remembered if they'd visited recently."

Tom stumbled behind them. Scott stopped and started to turn back, but the giant stepped forward and set the pilot back on his feet as if he weighed nothing.

Tom nodded at the creature, waved a hand, and moved to join Scott and Nogushi.

She continued talking. ". . . and I imagine our presence probably screwed up their plans."

Scott raised his eyebrows. "Screwed up their plans. Oh, that's great. I feel so much better knowing that this whole fucking mess was an accident."

Noguchi shrugged. "Hey, at least he's on our side."

"Until he gets hungry," Scott mumbled under his breath.

Noguchi stopped at the end of the alley and waited for the giant to catch up to them. She kept her revolver barrel pointed up.

"Okay. The stampede started just around the corner here; we're going to walk through its path and see if there's anything left alive that shouldn't be."

Swell.

Scott looked around for some kind of weapon. Besides a few small rocks, they were out of luck. They'd have to stick close to the woman.

The giant hefted a large spear and seemed to wait for Noguchi's signal.

"Go."

The alien and Noguchi crouched out into the open compound, weapons ready.

Scott's heart raced; he looked over at Tom, who shrugged. They stepped out together to join the other two. It wasn't as if they had a whole lot of choice here, now was it?

"Holy *shit*," Tom said.

Scott forgot his fear for a second or two.

The stretch of open ground was littered with dozens of bodies, rhynth, bug, and giant alien. Large patches of soil were eaten away to reveal charred black splatterlike stains, as if the blood from the corpses was toxic. The rhynth were cut or blown open, chests shattered, throats slit. The black bugs were mostly crushed, so also the giants.

The only light was from a sole street lamp that hadn't been broken or shot out. The resulting mix of dark and death and shadows was forbidding, ominous. Ugly.

"When you kill something, you don't fool around," said Scott.

Noguchi wasn't listening. Her gaze darted from side to side, her revolver still up.

The giant's head was cocked to one side, his stance ready. The two of them moved forward slowly.

The pilots stayed close.

The four of them made their way cautiously down the ravaged street, stepped over torn bodies and corpses smashed down deep into the cracked earth. Apparently this was where the fight had ended.

After a moment of tense silence, Tom whispered loudly to Scott as they followed their armed escorts.

"Do you think the stampede got them all?"

Scott started to reply, but stopped short. He had

heard something behind them—the cry of a bird, perhaps, a chittering sound—

Behind one of the storage buildings, sudden movement. Scott felt his mouth go dry. He had heard it before—

"Run," he said, hardly able to get the word out. *"Run."*

Dachande heard the Hard Meat and spun around. He sprinted past the two ooman strangers toward the threat, staff forward. He was dimly aware that the small warrior was right behind. It shouted something at the other two.

They came in a single-file stream, flowed from around a structure, ten, maybe twelve. Dachande leapt to greet them.

Two arrived first, angled in from the sides. Dachande spun, swung completely around, cut them both through their midsections in one strike. He didn't watch them hit the ground; there was no need—they were dead and all he need do was avoid the throes.

He extended his *ki'cti-pa* and slashed through the throat of the next drone nearest, to his right.

The drone's death cry was garbled through its own *thwei*.

A split second later, he jabbed the staff point through the jaws of another, twisted the sharp blade and dug a hole through the top of the skull. The weapon's metal was proof against the Hard Meat's *thwei*, but there was no time to hesitate and enjoy the kill—when you fought the ten thousand, you did so one at a time, but you also had to do so *quickly*—

He thrust the spear's butt back, hard, and knocked

one behind him down, then turned and slashed its gut. Digest *this*, foolish creature!

The *ki'cti-pa* blurred again, jammed backhand into yet another Hard Meat chest. The drone howled, fell, did not die but did not rise again. Acid pumped into the dark air, pooled, smoking.

Dachande jumped forward, stabbed the throat of yet another, and then spun to meet the next. Death fell all around his feet as he and the Hard Meat danced.

Noguchi heard what sounded like a bird and turned; Broken Tusk was faster—he ran past the two pilots toward the main storage shed. He was eager and if he had any fear of the dark monsters, it was not apparent.

"Follow the tower around to the east lock!"

She would just have to hope that the pilots listened. She hurled herself after the warrior.

Several of the bugs streamed from behind the shed and toward Broken Tusk. He stepped in to battle without hesitation. Too many of them, ten, twelve. She aimed at one of the bugs—

—and it was dead before she fired. She took aim again—and again, her target had fallen already.

She took a step back, transfixed by the swift movements of the giant warrior.

Here was no inexperienced novice; every step was measured, every strike timed and sure. Within the space of a few seconds, most of the bugs were down, dead or dying. She had enough training to recognize a Master when she saw one. This one's skill had been gained in battle, against deadly enemies.

Broken Tusk whirled and jabbed, crouched and

slashed with precision and confidence. Never a misstep, never a hesitation. He was no dojo tiger, covered in padding and fighting for points.

Wherever he had come from, they had a martial arts more complex and dangerous than any she'd ever seen. It was like a choreographed dance—

Except we don't have all day.

She aimed and fired several shots, then aimed and fired again. The last two shrieked and stumbled. Broken Tusk hesitated, confused perhaps, then finished them both with slashes to the gut.

"Sorry." Noguchi ejected the spent rounds and slapped in a loader. "But we've got to go."

Broken Tusk stared at her for a second, then raised one claw—in understanding or camaraderie, she couldn't know. She returned the move, then started toward the east lock.

The warrior caught up to her easily, then slowed and strode at her side as they rounded the front of the ops building toward the lock. He made thick growling noises, strange, but somehow not threatening.

Ahead, the lock was open. Conover stood by the control panel inside, face pale.

Noguchi heard now familiar chirping noises behind them, not far.

"Hurry!" Conover shouted.

Noguchi and Broken Tusk ran through the entry together. The door slammed down.

A second later there were several thundering crashes. The metal door shook as the nightmare creatures threw themselves at it, but it wouldn't give.

Noguchi collapsed against the frame and closed her eyes. They were safe, at least for the moment.

Safe—and fucked. They hadn't gotten them all.

The plan hadn't worked.

26

o what's the plan?"

Noguchi didn't answer. She continued to take deep breaths, her eyes closed. The giant alien stood at her side, still enough to be a statue. Its face was turned to watch the woman, but the odd mask it wore covered most of any expression it may have had. Given the faces of some of the dead ones who'd lost their masks in the stampede, Scott was just as happy about that. Ugly bastards.

He stepped away from the door and started to pace. He was feeling pretty goddamn tired of not knowing what was going on.

"Look, lady, I realize that you're under a lot of stress, but you do *have* some idea of what we're going to do, don't you? The stampede didn't work out quite the way it was supposed to, obviously. Now if I were you, I'd start worrying about what—"

"What?" Noguchi had opened her eyes to reveal an icy anger. "If you were me, you'd worry about what?"

He shut up. Then, "Well, shit. What next?"

"Lay off, Scott." Tom sounded bone-tired.

Scott looked at his friend and felt his anger spark higher. Tom looked worse than he had before. Whatever he'd picked up was making him really sick. The younger pilot had fallen into a chair and rested his head on a console; his body shook.

Scott stopped in front of Noguchi and lowered his voice. "My friend is sick, okay? We have to do *something*."

Noguchi smiled softly, humorlessly. "No shit. But unless you or your friend come up with some brilliant revelation, I suggest you *shut up*; I'll listen to you when you've got something to say."

She closed her eyes again.

The spark fizzled. She was a cold bitch, but he didn't have any ideas to contribute. And he sure as fuck didn't want to lead this little party.

"Right. Sorry, okay? I don't feel so good. It's been a bad day."

Noguchi nodded, then walked toward an ops panel. "The colonists made it out safely, that's something. We've got power here, and supplies; we can hold out for a while here and come up with something."

"There's a screen still on over here," Tom said.

Scott and Noguchi both walked over to where the ailing pilot sat. The giant remained at the door, motionless.

Across the top of the small console was a series of numbers.

"That's my code," said Noguchi. "It's a hyperstat

from the corporation substation! The æther driver got through."

She leaned in front of Tom and punched a few keys excitedly.

Scott blinked. Æther driver? What the hell was that? Some new equipment the company was too cheap to put on their ship? Shit.

He read over her shoulder.

Attn: Machiko Noguchi, Prosperity Wells/from BAE:683 Takashi Chigusa, New Osaka. re: possible XT specimens. Take steps to preserve all specimens of species described in Revna's report; nearest Marine ship will enter area at approx. 5/14. Keep BAE:683 apprised. Await further instructions.

YFNT677074/TC.

Noguchi slammed her fist against the screen and stalked over to a chair. She plopped down and put one hand to her forehead.

"Five weeks," she said softly. "All we have to do is survive for five weeks."

As if on cue, there was another slam to the lock. A creature screamed, the sound muffled through the thick metal.

"And preserve for them 'all specimens,'" she said. She laughed. It wasn't a funny noise.

Christ. Don't lose it, lady. We need you.

It was looking hopeless. Noguchi had never felt so frustrated in her life, or so angry. There was nothing she could do—

"Well, fuck this!" Conover had started pacing again. "I say we scram out of here and join the colonists!"

She looked up at the red-faced pilot and shook her

head. "Yeah? And how long before the bugs run out of food and head into the desert looking for more?"

Conover dropped his gaze and said nothing.

"I don't know about you two, but I'm tired of fucking with all of this. I want to finish this, and I want to finish it *now*." She wasn't sure how, but there had to be a way—

Conover snorted. "Sure, great. You gonna burn down the whole complex?"

Strandberg coughed loudly. "That wouldn't work, too many of them would"—he coughed again—"would get away. It'd have to be something fast."

Noguchi started running off possibilities in her head. Maybe they could formulate some kind of bomb, or gas—

Conover jerked his gaze at Broken Tusk. "Why don't we ask the hulk over there? Maybe he's got a death ray or something."

Strandberg shook his head. "I'm serious. I think Ms. Noguchi had the right idea with the stampede, crush them like bugs—" He broke into a fit of coughing.

Noguchi looked at Strandberg with sympathy; he really didn't look well, and he had at least tried to be helpful—

The pilot had regained his wind and raised one hand weakly. "Something big enough to take out the complex and the ship at once—"

Conover interrupted angrily, "Forget it! I can't even believe you'd bring it up!"

Noguchi stood and faced the asshole pilot. "Don't hold out on me, Conover! If you know something that might stop those things—"

Strandberg started coughing again.

Conover glared at her and jabbed a finger in her

general direction. "Look, I have some shares in this little investment along with everyone else! There is nothing we can do, okay?"

Strandberg tried to stand up, and fell to the floor. His coughing suddenly turned to hoarse choking sounds, and he spasmed and convulsed, clutched at his chest.

Heart attack or epileptic seizure—

Noguchi took one step toward him and felt a hand on her shoulder. Broken Tusk. He hissed and hefted his spear.

Conover rushed to his friend's side and then stepped back at the sight of blood on Strandberg's abdomen.

"Tommy—?!"

Noguchi gasped. The convulsing pilot screamed again and again. And at the same time, there was the sound of ripping, shredding, the sound of flesh parting—

A creature the size of Noguchi's forearm burst through Strandberg's chest in a spray of red. Dripping with blood and slime, the animal looked surreal, its head dominated by rows of teeth. It coiled its long, flesh-colored body in the frame of Strandberg's bloody rib cage and screeched at them.

And jumped—

27

Dachande watched from the door as the oomans battled verbally. Although they did not give off a musk, the anger was clear. He imagined they were worried about their deaths and the proper manner of them, not an unreasonable concern in the situation. There might not be any witnesses to carry the tale to their friends and relatives, no one would know if they had died bravely or not, a concern to any warrior, of course. But in the end, *they* would know, just as he would know. All beings died, later, sooner, no one escaped the Black Warrior. But—if it happened in battle, did you meet the gods with blood on your blade, your laughter at Death still echoing around you? That was the thing; that way lay honor.

He had counted five of his students crushed into

the soil on their way here, their weapons destroyed or missing. There was no way to know if there were more still alive, but he guessed not. He was vaguely disappointed in their performance, but they had been served with what they earned. Especially if they had followed Tichinde. The nature of would-be warriors was to obey the strongest among them and Tichinde had been that. Unfortunately, when a Hunt needed strategy and tactics, strength did not make up for stupidity. Even a good teacher could fail and that rankled, but one worked with what one was given.

Dachande watched the ooman debate with interest; the small warrior was in charge, and the other disagreed with whatever the small one wanted. He waited to see if there would be physical combat, but for some reason, the larger ooman did not strike. Dachande guessed the small one must be a Leader to merit such respect. He decided to support the warrior; from its actions so far, it was surely braver than the others. Certainly it stood in better balance, it flowed better.

When the third ooman fell and went into *z'skvy-de*, Dachande moved. The oomans had no experience with such things and did not recognize the eruptive phase. The small warrior stepped forward, but he stopped it, quickly explained the situation, and stepped past.

The larger ooman stood in his way. He pushed it aside and reached the ooman host just as the *kainde amedha* lunged forth.

The newborn creature snaked across the floor and almost made it under a table before Dachande lifted his spear and brought it down, hard.

He could feel the young drone's back snap beneath the weapon. Hot intestine squirted, blood hissed.

Dachande stepped away and looked at the oomans. He waited.

Scott couldn't seem to catch his breath. He was sprawled on the floor next to Tommy, where the giant had shoved him and Tommy was—

"Oh, Jesus, no," he whispered. His voice sounded faint, far away.

Tommy still quivered all over. His fingers clenched and unclenched, and then nothing.

The giant had squashed the alien parasite quickly and neatly. It was over, that fast. And Tommy lay next to him, the slick innards of his body exposed, his eyes open.

Scott turned away and dry-heaved a few times, the retching bringing only sour spit. And then he understood.

He sat up stiffly and put a hand on his stomach. And coughed. And started to cry.

Noguchi grabbed someone's coat off the back of one of the chairs and draped it over the dead pilot. She shuddered and stepped back.

Conover's shoulders shook with grief.

Noguchi looked up at Broken Tusk, who watched mutely, and then back at Conover.

Broken Tusk had known. Her theory had panned out. For what that was worth at this point.

She crouched down next to the crying pilot and put a hand across his back. She kept her voice low, but didn't hesitate.

"I'm sorry about your friend, Conover. But I need your help right now, okay? Before Strandberg—"

She cleared her throat and started again. "He was about to tell me something—something that could wipe out the bugs; I need—"

Conover turned his tear-streaked face up to look at her. "You don't get it, do you? What happened to Tommy—that thing that was inside of him. We were together on *The Lector*. That means I've got one of those things inside of—"

The pilot's face crumpled in despair. He buried his face in his hands and started to sob loudly.

Noguchi let him cry for a moment, then patted him gently on the back. She felt like a real bitch for what she was about to say, but there was no way around it.

"You're not dead yet, Conover. We still need your help."

He continued to rock back and forth. "Leave me alone. I'm doomed, I'm a dead man."

Noguchi stood up. "Maybe if you help us, I can help you."

Conover looked up at her and wiped his eyes with the back of one hand. "Are you a doctor? You gonna perform surgery and make me all better?"

Noguchi shook her head. "No, I can't do that. But you can have a shot at revenge—" She took a deep breath. "And I can make it quicker, easier for you."

The mixed look of pain and self-pity and gratitude on the pilot's face made her stomach clench. Conover was an asshole, but he didn't deserve to die for it. If she had one of those things inside of her . . .

"Okay," he said quietly. "Fuck it. Yeah, okay."

Scott sat at the terminal, his eyes gritty and his hands trembling. He was going to die. He was going to die. The thought was a repeating loop in his mind, a horrible and constant statement of looming black truth. He was pregnant with a monster, he was going to die—

Scott shook his head and finished the sentence he had typed onto the screen; almost done. His stomach hurt, and with each second, it got worse. He coughed into his hand and tapped a few more keys. Real, or in his mind?

"Everything you need is on the disk," he said. His voice sounded dead, too.

Noguchi nodded. She sat next to him and watched carefully as he worked.

"Thanks, Conover."

"Scott," he said softly. It suddenly seemed very important that she knew his name. Because he was going to die.

"Thanks, Scott."

He felt a few more tears trickle down his face and into his beard. It had been like that for the last twenty minutes. Knowing you were about to die was bad, very bad.

"It's going to be tough getting in," he said.

"We'll find a way."

Scott nodded and glanced at the giant. It was back by the door, spear at its side.

"I don't doubt it," he said. He coughed, the painful spasm filling him with dread. He took a deep breath and coughed again. It was getting worse.

He smiled weakly at Noguchi. "You know, if this works, the company's gonna be really pissed."

She straightened slightly and then laughed. She seemed surprised by the sound. So was Scott.

You can still make a pretty woman laugh, Scott.

"Fuck the company," she said.

"Yeah."

On a sudden impulse, Scott grabbed at a piece of paper on the console and a pen. He made a quick sketch, studied the drawing for a moment, and then added a few more details.

He folded the paper in half and handed it to Noguchi.

"It's a going away present," he said. He coughed and pressed one hand to his stomach. He tried not to think about it—

You're going to die—

"It's a map of the ship," he continued. "I should have thought of it before."

She slipped the paper into a chest pocket and nodded. Behind them, at the door, the shrieks of the alien bugs had gotten louder.

"Sounds like every bug in the place is trying to get in," he said. "Well. All but one of them. It's already in."

"We're ready to go." She stood.

Scott nodded and coughed again. He was going to die.

A kind of calm slipped over him, a sense of unreality that made him feel far away from all this. It didn't matter, not really. He should be scared, had been scared, but now, in this moment, he was somehow floating above it, watching himself as if he were someone else. It was a done deal, end of the line, and while he had never dreamed it would happen this way, here it was and what choice did he have?

At least he had helped. Maybe it would even make some kind of difference—he wouldn't be around to see, but at least he wouldn't be in pain, and the damn repeating line would end.

The giant alien walked over to meet them when Noguchi stood. It gestured with its spear at Scott.

Noguchi's voice came from the creature: "I can make it quicker, easier for you."

Noguchi held up one hand. "No. I made the promise, I'll do it."

The giant seemed to understand. It stepped back.

"Weird," said Scott. He coughed—and with it came an odd nauseous feeling. Like he had swallowed something alive.

"Just do it, okay?"

Noguchi held her pistol up. "Close your eyes, Scott. Count to three."

Scott closed his eyes. He sensed the barrel of the weapon behind his skull and he clenched his eyes tighter. He was afraid. But he was ready.

"I'll remember you," said Noguchi gently.

"One. Two—"

The warrior looked away from the fallen ooman and stood still for a moment. Dachande said nothing, but after a short span, he growled a time reminder at the standing ooman and motioned at the door. The Leader had done what a Leader had to do; there was no cure for an infected host and the larger ooman's death was quick and honorable. It had not fought or tried to run.

He moved to the dead ooman, judged where the unborn Hard Meat embryo was, and raised his spear. Looked at the remaining ooman.

The ooman nodded and turned away as Dachande drove the spear downward. Felt the blade hit the harder substance of the embryo. Felt it struggle to escape the point, then give up.

He pulled the blade free, hammered the shaft of the weapon with his free fist to shake the blood from it. Done.

The other ooman walked to join him. Glanced down at its dead comrade, then away. It looked tired. It motioned at a side entrance with its weapon and nodded at Dachande.

He nodded back and followed the small warrior to crouch by the entry. The drones still scrabbled madly outside the main door, but there were no sounds outside this one.

The warrior raised its burner. Dachande readied his staff.

The door opened.

28

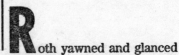oth yawned and glanced at her chrono for the third time in fifteen minutes. They were out in the middle of nowhere in a quick and dirty makeshift camp and she was watching the darkness for monsters. Monsters.

Life sure wasn't what you expected, at least never for more than a few minutes at a time.

The suns would be coming up soon, which meant her shift was about done. In the dim predawn light, she leaned against Ackland's AV and whistled softly for Creep. The mutt had wandered over to stand watch with Leo, an older Chinese man who always seemed to have candy in his pocket.

After a few seconds, Creep padded quietly through the maze of vehicles to join her. She scratched his head.

"How's Leo, dog? Still awake?"

Creep whuffled softly and sat down, tongue hanging out.

"I heard that, Roth," a voice crackled in her ear.

"You been feeding my dog crap again, Leo?" Roth spoke quietly. Most of the camp was still asleep, except for her and five others. On any normal night, they would've swapped jokes and insults, maybe taken turns napping. But the day before had been too long and too frightening. The shift had been tense and silent, and except for one false alarm when a few stray rhynth had wandered into camp, uneventful.

Leo chuckled. "Yep. You don't give him anything good; if I were him, I'd be hungry for something besides soypro in a can, too."

"You'd make a good dog, Leo."

There was a short pause and then Kaylor came online. "Sorry to interrupt, folks, but shouldn't Noguchi be here by now?"

Roth sighed. "Yeah, we know." Kaylor had a bad habit of stating the obvious.

Leo cut in. "Maybe someone should go back ..."

He trailed off. No one replied. Roth concentrated on the twins suns as they sneaked up on the far edge of the desert and began to lighten the clear sky.

Twenty minutes later, the door to Ackland's AV banged open.

Roth jumped. She had been lulled into a trance by the silence and purity of the early morning. Asshole.

Within a few minutes, the camp was up. Bleary-eyed ranchers and their children stumbled out into the almost-cool air and trotted off to relieve themselves behind various rocks and low shrub.

Roth shouldered her rifle and rubbed at her eyes.

Sleep would be bliss, but she wanted to stay awake for a while and watch for Noguchi.

"Jame?" Cathie walked over with two cups of coffee.

"Thanks, hon. Get any sleep?"

Cathie smiled. "An hour or two, at least."

She handed Roth a mug and kissed her lightly. "I figured you wouldn't be ready for bed quite yet."

Roth motioned with her head at a small group of people who had gathered by Luccini's AV, Ackland and Weaver among them.

"What's the deal?"

Cathie shrugged. "Ackland's being a dickhead, what else?"

Jenkins arrived and took over from Roth. They nodded at each other.

As soon as the shift was covered, Roth and Cathie walked over to join the circle; several other ranchers had also stopped.

". . . and I think it's suicide!" Ackland looked blustery and irritated, as usual; Cathie was right, he was a dickhead.

"What's suicide?" Roth asked.

Weaver's cheeks were flushed. "Oh, nothing. Ackland is being a coward, that's all."

"Bullshit," said Ackland. "There's nothing we can do until the Marines show up, that's all! If one of you wants to go back and get killed, that's fine by me!"

Paul Luccini spoke up. He didn't talk much, but people tended to listen when he did. "The Marines might take a while, Ackland."

Cathie stepped in. "In the meantime, she could be hurt, or in need of help."

"Those are the chances she took when she accepted the job," said Ackland. His voice was now patronizing and slow, as if he were addressing children. "The Chigusa Corporation is responsible for the safety of the colonists, not the other way around."

A red haze seemed to settle over everything for Roth. She took a deep breath, tried to control it, but something snapped while Ackland spoke.

"You *bastard!*" She stepped forward and poked him in the chest with one trembling finger. "You can't shove this off on the company! *You* had me lie to Doc Revna about where we found those creatures! And it was your idea to sneak those rhynth past quarantine!" She took another step toward him. "I'm ashamed to admit to my part in it, but I take responsibility for *my* stupidity! What's *your* excuse?"

Ackland held up his hands, as if to defend himself. "Hey, look—you know what a hardass Noguchi is, right?" He searched the assembled ranchers for support. "I was just trying to protect my investments. *Our* investments."

Luccini spoke again. "Fuck the investments. I've got a family."

Several others chorused agreement.

Weaver glared at Ackland. "You can say what you want about Noguchi, but when it came down to it, she risked her life to save all of us—including your ass!"

Ackland opened his mouth, his fat face angry—and then closed it again. He turned and walked away.

"He'd better pray she's still alive when this is all over," Cathie whispered to Roth.

Roth nodded. The rush of adrenaline was gone, had left her exhausted. She caught Weaver's gaze. "Are you looking for volunteers?"

Weaver considered it for a moment and then shook her head. "No. Not yet, anyway. Machiko told us to wait, so we'll wait. If she'd not here by late afternoon, though ..."

"Right. Let me know, okay?"

Roth and Cathie walked over to a makeshift table that had been assembled and stacked with trays of rolls and a couple of pots of coffee.

"Do you think she's still alive?" said Cathie.

Roth started to say no, but then thought better of it.

"If anyone could survive that place right now," she said carefully, "it'd be her."

Dawn had come.

Broken Tusk stepped past her, out into the open compound, and then motioned for her to follow.

Noguchi crouched outside of the door and pointed left, then right with her handgun. It was clear.

She could still hear the screaming bugs around the corner to her right; they continued to slam into the main door, apparently unaware their prey had escaped.

Noguchi and Broken Tusk circled to the back. From behind them, Noguchi heard several loud cracks as the door finally gave up the fight.

Looks like they got tired of waiting for us to let them in—

Broken Tusk glanced back at her.

She pointed forward and he moved on.

Noguchi covered the rear as they headed to the other side of the ops building. They hurried, but didn't run. She took her cues from the warrior; he had dealt with these things before, and he stepped cautiously.

In spite of the situation, part of Noguchi could appreciate the dawn. The compound was illuminated softly by the early light, so unlike the Prosperity Wells she had known, harsh and glaring. It seemed tranquil and cool, like a dream—

—or a memory—

Pay attention here, Noguchi. Daydream when you don't have to worry about being eaten.

Good thought, but a little late.

She didn't see the thing until it was almost on top of her.

Dachande heard the splintering of the weak door behind them as they circled. He wasn't sure of what the ooman warrior had planned, but he knew what he needed to know and it was simple: kill everything that got in their way.

The ooman pointed past him and then turned its back again; it watched for threats from the rear.

Dachande glanced upward and then went on. They should step a little faster. The drones would run through the ooman structure quickly, and then come back out. They were stupid, but good at finding live meat.

Dachande heard a cry from above and looked up again, too late.

A single drone howled and jumped, its long body twisted in the air. It landed behind him. In front of the ooman.

Noguchi spun. The hellish creature reached for her—

She whipped her arm around, tried to aim, no time, fired—

Missed.

The nightmare bug towered over her, shrieking.

Slime dripped from its metallic jaws. Its huge mouth opened, exposed a set of inner teeth, razor sharp.

Noguchi stumbled backward as the inner jaws snapped forward and smacked into her chest.

Something ripped. Hot pain seared her skin, blood flowed—

—she shoved the gun like a punch as the creature prepared to leap—

Before she could pull the trigger, the bug convulsed and shuddered wildly. A thick silver blade had suddenly appeared in the middle of its segmented torso. The thing's acid blood sprayed across the dusty floor, flowing toward her.

Noguchi passed out.

Dachande speared the drone in the back and then tossed the body across the ground. It wasn't dead yet, but it would be.

He spun, searched for others. He could hear the attacker's cry answered from structures all around. They would be here in seconds.

He scooped up the ooman and ran.

He had not had time to study the ooman dwellings properly, save the tower he had fallen from the night before—but the two larger oomans had been in one of the buildings nearby, he was sure of it. With luck, it was still safe. And the warrior had seemed to want them to head in that direction.

The warrior weighed almost nothing, hardly more than his staff. It made a low sound of pain as he pounded the dust. Speed was of the essence; he could not fight with it in his arms. The drone had clawed open the ooman's soft armor, armor now soaked in *thwei.* Red blood unlike his own. How different they were.

He heard screams from where he'd left the dying bug; it had been found.

Dachande ran faster.

She was flying.

Noguchi opened her eyes and blinked hard. Her abdomen felt shredded and her head ached.

Broken Tusk carried her. They ran through the compound, incredibly fast. Something had happened, she had been attacked—

She lifted her head slightly and panicked for a split second before she realized that the gun was still clenched in her fist. She winced at the pain in her chest and belly and closed her eyes again. Broken Tusk had saved her, but there was nothing she could do until he put her down.

From somewhere not so far away, the nightmare creatures howled.

Dachande saw the open entry to some long, low structure directly ahead.

The drones hadn't spotted him yet. He ran to the building, scanned the interior quickly, and ducked through the ooman-sized door.

It was empty. He set the warrior down carefully and then closed the door. He fumbled for a minute with the latch mechanism, and finally smashed the door hard enough to drive it into the frame. It was a flimsy barrier, the drones would get through it in seconds—but they didn't know where he was, not yet.

He turned to look at the ooman, and was surprised

to see it sitting up. It still held its small burner—not aimed at him, but not down, either.

He approached it carefully and crouched down next to it to study the wound. The ooman seemed to protest at first, but relented quickly; it lay down.

He pulled the soaked padding away from the warrior's body and touched it gently. The ooman moaned.

"It's not going to kill you," he said. The ooman didn't reply.

He tried again. "No *thei-de*, understand?"

It didn't understand. It babbled for a minute and then fell quiet again. Frustrating.

Dachande lifted the rest of the weak armor away from the warrior's chest and then hissed, surprised. If ooman anatomy was anywhere similar to yautja, this warrior was a female; he hadn't thought of it before. It had a pair of what were obviously milk glands.

Stupid! Of course it's female!

Yautja females were bigger than males; it was apparently the reverse for oomans. It had never occurred to him. That was stupid; simple mistakes like that could lead to bigger ones, fatal ones.

It also explained why this warrior was smarter than most of the yautja he taught. Females of any species were usually smarter than the males.

Dachande assessed the wounds; minor. There was a fair amount of blood, but it had already stopped flowing, and most of the acid burns had been slowed by the armor.

He used some of the torn armor to stanch the wound and then sat back on his heels and studied the ooman. It watched him, curious perhaps.

They didn't have much time, but Dachande thought they could spare a few seconds.

He pointed at his chest and gave her his honorary name. "Dachande."

The ooman shook her head.

"Dah-shann-day." He stretched it out.

The ooman tried, but couldn't make the right sounds. Dachande shook his head.

She reached out hesitantly and touched his shortened mandible. The new style masks covered only the nostrils, leaving the fighting tusks bare. She said something in her own language, then repeated it.

Dachande tilted his head. It wasn't his name, but she seemed to understand the meaning. "Brr-k'in dusg?"

The ooman exposed her teeth and then pointed at herself and spoke.

Dachande tried. "Nihkuo'te?"

The ooman shook its—no, *her* head.

He looked at the creature for a moment and then named her.

"Da'dtou-di." It was the feminine of "small knife." A brave name, and it suited her.

Da'dtou-di pointed at herself and did her best. "Dahdtoou-dee?"

Dachande hissed with pleasure. It was a start, and it was enough; it was all the time they could waste on pleasantries. Should they survive, they would talk later.

He stood. "Da'dtou-di," he said, "we must go."

The ooman got up, staggered slightly, and then nodded. She was all right.

Dachande turned and walked to the door. He listened.

The drones had run past their structure and were assembling elsewhere. Which likely meant their nest was close by.

The Leader waited for Da'dtou-di to join him, feeling older than he'd ever felt before. His bones ached. He had been on many Hunts, dangerous Hunts, but for the first time, the outcome was not obvious. There were more drones here than he'd ever fought, and where there was a nest, there would be a queen—the drones could do that, change to female when no others were around. And a queen was not an easy kill.

He sighed deeply. If his Final Hunt were not today, it would be soon.

Noguchi got to her feet carefully and fought off dizziness. Broken Tusk started to reach toward her, but she nodded and held up a hand. The wounds weren't as bad as she'd feared; the light-headedness was more exhaustion than anything else.

She joined Broken Tusk at the door and held her handgun ready. Her new name rang through her thoughts, Dahdtoudi. If someone had told her a year ago that she'd be fighting XTs with an alien warrior, the fate of a hundred people on their shoulders, she would have laughed for a week.

As it stood, she allowed herself a tight grin. It was actually pretty funny; she'd laugh later, if there was time. If she woke up.

Noguchi motioned at the door, then pointed toward the south, where *The Lector* sat. Broken Tusk tilted his head to one side in agreement.

Next thing you know, we'll be talking philosophy.

Broken Tusk growled something at her and then pushed her back from the door slightly. He had jammed it.

Noguchi stepped back and watched as the warrior took a deep breath—

—and the door flew open to expose one of the warriors, a twin to Broken Tusk, holding a spear, its arms raised to strike.

oguchi reacted without thinking.

She dropped her weapon to chest level and fired into the warrior's belly until her gun ran dry.

The warrior fell backward. Its strange gun discharged harmlessly into the air with a hollow thump and an eye-smiting flare. The spear it held in the other hand fell and clattered on the door stoop.

He had not had time to scream.

Broken Tusk jumped in a split second later, but it was done.

A low, guttural gurgle came from the dying warrior's throat, punctuated with a spew of thick, greenish, milky, almost glowing fluid.

Blood.

Broken Tusk hefted his staff and brought the

weighted end down on the warrior's skull. The head split with a dull, wet crack.

Broken Tusk's posture indicated anger and sorrow, his huge shoulders tensed, head bowed. She had killed one of his people. Would he be angry with her?

Noguchi scanned the immediate area for other dangers and then looked at Broken Tusk again.

He was much more adept than the one she'd shot had been.

It dawned on her.

It would explain the difference in prowess, the difference in behavior—

Broken Tusk must be the commander.

Dachande was disgusted with himself. He had been so intrigued with the ooman female, so intent on opening the door, he had not scented the yautja.

It was Oc'djy, one of his less adept students. The dead yautja's attack had been, as it seemed with all of their moves since they arrived, stupid. "Look before you shoot" was one of the cardinal rules. If you aren't *sure* of your target, the burner stays cold, the spear does not fly. Shooting a brother warrior accidentally was the height of bad manners.

And quarter-wit Oc'djy breathing his last on the ground would surely have killed them both if Da'dtou-di hadn't fired first. No doubt of it. He was embarrassed that his students were so inept.

Dachande clattered a respectful appreciation to Da'dtou-di and then cracked Oc'djy's head open. That his thick skull could no longer be any Hunter's trophy was a disgrace, and one he had earned. Too bad he had not broken Tichinde's. Ah, well. It was not likely anybody on this world would ever find the dead student, save for scavengers.

Dachande took a deep breath and frowned slightly. The yautja's musk, the *h'dui'se*, was weak, covered with the stench of dried feces and blood. At least that explained his inability to detect the student before . . .

He snatched the burner from the ground in irritation. A Leader should not make excuses; in Hunting, they did not matter—you died or you did not.

At least he had a decent weapon. Dachande checked it over and growled. Four more fires; not much, but better than his spear alone. Tichinde's burner had been empty.

He glanced at Da'dtou-di, who studied him carefully. He did not know contempt on an ooman face, but she probably felt it.

Da'dtou-di motioned again toward the nest as she finished reloading her weapon. Dachande tilted his head and stepped forward, slinging the burner over one shoulder. She was right; now was not the time for recriminations. He could dwell on his incompetencies later.

Maybe.

Noguchi pointed at the ship, only a few structures away, fifty or sixty meters.

Broken Tusk moved again to the fore position.

They edged forward, Noguchi careful to check the roof.

They made it past the south end of the pen they'd been in before the first attack.

Broken Tusk walked into the open space between two of the pens.

Noguchi backed toward him cautiously.

He hissed a warning.

Noguchi spun, handgun extended.

Broken Tusk crouched, hissed again, his arms spread wide, spear pointed at the sky.

Two of the bugs sprinted toward them from the shadows of the alley, joined by a third. Then a fourth. And a fifth.

Dachande counted them quickly, then stood. Only five.

As the first two rushed to attack him, he sidestepped and thrust the bladed staff out.

The closest one caught it in the throat; it screamed, collapsed, hit the ground.

The second rammed its head directly into the durable blade; the top of its head sliced neatly from its body. Acidic blood fountained.

Da'dtou-di fired her burner from behind him, the sounds loud and sharp.

Two of the running drones fell. Four of five.

Dachande stepped in again to take out the last.

It seemed not to see its fallen siblings. The creature ran straight at him, shrieking.

Dachande hopped to one side as the creature neared, spear held to the other side—

—except the drone hopped and matched his move.

And hit him, running full speed.

Noguchi aimed past Broken Tusk and fired. The first two shots missed, but the third took out one of the black bugs, still a dozen meters away.

She trained and fired again, this time right on the

target. A second fell, its corrosive blood sprayed and began to sizzle and eat into the nearest wall.

She tried for the last, but Broken Tusk was in the line of fire. Noguchi turned quickly, alert to other threats.

From *The Lector* or close to it, she heard what sounded like a hundred of the nightmares. They shrieked and howled and pounded the earth, but none came into view.

Noguchi spun, just in time to see the fifth bug barrel into Broken Tusk and knock him down.

Dachande felt ribs snap as the drone tackled him. He'd lost his spear—

The snarling bug drove its head downward, opened its mouth, exposed its inner jaws—

—he plunged his fist into its mouth.

The alien gagged and bit down. Dachande felt the dagger teeth pierce his arm but he drove his claws in deeper, dug deep into softer flesh—

The drone jerked its talons away from Dachande's throat and clutched at its own. The Leader brought up his other fist and slammed the bug's neck, hard.

The drone spilled to the side.

Dachande let the weight of the creature pull him over to land on top of it. He grabbed for the burner—that sent a shooting pain through his side—and brought the blunt end down on the bug's slender throat.

The drone let go of his arm and died.

Broken Tusk staggered to his feet and retrieved his spear. He turned and jogged toward her. His arm was dotted with green spots where the thing had bitten him.

If he felt any pain, Noguchi couldn't see it. She covered him until he reached her, and then turned toward the ship without her pointing to it.

He knew that much, and she had figured it out on the way.

They were going to where most of the creatures called home.

Dachande ignored the jabbing pain as they edged closer to the nest. The drones would surround their queen now, protect her. They made it past the second and third structure with no more attacks.

Da'dtou-di paused for a second to reload her burner. Dachande glanced at her thoughtfully.

She was the prey he had waited most of his life to Hunt. They were small but powerful, obviously more intelligent than the yautja had thought, and as brave as any warrior he had Hunted with.

Of course, Da'dtou-di could be an exception; she was obviously trained better than the other few oomans he had been in contact with. The kind one that had died, for instance—it was not trained to Hunt, and had been blind to the danger he could have represented.

He would have enjoyed Hunting oomans. But he was proud to Hunt at Da'dtou-di's side. This would be a tale to tell for generations to come ...

The ooman saw that he watched her and raised her fist into the air. She exposed her teeth again at the same time, probably a sign of aggression.

Dachande still wore his mask, but he raised his

arm also and then clattered, as loud as he dared, the Kiss of Midnight.

Kill or die. He was ready.

They crept into the open space in front of the shield wall as quietly as possible. Ryushi's suns beat down on the nearly lifeless compound. It seemed like hours ago that Noguchi had been thinking of how beautiful the town was. Not now. Especially since the heat of midmorning had taken on the cloying stench of rot and decay. A lot of bodies—humans, aliens, warriors—must be cooking in the hot sunshine.

The Lector seemed deserted from the outside. A lone dead rhynth lay on the ground in front of the ship, its intestines ripped out. It must have staggered from the stampede to die there ...

Noguchi figured the bugs had nested in the ship, and that they waited there now, grouped to attack. Their actions reminded her of a bee colony, the way the drones of a hive lived only to feed and protect their queen.

She shuddered slightly at the thought; she wouldn't want to meet with whatever those monstrosities called "mother."

The distance to the ship slowly dwindled as they crossed the compound. Noguchi's heart thumped louder with each step. She stifled an urge to go back to the empty holding pen and study Conover's map for a while longer.

Like five or ten years.

Broken Tusk walked cautiously, but not too much so; Noguchi figured he knew something she didn't. That wouldn't take much.

As they neared the main loading entrance, her wor-

ries about what they would do if the door was closed
vanished. The middle steel entry was halfway open as
it had been when she and Mason had gone in—

Another pleasant thought. They reached the bottom of the ramp and Noguchi looked up into the
black interior of the dock; the metal door was raised
horizontally, exactly the right height to let the bugs
come and go.

The bugs didn't seem too smart, but she wondered.
Conover had spoken of one that was much larger
than the others, that had slept near them when they
were captives.

Queen?

She might have stood there for a lot longer, but
Broken Tusk growled at her. Noguchi took it as impatience. She took a tentative step onto the ramp.

From somewhere inside the blackness, a low hiss.

Noguchi took another step, gun ready for the first
thing that moved. Broken Tusk was by her side, his
weapon also out. He had slung the spear over his
back.

The dark lock stirred, shadows shifted. She heard
the clatter of alien movement, and then silence.

Broken Tusk moved in front of her. She let him.

They were halfway up the ramp when a sudden
flurry of motion in the dark ahead of them surprised
her. She fired into the dock, twice.

The gunshots clapped loudly in the still air. Whatever had moved wasn't moving now.

Broken Tusk made a few guttural sounds and then
walked without hesitation to the top of the ramp. He
turned and motioned at her to follow.

Noguchi joined him and peered inside. Nothing, at
least nothing she could hear or see. It felt empty, too.
But there was alien spoor all around. An odd, wet-

metal smell. What looked like meaty chunks of slaughtered rhynth—or human.

She edged inside, adrenaline pumping. On the dark floor there were several of the unclassifieds that the Revnas had dissected, their spiderlike bodies curled and motionless. Dark shapes lined the walls. She looked closer and then shuddered. *The Lector*'s crew, at least some of them, with chests ruptured, webbed like flies in the nest of a demonic spider. Some of them had not died easily, from the expressions locked on to their dead faces.

Where—?

A jagged hole at the rear of the dock answered her. The edges of the torn metal looked melted, scorched. All around it were bizarre formations of shiny black material. It stretched and hung in thick ropes, appeared both organic and deliberate.

It seemed twice as hot as outside in the burning sunlight with the humidity added. Noguchi took a shaky breath and then moved into the darkness. Broken Tusk walked ahead of her to the hole and waited.

She heard a chittering movement come from deep inside the ship somewhere, and steeled her nerves as she approached.

They were going to have to find the control room. Which meant going in, navigating a labyrinth of corridors, climbing two flights of steps, and unlocking a locked door.

Broken Tusk watched her for a second and then stepped into the hole.

Noguchi prayed silently to anyone listening, and followed him.

30

achande went first.

He crouched down immediately and searched for life, sweeping back and forth with his burner. Nothing moved.

Da'dtou-di slipped in after him. He ignored her for the moment; she could take care of herself. What she lacked in skill, she made up for with intelligence; it would have to be enough.

He scanned the long dark corridor through the eyes of the mask. More of the alien spittle secretion, *te'dqi*, lined the steep walls. It was a brittle substance, but could provide camouflage for hiding drones.

The lenses showed nothing. He glanced at Da'dtou-di. Her sickly pale skin seemed whiter than before.

"Nothing," he said.

She babbled a short reply. The words were nonsense but the tone was watchful and ready.

They crept forward.

Da'dtou-di stumbled behind him. Apparently oomans didn't see well in the dark. She followed closer.

At the end of the corridor, another door, open. Dachande heard the *kainde amedha* as they skittered somewhere beyond. He ducked his head to get through the portal and discovered that he would have to move in a crouch through the next hall; the ooman ceiling was lower here.

Dachande had gone into three nests before this one. But always with fully stocked burners and at least a handful of armed yautja with him. Not to mention that he felt like a month old *rjet* turd—his side ached from the drone attack and each deep breath burned somewhere inside. From his experience and the way he felt, the wounds were fairly serious. Well. Nothing to be done about it.

He wasn't afraid, Blooded warriors seldom were in battle. But he accepted that dying could come easily here. He hoped it would come with honor. The real pity would be that there would be no one to tell the tale. No one except a small ooman—assuming she survived as well.

They moved forward in the thick dark.

Noguchi tripped on something and caught herself before she fell. There was virtually no light. Every dozen paces or so, a small dim emergency torch set high into the wall illuminated just enough to make it seem darker. She could make out her own weapon and Broken Tusk's back; beyond that, nothing.

The warrior seemed to be able to see better. He

must have done this a dozen times, and he obviously knew something about the aliens' behavior—

Noguchi felt her gut clench at the sound of movement ahead somewhere. She gripped her weapon tighter, her eyes wide and semiblind.

They stepped into a second corridor, the air grew muggier as they progressed. Their footsteps were oddly muffled by the strange alien material that lay thick on the floor.

She should be in front, she knew that; Dachande had looked at the map Conover had given her, but his understanding of it couldn't be clear. Then again, he could *see* better, and was stronger—

As they neared the end of the second hallway, Noguchi heard another alien chitter, close.

From *behind* them.

Dachande whipped around at the drone's cry and pointed his burner.

Da'dtou-di had also heard it. She fired at the bug as it ran for them.

The shot from her burner hit the drone in the shoulder and spun it around. It didn't fall.

Dachande aimed his burner at the screaming creature. Light and heat spewed in a tight beam.

The drone's back exploded outward in a spray of corrosive blood and cooked entrails.

Footfalls. He spun. Two drones attacked from the front.

Dachande turned, got the first with his bladed wrist, a sharp slashing jab to the bug's throat.

The second clambered over its falling brother and reached for him. Dachande knocked it down, used the burner as a club to crush its jaws. Blood hissed over the durable metal and dripped to the floor, ate holes in the hard material.

Da'dtou-di inhaled sharply and fired past him, at a third drone.

And missed. The Hard Meat turned and sprinted away from them, down the third winding corridor, shrieking an alarm to the others. It was too stupid to be afraid so it must be a sentry.

Dachande cursed. Behind him, he was pretty certain Da'dtou-di did the same in her own language. He didn't need a translator to understand that.

Well, it just meant they'd have to hurry. He had hoped to make it farther ...

The Leader picked up his pace and hit the hallway at a jog, Da'dtou-di right behind. Ahead, the Hard Meat waited.

She was terrified but ready. This had to be done or else the colonists would die—

And you, too, Machiko.

No shit.

At the end of the third hall, the corridor came to a T-junction. Noguchi pointed for Broken Tusk to turn left; she hoped she'd remember the rest as they came to it.

She moved blindly behind Broken Tusk. There would be a rung ladder on the right pretty soon—

—a bug hissed behind her. Noguchi turned and fired. The shots were deafening in the closed area. The alien's dying screams were quieter.

This was getting old real goddamn fast.

She turned again, just in time to see a bolt of hard light come from the warrior's weapon, accompanied by an echoey thud. It acted as a strobe, showed them a nightmare of dark limbs and shiny teeth.

More screaming.

Noguchi breathed the stifling air shallowly. Her body twitched and jumped as she searched the darkness for the ladder. Her chest had started to bleed again.

Maybe she was already dead and didn't realize it.

Maybe they were in hell.

Dachande felt the ooman slap him on the back and turned.

Da'dtou-di pointed up, her face distorted. She seemed disturbed, as far as he was able to read her expression.

He eyed the flimsy ladder and then started to climb; the narrow rungs allowed him to take three at a time.

Dachande reached the top and looked down at the small warrior. She swung her weapon in an arc; dull light glinted off the small metallic burner.

He looked up again, reached for the floor of the next level—

—a clawed hand dropped down to cover his own. The black talons etched into his wrist, raising small fountains of his blood.

The drone bent down and hissed into his face.

Noguchi looked up just in time.

The bug leaned toward Broken Tusk and opened its jaws.

She aimed and squeezed. The AP bullet went into the alien's mouth and out the back of its head. It fell forward, almost toppled Broken Tusk from the ladder, and then clattered to the floor. If the maker of this ammunition ever asked, she would give them a testimonial they wouldn't believe. This here stuff is a monster killer, never leave your cube without a few dozen rounds . . .

A shriek from her left.

She fired and fired again as they seemed to come at her from all sides. The noise was incredible—

Click.

That was louder.

Dachande stood up and hit the first drone to come at him with the weighted staff. It dropped, still alive but out of the fight. There was nothing behind it, at least for a few seconds.

He turned to cover Da'dtou-di on her climb, at the same time her weapon fire stopped.

A drone leapt at her, knocked her back against the ladder.

Dachande felt pure rage. He jumped from the second level, staff in front of him—

—and landed on the drone.

Like that, tarei hsan?

The drone did not. So he killed it.

Noguchi was dizzy. Broken Tusk stamped the life out of the bug that had grabbed her. He tucked her under his arm and ascended the rung ladder easily.

He set her down first and then pulled himself up after her. Noguchi reloaded her gun and then covered him, but the last few hissing shapes that were below backed away, then turned and scampered off. That didn't really seem like a victory, somehow.

She looked down the second level corridor. The next ladder would be at the end, but their escape was only a few meters away.

Much as she wanted Broken Tusk to come with her, someone needed to guard the escape pod. And Broken Tusk probably couldn't run a human computer—

At least the passage was clear for the moment.

They started down the second level.

The ooman paused midway down the hallway and then pointed at a doorway with odd figures scrawled on it. Ooman language.

She spoke something. Dachande hit the animal loop on his suit to record, in case it might later be helpful. Da'dtou-di motioned at him and then again at the door.

She wanted him to stay *here*?

Dachande growled, but Da'dtou-di was adamant. It was important to her.

It had been a long time since he had trusted another in battle. And now he was being asked to trust an *ooman*, not even an *un-Blooded* yautja!

She held up her clawless hand again and then backed away a few steps.

Dachande tilted his head at her.

Da'dtou-di spoke again and bared her teeth at him. And then she turned and ran ahead. He could take her head off with a swipe of his wrist blade and yet she showed him her teeth. Brave Little Knife. If she risked his wrath it must be important to her indeed. Well.

This was her kind's ship. She surely knew things about it he did not. She must have a plan.

Dachande stayed.

He tilted his head, which she thought meant affirmative.

Noguchi felt a rush of relief. She didn't want to part with him in this hot, deadly maze, but she'd need a clear path to get back. She only had maybe a dozen rounds left. It did not matter how good the ammo was if you were out of it; she hoped Broken Tusk had more for his weapon.

"Hold the fort," she said, and grinned tightly. She was scared and she hurt, but it felt powerful to be doing something. Something that might kill the infestation in her town . . .

You hope.

"I'll be back when I'm done."

With that, she turned and ran. And prayed that he would be there when she got back.

If she got back.

The second ladder looked empty, but she couldn't see the top. The strange alien formations were thicker here, looped around the rungs and covered the wall.

She checked behind her again and started to climb, revolver in hand.

A drop of odd, warm goo smacked onto her arm. Then another.

She looked up.

Da'dtou-di hadn't indicated if she wanted the door he guarded open, but Dachande opened it anyway. The ooman wanted him to watch it for *some* reason.

It was locked, so he pounded at the frame with the end of his staff until it cracked.

It was a *tyioe-ti*, an escape pod, small but large enough for the two of them. He stepped in and surveyed it quickly. Not a nesting area. Three ooman-sized chairs and a panel of controls. He'd never be able to squeeze into one of those tiny seats to fly this craft.

He turned and stood at the entry to wait for Da'dtou-di. And he heard a resounding crash from the direction they had come from, followed by a low, scratchy hiss.

Dachande tensed. It was a sound he had heard before.

A queen. Heading in this direction.

Was it the one they had brought on their ship, egg-layer of their prey? Or had one of the drones shifted hormones and metamorphosed into a female?

Not that it really mattered, just at the moment.

He waited.

Noguchi looked up and stopped breathing.

One of the bugs had leaned down from the third level, its long, misshapen skull right above her. Another drop of slime fell from its jaws—

She brought her pistol up and rammed the barrel into its mouth. She jerked the trigger again and again.

The creature didn't even cry out. It fell past her with a clattering thud. It was a small miracle that none of its acidic blood splashed onto her.

Her hands shook as she topped the ladder. Surely there would be another at the top, waiting to tear at her, to rip out her throat—

Noguchi pulled herself up and on to her knees. The

platform was coated heavily with the dark alien material, but otherwise empty.

She jumped to her feet and ran down the hall. At the end was another tee. Without hesitation, she took a right and continued on. The hot, sticky air made it a struggle to breathe. It smelled like rotten mushrooms in here.

It wasn't until two more turns in the twisted corridor that she realized she had gone the wrong way.

Dachande took a deep breath and waited. There was no doubt that it was the queen, or that she was headed toward him.

Drones were target practice, but a queen egg-layer—

No lone yautja had ever survived combat with one, unless he had a burner. Once, a dozen Blooded warriors had taken one down with only blades and spears, but the queen had killed nine of them before she died.

Metal creaked and groaned from below. At least he still had a fire in his burner. Two of them.

A crest of shiny black appeared at the top of the ladder . . .

Dachande pointed and fired.

Missed.

The Hard Meat ducked and screamed, but was uninjured. He took aim and waited for her to come up.

Nothing happened for several beats. Dachande remained ready.

Suddenly she howled and a dark shape sprang into view at the top of the ladder.

Dachande fired, his last shot.

The head of the creature exploded.

He roared in triumph and threw the empty burner at the bubbling mess. The useless weapon skipped over the platform and disappeared. He had killed her, had Hunted a queen and killed her! The stories of their intelligence and skill had been wrong, she had been an easy target—

The queen hissed again and the crest of her unmistakable skull rose into view.

Dachande's eyes widened. But he had blown her to pieces—!

Decoy. She had sent a drone to take the shots; he had been tricked.

But how could she know that—?

It didn't matter. The deadly queen was alive, and she was coming.

S'yuit-de!

He watched as two huge talons screeched across the metal platform and pulled the grinning monster into view.

Noguchi didn't bother with the map. She knew where she'd fucked up.

There was a second of initial panic. She'd actually *left* him there to wait for her, stupid, stupid—!

Noguchi brought it under control and turned back.

She was almost back to where she had taken the wrong turn when one of the nightmare creatures leapt out of nowhere to land in front of her.

She pointed and fired several times. The snarling animal shrieked and fell.

Behind it was another. She pulled the trigger again, and it toppled on top of the other. There were no others.

Idiot! Your ammo!

A cold hand clutched at her heart. The gun was empty.

She ejected the spent shells and loaded the final rounds, hands shaking harder now.

Six rounds.

Noguchi came to the tee and ran straight. For one terrifying moment she felt totally lost, but then she saw the door. Yellow and black lines, just as Conover had said.

She aimed as carefully as she could and blew the lock off of the door. Bits of plastic and metal spewed and stung her face and hands. The door opened to reveal a room full of panels and screens. This was the central computer room, according to what Conover told her. The ship's brains.

Noguchi slammed the door behind her and ran to the second chair.

Second chair, straight on, disk slot next to red and black strip—

She hit the transmitter's power switch and waited for the panel to light up. She took Scott's disk from her pocket and held it tightly. The seconds stretched like minutes. Hours. Eons . . .

There was an empty coffee cup on the console in front of her with "Conover" stenciled on the side. She felt a stab of pity for the pilot; he had died bravely.

The screen glowed to life with a stream of numbers and letters at the top. She carefully inserted the disk into the slot and pushed the lock button.

The computer hummed and blinked. Noguchi felt her breath catch.

If this doesn't work, you're dead—

A light flashed: *Dir. received/pil. S. Conover, 93630/navigational complete.*

She slapped the board. "Yes, yes, *yes!*"

It had worked.

She turned just as the door burst inward.

Dachande straightened his back and took a deep breath. If this was to be his Final Hunt, he would die fighting. Combat against a queen with only a staff—it was an honor. He would fight and he would lose but that was the only choice.

From the way Da'dtou-di had gone he heard her weapon crash several times. He tuned it out. She would have to complete her mission alone.

The queen was huge, twice as large as a drone. Her arms were longer—she had a second, smaller set protruding from her chest—her crown sleek and branched almost like antlers. Her double jaws held more than two rows of shiny teeth. And being female, she would know how to fight.

She moved toward him slowly. Her long, pointed tail dragged across the metal floor.

Dachande raised his staff and held it out slightly, legs spread wide. If she came at him like he thought she would, he would get in at least one clean cut.

The queen towered in the corridor, bent almost in half to move.

Dachande held steady. He said, "Come, Hard Meat. I killed your children. Come and join them." An unlikely boast and neither could she understand it, but smiling into the face of Death was said to sometimes unnerve even the Black Warrior.

A sudden noise behind him called for his attention, but he didn't take his eyes from her.

She swung her head to look past him and hissed.

Dachande's eyes flickered. Was there someone—?

The queen leapt—

* * *

Noguchi blew the bug's brains across the hall with two shots.

The dark jellied mass splatted against the corridor wall and ran down in clumps.

She jumped over the corpse and into the passageway. She sprinted for the tee.

It was over, or it would be soon. The barge was going to fall like a meteor, like an atomic-powered meteor and when it hit, it would take out what was left of Prosperity Wells. And the rest of the alien brood. There wouldn't be anything remaining here but a smoldering crater.

The escape pod should get them far enough out of town—

At the turn to get back to the ladder, the corridor beyond exploded into motion.

Noguchi let out a cry and then aimed at one of the bugs that sprang for her. The bullet knocked it down, still shrieking.

Two shots now, only two left—

Noguchi reached the top of the rung ladder down to the second level. The ladder was twisted, torn loose from the wall. Shit—!

"Broken T—!"

She stopped. Below her, the warrior stood. And faced one of the nightmare creatures, a giant, huge, it filled the entire corridor!

At the sound of her voice, the monster looked up and hissed, a horrible, raspy sound that chilled her to the pit of her soul.

—Queen—

It spun and lashed out at Broken Tusk as Noguchi aimed her handgun at it.

The impossibly long and heavy tail crashed against the warrior's chest. His spear flew and he was knocked flying.

She heard the sound of the impact from where she was. Broken Tusk smacked against the door he guarded and bounced off it. His blood seemed to glow against his dark armor. He didn't move.

Noguchi fired, her chest tight. The queen screamed and turned toward her.

The bullet missed.

Without thinking, Noguchi jumped to the second level, revolver in front of her. One shot left. One chance.

Her knees buckled as she hit the platform, but she didn't fall.

The queen shrieked and started for her.

Noguchi prayed that one bullet would stop her—
—fired—
—and the monster fell backward, screamed, and thrashed on the floor. Chest shot.

Not dead, but down.

Noguchi ran to Broken Tusk. She dropped the empty weapon. The nightmare queen's tail lashed out and would have knocked her down if she hadn't jumped.

Broken Tusk took the lash again in the chest. Blood spattered.

Noguchi kicked at the door to the escape pod and stumbled. The inner hatch was open.

The queen screamed, a piercing howl. Her death chant, Noguchi hoped.

She bent over the injured warrior and got one arm under him. With strength she didn't know she had, she lifted with a grunt—

—and he slid with her into the pod.

Sweat ran down her face. She pulled again, and his feet cleared the door.

No time, no time—

She half fell into a chair in front of the panel and searched frantically for the control.

Behind her, the alien screamed again in pain and fury.

Broken Tusk groaned and rolled toward Noguchi.

Noguchi found the button, right in front of her. In her panic she had missed it.

Movement behind her. A scream that sent hot, charnel, rotting air across her back.

She half turned, hand on the button—

—and the queen was *there*, her head in the pod, her huge claw came down—

—and embedded in the warrior's shoulder.

Broken Tusk screamed.

Noguchi slammed the door's override button.

The thick metal door closed. The grinning head seemed to rush at her—

—and then toppled to the floor as the pressure door, designed to seal the ship against hard vacuum, crunched the exoskeleton of the monster's relatively thin neck and beheaded the queen.

Her disembodied hand was still buried in the motionless warrior's back.

Noguchi hit the next button.

And they were free of the larger ship, flying.

The pain was bad, but Dachande let it happen.

He didn't understand it for a moment. It. Something. Da'dtou-di, was she here? Had they killed her?

He felt oddly weightless for a short time—

—flying—

And then the floor rose up and slammed against him.

There was a burst of new pain. Gravity returned, with more aches than he'd ever had. He was hurt, badly hurt.

Then a rush of hot, clean air. Light assaulted his eyes. His breathing mask was gone. Too much of the planet's combustive oxygen flooded into his lungs. He couldn't last more than a few hours breathing such potent air.

He coughed. Warm liquid ran down his throat, but it still felt raw, wounded.

A shadow moved over him. He was lifted slightly and pulled.

He growled in pain but couldn't seem to form a protest. The air blinded him. He was outside.

He opened his eyes slowly and focused on the face that hovered over his.

Da'dtou-di!

He felt a burst of pride. She had survived, had helped him.

Dachande started to speak and coughed again. More pain.

He reached for the loop on the arm of his suit, but his fingers had grown clumsy.

Da'dtou-di placed her fragile hand under his and moved it for him.

Noguchi's throat felt tight. There was a stone in her chest, heavy and painful. Pale blood covered the warrior, his breathing slow and labored. He was dying.

They had made it. The pod had landed with a jarring impact somewhere in the east desert, far from

Prosperity Wells; the chute had opened at least. But . . .

Broken Tusk raised a shaky hand toward his other wrist, but couldn't seem to maneuver it well. Noguchi guided it for him.

It was the recording device. She felt her eyes brim as her own voice spilled out.

"Hold the fort. I'll be back when I'm done."

Broken Tusk grabbed at the alien claw, still embedded in his shoulder. "Hang on," she said. "Help will be here soon, the colonists will come—" She faltered and choked. Then gave him what she felt he needed. "We did it. We killed the bugs. The queen. You and I." She waved her hand, feeling helpless.

He pulled the queen's claw loose and looked at it.

She pointed at it, nodded, made a throat-cutting gesture.

He understood. She was sure of it, because he nodded in return. Then he grasped one of the long, spidery digits and snapped it off, groaned with the exertion. Hissing blood dripped from the finger.

Broken Tusk then motioned at the mark on his face, a jagged bolt between his eyes. He motioned at her and then at the scar again.

Noguchi nodded and leaned closer.

Da'dtou-di had to be Blooded. It was his responsibility, as Leader.

Dachande tore off one of the queen's fingers. It hurt to move, to breathe, to live, but this was important; it was all he had left.

Da'dtou-di came closer, closed her eyes. Something wet splashed on Dachande' face; he ignored it. It was time.

The warrior dipped one claw into the alien blood and then spat on the claw. His own blood mixed with the alien's acidic ichor. That was part of it. His blood would partly neutralize the potent chemicals from the Hard Meat. Moving with great care, he reached out and etched his mark into her pale skin, on the forehead, between her eyes. He managed to keep his hand from shaking long enough to draw his symbol.

She hissed in pain, but didn't move. She was brave, Little Knife. She had helped him and they had killed the queen. That was something to take and lay at the feet of the Black Warrior.

Dachande dropped his hand, exhausted. The animal loop played again, some ooman speak from long before. It didn't matter; he had been ready for a long time and now was the moment. He had no complaints.

He wished he could talk in her language, teach her what he could—be brave, Hunt well, respect your Leader. But she already knew most of that. The rest, she would surely learn. She was Blooded now, and somehow she would learn. Even though they had only been together a short time, he knew all about her.

The best student he ever had.

Tears fell before Broken Tusk even touched her. She started to wipe at her eyes, but then closed them instead. The dying warrior was going to give her his mark, she understood what he wished. She leaned down.

The pain was short and burning. A trickle of green blood ran down her nose.

Broken Tusk dropped his hand, and her voice spoke again from the loop, softly this time.

"I'll remember you."

Noguchi lowered her head and started to sob, the first real tears she had cried in a long time.

Behind them, a light appeared in the sky. A ball of flame plummeted through the Ryushi sunlight, headed for Prosperity Wells.

Noguchi glanced behind her as the explosion thundered through the desert. The air around her compressed suddenly. Fiery air washed over them with the sound, the roar and rumble of it.

When the sound died, the town was gone. As quickly as that.

She turned back to the warrior. Buried her face in her hands and rocked slowly, back and forth.

Dachande had stopped breathing. Like the town, he was gone.

Epilogue

Dahdtoudi woke up early on the morning they came.

It was first light on the open plain that unfolded in front of her small home. She yawned and stretched as she climbed out of bed and glanced out the window. The air felt different somehow, electric—

Only two years before, she would have disregarded the sense of change as nonsense, superstition. But "quiet" didn't start to describe the experience of living on a world where she was the only human; she had developed a feel for Ryushi, the way an athlete could feel her body and its fluctuations. The air was different, no question. Something was going to happen.

Something.

She pulled on a coverall and slipped on her boots. She pulled her shaggy hair into a knot at the back of her neck as she walked into the tiny kitchen for a glass of water. The new well between her home and the near cliff was clean, the water sweet. No more riding twenty klicks for a shower at the old well, either.

Dahdtoudi drank the cool water slowly and thought about the day ahead. Yesterday, she had run through forms, so today was weight day. Also water day for the sheltered garden in the glassed shed behind the house. Tomorrow she would ride the east sector and check for visitors ...

She finished and set the glass in the sink. It was feeding time first.

Dahdtoudi walked outside and almost tripped on Creep. The dog jumped and wagged his tail, excited to see her.

She scruffed the dog behind his ears. "I'm excited, too, Creep. It's been what, six hours since last we met?"

Creep barked happily and followed her to the rhynth pen. He ran between her legs and almost knocked her over.

"Dumb dog," she said fondly. He barked again.

She couldn't look at the mutt without thanking Jame and Cathie silently. Creep had been good company, had kept loneliness from getting too big. They had acted as though it would be best for the dog, to be able to run free—but the gift had been for her, too.

"Good morning, kids."

The three rhynth that she kept turned their heads slowly to watch her approach. Spot, Milo, and Mim. They weren't as good at conversation as Creep, but they were tame. They also acted as transport; she had a flyer, but eventually her fuel would run out, so she saved it for emergencies. Keeping them as pets made it harder to eat meat, but it was a matter of survival. Besides, she only had to hunt once every two months or so ...

Dahdtoudi dumped some grain in their trough and scratched Mim behind her leathery ears. The beast snorted and started to eat as if she'd been starving.

"Should have called you 'pig,'" said Dahdtoudi. The rhynth ignored her.

She walked back to the house and sat down on the front porch to watch the suns rise. There was enough light for her to see the queen's skull, bleached by the hot suns where it perched on her roof. Her trophy, hers and Broken Tusk's.

Creep lay down next to her and nuzzled her legs.

"What's different today, dog? Something is different."

Creep glanced at her and then rested his head on his paws. She patted his side and smiled.

They had been here alone for almost two years. After Broken Tusk had died, she had joined the colonists for the long wait. It had taken nearly two months before help had arrived, and by then her decision was made, was firm. Was irrevocable.

At first a couple of the ranchers had argued with her, but they soon gave up.

The company hadn't tried to change her mind at all. She could have been charged with something, however trumped up the charges would have been, but the final word was that "her actions had been dictated by necessity." Her executive contract had been quietly bought out, which was fine by her. Chigusa was worried about liability and declared the whole thing a write-off. The old man wasn't stupid. He gave her a permanent, official position as a "caretaker," and pulled his interests out of the Cygni system. He never threw good money after bad, so it was said, and he was superstitious about staying on a world so cursed as this one. The galaxy was full of worlds and the old man owned hundreds of them. He would never miss this one.

Only Roth and her spouse and Weaver had seemed to understand why she wanted to stay.

So the colonists had gone to start over again in the Rigel system, and she was left alone to start over on Ryushi. And she had been happy. For the first time in her life, there had been no dragons. There was only peace.

"Everything I care about is right here," she said softly.

Creep sighed, most likely bored. She'd had a lot of time to replay conversations and events in her mind, and the dog had suffered the same stories for two years.

A flash of movement in the morning sky caught her attention. For several seconds she thought she was seeing things; it had been so long . . .

The flash grew brighter and brighter. She watched its progress as it ripped through the air, the sound far away. Creep sensed her excitement and sat up, whining softly.

The object fell gracefully in an arc to land to the west, maybe half a day's ride by rhynth, maybe less. Dahdtoudi Noguchi stood quickly and tried not to get her hopes up.

Probably a meteor, that's all . . .

But she didn't really think so. She went to get ready.

* * *

Seven hours later, she dismounted Milo and moved through the harsh sunlight toward a small stand of rocks. She carried her binoculars and carbine; the company had left her with plenty of supplies.

A thin stream of smoke still rose from where the object had landed, in a small valley set among a stand of steep rock walls.

Dahdtoudi slipped between the rocks silently and propped herself up on a baked stone. She scanned left to right until she picked up the smoke—

A small vehicle on treads buzzed across the cracked dirt, maybe a hundred meters away. She zoomed in, her heart hammering.

Behind it was a trail that extended beyond her range of vision. A trail of spheres, oval-shaped—

Dahdtoudi lowered the viewer and stood for a moment. She rubbed absently at the jagged scar between her eyes, faded white now.

"It won't be long," she said. She would make them understand, tell them of Broken Tusk's bravery and skill. And how everything had gone wrong ...

Milo gazed at her. She stretched her sore muscles and then mounted him for the ride home.

The Leader sighed inwardly at the yautja assembled before him. They were as ready as he could make them, pumped and hungry to kill. They stood in line next to the ship, their burners loaded and blades sharpened.

But he also had orders to seek after Dachande's group on this Hunt, an extra pain he could have done without. That ship had never returned.

He had known Dachande. Old broken tooth had been a good Leader and a strong warrior, but something had gone wrong, and those in charge wanted to know what. As they always did when it was not they who had to determine it.

Vk'leita shook his head as he reviewed the young yautja. He had Hunted with Dachande, he respected him, as had many—but he was surely dead, and dead was dead, all that mattered was the way of it. More than a long cycle had passed, probably too much time to ascertain much of anything. The dead from that trip would be sun-grayed bones scattered by the local scavengers by now.

He nodded at the other Blooded, Ci'tde. Ci'tde would take the group on the initial scouting trip. The Hunt would start in earnest after the light fell away.

The Leader stayed at the ship and ran through some practice drills while he was alone. Young males took a lot of energy to train, and he relished the time away from them. Besides, he would have to check the *ui'stbi*, the geography, for remnants of recent Hunting. He could do some through the ships' *gkinmara*, but much would have to be done on foot. He was looking forward to stretching himself, covering ground, loosening up the ship-stale muscles.

He finished practice and then sat on the ground to clean his armor. The yautja would not be back until the suns had passed through their high point, so he had plenty of time . . .

Behind him, a sound of movement.

Vk'leita was on his feet instantly. The sound had come from the other side of the ship. He snatched up his burner and started toward the sound.

He reached the front of the ship and let out a warning hiss.

Nothing.

Suddenly a small figure stepped into view. Vk'leita pointed at the creature and almost fired—

—he lowered the burner uncertainly. The creature was no yautja, it was the size of a child—but it wore armor and a wrist blade. The creature moved slowly toward him, hands out.

Ooman!

The Leader raised his weapon again. The sickly, pale, *ugly* face of it—

It stepped closer and tilted its head to one side.

He could have fired. Had the other yautja been there, he might have, that was the proper response to a threat. But this small creature did not seem particularly threatening, even though he knew the stories. And neither did it seem to be afraid. If anything, it carried itself proudly, almost as if it were a warrior. Oomans were supposed to be cowards, sneaky, deadly when cornered, but seldom stand-up face-on fighters. And it made him curious.

"Who are you?" said Vk'leita.

The ooman pointed at itself. "Da'dtou-di."

Vk'leita flared his mandibles. The creature's accent was awful, strange, but he understood. Female? An ooman female? The name was "small knife," feminine form—

Going against a lifetime of training, the Leader reslung his burner and moved closer. This bore investigation. The ooman stood still.

When he was a few paces away, he stopped and eyed the ooman carefully. It wore tresses like yautja, and carried the weapon; its pieced-together armor was part warrior—he recognized the Hard Meat shell—and part unknown.

The ooman motioned at itself again. "Da'dtou-di," it said again. It reached up and touched its face.

The Leader peered closer. It had a mark on its head. It looked like—no, it couldn't be. He took another two steps and bent to stare at the ooman. It did not flinch as he practically stuck his mask in the thing's face.

The mark—

It was *Blooded*! A Blooded ooman! That couldn't be! It was not possible. But there was the mark, right *there*! and, and—the mark was—

Dachande's.

What the unholy *pauk*?

Vk'leita growled. "You know Dachande? Where is he?"

Da'dtou-di shook her head and then pointed at him. She touched her own face again, now where mandibles would be if she were yautja. With one of her fingers, she mimed a break.

As if a mandible were broken. Dachande.

"Go on."

The ooman used her hands as teeth and made tearing movements with them. Then motioned "Dachande" again. *Thei-de*. Dachande was dead.

Da'dtou-di moved closer to him and then cautiously reached up to rest her tiny hand on his shoulder. She *greeted* him.

Vk'leita tilted his head, fascinated, and returned the gesture. This was unheard of. He was standing here as if he had a brain listening to a *pauking* ooman talk to him in sign language, telling him about the death of a Blooded warrior. She was *ooman*, but she called herself Da'dtou-di in the warrior's tongue. She bore Dachande's mark, no way around that, no warrior would tell an alien what that mark meant, much less how to apply it, not under any circumstances. And she had come to him to speak of Dachande's death. But something else, too . . .

"Hunt?" Vk'leita asked. "You've come to Hunt with us?" He unsheathed his blade and made jabbing movements in the air.

Da'dtou-di tilted her head and exposed her small teeth. She raised one arm into the air and threw back her head. A long, strange cry came from her, of aggression and eagerness, he guessed.

The Leader listened to the eerie sound and then circled the ooman. She was little, but moved well; she carried the marks of a warrior, and she had known Dachande. He studied her thoughtfully.

This was unprecedented, but there was really only one option. She was Blooded. However it had come to be, there it was. The rules of the Hunt had never been stretched so much, he was sure of that. But what could he do? He was a warrior, he had his code and he had lived his life with it too long to deny it now. He would let her Hunt with them. Perhaps they could exchange languages, and he would learn Dachande's fate. Perhaps she would choose to leave with them, to return to their home and teach them ooman ways—surely that would be a great victory, to have found an ooman warrior?

Well. Perhaps covered much of the galaxy, didn't it? Who could say?

The Leader raised his own arm and howled. After a moment, Da'dtou-di joined him.

There was much that they could teach one another.

Joseph Conrad

Heart of Darkness

Herausgegeben von
Bernhard Reitz

Philipp Reclam jun. Stuttgart

RECLAMS UNIVERSAL-BIBLIOTHEK Nr. 9161
Alle Rechte vorbehalten
© 1984 Philipp Reclam jun. GmbH & Co. KG, Stuttgart
Gesamtherstellung: Reclam, Ditzingen. Printed in Germany 2010
RECLAM, UNIVERSAL-BIBLIOTHEK und RECLAMS
UNIVERSAL-BIBLIOTHEK sind eingetragene Marken
der Philipp Reclam jun. GmbH & Co. KG, Stuttgart
ISBN 978-3-15-009161-6

www.reclam.de

Heart of Darkness

I

The *Nellie*[1], a cruising yawl, swung to her anchor without a flutter of the sails, and was at rest. The flood had made, the wind was nearly calm, and being bound down the river, the only thing for it was to come to and wait for the turn of the tide.

The sea-reach of the Thames stretched before us like the beginning of an interminable waterway. In the offing the sea and the sky were welded together without a joint, and in the luminous space the tanned sails of the barges drifting up with the tide seemed to stand still in red clusters of canvas sharply peaked, with gleams of varnished spirits. A haze rested on the low shores that ran out to sea in vanishing flatness. The air was dark above Gravesend[2], and farther back still seemed con-

---

3 **cruising yawl:** Segeljacht.
8 **sea-reach:** Mündungsgebiet.
9 **interminable:** endlos.
    offing: Seeraum, offene See.
10 **to weld:** zusammenschmieden, verschmelzen.
11 **luminous:** lichterfüllt.
    tanned: lohfarben.
12 **barge:** Lastkahn.
13 **cluster:** Schwarm.
    canvas: Segeltuch.
14 **to varnish:** lackieren.
    haze: Dunst.

densed into a mournful gloom, brooding motionless over the biggest, and the greatest, town on earth.

The Director of Companies was our captain and our host. We four affectionately watched his back as he
5 stood in the bows looking to seaward. On the whole river there was nothing that looked half so nautical. He resembled a pilot, which to a seaman is trustworthiness personified. It was difficult to realize his work was not out there in the luminous estuary, but behind him,
10 within the brooding gloom.

Between us there was, as I have already said somewhere, the bond of the sea. Besides holding our hearts together through long periods of separation, it had the effect of making us tolerant of each other's yarns – and
15 even convictions. The Lawyer – the best of old fellows – had, because of his many years and many virtues, the only cushion on deck, and was lying on the only rug. The Accountant had brought out already a box of dominoes, and was toying architecturally with the
20 bones. Marlow sat cross-legged right aft, leaning against the mizzen-mast. He had sunken cheeks, a yellow

---

1 **mournful:** traurig.
  to brood: brüten.
4 **affectionately** (adv.): liebevoll.
5 **in the bows:** am Bug.
6 **nautical:** nautisch.
9 **estuary:** Flußmündung, Meeresbucht.
14 **tolerant:** duldsam.
  yarn: Seemannsgarn.
15 **Lawyer:** Rechtsanwalt.
18 **Accountant:** Buchhalter, Wirtschaftsprüfer.
19 f. **to toy architecturally with the bones:** mit den Dominosteinen bauen.
20 **aft:** achtern.
21 **mizzen-mast:** Besanmast.

complexion, a straight back, an ascetic aspect, and, with his arms dropped, the palms of hands outwards, resembled an idol. The director, satisfied the anchor had good hold, made his way aft and sat down amongst us. We exchanged a few words lazily. Afterwards there was silence on board the yacht. For some reason or other we did not begin that game of dominoes. We felt meditative, and fit for nothing but placid staring. The day was ending in a serenity of still and exquisite brilliance. The water shone pacifically; the sky, without a speck, was a benign immensity of unstained light; the very mist on the Essex marshes was like a gauzy and radiant fabric, hung from the wooded rises inland, and draping the low shores in diaphanous folds. Only the gloom to the west, brooding over the upper reaches, became more sombre every minute, as if angered by the approach of the sun.

And at last, in its curved and imperceptible fall, the sun

1 **complexion:** Gesichtsfarbe.
  ascetic: asketisch.
3 **idol:** Götzenbild.
7 **meditative:** besinnlich.
8 **placid:** gelassen.
9 **serenity:** Klarheit.
  exquisite: außergewöhnlich.
10 **pacifically** (adv.): friedlich.
11 **immensity:** Unermeßlichkeit.
  unstained: fleckenlos.
12 **marsh:** Marschland.
  gauzy: gazeartig.
  fabric: Gewebe.
13 **to drape:** drapieren.
14 **diaphanous:** durchsichtig.
15 **reach:** Bereich.
  sombre: düster.
17 **imperceptible:** unmerklich.

sank low, and from glowing white changed to a dull red
without rays and without heat, as if about to go out
suddenly, stricken to death by the touch of that gloom
brooding over a crowd of men.

5 Forthwith a change came over the waters, and the
serenity became less brilliant but more profound. The
old river in its broad reach rested unruffled at the
decline of day, after ages of good service done to the
race that peopled its banks, spread out in the tranquil
10 dignity of a waterway leading to the uttermost ends of
the earth. We looked at the venerable stream not in the
vivid flush of a short day that comes and departs for
ever, but in the august light of abiding memories. And
indeed nothing is easier for a man who has, as the
15 phrase goes, "followed the sea" with reverence and
affection, than to evoke the great spirit of the past upon
the lower reaches of the Thames. The tidal current runs
to and fro in its unceasing service, crowded with
memories of men and ships it had borne to the rest of
20 home or to the battles of the sea. It had known and
served all the men of whom the nation is proud, from
Sir Francis Drake to Sir John Franklin[3], knights all,

---

5 **forthwith:** sogleich.
6 **profound:** tiefgründig.
7 **unruffled:** glatt.
9 **tranquil:** ruhig.
10 **uttermost:** äußerst.
11 **venerable:** ehrwürdig.
12 **vivid:** lebhaft.
   flush: Erröten.
13 **august:** erhaben.
   to abide: fortdauern, bleiben.
16 **to evoke:** beschwören.
17 **tidal current:** Gezeitenstrom.

titled and untitled – the great knights-errant of the sea. It had borne all the ships whose names are like jewels flashing in the night of time, from the *Golden Hind* returning with her round flanks full of treasure, to be
5 visited by the Queen's Highness and thus pass out of the gigantic tale, to the *Erebus* and *Terror*, bound on other conquests – and that never returned. It had known the ships and the men. They had sailed from Deptford, from Greenwich, from Erith[4] – the adventurers and the
10 settlers; kings' ships and the ships of men on 'Change; captains, admirals, the dark "interlopers" of the Eastern trade, and the commissioned "generals" of East India fleets[5]. Hunters for gold or pursuers of fame, they all had gone out on that stream, bearing the sword, and
15 often the torch, messengers of the might within the land, bearers of a spark from the sacred fire. What greatness had not floated on the ebb of that river into the mystery of an unknown earth! ... The dreams of men, the seed of commonwealths, the germs of
20 empires.
The sun set; the dusk fell on the stream, and lights began to appear along the shore. The Chapman lighthouse,

---

1 **knight-errant:** fahrender Ritter.
3 **Hind:** Hirschkuh, Hindin.
4 **flank:** Flanke.
6 **gigantic:** gigantisch, riesenhaft.
10 **men on 'Change:** Makler.
11 **interloper:** Schleichhändler.
12 **to comission:** bestallen.
15 **torch:** Fackel.
17 **ebb:** Ebbe.
19 **commonwealth:** Gemeinwesen.
   germ: Keim.
22 **lighthouse:** Leuchtturm.

7

a three-legged thing erect on a mud-flat, shone strongly. Lights of ships moved in the fairway – a great stir of lights going up and going down. And farther west on the upper reaches the place of the monstrous town was still
5 marked ominously on the sky, a brooding gloom in sunshine, a lurid glare under the stars.

"And this also," said Marlow suddenly, "has been one of the dark places of the earth."

He was the only man of us who still "followed the sea."
10 The worst that could be said of him was that he did not represent his class. He was a seaman, but he was a wanderer, too, while most seamen lead, if one may so express it, a sedentary life. Their minds are of the stay-at-home order, and their home is always with them – the
15 ship; and so is their country – the sea. One ship is very much like another, and the sea is always the same. In the immutability of their surroundings the foreign shores, the foreign faces, the changing immensity of life, glide past, veiled not by a sense of mystery but by a
20 slightly disdainful ignorance; for there is nothing mysterious to a seaman unless it be the sea itself, which is the mistress of his existence and as inscrutable as Destiny. For the rest, after his hours of work, a casual

---

1 **mud-flat:** Watt.
2 **fairway:** Fahrwasser.
4 **monstrous:** ungeheuerlich.
6 **lurid:** gespenstisch.
  glare: Glanz.
13 **sedentary:** seßhaft.
17 **immutability:** Unveränderlichkeit.
19 **to veil:** verschleiern.
20 **disdainful:** verächtlich.
22 **inscrutable:** unergründlich.
23 **casual:** gelegentlich.

8

stroll or a casual spree on shore suffices to unfold for him the secret of a whole continent, and generally he finds the secret not worth knowing. The yarns of seamen have a direct simplicity, the whole meaning of which lies within the shell of a cracked nut. But Marlow was not typical (if his propensity to spin yarns be excepted), and to him the meaning of an episode was not inside like a kernel but outside, enveloping the tale which brought it out only as a glow brings out a haze, in the likeness of one of these misty halos that sometimes are made visible by the spectral illumination of moonshine.

His remark did not seem at all surprising. It was just like Marlow. It was accepted in silence. No one took the trouble to grunt even; and presently he said, very slow –

"I was thinking of very old times, when the Romans first came here, nineteen hundred years ago[6] – the other day ... Light came out of this river since – you say Knights? Yes; but it is like a running blaze on a plain, like a flash of lightning in the clouds. We live in the flicker – may it last as long as the old earth keeps rolling! But darkness was here yesterday. Imagine the feelings of a commander of a fine – what d'ye call 'em? –

1 **stroll:** Bummel.
  spree: vergnügter Abend.
6 **typical:** typisch.
  propensity: Neigung.
8 **kernel:** Kern.
  to envelop: umhüllen.
10 **halo:** Hof, Ring.
11 **spectral:** geisterhaft.
15 **to grunt:** knurren, brummen.
22 **flicker:** Aufflackern.

trireme in the Mediterranean, ordered suddenly to the
north; run overland across the Gauls in a hurry; put in
charge of one of these craft the legionaries – a wonderful lot of handy men they must have been, too – used to
build, apparently by the hundred, in a month or two, if
we may believe what we read[7]. Imagine him here – the
very end of the world, a sea the colour of lead, a sky the
colour of smoke, a kind of ship about as rigid as a
concertina – and going up this river with stores, or
orders, or what you like. Sand-banks, marshes, forests,
savages, – precious little to eat fit for a civilized man,
nothing but Thames water to drink. No Falernian wine[8]
here, no going ashore. Here and there a military camp
lost in a wilderness, like a needle in a bundle of hay –
cold, fog, tempests, disease, exile, and death, – death
skulking in the air, in the water, in the bush. They must
have been dying like flies here. Oh, yes – he did it. Did
it very well, too, no doubt, and without thinking much
about it either, except afterwards to brag of what he had
gone through in his time, perhaps. They were men
enough to face the darkness. And perhaps he was
cheered by keeping his eye on a chance of promotion to
the fleet at Ravenna[9] by-and-by, if he had good friends
in Rome and survived the awful climate. Or think of a

---

1 **trireme:** Triere, Dreiruderer.
2 **the Gauls:** die beiden Gallien in römischer Zeit.
3 **craft:** Fahrzeug.
  legionary: Legionär.
9 **concertina:** Ziehharmonika.
11 **precious little:** kaum etwas.
15 **exile:** Verbannung.
16 **to skulk:** lauern.
19 **to brag:** prahlen.
22 **promotion:** Beförderung.

10

decent young citizen in a toga – perhaps too much dice,
you know – coming out here in the train of some
prefect, or tax-gatherer, or trader even, to mend his
fortunes. Land in a swamp, march through the woods,
5 and in some inland post feel the savagery, the utter
savagery, had closed round him, – all that mysterious
life of the wilderness that stirs in the forest, in the
jungles, in the hearts of wild men. There's no initiation
either into such mysteries. He has to live in the midst of
10 the incomprehensible, which is also detestable. And it
has a fascination, too, that goes to work upon him. The
fascination of the abomination – you know, imagine the
growing regrets, the longing to escape, the powerless
disgust, the surrender, the hate."
15 He paused.
"Mind," he began again, lifting one arm from the
elbow, the palm of the hand outwards, so that, with his
legs folded before him, he had the pose of a Buddha
preaching in European clothes and without a lotus-
20 flower[10] – "Mind, none of us would feel exactly like this.
What saves us is efficiency – the devotion to efficiency.
But these chaps were not much account, really. They
were no colonists; their administration was merely a

---

1 **dice:** Würfel, würfeln.
3 **prefect:** Präfekt.
  tax-gatherer: Steuereintreiber.
5 **savagery:** Barbarei.
8 **initiation:** Einweihung, Aufnahmezeremonie.
10 **incomprehensible:** unfaßbar, unbegreiflich.
   detestable: verabscheuungswürdig.
12 **abomination:** Abscheu, Greuel.
17 **palm:** Handfläche.
21 **efficiency:** Leistung, Tüchtigkeit.
22 **chap:** Bursche, Kerl.

11

squeeze, and nothing more, I suspect. They were conquerors, and for that you want only brute force – nothing to boast of, when you have it, since your strength is just an accident arising from the weakness of
5 others. They grabbed what they could get for the sake of what was to be got. It was just robbery with violence, aggravated murder on a great scale, and men going at it blind – as is very proper for those who tackle a darkness. The conquest of the earth, which mostly means
10 the taking it away from those who have a different complexion or slightly flatter noses than ourselves, is not a pretty thing when you look into it too much. What redeems it is the idea only. An idea at the back of it; not a sentimental pretence but an idea; and an unselfish
15 belief in the idea – something you can set up, and bow down before, and offer a sacrifice to . . ."
He broke off. Flames glided in the river, small green flames, red flames, white flames, pursuing, overtaking, joining, crossing each other – then separating slowly or
20 hastily. The traffic of the great city went on in the deepening night upon the sleepless river. We looked on, waiting patiently – there was nothing else to do till the end of the flood; but it was only after a long silence, when he said, in a hesitating voice, "I suppose you
25 fellows remember I did once turn fresh-water sailor for a bit," that we knew we were fated, before the ebb

1 **squeeze:** Ausbeutung.
2 **brute:** roh.
7 **to aggravate:** erschweren.
   scale: Maßstab.
8 **to tackle:** anpacken, in Angriff nehmen.
13 **to redeem:** erlösen, wiedergutmachen.
14 **pretence:** Vorwand.

12

began to run, to hear about one of Marlow's inconclusive experiences.

"I don't want to bother you much with what happened to me personally," he began, showing in this remark the
5 weakness of many tellers of tales who seem so often unaware of what their audience would best like to hear; "yet to understand the effect of it on me you ought to know how I got out there, what I saw, how I went up that river to the place where I first met the poor chap. It
10 was the farthest point of navigation and the culminating point of my experience. It seemed somehow to throw a kind of light on everything about me – and into my thoughts. It was sombre enough, too – and pitiful – not extraordinary in any way – not very clear either. No, not
15 very clear. And yet it seemed to throw a kind of light.

"I had then, as you remember, just returned to London after a lot of Indian Ocean, Pacific, China Seas – a regular dose of the East – six years or so[11], and I was
20 loafing about, hindering you fellows in your work and invading your homes, just as though I had got a heavenly mission to civilize you. It was very fine for a time, but after a bit I did get tired of resting. Then I began to look for a ship – I should think the hardest
25 work on earth. But the ships wouldn't even look at me. And I got tired of that game, too.

"Now when I was a little chap I had a passion for maps. I would look for hours at South America, or Africa, or Australia, and lose myself in all the glories of explora-

---

1 f. **inconclusive:** nicht überzeugend, ergebnislos.
10 **to culminate:** gipfeln.
20 **to loaf:** herumlungern.

tion. At that time there were many blank spaces on the earth, and when I saw one that looked particularly inviting on a map (but they all look that) I would put my finger on it and say, When I grow up I will go there. The
5 North Pole was one of these places, I remember. Well, I haven't been there yet, and shall not try now. The glamour's off[12]. Other places were scattered about the Equator, and in every sort of latitude all over the two hemispheres. I have been in some of them, and . . .
10 well, we won't talk about that. But there was one yet – the biggest, the most blank, so to speak – that I had a hankering after.

"True, by this time it was not a blank space any more. It had got filled since my boyhood with rivers and lakes
15 and names. It had ceased to be a blank space of delightful mystery – a white patch for a boy to dream gloriously over. It had become a place of darkness. But there was in it one river especially, a mighty big river, that you could see on the map, resembling an immense snake
20 uncoiled, with its head in the sea, its body at rest curving afar over a vast country, and its tail lost in the depths of the land. And as I looked at the map of it in a shop-window, it fascinated me as a snake would a bird – a silly little bird. Then I remembered there was a big
25 concern, a Company for trade on that river. Dash it all! I thought to myself, they can't trade without using some kind of craft on that lot of fresh water – steamboats!

---

7 **glamour:** Zauber, Glanz.
8 **latitude:** geographische Breite.
9 **hemisphere:** Hemisphäre, Erdhalbkugel.
12 **to hanker:** sich sehnen nach.
20 **to uncoil:** entrollen.
25 **concern:** Konzern.

Why shouldn't I try to get charge of one? I went on along Fleet Street, but could not shake off the idea. The snake had charmed me.

"You understand it was a Continental concern, that
5 Trading society; but I have a lot of relations living on the Continent, because it's cheap and not so nasty as it looks, they say.

"I am sorry to own I began to worry them. This was already a fresh departure for me. I was not used to get
10 things that way, you know. I always went my own road and on my own legs where I had a mind to go. I wouldn't have believed it of myself; but, then – you see – I felt somehow I must get there by hook or by crook. So I worried them. The men said 'My dear
15 fellow,' and did nothing. Then – would you believe it? – I tried the women. I, Charlie Marlow, set the women to work – to get a job. Heavens! Well, you see, the notion drove me. I had an aunt, a dear enthusiastic soul. She wrote: 'It will be delightful. I am ready to do anything,
20 anything for you. It is a glorious idea. I know the wife of a very high personage in the Administration, and also a man who has lots of influence with,' etc., etc. She was determined to make no end of fuss to get me appointed skipper of a river steamboat, if such was my
25 fancy[13].

"I got my appointment – of course; and I got it very quick. It appears the Company had received news that one of their captains had been killed in a scuffle with the

6 **nasty:** garstig.
13f. **by hook or by crook:** auf Biegen und Brechen.
21 **personage:** Persönlichkeit.
24 **skipper:** Kapitän.
28 **scuffle:** Rauferei.

natives. This was my chance, and it made me the more
anxious to go. It was only months and months afterwards, when I made the attempt to recover what was
left of the body, that I heard the original quarrel arose
5 from a misunderstanding about some hens. Yes, two
black hens. Fresleven – that was the fellow's name, a
Dane[14] – thought himself wronged somehow in the
bargain, so he went ashore and started to hammer the
chief of the village with a stick. Oh, it didn't surprise me
10 in the least to hear this, and at the same time to be told
that Fresleven was the gentlest, quietest creature that
ever walked on two legs. No doubt he was; but he had
been a couple of years already out there engaged in the
noble cause, you know, and he probably felt the need at
15 last of asserting his self-respect in some way. Therefore
he whacked the old nigger mercilessly, while a big
crowd of his people watched him, thunderstruck, till
some man – I was told the chief's son – in desperation at
hearing the old chap yell, made a tentative jab with a
20 spear at the white man – and of course it went quite easy
between the shoulderblades. Then the whole population cleared into the forest, expecting all kinds of
calamities to happen, while, on the other hand, the
steamer Fresleven commanded left also in a bad panic,
25 in charge of the engineer, I believe. Afterwards nobody
seemed to trouble much about Fresleven's remains, till I
got out and stepped into his shoes. I couldn't let it rest,

16 **to whack:** verprügeln.
17 **thunderstruck:** wie vom Donner gerührt.
19 **tentative:** zaghaft.
   jab: Stoß.
23 **calamity:** Unheil.
26 **remains:** sterbliche Überreste.

16

though; but when an opportunity offered at last to meet my predecessor, the grass growing through his ribs was tall enough to hide his bones. They were all there. The supernatural being had not been touched
5 after he fell. And the village was deserted, the huts gaped black, rotting, all askew within the fallen enclosures. A calamity had come to it, sure enough. The people had vanished. Mad terror had scattered them, men, women, and children, through the bush, and they
10 had never returned. What became of the hens I don't know either. I should think the cause of progress got them, anyhow. However, through this glorious affair I got my appointment, before I had fairly begun to hope for it.

15 "I flew around like mad to get ready, and before forty-eight hours I was crossing the Channel to show myself to my employers, and sign the contract. In a very few hours I arrived in a city that always makes me think of a whited sepulchre. Prejudice no doubt. I had no diffi-
20 culty in finding the Company's offices. It was the biggest thing in the town, and everybody I met was full of it. They were going to run an over-sea empire, and make no end of coin by trade.

"A narrow and deserted street in deep shadow, high
25 houses, innumerable windows with venetian blinds, a

---

4 **supernatural:** übernatürlich.
6 **to gape:** klaffen, gähnen.
  askew: schief.
6 f. **enclosure:** Umzäunung.
19 **sepulchre:** Grabmal.
  prejudice: Vorurteil.
25 **innumerable:** zahllos.
  venetian blind: Jalousie, Rolladen.

dead silence, grass sprouting between the stones, imposing carriage archways right and left, immense double doors standing ponderously ajar. I slipped through one of these cracks, went up a swept and
5 ungarnished staircase, as arid as a desert, and opened the first door I came to. Two women, one fat and the other slim, sat on straw-bottomed chairs, knitting black wool. The slim one got up and walked straight at me – still knitting with down-cast eyes – and only just as I
10 began to think of getting out of her way, as you would for a somnambulist, stood still, and looked up. Her dress was as plain as an umbrella-cover, and she turned round without a word and preceded me into a waiting-room. I gave my name, and looked about. Deal table in
15 the middle, plain chairs all round the walls, on one end a large shining map, marked with all the colours of a rainbow. There was a vast amount of red – good to see at any time, because one knows that some real work is done in there, a deuce of a lot of blue, a little green,
20 smears of orange, and, on the East Coast, a purple patch, to show where the jolly pioneers of progress

---

1 **to sprout:** sprießen.
2 **to impose:** beeindrucken.
  archway: Arkade, Bogengang.
3 **ponderously** (adv.): massig, gewichtig.
  ajar: angelehnt, halb offen.
5 **ungarnished:** schmucklos.
  arid: reizlos.
7 **slim:** schlank.
  straw-bottomed chair: Stuhl mit geflochtenem Sitz.
11 **somnambulist:** Schlafwandler.
14 **deal table:** Holztisch.
19 **a deuce of a lot:** verteufelt viel.
21 **pioneer:** Pionier.

drink the jolly lager-beer. However, I wasn't going into any of these. I was going into the yellow. Dead in the centre. And the river was there – fascinating – deadly – like a snake. Ough! A door opened, a whitehaired secretarial head, but wearing a compassionate expression, appeared, and a skinny forefinger beckoned me into the sanctuary. Its light was dim, and a heavy writing-desk squatted in the middle. From behind that structure came out an impression of pale plumpness in a frock-coat. The great man himself. He was five feet six, I should judge, and had his grip on the handle-end of ever so many millions. He shook hands, I fancy, murmured vaguely, was satisfied with my French. *Bon voyage.*

"In about forty-five seconds I found myself again in the waiting-room with the compassionate secretary, who, full of desolation and sympathy, made me sign some document. I believe I undertook amongst other things not to disclose any trade secrets. Well, I am not going to.

"I began to feel slightly uneasy. You know I am not used to such ceremonies, and there was something ominous in the atmosphere. It was just as though I had

---

5 **compassionate:** mitleidig.
6 **to beckon:** winken.
7 **sanctuary:** Allerheiligste.
8 **to squat:** hocken, gedrungen dastehen.
9 **structure:** Bauwerk, Gefüge.
  plumpness: Drallheit.
10 **frock-coat:** Gehrock.
13 **vaguely** (adv.): unbestimmt, unklar.
13f. **Bon voyage** (frz.): Gute Reise.
17 **desolation:** Vereinsamung, Trostlosigkeit.
19 **to disclose:** verraten.

been let into some conspiracy – I don't know – something not quite right; and I was glad to get out. In the outer room the two women knitted black wool feverishly. People were arriving, and the younger one was walking back and forth introducing them. The old one sat on her chair. Her flat cloth slippers were propped up on a foot-warmer, and a cat reposed on her lap. She wore a starched white affair on her head, had a wart on one cheek, and silver-rimmed spectacles hung on the tip of her nose. She glanced at me above the glasses. The swift and indifferent placidity of that look troubled me. Two youths with foolish and cheery countenances were being piloted over, and she threw at them the same quick glance of unconcerned wisdom. She seemed to know all about them and about me, too. An eerie feeling came over me. She seemed uncanny and fateful. Often far away there I thought of these two, guarding the door of Darkness, knitting black wool as for a warm pall, one introducing, introducing continuously to the unknown, the other scrutinizing the cheery and foolish faces with unconcerned old eyes. *Ave!* Old knitter of

---

1 **conspiracy:** Verschwörung.
6 **to prop:** stützen.
7 **to repose:** ruhen.
8 **to starch:** stärken.
  wart: Warze.
9 **silver-rimmed:** silbergefaßt.
11 **placidity:** Gelassenheit.
15 **eerie:** unheimlich.
16 **uncanny:** nicht geheuer.
19 **pall:** Decke.
20 **to scrutinize:** genau prüfen.
21 **Ave!** (lat.): Sei gegrüßt!

black wool. *Morituri te salutant.* Not many of those she looked at ever saw her again – not half, by a long way.

"There was yet a visit to the doctor. 'A simple formality,' assured me the secretary, with an air of taking an immense part in all my sorrows. Accordingly a young chap wearing his hat over the left eyebrow, some clerk I suppose, – there must have been clerks in the business, though the house was as still as a house in a city of the dead – came from somewhere upstairs, and led me forth. He was shabby and careless, with inkstains on the sleeves of his jacket, and his cravat was large and billowy, under a chin shaped like the toe of an old boot. It was a little too early for the doctor, so I proposed a drink, and thereupon he developed a vein of joviality. As we sat over our vermuths he glorified the Company's business, and by-and-by I expressed casually my surprise at him not going out there. He became very cool and collected all at once. 'I am not such a fool as I look, quoth Plato to his disciples,' he said sententiously, emptied his glass with great resolution, and we rose.

"The old doctor felt my pulse, evidently thinking of something else the while. 'Good, good for there,' he

---

1 **Morituri te salutant** (lat.): Die Todgeweihten grüßen dich.
3 f. **formality:** Formalität.
9 **upstairs:** in einem oberen Stockwerk.
10 **shabby:** schäbig. .
11 **cravat:** Halsbinde, Krawatte.
12 **billowy:** wellig, wogend.
14 **joviality:** Heiterkeit.
16 **by-and-by:** allmählich.
19 **disciple:** Schüler.
   sententiously (adv.): lehrhaft.
21 **pulse:** Pulsschlag.

mumbled, and then with a certain eagerness asked me whether I would let him measure my head. Rather surprised, I said Yes, when he produced a thing like calipers and got the dimensions back and front and every way, taking notes carefully. He was an unshaven little man in a threadbare coat like a gaberdine, with his feet in slippers, and I thought him a harmless fool. 'I always ask leave, in the interests of science, to measure the crania of those going out there,' he said. 'And when they come back, too?' I asked. 'Oh, I never see them,' he remarked; 'and, moreover, the changes take place inside, you know.' He smiled, as if at some quiet joke. 'So you are going out there. Famous. Interesting, too.' He gave me a searching glance, and made another note. 'Ever any madness in your family?' he asked, in a matter-of-fact tone. I felt very annoyed. 'Is that question in the interests of science, too?' 'It would be,' he said, without taking notice of my irritation, 'interesting for science to watch the mental changes of individuals, on the spot, but . . .' 'Are you an alienist?' I interrupted. 'Every doctor should be – a little,' answered that original, imperturbably. 'I have a little theory which you Messieurs who go out there must help me to prove. This is my share in the advantages my country shall reap

---

1 **to mumble:** murmeln.
4 **caliper:** Greifzirkel.
   dimension: Abmessung.
6 **threadbare:** abgetragen.
   gaberdine: Gabardine, Kammgarn.
9 **cranium** (lat., pl. *crania*): Schädel.
16 **matter of fact:** selbstverständlich.
18 **irritation:** Aufregung, Reizung.
20 **alienist:** Nervenarzt.
22 **imperturbably** (adv.): unerschütterlich.

22

from the possession of such a magnificent dependency. The mere wealth I leave to others. Pardon my questions, but you are the first Englishman coming under my observation ...' I hastened to assure him I was not in the least typical. 'If I were,' said I, 'I wouldn't be talking like this with you.' 'What you say is rather profound, and probably erroneous,' he said, with a laugh. 'Avoid irritation more than exposure to the sun. Adieu. How do you English say, eh? Good-bye. Ah! Good-bye. Adieu. In the tropics one must before everything keep calm.' ... He lifted a warning forefinger. ... *'Du calme, du calme. Adieu.'*

"One thing more remained to do – say good-bye to my excellent aunt. I found her triumphant. I had a cup of tea – the last decent cup of tea for many days – and in a room that most soothingly looked just as you would expect a lady's drawing-room to look, we had a long quiet chat by the fireside. In the course of these confidences it became quite plain to me I had been represented to the wife of the high dignitary, and goodness knows to how many more people besides, as an exceptional and gifted creature – a piece of good fortune for the Company – a man you don't get hold of every day. Good heavens! and I was going to take charge of a two-penny-half-penny river-steamboat with a penny whistle

1 **dependency:** abhängiges Gebiet, Kolonie.
7 **erroneous:** irrig, falsch.
8 **exposure:** Aussetzung.
10 **tropics:** die Tropen.
11f. **Du calme** (frz.): Ruhe.
14 **triumphant:** triumphierend.
16 **soothingly** (adv.): beruhigend.
20 **dignitary:** Würdenträger.
22 **gifted:** begabt.

attached! It appeared, however, I was also one of the Workers, with a capital – you know. Something like an emissary of light, something like a lower sort of apostle. There had been a lot of such rot let loose in print and
5 talk just about that time, and the excellent woman, living right in the rush of all that humbug, got carried off her feet. She talked about 'weaning those ignorant millions from their horrid ways,' till, upon my word, she made me quite uncomfortable. I ventured to hint that
10 the Company was run for profit.

"'You forget, dear Charlie, that the labourer is worthy of his hire,' she said, brightly. It's queer how out of touch with truth women are. They live in a world of their own, and there had never been anything like it,
15 and never can be. It is too beautiful altogether, and if they were to set it up it would go to pieces before the first sunset. Some confounded fact we men have been living contentedly with ever since the day of creation would start up and knock the whole thing over.

20 "After this I got embraced, told to wear flannel, be sure to write often, and so on – and I left. In the street – I don't know why – a queer feeling came to me that I was an impostor. Odd thing that I, who used to clear out for

---

3 **emissary:** Bote, Abgesandter.
   apostle: Apostel.
4 **rot:** kompletter Blödsinn.
6 **humbug:** Humbug, Unsinn.
7 **to wean:** entwöhnen, abbringen (von).
8 **horrid:** entsetzlich.
12 **hire:** Lohn.
17 **to confound:** verwirren.
20 **flannel:** Flanell.
23 **impostor:** Betrüger.
   to clear out: davonmachen, verschwinden.

24

any part of the world at twenty-four hours' notice, with less thought than most men give to the crossing of a street, had a moment – I won't say of hesitation, but of startled pause, before this commonplace affair. The best way I can explain it to you is by saying that, for a second or two, I felt, as though, instead of going to the centre of a continent, I were about to set off for the centre of the earth.

"I left in a French steamer, and she called in every blamed port they have out there[15], for, as far as I could see, the sole purpose of landing soldiers and custom-house officers. I watched the coast. Watching a coast as it slips by the ship is like thinking about an enigma. There it is before you – smiling, frowning, inviting, grand, mean, insipid, or savage, and always mute with an air of whispering, Come and find out. This one was almost featureless, as if still in the making, with an aspect of monotonous grimness. The edge of a colossal jungle, so dark-green as to be almost black, fringed with white surf, ran straight, like a ruled line, far, far away along a blue sea whose glitter was blurred by a creeping

---

3 **hesitation:** Zögern, Bedenken.
4 **commonplace:** alltäglich.
10 **blamed:** verflucht, verdammt.
11 f. **custom-house officer:** Zollbeamter.
13 **enigma:** Rätsel.
15 **insipid:** abgeschmackt.
   mute: stumm.
17 **featureless:** gesichtslos, konturlos.
18 **grimness:** Unerbittlichkeit.
   colossal: gewaltig.
19 **to fringe:** säumen.
20 **surf:** Brandung.
   ruled line: mit dem Lineal gezogene Linie.
21 **to blur:** verwischen.

mist. The sun was fierce, the land seemed to glisten and
drip with steam. Here and there grayish-whitish specks
showed up clustered inside the white surf, with a flag
flying above them perhaps. Settlements some centuries
5 old, and still no bigger than pinheads on the untouched
expanse of their background. We pounded along, stopped, landed soldiers; went on, landed custom-house
clerks to levy toll in what looked like a God-forsaken
wilderness, with a tin shed and a flag-pole lost in it;
10 landed more soldiers – to take care of the custom-house
clerks, presumably. Some, I heard, got drowned in the
surf; but whether they did or not, nobody seemed
particularly to care. They were just flung out there, and
on we went. Every day the coast looked the same, as
15 though we had not moved; but we passed various places
– trading places – with names like Gran' Bassam, Little
Popo; names that seemed to belong to some sordid
farce acted in front of a sinister back-cloth. The idleness
of a passenger, my isolation amongst all these men with
20 whom I had no point of contact, the oily and languid
sea, the uniform sombreness of the coast, seemed to

---

1 **to glisten:** gleißen, glänzen.
2 **to drip:** triefen.
   speck: Fleck.
5 **pinhead:** Nadelkopf.
6 **expanse:** Weite.
   we pounded along: (fig.) das Schiff stampfte weiter.
8 **to levy toll:** Steuern erheben.
17 **sordid:** schmutzig.
18 **farce:** Posse, Farce.
   sinister: unheilvoll, böse.
   idleness: Trägheit.
19 **isolation:** Isolation.
20 **languid:** träge.

26

keep me away from the truth of things, within the toil of a
mournful and senseless delusion. The voice of the surf
heard now and then was a positive pleasure, like the
speech of a brother. It was something natural, that had its
5 reason, that had a meaning. Now and then a boat from
the shore gave one a momentary contact with reality. It
was paddled by black fellows. You could see from afar
the white of their eyeballs glistening. They shouted,
sang; their bodies streamed with perspiration; they had
10 faces like grotesque masks – these chaps; but they had
bone, muscle, a wild vitality, an intense energy of
movement, that was as natural and true as the surf along
their coast. They wanted no excuse for being there.
They were a great comfort to look at. For a time I would
15 feel I belonged still to a world of straightforward facts;
but the feeling would not last long. Something would
turn up to scare it away. Once, I remember, we came
upon a man-of-war anchored off the coast. There wasn't
even a shed there, and she was shelling the bush. It
20 appears the French had one of their wars going on thereabouts. Her ensign dropped limp like a rag; the muzzles

2 **delusion:** Verblendung.
6 **momentary:** vorübergehend.
7 **to paddle:** rudern, paddeln.
8 **eyeball:** Augapfel.
9 **perspiration:** Schweiß.
10 **grotesque:** grotesk.
   mask: Maske.
11 **vitality:** Lebenskraft.
18 **man-of-war:** Kriegsschiff.
19 **shed:** Schuppen.
21 **ensign:** Fahne.
   limp: schlaff.
   muzzle: Mündung.

of the long six-inch guns stuck out all over the low hull;
the greasy, slimy swell swung her up lazily and let her
down, swaying her thin masts. In the empty immensity
of earth, sky, and water, there she was, incomprehen-
5 sible, firing into a continent. Pop, would go one of the
six-inch guns; a small flame would dart and vanish, a
little white smoke would disappear, a tiny projectile
would give a feeble screech – and nothing happened.
Nothing could happen. There was a touch of insanity
10 in the proceeding, a sense of lugubrious drollery in the
sight; and it was not dissipated by somebody on board
assuring me earnestly there was a camp of natives – he
called them enemies! – hidden out of sight somewhere.

15 "We gave her her letters (I heard the men in that lonely
ship were dying of fever at the rate of three a-day) and
went on. We called at some more places with farcical
names[16], where the merry dance of death and trade
goes on in a still and earthy atmosphere as of an
20 overheated catacomb; all along the formless coast bor-
dered by dangerous surf, as if Nature herself had tried

---

2 **greasy:** schmierig, ölig.
  swell: Dünung.
3 **to sway:** schaukeln, schwanken.
6 **to dart:** hervorschießen.
7 **projectile:** Projektil, Geschoß.
8 **screech:** Schrei.
9 **insanity:** Wahnsinn.
10 **proceeding:** Verfahren.
  lugubrious: kläglich, erbärmlich.
  drollery: Komik.
11 **to dissipate:** zerstreuen.
17 **farcical:** farcenhaft, absurd, lächerlich.
20 **catacomb:** Katakombe.

28

to ward off intruders; in and out of rivers, streams of
death in life, whose banks were rotting into mud, whose
waters, thickened into slime, invaded the contorted
mangroves, that seemed to writhe at us in the extremity
5 of an impotent despair. Nowhere did we stop long
enough to get a particularized impression, but the general sense of vague and oppressive wonder grew upon
me. It was like a weary pilgrimage amongst hints for
nightmares.

10 "It was upward of thirty days before I saw the mouth of
the big river. We anchored off the seat of the government[17]. But my work would not begin till some two
hundred miles farther on. So as soon as I could I made a
start for a place thirty miles higher up.

15 "I had my passage on a little sea-going steamer. Her
captain was a Swede, and knowing me for a seaman,
invited me on the bridge. He was a young man, lean,
fair, and morose, with lanky hair and a shuffling gait.
As we left the miserable little wharf, he tossed his head
20 contemptuously at the shore. 'Been living there?' he

1 **to ward off:** abwehren.
  intruder: Eindringling.
3 **contorted:** gewunden, verdreht.
4 **to writhe:** sich winden.
5 **impotent:** unvermögend, machtlos.
6 **particularized:** ins einzelne gehend.
7 **vague:** unbestimmt, unklar.
9 **nightmare:** Alptraum.
15 **sea-going:** seetüchtig.
18 **morose:** mürrisch.
  lanky: strähnig.
  to shuffle: schlurfen.
  gait: Gangart.
19 **wharf:** Kai.
20 **contemptuously** (adv.): verächtlich.

asked. I said, 'Yes.' 'Fine lot these government chaps –
are they not?' he went on, speaking English with great
precision and considerable bitterness. 'It is funny what
some people will do for a few francs a month. I wonder
5 what becomes of that kind when it goes up country?' I said
to him I expected to see that soon. 'So-o-o!' he exclaimed.
He shuffled athwart, keeping one eye ahead vigilantly.
'Don't be too sure,' he continued. 'The other day I took up
a man who hanged himself on the road. He was a Swede,
10 too.' 'Hanged himself! Why, in God's name?' I cried. He
kept on looking out watchfully. 'Who knows? The sun
too much for him, or the country perhaps.'

"At last we opened a reach. A rocky cliff appeared,
mounds of turned-up earth by the shore, houses on a
15 hill, others with iron roofs, amongst a waste of excava-
tions, or hanging to the declivity. A continuous noise of
the rapids above hovered over this scene of inhabited
devastation. A lot of people, mostly black and naked,
moved about like ants. A jetty projected into the river.
20 A blinding sunlight drowned all this at times in a sudden
recrudescence of glare. 'There's your Company's sta-

---

4 **franc:** Belgischer Franc.
7 **athwart:** quer über.
  vigilantly (adv.): wachsam.
14 **mound:** Wall.
15 f. **excavation:** Ausschachtung.
16 **declivity:** Abhang.
17 **rapid:** Stromschnelle.
  to hover: schweben über.
18 **devastation:** Wüstenei.
19 **ant:** Ameise.
  jetty: Mole.
  to project: hineinragen.
21 **recrudescence:** Wiederausbrechen.

tion[18],' said the Swede, pointing to three wooden barrack-like structures on the rocky slope. 'I will send your things up. Four boxes did you say? So. Farewell.'

"I came upon a boiler wallowing in the grass, then found a path leading up the hill. It turned aside for the boulders, and also for an undersized railway-truck lying there on its back with its wheels in the air. One was off. The thing looked as dead as the carcass of some animal. I came upon more pieces of decaying machinery, a stack of rusty rails. To the left a clump of trees made a shady spot, where dark things seemed to stir feebly. I blinked, the path was steep. A horn tooted to the right, and I saw the black people run. A heavy and dull detonation shook the ground, a puff of smoke came out of the cliff, and that was all. No change appeared on the face of the rock. They were building a railway. The cliff was not in the way or anything; but this objectless blasting was all the work going on.

"A slight clinking behind me made me turn my head. Six black men advanced in a file, toiling up the path. They walked erect and slow, balancing small baskets

---

1 f. **barrack:** Baracke, Kaserne.
4 **boiler:** Dampfkessel.
  to wallow: sich wälzen.
6 **boulder:** Felsblock.
8 **carcass:** Kadaver.
10 **clump:** Gruppe.
11 **to blink:** blinzeln.
12 **to toot:** tuten, blasen.
13 **detonation:** Detonation, Explosion.
17 **objectless:** ziellos.
  blasting: Sprengen.
19 **clinking:** Klirren.
20 **in a file:** hintereinander.

full of earth on their heads, and the clink kept time with their footsteps. Black rags were wound round their loins, and the short ends behind waggled to and fro like tails. I could see every rib, the joints of their limbs were like knots in a rope; each had an iron collar on his neck, and all were connected together with a chain whose bights swung between them, rhythmically clinking. Another report from the cliff made me think suddenly of that ship of war I had seen firing into a continent. It was the same kind of ominous voice; but these men could by no stretch of imagination be called enemies. They were called criminals, and the outraged law, like the bursting shells, had come to them, an insoluble mystery from the sea. All their meagre breasts panted together, the violently dilated nostrils quivered, the eyes stared stonily up-hill. They passed me within six inches, without a glance, with that complete, deathlike indifference of unhappy savages. Behind this raw matter one of the reclaimed, the product of the new forces at work, strolled despondently, carrying a rifle by its middle. He had a uniform jacket with one button off,

---

3 **loin:** Lende.
  to waggle to and fro: hin- und herwackeln.
7 **bight:** Krümmung, durchhängender Teil.
  rhythmically (adv.): rhythmisch.
13 **insoluble:** unlösbar.
14 **meagre:** mager, dürr.
  to pant: keuchen.
15 **dilated:** gebläht, gedehnt.
  to quiver: zittern.
16 **stonily** (adv.): versteinert.
19 **to reclaim:** bekehren.
20 **to stroll:** schlendern.
  despondently (adv.): verdrossen.

and seeing a white man on the path, hoisted his weapon
to his shoulder with alacrity. This was simple prudence,
white men being so much alike at a distance that he
could not tell who I might be. He was speedily reas-
5 sured, and with a large, white, rascally grin, and a
glance at his charge, seemed to take me into partnership
in his exalted trust. After all, I also was a part of the
great cause of these high and just proceedings.

"Instead of going up, I turned and descended to the
10 left. My idea was to let that chain-gang get out of
sight before I climbed the hill. You know I am not
particularly tender; I've had to strike and to fend off.
I've had to resist and to attack sometimes – that's only
one way of resisting – without counting the exact cost,
15 according to the demands of such sort of life as I had
blundered into. I've seen the devil of violence, and the
devil of greed, and the devil of hot desire; but, by all
the stars! these were strong, lusty, red-eyed devils,
that swayed and drove men – men, I tell you. But as
20 I stood on this hillside, I foresaw that in the blinding
sunshine of that land I would become acquainted with
a flabby, pretending, weak-eyed devil of a rapacious

---

1 **to hoist:** hochziehen, hieven.
2 **alacrity:** Eifer.
  prudence: Vorsicht.
5 **rascally:** schurkisch.
7 **exalted:** erhaben.
10 **chain-gang:** Kettensträflinge.
16 **to blunder into s.th.:** zufällig auf etwas stoßen, in etwas hineinstol-
  pern.
17 **greed:** Habgier.
21 **to become acquainted with s.o./s.th.:** jdn./etwas kennenlernen.
22 **flabby:** schlaff.
  rapacious: raubgierig.

and pitiless folly. How insidious he could be, too, I was only to find out several months later and a thousand miles farther. For a moment I stood appalled, as though by a warning. Finally I descended the hill, obliquely,
5 towards the trees I had seen.

"I avoided a vast artificial hole somebody had been digging on the slope, the purpose of which I found it impossible to divine. It wasn't a quarry or a sand-pit, anyhow. It was just a hole. It might have been
10 connected with the philanthropic desire of giving the criminals something to do. I don't know. Then I near-ly fell into a very narrow ravine, almost no more than a scar in the hillside. I discovered that a lot of imported drainage-pipes for the settlement had been tumbled
15 in there. There wasn't one that was not broken. It was a wanton smash-up. At last I got under the trees. My purpose was to stroll into the shade for a moment; but no sooner within than it seemed to me I had stepped into the gloomy circle of some Inferno[19].
20 The rapids were near, and an uninterrupted, uniform,

---

1 **pitiless:** unbarmherzig.
  insidious: heimtückisch, hinterhältig.
3 **appalled:** entsetzt, erschreckt.
4 **obliquely** (adv.): schräg.
8 **quarry:** Steinbruch.
8f. **sandpit:** Sandgrube.
10 **philantropic:** menschenfreundlich.
12 **ravine:** Hohlweg, Schlucht.
13 **scar:** Narbe, Schramme.
14 **drainage-pipe:** Abflußrohr.
  to tumble: durcheinander-, hinwerfen.
16 **wanton:** mutwillig.
  smash-up: Zerstörung.
19 **Inferno** (ital.): Hölle.

34

headlong, rushing noise filled the mournful stillness of the grove, where not a breath stirred, not a leaf moved, with a mysterious sound – as though the tearing pace of the launched earth had suddenly become
5 audible.

"Black shapes crouched, lay, sat between the trees leaning against the trunks, clinging to the earth, half coming out, half effaced within the dim light, in all the attitudes of pain, abandonment, and despair. Another
10 mine on the cliff went off, followed by a slight shudder of the soil under my feet. The work was going on. The work! And this was the place where some of the helpers had withdrawn to die.

"They were dying slowly – it was very clear. They were
15 not enemies, they were not criminals, they were nothing earthly now, – nothing but black shadows of disease and starvation, lying confusedly in the greenish gloom. Brought from all the recesses of the coast in all the legality of time contracts, lost in uncongenial surround-
20 ings, fed on unfamiliar food, they sickened, became inefficient, and were then allowed to crawl away and

---

1 **mournful:** traurig.
2 **grove:** Gehölz, Hain.
4 **to launch:** ins Wasser lassen.
6 **to crouch:** sich ducken.
8 **to efface:** auslöschen.
9 **abandonment:** Verlassenheit.
10 **mine:** Mine, Sprengsatz.
   shudder: Erbeben.
17 **starvation:** Hunger.
18 **recess:** Winkel.
19 **legality:** Rechtmäßigkeit.
   uncongenial: ungünstig, ungeeignet.
21 **inefficient:** unbrauchbar.

rest. These moribund shapes were free as air – and
nearly as thin. I began to distinguish the gleam of the
eyes under the trees. Then, glancing down, I saw a face
near my hand. The black bones reclined at full length
5 with one shoulder against the tree, and slowly the
eyelids rose and the sunken eyes looked up at me,
enormous and vacant, a kind of blind, white flicker in
the depths of the orbs, which died out slowly. The man
seemed young – almost a boy – but you know with them
10 it's hard to tell. I found nothing else to do but to offer
him one of my good Swede's ship's biscuits I had in my
pocket. The fingers closed slowly on it and held – there
was no other movement and no other glance. He had
tied a bit of white worsted round his neck – Why?
15 Where did he get it? Was it a badge – an ornament – a
charm – a propitiatory act? Was there any idea at all
connected with it? It looked startling round his black
neck, this bit of white thread from beyond the seas.

"Near the same tree two more bundles of acute angles
20 sat with their legs drawn up. One, with his chin propped
on his knees, stared at nothing, in an intolerable and
appalling manner: his brother phantom rested its fore-

---

1 **moribund:** todgeweiht.
4 **to recline:** lehnen an.
7 **vacant:** leer.
8 **orb:** Augapfel.
11 **ship's biscuit:** Schiffszwieback.
14 **worsted:** Wollfaden.
15 **badge:** Abzeichen.
16 **charm:** Zauber.
   propitiatory: sühnend.
19 **acute angle:** spitzer Winkel.
21 **intolerable:** unerträglich.
22 **phantom:** Phantom, Trugbild.

head, as if overcome with a great weariness; and all about others were scattered in every pose of contorted collapse, as in some picture of a massacre or a pestilence. While I stood horror-struck, one of these creatures rose to his hands and knees, and went off on all-fours towards the river to drink. He lapped out of his hand, then sat up in the sunlight, crossing his shins in front of him, and after a time let his woolly head fall on his breastbone.

"I didn't want any more loitering in the shade, and I made haste towards the station. When near the buildings I met a white man, in such an unexpected elegance of get-up that in the first moment I took him for a sort of vision. I saw a high starched collar, white cuffs, a light alpaca jacket, snowy trousers, a clear necktie, and varnished boots. No hat. Hair parted, brushed, oiled, under a green-lined parasol held in a big white hand. He was amazing, and had a penholder behind his ear.

"I shook hands with this miracle, and I learned he was the Company's chief accountant, and that all the book-keeping was done at this station. He had come out for a moment, he said, 'to get a breath of fresh air.' The expression sounded wonderfully odd, with its suggestion of sedentary desk-life. I wouldn't have mentioned

---

3 **collapse:** Zusammenbruch.
 massacre: Gemetzel, Massaker.
 6 **to lap:** lecken.
 7 **shin:** Schienbein.
10 **loitering:** Umherschlendern.
13 **get-up:** Ausstaffierung.
14 **cuff:** Manschette.
16 **varnished boots:** Lackstiefel.
17 **parasol:** Sonnenschirm.
24 **sedentary desk-life:** (Schreibtisch-)Tätigkeit.

the fellow to you at all, only it was from his lips that I
first heard the name of the man who is so indissolubly
connected with the memories of that time. Moreover, I
respected the fellow. Yes; I respected his collars, his
5 vast cuffs, his brushed hair. His appearance was certainly that of a hairdresser's dummy; but in the great
demoralization of the land he kept up his appearance.
That's backbone. His starched collars and got-up shirt-
fronts were achievements of character. He had been out
10 nearly three years; and, later, I could not help asking
him how he managed to sport such linen. He had just
the faintest blush, and said modestly, 'I've been teaching one of the native women about the station. It was
difficult. She had a distaste for the work.' Thus this man
15 had verily accomplished something. And he was
devoted to his books, which were in applepie order.
"Everything else in the station was in a muddle, –
heads, things, buildings. Strings of dusty niggers with
splay feet arrived and departed; a stream of manufac-
20 tured goods, rubbishy cottons, beads, and brass-wire set
into the depths of darkness, and in return came a
precious trickle of ivory.
"I had to wait in the station for ten days – an eternity. I
lived in a hut in the yard, but to be out of the chaos I

2 **indissolubly** (adv.): unlöslich.
6 **hairdresser's dummy:** Friseurpuppe.
7 **demoralization:** Verwahrlosung.
8 **backbone:** Rückgrat.
8f. **shirt-front:** Hemdbrust.
11 **to sport s.th.:** sich sehen lassen mit etwas.
17 **muddle:** Durcheinander.
19 **splay foot:** Spreizfuß.
20 **brass-wire:** Messingdraht.
22 **ivory:** Elfenbein.

38

would sometimes get into the accountant's office. It was
built of horizontal planks, and so badly put together
that, as he bent over his high desk, he was barred from
neck to heels with narrow strips of sunlight. There was
no need to open the big shutter to see. It was hot there,
too; big flies buzzed fiendishly, and did not sting, but
stabbed. I sat generally on the floor, while, of faultless
appearance (and even slightly scented), perching on a
high stool, he wrote, he wrote. Sometimes he stood up
for exercise. When a truckle-bed with a sick man (some
invalid agent from up-country) was put in there, he
exhibited a gentle annoyance. 'The groans of this sick
person,' he said, 'distract my attention. And without
that it is extremely difficult to guard against clerical
errors in this climate.'

"One day he remarked, without lifting his head, 'In the
interior you will no doubt meet Mr. Kurtz[20].' On my
asking who Mr. Kurtz was, he said he was a first-class
agent; and seeing my disappointment at this information, he added slowly, laying down his pen, 'He is a very

---

2 **plank:** Bohle.
3 **to bar:** mit Streifen versehen.
5 **shutter:** Fensterladen.
6 **to buzz:** summen.
  fiendishly (adv.): teuflisch.
7 **to stab:** zustoßen, durchbohren.
  faultless: fehlerfrei.
8 **scented:** parfümiert.
  to perch: hocken.
10 **truckle-bed:** niedriges Rollbett.
11 **invalid:** Kranker.
12 **annoyance:** Verärgerung.
13 **to distract:** ablenken.
14f. **clerical error:** Schreibfehler.

remarkable person.' Further questions elicited from him that Mr. Kurtz was at present in charge of a trading post, a very important one, in the true ivory-country, at 'the very bottom of there. Sends in as much ivory as all the others put together . . .' He began to write again. The sick man was too ill to groan. The flies buzzed in a great peace.

"Suddenly there was a growing murmur of voices and a great tramping of feet. A caravan had come in. A violent babble of uncouth sounds burst out on the other side of the planks. All the carriers were speaking together, and in the midst of the uproar the lamentable voice of the chief agent was heard 'giving it up' tearfully for the twentieth time that day. . . . He rose slowly. 'What a frightful row,' he said. He crossed the room gently to look at the sick man, and returning, said to me, 'He does not hear.' 'What! Dead?' I asked, startled. 'No, not yet,' he answered, with great composure. Then, alluding with a toss of the head to the tumult in the station-yard. 'When one has got to make correct entries, one comes to hate those savages – hate them to the death.' He remained thoughtful for a moment. 'When you see Mr. Kurtz,' he went on, 'tell him from me that everything here' – he glanced at the desk – 'is

---

1 **to elicit:** entlocken.
9 **tramping:** Getrampel.
  caravan: Karawane.
10 **babble:** Geplapper.
  uncouth: ungeschlacht, grob.
12 **uproar:** Aufruhr, Tumult.
  lamentable: kläglich.
15 **row:** Streit.
18 **composure:** Gelassenheit.
19 **to allude to:** auf etwas anspielen.

40

very satisfactory. I don't like to write to him – with those messengers of ours you never know who may get hold of your letter – at that Central Station.' He stared at me for a moment with his mild, bulging eyes. 'Oh, he will go far, very far,' he began again. 'He will be a somebody in the Administration before long. They, above – the Council in Europe, you know – mean him to be.'

"He turned to his work. The noise outside had ceased, and presently in going out I stopped at the door. In the steady buzz of flies the homeward-bound agent was lying flushed and insensible; the other, bent over his books, was making correct entries of perfectly correct transactions; and fifty feet below the doorstep I could see the still tree-tops of the grove of death.

"Next day I left that station at last, with a caravan of sixty men, for a two-hundred-mile tramp.

"No use telling you much about that. Paths, paths, everywhere; a stamped-in network of paths spreading over the empty land, through long grass, through burnt grass, through thickets, down and up chilly ravines, up and down stony hills ablaze with heat; and a solitude, a solitude, nobody, not a hut. The population had cleared out a long time ago. Well, if a lot of mysterious niggers armed with all kinds of fearful weapons suddenly took to travelling on the road between Deal and

---

12 **to flush:** erröten.
   insensible: bewußtlos.
14 **transaction:** Geschäftsvorgang.
19 **network:** Netz.
21 **thicket:** Dickicht.
22 **ablaze:** lodernd.
23 **solitude:** Einsamkeit.

Gravesend[21], catching the yokels right and left to carry heavy loads for them, I fancy every farm and cottage thereabouts would get empty very soon. Only here the dwellings were gone, too. Still I passed through several abandoned villages. There's something pathetically childish in the ruins of grass walls. Day after day, with the stamp and shuffle of sixty pair of bare feet behind me, each pair under a 60-lb. load. Camp, cook, sleep, strike camp, march. Now and then a carrier dead in harness, at rest in the long grass near the path, with an empty water-gourd and his long staff lying by his side. A great silence around and above. Perhaps on some quiet night the tremor of far-off drums, sinking, swelling, a tremor vast, faint; a sound weird, appealing, suggestive, and wild – and perhaps with as profound a meaning as the sound of bells in a Christian country. Once a white man in an unbuttoned uniform, camping on the path with an armed escort of lank Zanzibaris[22], very hospitable and festive – not to say drunk. Was looking after the upkeep of the road he declared. Can't say I saw any road or any upkeep, unless the body of a middle-aged negro, with a bullet-hole in the forehead, upon which I

---

1 **yokel:** Bauernlümmel.
5 **pathetically** (adv.): pathetisch.
10 **harness:** Geschirr.
11 **gourd:** Kürbisflasche.
13 **tremor:** Beben.
14 **weird:** unheimlich.
18 **escort:** Eskorte.
   lank: hager.
18 f. **hospitable:** gastfreundlich.
19 **festive:** festlich.
21 **upkeep:** Instandhaltung.
22 **bullet:** Kugel.

absolutely stumbled three miles farther on, may be considered as a permanent improvement. I had a white companion, too, not a bad chap, but rather too fleshy and with the exasperating habit of fainting on the hot
5 hillsides, miles away from the least bit of shade and water. Annoying, you know, to hold your own coat like a parasol over a man's head while he is coming-to. I couldn't help asking him once what he meant by coming there at all. 'To make money, of course. What do you
10 think?' he said, scornfully. Then he got fever, and had to be carried in a hammock slung under a pole. As he weighed sixteen stone I had no end of rows with the carriers. They jibbed, ran away, sneaked off with their loads in the night – quite a mutiny. So, one evening, I
15 made a speech in English with gestures, not one of which was lost to the sixty pairs of eyes before me, and the next morning I started the hammock off in front all right. An hour afterwards I came upon the whole concern wrecked in a bush – man, hammock, groans,
20 blankets, horrors. The heavy pole had skinned his poor nose. He was very anxious for me to kill somebody, but there wasn't the shadow of a carrier near. I remember the old doctor, – 'It would be interesting for science to watch the mental changes of individuals, on the spot.' I
25 felt I was becoming scientifically interesting. However, all that is to no purpose. On the fifteenth day I came in sight of the big river again, and hobbled into the Central

---

4 **to exasperate:** erbittern.
7 **to come to:** aus der Bewußtlosigkeit erwachen.
11 **hammock:** Hängematte.
13 **to jib:** bocken, störrisch sein.
14 **mutiny:** Meuterei.
27 **to hobble:** humpeln, hinken.

43

Station[23]. It was on a back water surrounded by scrub and forest, with a pretty border of smelly mud on one side, and on the three others enclosed by a crazy fence of rushes. A neglected gap was all the gate it had, and the first glance at the place was enough to let you see the flabby devil was running that show. White men with long staves in their hands appeared languidly from amongst the buildings, strolling up to take a look at me, and then retired out of sight somewhere. One of them, a stout, excitable chap with black moustache, informed me with great volubility and many digressions, as soon as I told him who I was, that my steamer was at the bottom of the river[24]. I was thunderstruck. What, how, why? Oh, it was 'all right.' The 'manager himself' was there. All quite correct. 'Everybody had behaved splendidly! splendidly!' – 'you must,' he said in agitation, 'go and see the general manager at once. He is waiting!'

"I did not see the real significance of that wreck at once. I fancy I see it now, but I am not sure – not at all. Certainly the affair was too stupid – when I think of it – to be altogether natural. Still . . . But at the moment it presented itself simply as a confounded nuisance. The steamer was sunk. They had started two days before in a sudden hurry up the river with the manager on board, in

---

4 **rush:** Binse.
  gap: Lücke, Spalte.
10 **moustache:** Schnurrbart.
11 **volubility:** Zungenfertigkeit, Redefluß.
  digression: Abschweifung.
19 **significance:** Bedeutung.
23 **confounded:** verwünscht.
  nuisance: Ärgernis, Mißgeschick.

charge of some volunteer skipper, and before they had
been out three hours they tore the bottom out of her on
stones, and she sank near the south bank. I asked
myself what I was to do there, now my boat was lost. As
5 a matter of fact, I had plenty to do in fishing my
command out of the river. I had to set about it the very
next day. That, and the repairs when I brought the
pieces to the station, took some months.

"My first interview with the manager was curious. He
10 did not ask me to sit down after my twenty-mile walk
that morning. He was commonplace in complexion, in
feature, in manners, and in voice. He was of middle size
and of ordinary build. His eyes, of the usual blue, were
perhaps remarkably cold, and he certainly could make
15 his glance fall on one as trenchant and heavy as an axe.
But even at these times the rest of his person seemed to
disclaim the intention. Otherwise there was only an indefinable, faint expression of his lips, something stealthy
– a smile – not a smile – I remember it, but I can't
20 explain. It was unconscious, this smile was, though just
after he had said something it got intensified for an
instant. It came at the end of his speeches like a seal
applied on the words to make the meaning of the
commonest phrase appear absolutely inscrutable. He

---

1 **volunteer:** Freiwilliger.
7 **repairs:** Ausbesserung, Instandsetzung.
13 **build:** Körperbau, Figur.
15 **trenchant:** schneidend.
17 **to disclaim:** verleugnen.
17 f. **indefinable:** unbestimmbar.
18 **stealthy:** verstohlen.
21 **to intensify:** verstärken.
24 **inscrutable:** unergründlich.

was a common trader, from his youth up employed in these parts – nothing more. He was obeyed, yet he inspired neither love nor fear, nor even respect. He inspired uneasiness. That was it! Uneasiness. Not a
5 definite mistrust – just uneasiness – nothing more. You have no idea how effective such a ... a ... faculty can be. He had no genius for organizing, for initiative, or for order even. That was evident in such things as the deplorable state of the station. He had no learning, and
10 no intelligence. His position had come to him – why? Perhaps because he was never ill ... He had served three terms of three years out there ... Because triumphant health in the general rout of constitutions is a kind of power in itself. When he went home on leave he
15 rioted on a large scale – pompously. Jack[25] ashore – with a difference – in externals only. This one could gather from his casual talk. He originated nothing, he could keep the routine going – that's all. But he was great. He was great by this little thing that it was
20 impossible to tell what could control such a man. He never gave that secret away. Perhaps there was nothing within him. Such a suspicion made one pause – for out

---

4 **uneasiness:** Unbehagen.
5 **definite:** bestimmt.
  mistrust: Mißtrauen.
6 **faculty:** Eigenschaft.
7 **initiative:** Initiative, Anstoßgeben.
9 **deplorable:** erbärmlich.
13 **rout:** Niederlage.
  constitution: Konstitution, Gesundheitszustand.
15 **to riot:** schwelgen.
  pompously (adv.): großspurig, pompös.
16 **externals:** das Äußere.
17 **to originate:** hervorbringen, ins Leben rufen.

there there were no external checks. Once when various
tropical diseases had laid low almost every 'agent' in
the station, he was heard to say, 'Men who come out
here should have no entrails.' He sealed the utterance
5 with that smile of his, as though it had been a door
opening into a darkness he had in his keeping. You
fancied you had seen things – but the seal was on. When
annoyed at meal-times by the constant quarrels of the
white men about precedence, he ordered an immense
10 round table to be made, for which a special house
had to be built. This was the station's mess-room. Where
he sat was the first place – the rest were nowhere.
One felt this to be his unalterable conviction. He was
neither civil nor uncivil. He was quiet. He allowed his
15 'boy' – an overfed young negro from the coast – to
treat the white men, under his very eyes, with provoking
insolence.

"He began to speak as soon as he saw me. I had been
very long on the road. He could not wait. Had to start
20 without me. The up-river stations had to be relieved.
There had been so many delays already that he did
not know who was dead and who was alive, and how
they got on – and so on, and so on. He paid no attention to my explanations, and, playing with a stick of

1 **check:** Hemmnis.
2 **to lay low:** niederstrecken.
4 **entrails:** Eingeweide.
  utterance: Äußerung.
9 **precedence:** Rangordnung, Vorrang.
11 **mess-room:** Kantine.
13 **unalterable:** unabänderlich.
17 **insolence:** Unverschämtheit.
20 **to relieve:** ablösen.

sealing-wax, repeated several times that the situation was 'very grave, very grave.' There were rumours that a very important station was in jeopardy, and its chief, Mr. Kurtz, was ill. Hoped it was not true. Mr. Kurtz was . . .
5 I felt weary and irritable. Hang Kurtz, I thought. I interrupted him by saying I had heard of Mr. Kurtz on the coast. 'Ah! So they talk of him down there,' he murmured to himself. Then he began again, assuring me Mr. Kurtz was the best agent he had, an exceptional
10 man, of the greatest importance to the Company; therefore I could understand his anxiety. He was, he said, 'very, very uneasy.' Certainly he fidgeted on his chair a good deal, exclaimed, 'Ah, Mr. Kurtz!' broke the stick of sealing-wax and seemed dumbfounded by the acci-
15 dent. Next thing he wanted to know 'how long it would take to' . . . I interrupted him again. Being hungry, you know, and kept on my feet, too, I was getting savage. 'How could I tell?' I said. 'I hadn't even seen the wreck yet – some months, no doubt.' All this talk seemed to
20 me so futile. 'Some months,' he said. 'Well, let us say three months before we can make a start. Yes. That ought to do the affair.' I flung out of his hut (he lived all alone in a clay hut with a sort of verandah) muttering to myself my opinion of him. He was a chattering idiot.
25 Afterwards I took it back when it was borne in upon me

---

1 **sealing-wax:** Siegellack.
2 **rumour:** Gerücht.
3 **jeopardy:** Gefahr.
5 **irritable:** gereizt.
12 **to fidget:** herumzappeln.
14 **dumbfounded:** sprachlos, zutiefst betroffen.
20 **futile:** nichtig, vergeblich.
22 **to fling:** eilen, stürzen.

startlingly with what extreme nicety he had estimated the time requisite for the 'affair.'

"I went to work the next day, turning, so to speak, my back on that station. In that way only it seemed to me I
5 could keep my hold on the redeeming facts of life. Still, one must look about sometimes; and then I saw this station, these men strolling aimlessly about in the sunshine of the yard. I asked myself sometimes what it all meant. They wandered here and there with their absurd
10 long staves in their hands, like a lot of faithless pilgrims bewitched inside a rotten fence. The word 'ivory' rang in the air, was whispered, was sighed. You would think they were praying to it. A taint of imbecile rapacity blew through it all, like a whiff from some corpse. By
15 Jove! I've never seen anything so unreal in my life. And outside, the silent wilderness surrounding this cleared speck on the earth struck me as something great and invincible, like evil or truth, waiting patiently for the passing away of this fantastic invasion.

20 "Oh, these months! Well, never mind. Various things happened. One evening a grass shed full of calico, cotton prints, beads, and I don't know what else, burst into a blaze so suddenly that you would have thought the earth had opened to let an avenging fire consume all

---

2 **requisite:** erforderlich.
11 **to bewitch:** behexen.
13 **imbecile:** schwachsinnig.
 rapacity: Habgier.
14 **whiff:** Aasgeruch.
18 **invincible:** unbesiegbar.
21 **calico:** Kattun.
22 **cotton print:** Baumwolldruck.
 bead: Glasperle.
24 **to avenge:** rächen.

49

that trash. I was smoking my pipe quietly by my dismantled steamer, and saw them all cutting capers in the light, with their arms lifted high, when the stout man with moustaches came tearing down to the river, a tin
5 pail in his hand, assured me that everybody was 'behaving splendidly, splendidly,' dipped about a quart of water and tore back again. I noticed there was a hole in the bottom of his pail.

"I strolled up. There was no hurry. You see the thing
10 had gone off like a box of matches. It had been hopeless from the very first. The flame had leaped high, driven everybody back, lighted up everything – and collapsed. The shed was already a heap of embers glowing fiercely. A nigger was being beaten near by. They said he had
15 caused the fire in some way; be that as it may, he was screeching most horribly. I saw him, later, for several days, sitting in a bit of shade looking very sick and trying to recover himself: afterwards he arose and went out – and the wilderness without a sound took
20 him into its bosom again. As I approached the glow from the dark I found myself at the back of two men, talking. I heard the name of Kurtz pronounced, then the words, 'take advantage of this unfortunate accident.' One of the men was the manager. I wished him a good
25 evening. 'Did you ever see anything like it – eh? it is

1 **trash:** Abfall, Plunder.
1f. **to dismantle:** auseinandernehmen, zerlegen.
2 **to cut capers:** Sprünge machen.
4 **to tear:** rasen, eilen.
6 **quart:** Quart, = 1,136 l.
12 **to collapse:** zusammenfallen.
13 **embers:** glühende Asche.
16 **to screech:** kreischen.

incredible,' he said, and walked off. The other man remained. He was a first-class agent, young, gentlemanly, a bit reserved, with a forked little beard and a hooked nose. He was stand-offish with the other agents,
5 and they on their side said he was the manager's spy upon them. As to me, I had hardly ever spoken to him before. We got into talk, and by-and-by we strolled away from the hissing ruins. Then he asked me to his room, which was in the main building of the station. He struck a
10 match, and I perceived that this young aristocrat had not only a silver-mounted dressing-case but also a whole candle all to himself. Just at that time the manager was the only man supposed to have any right to candles. Native mats covered the clay walls; a collection of spears,
15 assegais, shields, knives was hung up in trophies. The business intrusted to this fellow was the making of bricks – so I had been informed; but there wasn't a fragment of a brick anywhere in the station, and he had been there more than a year – waiting. It seems he could not make
20 bricks without something, I don't know what – straw maybe. Anyways, it could not be found there, and as it was not likely to be sent from Europe, it did not appear clear to me what he was waiting for. An act of special creation perhaps. However, they were all waiting – all

1 **incredible:** unglaublich.
4 **stand-offish:** distanziert.
8 **to hiss:** zischen.
10 **aristocrat:** Aristokrat.
11 **silver-mounted:** silberbeschlagen.
   dressing-case: Reisenecessaire.
14 **mat:** Matte.
15 **assegai:** Assagai (Wurfspieß).
   trophy: Trophäe.
16 **to entrust:** anvertrauen, betrauen mit.

the sixteen or twenty pilgrims of them – for something; and upon my word it did not seem an uncongenial occupation, from the way they took it, though the only thing that ever came to them was disease – as far as I could see. They beguiled the time by backbiting and intriguing against each other in a foolish kind of way. There was an air of plotting about that station, but nothing came of it, of course. It was as unreal as everything else – as the philanthropic pretence of the whole concern, as their talk, as their government, as their show of work. The only real feeling was a desire to get appointed to a trading-post where ivory was to be had, so that they could earn percentages. They intrigued and slandered and hated each other only on that account, – but as to effectually lifting a little finger – oh, no. By heavens! there is something after all in the world allowing one man to steal a horse while another must not look at a halter. Steal a horse straight out. Very well. He has done it. Perhaps he can ride. But there is a way of looking at a halter that would provoke the most charitable of saints into a kick.

"I had no idea why he wanted to be sociable, but as we chatted in there it suddenly occurred to me the fellow

2 **uncongenial:** unpassend.
5 **to beguile:** verkürzen, vertreiben.
  to backbite: verleumden.
6 **to intrigue:** Ränke schmieden.
7 **to plot:** anzetteln, planen.
13 **percentage:** Anteil, Prozentsatz.
14 **to slander:** verleumden.
15 **effectually** (adv.): wirksam.
18 **halter:** Halfter.
21 **charitable:** barmherzig, nachsichtig.
22 **sociable:** gesellig.

was trying to get at something – in fact, pumping me. He alluded constantly to Europe, to the people I was supposed to know there – putting leading questions as to my acquaintances in the sepulchral city, and so on.
5 His little eyes glittered like mica discs – with curiosity – though he tried to keep up a bit of superciliousness. At first I was astonished, but very soon I became awfully curious to see what he would find out from me. I couldn't possibly imagine what I had in me to make it
10 worth his while. It was very pretty to see how he baffled himself, for in truth my body was full only of chills, and my head had nothing in it but that wretched steamboat business. It was evident he took me for a perfectly shameless prevaricator. At last he got angry, and, to
15 conceal a movement of furious annoyance, he yawned. I rose. Then I noticed a small sketch in oils, on a panel, representing a woman, draped and blindfolded, carrying a lighted torch. The background was sombre – almost black. The movement of the woman was stately,
20 and the effect of the torch-light on the face was sinister.
"It arrested me, and he stood by civilly, holding an empty half-pint champagne bottle (medical comforts) with the candle stuck in it. To my question he said Mr.

---

1 **to pump:** aushorchen.
5 **mica discs:** Glimmerplättchen.
6 **superciliousness:** Hochnäsigkeit.
10 **to baffle:** völlig verwirren.
11 **chill:** Schüttelfrost, Fieberschauer.
14 **prevaricator:** Wortverdreher.
16 **panel:** Holztafel, Täfelung.
17 **blindfolded:** mit verbundenen Augen.
21 **sinister:** drohend, unheimlich.
23 **half-pint:** 0,28 Liter.

Kurtz had painted this – in this very station more than a year ago – while waiting for means to go to his trading-post. 'Tell me, pray,' said I, 'who is this Mr. Kurtz?'

5 " 'The chief of the Inner Station,' he answered in a short tone, looking away. 'Much obliged,' I said, laughing. 'And you are the brickmaker of the Central Station. Everyone knows that.' He was silent for a while. 'He is a prodigy,' he said at last. 'He is an emissary of pity, and
10 science, and progress, and devil knows what else. We want,' he began to declaim suddenly, 'for the guidance of the cause intrusted to us by Europe, so to speak, higher intelligence, wide sympathies, a singleness of purpose.' 'Who says that?' I asked. 'Lots of them,' he
15 replied. 'Some even write that; and so *he* comes here, a special being, as you ought to know.' 'Why ought I to know?' I interrupted, really surprised. He paid no attention. 'Yes. To-day he is chief ot the best station, next year he will be assistant-manager, two years more
20 and . . . but I daresay you know what he will be in two years' time. You are of the new gang – the gang of virtue. The same people who sent him specially also recommended you. Oh, don't say no. I've my own eyes to trust.' Light dawned upon me. My dear aunt's in-
25 fluential acquaintances were producing an unexpected effect upon that young man. I nearly burst into a laugh. 'Do you read the Company's confidential correspon-

9 **prodigy:** Wunder.
11 **to declaim:** deklamieren.
13 **singleness:** Redlichkeit, Aufrichtigkeit.
20 **I daresay:** ich darf wohl behaupten.
21 **gang:** Bande.

dence?' I asked. He hadn't a word to say. It was great
fun. 'When Mr. Kurtz,' I continued, severely, 'is General Manager, you won't have the opportunity.'

"He blew the candle out suddenly, and we went outside.
5 The moon had risen. Black figures strolled about listlessly, pouring water on the glow, whence proceeded a
sound of hissing; steam ascended in the moonlight, the
beaten nigger groaned somewhere. 'What a row the
brute makes!' said the indefatigable man with the mous-
10 taches, appearing near us. 'Serve him right. Transgression – punishment – bang! Pitiless, pitiless. That's the
only way. This will prevent all conflagrations for the
future. I was just telling the manager . . .' He noticed
my companion, and became crestfallen all at once. 'Not
15 in bed yet,' he said, with a kind of servile heartiness;
'it's so natural. Ha! Danger – agitation.' He vanished. I
went on to the river-side, and the other followed me. I
heard a scathing murmur at my ear, 'Heap of muffs – go
to.' The pilgrims could be seen in knots gesticulating,
20 discussing. Several had still their staves in their hands. I
verily believe they took these sticks to bed with them.
Beyond the fence the forest stood up spectrally in the
moonlight, and through the dim stir, through the faint
sounds of that lamentable courtyard, the silence of

5f. **listlessly** (adv.): verdrossen.
9 **indefatigable**: unermüdlich.
10f. **transgression**: Vergehen.
12 **conflagration**: Brand(stiftung).
14 **crestfallen**: niedergeschlagen.
15 **servile**: unterwürfig.
18 **scathing**: ätzend.
   muff: tölpelhafter Versager.
19 **to gesticulate**: gestikulieren.

the land went home to one's very heart – its mystery, its greatness, the amazing reality of its concealed life. The hurt nigger moaned feebly somewhere near by, and then fetched a deep sigh that made me mend my pace away
5 from there. I felt a hand introducing itself under my arm. 'My dear sir,' said the fellow, 'I don't want to be misunderstood, and especially by you, who will see Mr. Kurtz long before I can have that pleasure. I wouldn't like him to get a false idea of my disposition. . . .'

10 "I let him run on, this papier-maché Mephistopheles, and it seemed to me that if I tried I could poke my forefinger through him, and would find nothing inside but a little loose dirt, maybe. He, don't you see, had been planning to be assistant-manager by-and-by under
15 the present man, and I could see that the coming of that Kurtz had upset them both not a little. He talked precipitately, and I did not try to stop him. I had my shoulders against the wreck of my steamer, hauled up on the slope like a carcass of some big river animal. The
20 smell of mud, of primeval mud, by Jove! was in my nostrils, the high stillness of primeval forest was before my eyes; there were shiny patches on the black creek. The moon had spread over everything a thin layer of silver – over the rank grass, over the mud, upon the wall

3 **to moan:** klagen.
4 **to mend one's pace:** den Schritt beschleunigen.
10 **papier-maché** (frz.): Pappmaché.
11 **to poke:** stoßen, stochern.
17 **precipitately** (adv.): überstürzt.
18 **to haul:** ziehen, schleppen.
20 **primeval:** urzeitlich.
21 **nostril:** Nasenloch.
22 **creek:** schmale Bucht.
24 **rank:** üppig.

56

of matted vegetation standing higher than the wall of a temple, over the great river I could see through a sombre gap glittering, glittering, as it flowed broadly by without a murmur. All this was great, expectant, mute, while the man jabbered about himself. I wondered whether the stillness on the face of the immensity looking at us two were meant as an appeal or as a menace. What were we who had strayed in here? Could we handle that dumb thing, or would it handle us? I felt how big, how confoundedly big, was that thing that couldn't talk, and perhaps was deaf as well. What was in there? I could see a little ivory coming out from there, and I had heard Mr. Kurtz was in there. I had heard enough about it, too – God knows! Yet somehow it didn't bring any image with it – no more than if I had been told an angel or a fiend was in there. I believed it in the same way one of you might believe there are inhabitants in the planet Mars. I knew once a Scotch sailmaker who was certain, dead sure, there were people in Mars. If you asked him for some idea how they looked and behaved, he would get shy and mutter something about 'walking on all-fours.' If you as much as smiled, he would – though a man of sixty – offer to fight you. I would not have gone so far as to fight for Kurtz, but I went for him near enough to a lie. You know I hate, detest, and can't bear a lie, not because I am straighter than the rest of us, but simply because it

---

1 **matted:** verfilzt.
  vegetation: Vegetation.
5 **to jabber:** quasseln, plappern.
8 **menace:** Bedrohung.
16 **fiend:** Teufel.
26 **to detest:** verabscheuen.

appals me. There is a taint of death, a flavour of mortality in lies – which is exactly what I hate and detest in the world – what I want to forget. It makes me miserable and sick, like biting something rotten would
5 do. Temperament, I suppose. Well, I went near enough to it by letting the young fool there believe anything he liked to imagine as to my influence in Europe. I became in an instant as much of a pretence as the rest of the bewitched pilgrims. This simply because I had a notion
10 it somehow would be of help to that Kurtz whom at the time I did not see – you understand. He was just a word for me. I did not see the man in the name any more than you do. Do you see him? Do you see the story? Do you see anything? It seems to me I am trying to tell you a
15 dream – making a vain attempt, because no relation of a dream can convey the dream-sensation, that commingling of absurdity, surprise, and bewilderment in a tremor of struggling revolt, that notion of being captured by the incredible which is of the very essence of
20 dreams. . . ."

He was silent for a while.

". . . No, it is impossible; it is impossible to convey the life-sensation of any given epoch of one's existence – that which makes its truth, its meaning – its subtle and
25 penetrating essence. It is impossible. We live, as we dream – alone. . . ."

He paused again as if reflecting, then added –

2 **mortality:** Sterblichkeit.
16f. **commingling:** Mischung.
17 **absurdity:** Absurdität.
19 **essence:** Wesen.
23 **life-sensation:** Lebensgefühl.

"Of course in this you fellows see more than I could then. You see me, whom you know. . . ."

It had become so pitch dark that we listeners could hardly see one another. For a long time already he, sitting apart, had been no more to us than a voice. There was not a word from anybody. The others might have been asleep, but I was awake. I listened, I listened on the watch for the sentence, for the word, that would give me the clue to the faint uneasiness inspired by this narrative that seemed to shape itself without human lips in the heavy night-air of the river.

". . . Yes – I let him run on," Marlow began again, "and think what he pleased about the powers that were behind me. I did! And there was nothing behind me! There was nothing but that wretched, old, mangled steamboat I was leaning against, while he talked fluently about 'the necessity for every man to get on.' 'And when one comes out here, you conceive, it is not to gaze at the moon.' Mr. Kurtz was a 'universal genius,' but even a genius would find it easier to work with 'adequate tools – intelligent men.' He did not make bricks – why, there was a physical impossibility in the way – as I was well aware; and if he did secretarial work for the manager, it was because 'no sensible man rejects wantonly the confidence of his superiors.' Did I see it? I saw it. What more did I want? What I really wanted was rivets, by heaven! Rivets. To get on with the work – to stop the hole. Rivets I wanted. There were cases of

3 **pitch:** Pech.
15 **to mangle:** verstümmeln, zerstückeln.
25 **wantonly** (adv.): mutwillig.
   superior: Vorgesetzter.

them down at the coast – cases – piled up – burst – split!
You kicked a loose rivet at every second step in that
station yard on the hillside. Rivets had rolled into the
grove of death. You could fill your pockets with rivets
5 for the trouble of stooping down – and there wasn't one
rivet to be found where it was wanted. We had plates
that would do, but nothing to fasten them with. And
every week the messenger, a lone negro, letter-bag on
shoulder and staff in hand, left our station for the coast.
10 And several times a week a coast caravan came in
with trade goods – ghastly glazed calico that made
you shudder only to look at it, glass beads value
about a penny a quart, confounded spotted cotton
handkerchiefs. And no rivets. Three carriers could
15 have brought all that was wanted to set that steamboat
afloat.
"He was becoming confidential now, but I fancy my
unresponsive attitude must have exasperated him at
last, for he judged it necessary to inform me he feared
20 neither God nor devil, let alone any mere man. I said I
could see that very well, but what I wanted was a certain
quantity of rivets – and rivets were what really Mr.
Kurtz wanted, if he had only known it. Now letters went
to the coast every week. . . . 'My dear sir,' he cried, 'I
25 write from dictation.' I demanded rivets. There was a
way – for an intelligent man. He changed his manner;
became very cold, and suddenly began to talk about a

3 **rivet:** Niete.
6 **plate:** Stahlplatte.
11 **ghastly:** grausig.
   to glaze: satinieren.
12 **to shudder:** schaudern.
18 **unresponsive:** unempfänglich.

60

hippopotamus; wondered whether sleeping on board the steamer (I stuck to my salvage night and day) I wasn't disturbed. There was an old hippo that had the bad habit of getting out on the bank and roaming at night over the station grounds. The pilgrims used to turn out in a body and empty every rifle they could lay hands on at him. Some even had sat up o'nights for him. All this energy was wasted, though. 'That animal has a charmed life,' he said; 'but you can say this only of brutes in this country. No man – you apprehend me? – no man here bears a charmed life.' He stood there for a moment in the moonlight with his delicate hooked nose set a little askew, and his mica eyes glittering without a wink, then, with a curt Goodnight, he strode off. I could see he was disturbed and considerably puzzled, which made me feel more hopeful than I had been for days. It was a great comfort to turn from that chap to my influential friend, the battered, twisted, ruined, tin-pot steamboat. I clambered on board. She rang under my feet like an empty Huntley & Palmer biscuit-tin kicked along a gutter; she was nothing so solid in make, and rather less pretty in shape, but I had expended enough hard work on her to make me love her. No influential friend would have served me better. She had given me a chance to come out a bit – to find out what I could do.

---

1 **hippopotamus:** Flußpferd.
2 **salvage:** Bergungsgut.
4 **to roam:** umherstreifen.
6 **rifle:** Gewehr, Büchse.
9 **to charm:** verzaubern.
10 **brute:** Tier, Vieh.
18 **battered:** verbeult.
21 **gutter:** Gosse.

No, I don't like work. I had rather laze about and think of all the fine things that can be done. I don't like work – no man does – but I like what is in the work, – the chance to find yourself. Your own reality – for yourself, not for others – what no other man can ever know. They can only see the mere show, and never can tell what it really means.

"I was not surprised to see somebody sitting aft, on the deck, with his legs dangling over the mud. You see I rather chummed with the few mechanics there were in that station, whom the other pilgrims naturally despised – on account of their imperfect manners, I suppose. This was the foreman – a boiler-maker by trade – a good worker. He was a lank, bony, yellow-faced man, with big intense eyes. His aspect was worried, and his head was as bald as the palm of my hand; but his hair in falling seemed to have stuck to his chin, and had prospered in the new locality, for his beard hung down to his waist. He was a widower with six young children (he had left them in charge of a sister of his to come out there), and the passion of his life was pigeon-flying. He was an enthusiast and a connoisseur. He would rave about pigeons. After work hours he used sometimes to

1 **to laze about:** herumfaulenzen.
9 **to dangle:** baumeln.
10 **to chum:** kumpeln.
12 **imperfect:** unvollkommen.
16 **bald:** kahl.
18 **locality:** Ort.
19 **widower:** Witwer.
20 **in charge of:** in der Obhut von.
21 **pigeon-flying:** Taubenflug.
22 **enthusiast:** Enthusiast, Schwärmer.
 connoisseur: Kenner.
 to rave: schwärmen.

come over from his hut for a talk about his children and
his pigeons; at work, when he had to crawl in the mud
under the bottom of the steamboat, he would tie up that
beard of his in a kind of white serviette he brought for
the purpose. It had loops to go over his ears. In the
evening he could be seen squatted on the bank rinsing
that wrapper in the creek with great care, then spreading it solemnly on a bush to dry.

"I slapped him on the back and shouted 'We shall have
rivets!' He scrambled to his feet exclaiming 'No!
Rivets!' as though he couldn't believe his ears. Then in a
low voice, 'You . . . eh?' I don't know why we behaved
like lunatics. I put my finger to the side of my nose and
nodded mysteriously. 'Good for you!' he cried, snapped
his fingers above his head, lifting one foot. I tried a jig.
We capered on the iron deck. A frightful clatter came
out of that hulk, and the virgin forest on the other bank
of the creek sent it back in a thundering roll upon the
sleeping station. It must have made some of the pilgrims
sit up in their hovels. A dark figure obscured the lighted

5 **loop:** Schlaufe.
6 **to squat:** hocken.
  to rinse: spülen.
7 **wrapper:** Hülle.
9 **to slap:** klopfen, einen Klaps geben.
10 **to scramble:** krabbeln.
13 **lunatic:** Verrückter.
14 **to snap:** knipsen, schnalzen.
15 **jig:** Gigue.
16 **to caper:** Sprünge machen.
  clatter: Geklapper.
17 **hulk:** nicht seetüchtiges Schiff.
  virgin: jungfräulich.
20 **hovel:** Hütte.
  to obscure: verdunkeln.

doorway of the manager's hut, vanished, then, a second or so after, the doorway itself vanished, too. We stopped, and the silence driven away by the stamping of our feet flowed back again from the recesses of the land.
5 The great wall of vegetation, an exuberant and entangled mass of trunks, branches, leaves, boughs, festoons, motionless in the moonlight, was like a rioting invasion of soundless life, a rolling wave of plants, piled up, crested, ready to topple over the creek, to sweep every
10 little man of us out of his little existence. And it moved not. A deadened burst of mighty splashes and snorts reached us from afar, as though an ichthyosaurus had been taking a bath of glitter in the great river. 'After all,' said the boiler-maker in a reasonable tone, 'why
15 shouldn't we get the rivets?' Why not, indeed! I did not know of any reason why we shouldn't. 'They'll come in three weeks,' I said, confidently.

"But they didn't. Instead of rivets there came an invasion, an infliction, a visitation. It came in sections
20 during the next three weeks, each section headed by a donkey carrying a white man in new clothes and tan

---

5 **exuberant:** üppig.
5f. **entangled:** verwickelt, verstrickt.
6 **festoon:** Ranke.
9 **to crest:** den Gipfel erreichen.
  to topple over: umkippen.
11 **to deaden:** dämpfen.
  burst: Ausbruch.
  splash: Platschen.
  snort: Schnauben.
12 **ichthyosaurus:** fossile Fischeidechse.
19 **infliction:** Plage.
  visitation: Heimsuchung.
21 **tan:** gelbbraun.

shoes, bowing from that elevation right and left to the
impressed pilgrims. A quarrelsome band of footsore
sulky niggers trod on the heels of the donkey; a lot of
tents, camp-stools, tin boxes, white cases, brown bales
would be shot down in the courtyard, and the air of
mystery would deepen a little over the muddle of the
station. Five such instalments came, with their absurd
air of disorderly flight with the loot of innumerable
outfit shops and provision stores, that, one would think,
they were lugging, after a raid, into the wilderness for
equitable division. It was an inextricable mess of things
decent in themselves but that human folly made look
like spoils of thieving.

"This devoted band called itself the Eldorado Exploring
Expedition[26], and I believe they were sworn to secrecy.
Their talk, however, was the talk of sordid buccaneers:
it was reckless without hardihood, greedy without
audacity, and cruel without courage; there was not an

1 **elevation:** Erhebung.
2 **footsore:** fußkrank.
3 **sulky:** verdrießlich.
4 **camp-stool:** Klappstuhl.
  bale: Ballen, Bündel.
7 **instalment:** Teillieferung.
8 **loot:** Beute.
10 **to lug:** schleppen.
  raid: Überfall.
11 **equitable:** gerecht.
13 **spoils:** Beute.
  thieving: Diebstahl.
16 **buccaneer:** Freibeuter.
17 **reckless:** rücksichtslos.
  hardihood: Tapferkeit.
18 **audacity:** Kühnheit.

atom of foresight or of serious intention in the whole batch of them, and they did not seem aware these things are wanted for the work of the world. To tear treasure out of the bowels of the land was their desire, with no more moral purpose at the back of it than there is in burglars breaking into a safe. Who paid the expenses of the noble enterprise I don't know; but the uncle of our manager was leader of that lot.

"In exterior he resembled a butcher in a poor neighbourhood, and his eyes had a look of sleepy cunning. He carried his fat paunch with ostentation on his short legs, and during the time his gang infested the station spoke to no one but his nephew. You could see these two roaming about all day long with their heads close together in an everlasting confab.

"I had given up worrying myself about the rivets. One's capacity for that kind of folly is more limited than you would suppose. I said Hang! – and let things slide. I had plenty of time for meditation, and now and then I would give some thought to Kurtz. I wasn't very interested in him. No. Still, I was curious to see whether this man, who had come out equipped with moral ideas of some sort, would climb to the top after all and how he would set about his work when there."

---

1 **foresight:** Vorsorge.
2 **batch:** Trupp.
4 **bowels:** Eingeweide.
6 **burglar:** Einbrecher.
11 **paunch:** Bauch, Wampe.
　　ostentation: Prahlerei.
12 **to infest:** heimsuchen.
15 **confab(ulation):** Plauderei.

II

"One evening as I was lying flat on the deck of my steamboat, I heard voices approaching – and there were the nephew and the uncle strolling along the bank. I laid my head on my arm again, and had nearly lost myself in a doze, when somebody said in my ear, as it were: 'I am as harmless as a little child, but I don't like to be dictated to. Am I the manager – or am I not? I was ordered to send him there. It's incredible.' . . . I became aware that the two were standing on the shore alongside the forepart of the steamboat, just below my head. I did not move; it did not occur to me to move: I was sleepy. 'It *is* unpleasant,' grunted the uncle. 'He has asked the Administration to be sent here,' said the other, 'with the idea of showing what he could do; and I was instructed accordingly. Look at the influence that man must have. Is it not frightful?' They both agreed it was frightful, then made several bizarre remarks: 'Make rain and fine weather – one man – the Council – by the nose' – bits of absurd sentences that got the better of my drowsiness, so that I had pretty near the whole of my wits about me when the uncle said, 'The climate may do away with this difficulty for you. Is he alone there?' 'Yes,' answered the manager; 'he sent his assistant down the river with a note to me in these terms: "Clear this poor devil out of the country, and don't bother sending more of that sort. I had rather be alone than have the kind of men you can dispose of with me." It was more than a year ago. Can you imagine such

18 **bizarre:** exzentrisch, wunderlich, phantastisch.
21 **drowsiness:** Schläfrigkeit.

impudence!' 'Anything since then?' asked the other, hoarsely. 'Ivory,' jerked the nephew; 'lots of it – prime sort – lots – most annoying, from him.' 'And with that?' questioned the heavy rumble. 'Invoice,' was the reply
5 fired out, so to speak. Then silence. They had been talking about Kurtz.

"I was broad awake by this time, but, lying perfectly at ease, remained still, having no inducement to change my position. 'How did that ivory come all this way?'
10 growled the elder man, who seemed very vexed. The other explained that it had come with a fleet of canoes in charge of an English half-caste clerk Kurtz had with him; that Kurtz had apparently intended to return himself, the station being by that time bare of goods and
15 stores, but after coming three hundred miles, had suddenly decided to go back, which he started to do alone in a small dugout with four paddlers, leaving the half-caste to continue down the river with the ivory. The two fellows there seemed astounded at anybody attempting
20 such a thing. They were at a loss for an adequate motive. As to me, I seemed to see Kurtz for the first time. It was a distinct glimpse: the dugout, four paddl-

---

1 **impudence:** Unverschämtheit.
2 **hoarsely** (adv.): heiser, rauh.
   to jerk: hervorstoßen.
4 **rumble:** Poltern, Rumpeln.
   invoice: Rechnung.
8 **inducement:** Anlaß.
10 **to growl:** brummen, knurren.
   vexed: verärgert.
12 **half-caste:** Halbblut.
17 **dugout:** Einbaum.
19 **to astound:** verblüffen, überraschen.

ing savages, and the lone white man turning his back suddenly on the headquarters, on relief, on thoughts of home – perhaps; setting his face towards the depths of the wilderness, towards his empty and desolate station. I did not know the motive. Perhaps he was just simply a fine fellow who stuck to his work for its own sake. His name, you understand, had not been pronounced once. He was 'that man.' The half-caste, who, as far as I could see, had conducted a difficult trip with great prudence and pluck, was invariably alluded to as 'that scoundrel.' The 'scoundrel' had reported that the 'man' had been very ill – had recovered imperfectly. ... The two below me moved away then a few paces, and strolled back and forth at some little distance. I heard: 'Military post – doctor – two hundred miles – quite alone now – unavoidable delays – nine months – no news – strange rumours.' They approached again, just as the manager was saying, 'No one, as far as I know, unless a species of wandering trader – a pestilential fellow, snapping ivory from the natives.' Who was it they were talking about now? I gathered in snatches that this was some man supposed to be in Kurtz's district, and of whom the manager did not approve. 'We will not be free from unfair competition till one of these fellows is hanged for an example,' he said. 'Certainly,' grunted the other; 'get him hanged! Why not? Anything – anything can be

---

4 **desolate:** einsam, verlassen.
10 **invariably** (adv.): unveränderlich.
   scoundrel: Schurke.
18 **species:** Art.
19 **pestilential:** ekelhaft, schädlich.
21 **snatch:** Gesprächsfetzen.

done in this country. That's what I say; nobody here, you understand, *here*, can endanger your position. And why? You stand the climate – you outlast them all. The danger is in Europe; but there before I left I took care to —' They moved off and whispered, then their voices rose again. 'The extraordinary series of delays is not my fault. I did my best.' The fat man sighed. 'Very sad.' 'And the pestiferous absurdity of his talk,' continued the other; 'he bothered me enough when he was here. "Each station should be like a beacon on the road towards better things, a centre for trade of course, but also for humanizing, improving, instructing." Conceive you – that ass! And he wants to be manager! No, it's —' Here he got choked by excessive indignation, and I lifted my head the least bit. I was surprised to see how near they were – right under me. I could have spat upon their hats. They were looking on the ground, absorbed in thought. The manager was switching his leg with a slender twig: his sagacious relative lifted his head. 'You have been well since you came out this time?' he asked. The other gave a start. 'Who? I? Oh! Like a charm – like a charm. But the rest – oh, my goodness! All sick. They die so quick, too, that I haven't the time to send them out of the country – it's incredible!' 'H'm. Just so,' grunted the uncle. 'Ah! my boy, trust to this – I say,

---

2 **to endanger:** gefährden.
3 **to outlast:** überdauern.
8 **pestiferous:** aufdringlich, lästig.
10 **beacon:** Leuchtfeuer.
14 **indignation:** Entrüstung.
18 **to switch:** schlagen.
19 **twig:** Zweig.
   sagacious: scharfsinnig.

trust to this.' I saw him extend his short flipper of an arm for a gesture that took in the forest, the creek, the mud, the river, – seemed to beckon with a dishonouring flourish before the sunlit face of the land a treacherous appeal to the lurking death, to the hidden evil, to the profound darkness of its heart. It was so startling that I leaped to my feet and looked back at the edge of the forest, as though I had expected an answer of some sort to that black display of confidence. You know the foolish notions that come to one sometimes. The high stillness confronted these two figures with its ominous patience, waiting for the passing away of a fantastic invasion.

"They swore aloud together – out of sheer fright, I believe – then pretending not to know anything of my existence, turned back to the station. The sun was low; and leaning forward side by side, they seemed to be tugging painfully uphill their two ridiculous shadows of unequal length, that trailed behind them slowly over the tall grass without bending a single blade.

"In a few days the Eldorado Expedition went into the patient wilderness, that closed upon it as the sea closes over a diver. Long afterwards the news came that all the donkeys were dead. I know nothing as to the fate of the less valuable animals. They, no doubt, like the rest of us, found what they deserved. I did not inquire. I was then rather excited at the prospect of meeting Kurtz

---

1 **flipper:** Flosse.
3 **to dishonour:** entehren.
4 **flourish:** Schwenken.
   treacherous: verräterisch.
18 **to tug:** ziehen, zerren.
19 **to trail:** sich hinziehen.

very soon. When I say very soon I mean it comparatively. It was just two months from the day we left the creek when we came to the bank below Kurtz's station[27].

5 "Going up that river was like travelling back to the earliest beginnings of the world, when vegetation rioted on the earth and the big trees were kings. An empty stream, a great silence, an impenetrable forest. The air was warm, thick, heavy, sluggish. There was no joy in
10 the brilliance of sunshine. The long stretches of the waterway ran on, deserted, into the gloom of overshadowed distances. On silvery sandbanks hippos and alligators sunned themselves side by side. The broadening waters flowed through a mob of wooded islands; you
15 lost your way on that river as you would in a desert, and butted all day long against shoals, trying to find the channel, till you thought yourself bewitched and cut off for ever from everything you had known once – somewhere – far away – in another existence perhaps. There
20 were moments when one's past came back to one, as it will sometimes when you have not a moment to spare to yourself; but it came in the shape of an unrestful and noisy dream, remembered with wonder amongst the overwhelming realities of this strange world of plants,
25 and water, and silence. And this stillness of life did not

---

1f. **comparative:** relativ, vergleichsweise.
8 **impenetrable:** undurchdringlich.
9 **sluggish:** träge, stagnierend.
13 **alligator:** Krokodil.
14 **mob:** Haufen.
16 **to butt:** stoßen.
    shoal: Untiefe.
24 **to overwhelm:** überwältigen.

72

in the least resemble a peace. It was the stillness of an
implacable force brooding over an inscrutable intention. It looked at you with a vengeful aspect. I got used
to it afterwards; I did not see it any more; I had no time.
I had to keep guessing at the channel; I had to discern,
mostly by inspiration, the signs of hidden banks; I
watched for sunken stones; I was learning to clap my
teeth smartly before my heart flew out, when I shaved
by a fluke some infernal sly old snag that would have
ripped the life out of the tin-pot steamboat and drowned
all the pilgrims; I had to keep a look-out for the signs of
dead wood we could cut up in the night for next day's
steaming. When you have to attend to things of that
sort, to the mere incidents of the surface, the reality –
the reality, I tell you – fades. The inner truth is hidden –
luckily, luckily. But I felt it all the same; I felt often its
mysterious stillness watching me at my monkey tricks,
just as it watches you fellows performing on your
respective tight-ropes for – what is it? half-a-crown a
tumble —"

"Try to be civil, Marlow," growled a voice, and I knew
there was at least one listener awake besides myself.

"I beg your pardon. I forgot the heartache which makes
up the rest of the price. And indeed what does the price

2 **implacable:** unversöhnlich.
3 **vengeful:** rachsüchtig.
5 **to discern:** erkennen.
9 **fluke:** glücklicher Zufall.
  infernal: höllisch.
  snag: Baumstamm.
10 **to rip:** reißen.
17 **monkey trick:** Posse, Kunststück.
19 **tight-rope:** Hochseil.
20 **tumble:** Purzelbaum.

matter, if the trick be well done? You do your tricks
very well. And I didn't do badly either, since I managed
not to sink that steamboat on my first trip. It's a wonder
to me yet. Imagine a blindfolded man set to drive a van
5 over a bad road. I sweated and shivered over that
business considerably, I can tell you. After all, for a
seaman, to scrape the bottom of the thing that's supposed to float all the time under his care is the unpardonable sin. No one may know of it, but you never
10 forget the thump – eh? A blow on the very heart. You
remember it, you dream of it, you wake up at night and
think of it – years after – and go hot and cold all over. I
don't pretend to say that steamboat floated all the time.
More than once she had to wade for a bit, with twenty
15 cannibals splashing around and pushing. We had
enlisted some of these chaps on the way for a crew[28].
Fine fellows – cannibals – in their place. They were men
one could work with, and I am grateful to them. And,
after all, they did not eat each other before my face:
20 they had brought along a provision of hippo-meat which
went rotten, and made the mystery of the wilderness
stink in my nostrils. Phoo! I can sniff it now. I had the
manager on board and three or four pilgrims with their
staves – all complete. Sometimes we came upon a
25 station close by the bank, clinging to the skirts of the
unknown, and the white men rushing out of a tumbledown hovel, with great gestures of joy and surprise

8 f. **unpardonable:** unverzeihlich.
10 **thump:** Ruck.
14 **to wade:** waten.
16 **to enlist:** anwerben.
22 **to sniff:** schnuppern.
26 f. **tumbledown:** baufällig.

and welcome, seemed very strange – had the appearance of being held there captive by a spell. The word ivory would ring in the air for a while – and on we went again into the silence, along empty reaches, round the
5 still bends, between the high walls of our winding way, reverberating in hollow claps the ponderous beat of the stern-wheel. Trees, trees, millions of trees, massive, immense, running up high; and at their foot, hugging the bank against the stream, crept the little begrimed
10 steamboat, like a sluggish beetle crawling on the floor of a lofty portico. It made you feel very small, very lost, and yet it was not altogether depressing, that feeling. After all, if you were small, the grimy beetle crawled on – which was just what you wanted it to do. Where the
15 pilgrims imagined it crawled to I don't know. To some place where they expected to get something, I bet! For me it crawled towards Kurtz – exclusively; but when the steam-pipes started leaking we crawled very slow. The reaches opened before us and closed behind, as if the
20 forest had stepped leisurely across the water to bar the way for our return. We penetrated deeper and deeper into the heart of darkness. It was very quiet there. At

---

2 **spell:** Zauber.
6 **to reverberate:** widerhallen.
  ponderous: schwerfällig.
7 **stern-wheel:** Schaufelrad am Heck.
  massive: massig.
8 **to hug:** sich dicht halten an.
9 **begrimed:** verdreckt.
11 **lofty:** hoch, erhaben.
  portico: Portikus, Säulengang.
18 **steam-pipe:** Dampfrohr.
  to leak: lecken.
20 **leisurely** (adv.): gemächlich.

night sometimes the roll of drums behind the curtain of trees would run up the river and remain sustained faintly, as if hovering in the air high over our heads, till the first break of day. Whether it meant war, peace, or
5 prayer we could not tell. The dawns were heralded by the descent of a chill stillness; the wood-cutters slept, their fires burned low; the snapping of a twig would make you start. We were wanderers on prehistoric earth, on an earth that wore the aspect of an unknown
10 planet. We could have fancied ourselves the first of men taking possession of an accursed inheritance, to be subdued at the cost of profound anguish and of excessive toil. But suddenly, as we struggled round a bend, there would be a glimpse of rush walls, of peaked grass-
15 roofs, a burst of yells, a whirl of black limbs, a mass of hands clapping, of feet stamping, of bodies swaying, of eyes rolling, under the droop of heavy and motionless foliage. The steamer toiled along slowly on the edge of a black and incomprehensible frenzy. The prehistoric
20 man was cursing us, praying to us, welcoming us – who could tell? We were cut off from the comprehension of our surroundings; we glided past like phantoms, wondering and secretly appalled, as sane men would be before an enthusiastic outbreak in a madhouse. We

---

1 **roll of drums:** Trommelwirbel.
5 **to herald:** ankündigen.
8 **prehistoric:** vorgeschichtlich.
11 **accursed:** verflucht.
   inheritance: Erbe.
12 **to subdue:** unterwerfen, bewältigen.
18 **foliage:** Laubwerk.
19 **frenzy:** Raserei.
21 **comprehension:** Verständnis.

could not understand because we were too far and could
not remember, because we were travelling in the night
of first ages, of those ages that are gone, leaving hardly
a sign – and no memories.

5 "The earth seemed unearthly. We are accustomed to
look upon the shackled form of a conquered monster,
but there – there you could look at a thing monstrous
and free. It was unearthly, and the men were — No,
they were not inhuman. Well, you know, that was the
10 worst of it – this suspicion of their not being inhuman. It
would come slowly to one. They howled and leaped,
and spun, and made horrid faces; but what thrilled you
was just the thought of their humanity – like yours – the
thought of your remote kinship with this wild and
15 passionate uproar. Ugly. Yes, it was ugly enough; but if
you were man enough you would admit to yourself that
there was in you just the faintest trace of a response to
the terrible frankness of that noise, a dim suspicion of
there being a meaning in it which you – you so remote
20 from the night of first ages – could comprehend. And
why not? The mind of man is capable of anything –
because everything is in it, all the past as well as all the
future. What was there after all? Joy, fear, sorrow,
devotion, valour, rage – who can tell? – but truth – truth
25 stripped of its cloak of time. Let the fool gape and
shudder – the man knows, and can look on without a

5 **unearthly:** unirdisch.
6 **to shackle:** fesseln, halten.
7 **monstrous:** ungeheuerlich.
14 **remote:** entfernt.
   kinship: Verwandtschaft.
15 **uproar:** Aufruhr, Tumult.
18 **frankness:** Freimut, Offenheit.

wink. But he must at least be as much of a man as these
on the shore. He must meet that truth with his own true
stuff – with his own inborn strength. Principles won't
do. Acquisitions, clothes, pretty rags – rags that would
5 fly off at the first good shake. No; you want a deliberate
belief. An appeal to me in this fiendish row – is there?
Very well; I hear; I admit, but I have a voice, too, and
for good or evil mine is the speech that cannot be
silenced. Of course, a fool, what with sheer fright and
10 fine sentiments, is always safe. Who's that grunting?
You wonder I didn't go ashore for a howl and a dance?
Well, no – I didn't. Fine sentiments, you say? Fine
sentiments, be hanged! I had no time. I had to mess
about with white-lead and strips of woollen blanket
15 helping to put bandages on those leaky steampipes – I
tell you. I had to watch the steering, and circumvent
those snags, and get the tin-pot along by hook or
by crook. There was surface-truth enough in these
things to save a wiser man. And between whiles I had
20 to look after the savage who was fireman. He was an
improved specimen; he could fire up a vertical boiler.
He was there below me, and, upon my word, to look
at him was as edifying as seeing a dog in a parody of

---

5 **deliberate:** wohlüberlegt, bewußt.
13f. **to mess about:** herumpfuschen.
14 **white-lead:** Bleiweiß.
15 **bandage:** Binde, Verband.
16 **to circumvent:** umgehen, ausweichen.
19 **between whiles:** zwischendurch.
20 **fireman:** Heizer.
21 **specimen:** Exemplar.
 vertical: aufrecht.
23 **edifying:** erbaulich.
 parody: Parodie.

breeches and a feather hat, walking on his hind-legs. A
few months of training had done for that really fine chap.
He squinted at the steam-gauge and at the water-gauge
with an evident effort of intrepidity – and he had filed
5 teeth, too, the poor devil, and the wool of his pate shaved
into queer patterns, and three ornamental scars on each
of his cheeks. He ought to have been clapping his hands
and stamping his feet on the bank, instead of which he
was hard at work, a thrall to strange witchcraft, full of
10 improving knowledge. He was useful because he had
been instructed; and what he knew was this – that should
the water in that transparent thing disappear, the evil
spirit inside the boiler would get angry through the
greatness of his thirst, and take a terrible vengeance. So
15 he sweated and fired up and watched the glass fearfully
(with an impromptu charm, made of rags, tied to his
arm, and a piece of polished bone, as big as a watch,
stuck flatways through his lower lip), while the wooded
banks slipped past us slowly, the short noise was left
20 behind, the interminable miles of silence – and we crept

1 **breeches:** Kniehose.
  hind-leg: Hinterbein.
3 **to squint:** schielen.
  steam-gauge: Dampfdruckmesser, Manometer.
  water-gauge: Wasserstandsanzeiger.
4 **intrepidity:** Unerschrockenheit.
  to file: feilen.
5 **pate:** Schädel.
6 **ornamental scar:** Schmucknarbe.
9 **thrall:** Sklave, Knecht,
  witchcraft: Hexerei.
12 **transparent:** durchsichtig.
14 **vengeance:** Rache.
16 **impromptu:** improvisiert.
18 **flatways:** der Länge nach.

on, towards Kurtz. But the snags were thick, the water was treacherous and shallow, the boiler seemed indeed to have a sulky devil in it, and thus neither that fireman nor I had any time to peer into our creepy
5 thoughts.

"Some fifty miles below the Inner Station we came upon a hut of reeds, an inclined and melancholy pole, with the unrecognizable tatters of what had been a flag of some sort flying from it, and a neatly stacked wood-
10 pile[29]. This was unexpected. We came to the bank, and on the stack of firewood found a flat piece of board with some faded pencil-writing on it. When deciphered it said: 'Wood for you. Hurry up. Approach cautiously.' There was a signature, but it was illegible – not Kurtz –
15 a much longer word. Hurry up. Where? Up the river? 'Approach cautiously.' We had not done so. But the warning could not have been meant for the place where it could be only found after approach. Something was wrong above. But what – and how much? That was the
20 question. We commented adversely upon the imbecility of that telegraphic style. The bush around said nothing, and would not let us look very far, either. A torn curtain

2 **shallow:** seicht.
4 **to peer:** suchend schauen.
  creepy: unheimlich, gruselig.
7 **melancholy:** schwermütig.
8 **tatter:** Fetzen.
9 **to stack:** aufstapeln.
12 **to decipher:** entziffern.
14 **signature:** Unterschrift.
  illegible: unleserlich.
20 **adverse:** gegensätzlich, widersprüchlich.
  imbecility: Schwachsinn.
21 **telegraphic style:** Telegrammstil.

80

of red twill hung in the doorway of the hut, and flapped
sadly in our faces. The dwelling was dismantled; but we
could see a white man had lived there not very long ago.
There remained a rude table – a plank on two posts; a
5 heap of rubbish reposed in a dark corner, and by the
door I picked up a book. It had lost its covers, and the
pages had been thumbed into a state of extremely dirty
softness; but the back had been lovingly stitched afresh
with white cotton thread, which looked clean yet. It was
10 an extraordinary find. Its title was, *An Inquiry into
some Points of Seamanship*[30], by a man Tower, Towson –
some such name – Master in his Majesty's Navy. The
matter looked dreary reading enough, with illustrative
diagrams and repulsive tables of figures, and the copy
15 was sixty years old. I handled this amazing antiquity
with the greatest possible tenderness, lest it should
dissolve in my hands. Within, Towson or Towser was
inquiring earnestly into the breaking strain of ships'
chains and tackle, and other such matters. Not a very
20 enthralling book; but at the first glance you could see

---

1 **twill:** Köperstoff.
   to flap: baumeln.
6 **covers:** Einband.
7 **to thumb:** mit dem Daumen abnützen, (passivisch) ›abgegriffen
   sein‹.
8 **to stitch:** heften, nähen.
13 **dreary:** traurig, öde.
   illustrative: erläuternd.
14 **diagram:** Diagramm, graphische Darstellung.
   repulsive: abstoßend.
15 **antiquity:** Antiquität.
18 **breaking strain:** maximale Belastbarkeit.
19 **tackle:** Tauwerk.
20 **to enthrall:** fesseln, einnehmen.

there a singleness of intention, an honest concern for
the right way of going to work, which made these
humble pages, thought out so many years ago, luminous with another than a professional light. The simple
5 old sailor, with his talk of chains and purchases, made
me forget the jungle and the pilgrims in a delicious
sensation of having come upon something unmistak-
ably real. Such a book being there was wonderful enough;
but still more astounding were the notes pencilled in the
10 margin, and plainly referring to the text. I couldn't
believe my eyes! They were in cipher! Yes, it looked
like cipher. Fancy a man lugging with him a book of
that description into this nowhere and studying it – and
making notes – in cipher at that! It was an extravagant
15 mystery.
"I had been dimly aware for some time of a worrying
noise, and when I lifted my eyes I saw the wood-pile was
gone, and the manager, aided by all the pilgrims, was
shouting at me from the river-side. I slipped the book
20 into my pocket. I assure you to leave off reading was
like tearing myself away from the shelter of an old and
solid friendship.
"I started the lame engine ahead. 'It must be this
miserable trader – this intruder,' exclaimed the man-
25 ager, looking back malevolently at the place we had
left. 'He must be English,' I said. 'It will not save him
from getting into trouble if he is not careful,' muttered

5 **purchase:** Talje, Takel.
9 **astounding:** überraschend, erstaunlich.
10 **margin:** Rand.
11 **cipher:** Geheimschrift.
14 **extravagant:** überspannt.
25 **malevolent:** böswillig.

the manager darkly. I observed with assumed innocence
that no man was safe from trouble in this world.

"The current was more rapid now, the steamer seemed
at her last gasp, the stern-wheel flopped languidly, and I
caught myself listening on tiptoe for the next beat of the
boat, for in sober truth I expected the wretched thing to
give up every moment. It was like watching the last
flickers of a life. But still we crawled. Sometimes I
would pick out a tree a little way ahead to measure our
progress towards Kurtz by, but I lost it invariably before
we got abreast. To keep the eyes so long on one thing
was too much for human patience. The manager dis-
played a beautiful resignation. I fretted and fumed and
took to arguing with myself whether or no I would talk
openly with Kurtz; but before I could come to any
conclusion it occurred to me that my speech or my
silence, indeed any action of mine, would be a mere
futility. What did it matter what any one knew or
ignored? What did it matter who was manager? One
gets sometimes such a flash of insight. The essentials of
this affair lay deep under the surface, beyond my reach,
and beyond my power of meddling.

1 **assumed:** vorgetäuscht, geheuchelt.
   innocence: Harmlosigkeit.
4 **to flop:** träge schlagen.
   languidly (adv.): schlaff, matt.
10 **invariably** (adv.): stets, beständig.
11 **abreast:** auf gleicher Höhe.
13 **resignation:** Ergebung.
   to fret: sich ärgern, grämen.
   to fume: wütend, ungeduldig sein.
18 **futility:** Vergeblichkeit.
20 **essentials:** das Wesentliche.
22 **to meddle:** sich einmischen.

"Towards the evening of the second day we judged ourselves about eight miles from Kurtz's station. I wanted to push on; but the manager looked grave, and told me the navigation up there was so dangerous that it would be advisable, the sun being very low already, to wait where we were till next morning. Moreover, he pointed out that if the warning to approach cautiously were to be followed, we must approach in daylight – not at dusk, or in the dark. This was sensible enough. Eight miles meant nearly three hours' steaming for us, and I could also see suspicious ripples at the upper end of the reach. Nevertheless, I was annoyed beyond expression at the delay, and most unreasonably, too, since one night more could not matter much after so many months. As we had plenty of wood, and caution was the word, I brought up in the middle of the stream. The reach was narrow, straight, with high sides like a railway cutting. The dusk came gliding into it long before the sun had set. The current ran smooth and swift, but a dumb immobility sat on the banks. The living trees, lashed together by the creepers and every living bush of the undergrowth, might have been changed into stone, even to the slenderest twig, to the lightest leaf. It was not sleep – it seemed unnatural, like a state of trance. Not the faintest sound of any kind could be heard. You

---

4 **navigation:** das Steuern des Schiffes.
11 **ripple:** Wellengekräusel.
16 **to bring up:** beidrehen.
17 f. **railway cutting:** Abgrabung, Durchstich für eine Eisenbahntrasse.
20 **immobility:** Unbeweglichkeit, Bewegungslosigkeit.
21 **to lash together:** zusammenbinden.
22 **undergrowth:** Unterholz.
24 **trance:** Trance, hypnotischer Schlaf.

84

looked on amazed, and began to suspect yourself of
being deaf – then the night came suddenly, and struck
you blind as well. About three in the morning some
large fish leaped, and the loud splash made me jump as
5 though a gun had been fired. When the sun rose there
was a white fog, very warm and clammy, and more
blinding than the night. It did not shift or drive; it was
just there, standing all round you like something solid.
At eight or nine, perhaps, it lifted as a shutter lifts. We
10 had a glimpse of the towering multitude of trees, of the
immense matted jungle, with the blazing little ball of
the sun hanging over it – all perfectly still – and then the
white shutter came down again, smoothly, as if sliding
in greased grooves. I ordered the chain, which we had
15 begun to heave in, to be paid out again. Before it
stopped running with a muffled rattle, a cry, a very loud
cry, as of infinite desolation, soared slowly in the opaque air. It ceased. A complaining clamour, modulated
in savage discords, filled our ears. The sheer unexpect-
20 edness of it made my hair stir under my cap. I don't
know how it struck the others: to me it seemed as
though the mist itself had screamed, so suddenly, and
apparently from all sides at once, did this tumultuous

6 **clammy:** klamm, feuchtkalt.
14 **groove:** Rille, Fuge.
15 **to pay out the chain:** ausbringen.
16 **to muffle:** dämpfen.
17 **to soar:** sich aufschwingen.
17f. **opaque:** undurchdringlich.
18 **clamour:** Geschrei.
    to modulate: modulieren, abstufen.
19 **discord:** Mißklang.
23 **tumultuous:** lärmend.

and mournful uproar arise. It culminated in a hurried outbreak of almost intolerably excessive shrieking, which stopped short, leaving us stiffened in a variety of silly attitudes, and obstinately listening to the nearly as
5 appalling and excessive silence. 'Good God! What is the meaning —' stammered at my elbow one of the pilgrims, – a little fat man, with sandy hair and red whiskers, who wore side-spring boots, and pink pyjamas tucked into his socks. Two others remained
10 open-mouthed a whole minute, then dashed into the little cabin, to rush out incontinently and stand darting scared glances, with Winchesters[31] at 'ready' in their hands. What we could see was just the steamer we were on, her outlines blurred as though she had been on the
15 point of dissolving, and a misty strip of water, perhaps two feet broad, around her – and that was all. The rest of the world was nowhere, as far as our eyes and ears were concerned. Just nowhere. Gone, disappeared; swept off without leaving a whisper or a shadow
20 behind.
"I went forward, and ordered the chain to be hauled in short, so as to be ready to trip the anchor and move the steamboat at once if necessary. 'Will they attack?' whis-

---

1 **to culminate:** gipfeln.
4 **obstinately** (adv.): hartnäckig.
6 **to stammer:** stammeln, stottern.
8 **side-spring boot:** Stiefel mit elastischem Schaft.
9 **to tuck into:** einschlagen, einstecken in.
11 **incontinently** (adv.): unverzüglich.
   to dart: schleudern.
12 **at "ready":** schußbereit.
21 **to haul in:** einholen.
22 **to trip the anchor:** den Anker schlippen.

pered an awed voice. 'We will be all butchered in this fog,' murmured another. The faces twitched with the strain, the hands trembled slightly, the eyes forgot to wink. It was very curious to see the contrast of expressions of the white men and of the black fellows of our crew, who were as much strangers to that part of the river as we, though their homes were only eight hundred miles away. The whites, of course greatly discomposed, had besides a curious look of being painfully shocked by such an outrageous row. The others had an alert, naturally interested expression; but their faces were essentially quiet, even those of the one or two who grinned as they hauled at the chain. Several exchanged short, grunting phrases, which seemed to settle the matter to their satisfaction. Their headman, a young, broad-chested black, severely draped in dark-blue fringed cloths, with fierce nostrils and his hair all done up artfully in oily ringlets, stood near me. 'Aha!' I said, just for good fellowship's sake. 'Catch 'im,' he snapped, with a bloodshot widening of his eyes and a flash of sharp teeth – 'catch 'im. Give 'im to us.' 'To you, eh?' I asked; 'what would you do with them?' 'Eat 'im!' he said, curtly, and, leaning his elbow on the

---

2 **to twitch:** zucken.
9 **to discompose:** aus der Fassung bringen.
10 **outrageous:** unerhört, ungeheuerlich.
11 **alert:** wachsam, munter.
13 **to grin:** grinsen.
15 **headman:** Anführer.
16 **broad-chested:** breitbrüstig.
18 **artfully** (adv.): kunstvoll.
   ringlet: Ringellöckchen.
20 **bloodshot:** blutunterlaufen.

rail, looked out into the fog in a dignified and pro-
foundly pensive attitude. I would no doubt have been
properly horrified, had it not occurred to me that he and
his chaps must be very hungry: that they must have been
growing increasingly hungry for at least this month past.
They had been engaged for six months (I don't think a
single one of them had any clear idea of time, as we at
the end of countless ages have. They still belonged to
the beginnings of time – had no inherited experience to
teach them as it were), and of course, as long as there
was a piece of paper written over in accordance with
some farcical law or other made down the river, it didn't
enter anybody's head to trouble how they would live.
Certainly they had brought with them some rotten
hippo-meat, which couldn't have lasted very long, anyway, even if the pilgrims hadn't, in the midst of a
shocking hullabaloo, thrown a considerable quantity of
it overboard. It looked like a high-handed proceeding;
but it was really a case of legitimate self-defence. You
can't breathe dead hippo waking, sleeping, and eating,
and at the same time keep your precarious grip on
existence. Besides that, they had given them every week
three pieces of brass wire, each about nine inches long;
and the theory was they were to buy their provisions
with that currency in river-side villages[32]. You can see
how *that* worked. There were either no villages, or the

---

1 **rail:** Reling.
2 **pensive:** nachdenklich.
17 **hullabaloo:** Tumult.
18 **high-handed:** willkürlich, anmaßend.
19 **legitimate:** rechtmäßig.
21 **precarious:** unsicher.
25 **currency:** Währung.

people were hostile, or the director, who like the rest of
us fed out of tins, with an occasional old he-goat thrown
in, didn't want to stop the steamer for some more or less
recondite reason. So, unless they swallowed the wire
itself, or made loops of it to snare the fishes with, I don't
see what good their extravagant salary could be to
them. I must say it was paid with a regularity worthy of
a large and honourable trading company. For the rest,
the only thing to eat – though it didn't look eatable in
the least – I saw in their possession was a few lumps of
some stuff like half-cooked dough, of a dirty lavender
colour, they kept wrapped in leaves[33], and now and
then swallowed a piece of, but so small that it seemed
done more for the looks of the thing than for any serious
purpose of sustenance. Why in the name of all the
gnawing devils of hunger they didn't go for us – they
were thirty to five – and have a good tuck-in for once,
amazes me now when I think of it. They were big
powerful men, with not much capacity to weigh the
consequences, with courage, with strength, even yet,
though their skins were no longer glossy and their
muscles no longer hard. And I saw that something
restraining, one of those human secrets that baffle

2 **he-goat:** Ziegenbock.
2 f. **to throw in:** dazugeben.
4 **recondite:** verborgen, undurchsichtig.
7 **regularity:** Regelmäßigkeit.
11 **dough:** Teig.
 lavender: Lavendel.
15 **sustenance:** Ernährung.
16 **to gnaw:** zernagen.
17 **tuck-in:** Fresserei, Schwelgerei.
21 **glossy:** glänzend.
23 **to baffle:** narren.

probability, had come into play there. I looked at them with a swift quickening of interest – not because it occurred to me I might be eaten by them before very long, though I own to you that just then I perceived – in a new light, as it were – how unwholesome the pilgrims looked, and I hoped, yes, I positively hoped, that my aspect was not so – what shall I say? – so – unappetizing: a touch of fantastic vanity which fitted well with the dream-sensation that pervaded all my days at that time. Perhaps I had a little fever, too. One can't live with one's finger everlastingly on one's pulse. I had often 'a little fever,' or a little touch of other things – the playful paw-strokes of the wilderness, the preliminary trifling before the more serious onslaught which came in due course. Yes; I looked at them as you would on any human being, with a curiosity of their impulses, motives, capacities, weaknesses, when brought to the test of an inexorable physical necessity. Restraint! What possible restraint? Was it superstition, disgust, patience, fear – or some kind of primitive honour? No fear can stand up to hunger, no patience can wear it out, disgust simply does not exist where hunger is; and as to superstition, beliefs, and what you may call principles, they are less than chaff in a breeze. Don't you know the

---

1 **probability:** Wahrscheinlichkeit.
5 **unwholesome:** ungesund.
9 **to pervade:** durchdringen.
13 **preliminary:** einleitend.
   trifling: Tändelei, Geplänkel.
14 **onslaught:** Ansturm.
18 **inexorable:** unerbittlich.
   restraint: Zurückhaltung.
19 **superstition:** Aberglaube.
24 **chaff:** Spreu.

devilry of lingering starvation, its exasperating torment, its black thoughts, its sombre and brooding ferocity? Well, I do. It takes a man all his inborn strength to fight hunger properly. It's really easier to face bereavement, dishonour, and the perdition of one's soul – than this kind of prolonged hunger. Sad, but true. And these chaps, too, had no earthly reason for any kind of scruple. Restraint! I would just as soon have expected restraint from a hyena prowling amongst the corpses of a battlefield. But there was the fact facing me – the fact dazzling, to be seen, like the foam on the depths of the sea, like a ripple on an unfathomable enigma, a mystery greater – when I thought of it – than the curious, inexplicable note of desperate grief in this savage clamour that had swept by us on the river-bank, behind the blind whiteness of the fog.

"Two pilgrims were quarrelling in hurried whispers as to which bank. 'Left.' 'No, no; how can you? Right, right, of course.' 'It is very serious,' said the manager's voice behind me; 'I would be desolated if anything should

---

1 **to exasperate:** erbittern.
  torment: Qual, Marter.
2 **ferocity:** Wildheit.
3 **inborn:** angeboren.
4 **bereavement:** schmerzlicher Verlust.
5 **dishonour:** Schande.
  perdition: Verdammnis.
6 **to prolong:** verlängern.
8 **scruple:** Gewissensbiß.
9 **hyena:** Hyäne.
  to prowl: umherstreichen.
11 **dazzling:** blendend, verwirrend.
12 **unfathomable:** unergründlich.
14 **inexplicable:** unerklärlich.
20 **to desolate:** betrüben, traurig machen.

happen to Mr. Kurtz before we came up.' I looked at
him, and had not the slightest doubt he was sincere. He
was just the kind of man who would wish to preserve
appearances. That was his restraint. But when he
5 muttered something about going on at once, I did not
even take the trouble to answer him. I knew, and he
knew, that it was impossible. Were we to let go our hold
of the bottom, we would be absolutely in the air – in
space. We wouldn't be able to tell where we were going
10 to – whether up or down stream, or across – till we
fetched against one bank or the other, – and then we
wouldn't know at first which it was. Of course I made no
move. I had no mind for a smash-up. You couldn't
imagine a more deadly place for a shipwreck. Whether
15 drowned at once or not, we were sure to perish speedily
in one way or another. 'I authorize you to take all the
risks,' he said, after a short silence. 'I refuse to take
any,' I said, shortly; which was just the answer he
expected, though its tone might have surprised him.
20 'Well, I must defer to your judgment. You are captain,'
he said, with marked civility. I turned my shoulder to
him in sign of my appreciation, and looked into the fog.
How long would it last? It was the most hopeless look-
out. The approach to this Kurtz grubbing for ivory in
25 the wretched bush was beset by as many dangers as
though he had been an enchanted princess sleeping in a

11 **to fetch:** gelangen.
13 **smash-up:** Zusammenstoß.
14 **shipwreck:** Schiffbruch.
16 **to authorize:** ermächtigen.
20 **to defer:** nachgeben, sich beugen.
26 **to enchant:** verzaubern.

fabulous castle. 'Will they attack, do you think?' asked the manager, in a confidential tone.

"I did not think they would attack, for several obvious reasons. The thick fog was one. If they left the bank in their canoes they would get lost in it, as we would be if we attempted to move. Still, I had also judged the jungle of both banks quite impenetrable – and yet eyes were in it, eyes that had seen us. The river-side bushes were certainly very thick; but the undergrowth behind was evidently penetrable. However, during the short lift I had seen no canoes anywhere in the reach – certainly not abreast of the steamer. But what made the idea of attack inconceivable to me was the nature of the noise – of the cries we had heard. They had not the fierce character boding of immediate hostile intention. Unexpected, wild, and violent as they had been, they had given me an irresistible impression of sorrow. The glimpse of the steamboat had for some reason filled those savages with unrestrained grief. The danger, if any, I expounded, was from our proximity to a great human passion let loose. Even extreme grief may ultimately vent itself in violence – but more generally takes the form of apathy. . . .

"You should have seen the pilgrims stare! They had no heart to grin, or even to revile me: but I believe they

---

1 **fabulous:** sagenhaft, legendär.
12 **inconceivable:** unbegreiflich, undenkbar.
14 **to bode:** prophezeien, ahnen lassen.
16 **irresistible:** unwiderstehlich.
19 **to expound:** erklären.
20 **proximity:** Nähe.
21 **to vent:** Luft machen.
22 **apathy:** Teilnahmslosigkeit, Gleichgültigkeit.
24 **to revile:** schmähen.

thought me gone mad – with fright, maybe. I delivered a
regular lecture. My dear boys, it was no good bothering.
Keep a look-out? Well, you may guess I watched the fog
for the signs of lifting as a cat watches a mouse; but for
anything else our eyes were of no more use to us than if
we had been buried miles deep in a heap of cotton-wool.
It felt like it, too – choking, warm, stifling. Besides, all I
said, though it sounded extravagant, was absolutely true
to fact. What we afterwards alluded to as an attack was
really an attempt at repulse. The action was very far from
being aggressive – it was not even defensive, in the usual
sense: it was undertaken under the stress of desperation,
and in its essence was purely protective.

"It developed itself, I should say, two hours after the
fog lifted, and its commencement was at a spot, roughly
speaking, about a mile and a half below Kurtz's station.
We had just floundered and flopped round a bend,
when I saw an islet, a mere grassy hummock of bright
green, in the middle of the stream. It was the only thing
of the kind; but as we opened the reach more, I perceived it was the head of a long sandbank, or rather of a
chain of shallow patches stretching down the middle of
the river. They were discoloured, just awash, and the

2 **to bother:** beunruhigen.
3 **to keep a look-out:** Ausschau, Wache halten.
7 **to stifle:** ersticken.
9 **to allude to:** hinstellen als.
10 **repulse:** Zurücktreiben, Abwehr eines Angriffs.
11 **aggressive:** angreifend, aggressiv.
   defensive: verteidigend.
17 **to flounder:** sich abquälen, taumeln.
18 **islet:** Inselchen.
   hummock: Hügel.
23 **awash:** überflutet.

whole lot was seen just under the water, exactly as a man's backbone is seen running down the middle of his back under the skin. Now, as far as I did see, I could go to the right or to the left of this. I didn't know either channel, of course. The banks looked pretty well alike, the depth appeared the same; but as I had been informed the station was on the west side, I naturally headed for the western passage.

"No sooner had we fairly entered it than I became aware it was much narrower than I had supposed. To the left of us there was the long uninterrupted shoal, and to the right a high, steep bank heavily overgrown with bushes. Above the bush the trees stood in serried ranks. The twigs overhung the current thickly, and from distance to distance a large limb of some tree projected rigidly over the stream. It was then well on in the afternoon, the face of the forest was gloomy, and a broad strip of shadow had already fallen on the water. In this shadow we steamed up – very slowly, as you may imagine. I sheered her well inshore – the water being deepest near the bank, as the sounding-pole informed me.

"One of my hungry and forbearing friends was sounding in the bows just below me. This steamboat was exactly like a decked scow. On the deck, there were two little teak-wood houses, with doors and windows. The boiler

11 **shoal:** Untiefe.
13 **serried:** dicht geschlossen.
15 **to project:** herausragen.
16 **rigid:** starr, steif.
20 **to sheer:** steuern.
21 **sounding-pole:** Peilstab.
22 **to forbear:** sich enthalten.
   to sound: loten, peilen.
24 **scow:** Prahm, Leichter.

95

was in the fore-end, and the machinery right astern. Over the whole there was a light roof, supported on stanchions. The funnel projected through that roof, and in front of the funnel a small cabin built of light planks
5 served for a pilot-house. It contained a couch, two camp-stools, a loaded Martini-Henry leaning in one corner, a tiny table, and the steering-wheel. It had a wide door in front and a broad shutter at each side. All these were always thrown open, of course. I spent my
10 days perched up there on the extreme fore-end of that roof, before the door. At night I slept, or tried to, on the couch. An athletic black belonging to some coast tribe, and educated by my poor predecessor, was the helmsman. He sported a pair of brass earrings, wore a
15 blue cloth wrapper from the waist to the ankles, and thought all the world of himself. He was the most unstable kind of fool I had ever seen. He steered with no end of a swagger while you were by; but if he lost sight of you, he became instantly the prey of an abject
20 funk, and would let that cripple of a steamboat get the upper hand of him in a minute.

---

1 **fore-end:** vorn, am Bug.
  astern: achtern.
3 **stanchion:** Pfosten.
  funnel: Schornstein.
5 **pilot-house:** Ruderhaus.
7 **steering-wheel:** Steuerrad.
12 **athletic:** athletisch.
14 **helmsman:** Rudergänger.
15 **ankle:** Fußknöchel.
17 **unstable:** instabil, unbeständig.
18 **swagger:** Großtuerei, Prahlerei.
19 **abject:** tiefste, äußerste.
20 **funk:** riesige Angst.

"I was looking down at the sounding-pole, and feeling much annoyed to see at each try a little more of it stick out of that river, when I saw my poleman give up the business suddenly, and stretch himself flat on the deck, without even taking the trouble to haul his pole in. He kept hold on it though, and it trailed in the water. At the same time the fireman, whom I could also see below me, sat down abruptly before his furnace and ducked his head. I was amazed. Then I had to look at the river mighty quick, because there was a snag in the fairway. Sticks, little sticks, were flying about – thick: they were whizzing before my nose, dropping below me, striking behind me against my pilot-house. All this time the river, the shore, the woods, were very quiet – perfectly quiet. I could only hear the heavy splashing thump of the stern-wheel and the patter of these things. We cleared the snag clumsily. Arrows, by Jove! We were being shot at! I stepped in quickly to close the shutter on the land-side. That fool-helmsman, his hands on the spokes, was lifting his knees high, stamping his feet, champing his mouth, like a reined-in horse. Confound him! And we were staggering within ten feet of the bank. I had to lean right out to swing the heavy shutter, and I saw a face amongst the leaves on the level with my own, looking at me very fierce and steady; and then suddenly, as though a veil had been removed from my eyes, I made out, deep in the tangled gloom, naked breasts, arms, legs, glaring eyes, – the bush was swarm-

---

3 **poleman:** Lotgast (der mit dem Loten beauftragte Seemann).
8 **furnace:** Kessel.
12 **to whiz:** zischen, schwirren.
21 **to champ:** heftig kauen.
   to rein in: anhalten.

ing with human limbs in movement, glistening, of
bronze colour. The twigs shook, swayed, and rustled,
the arrows flew out of them, and then the shutter came
to. 'Steer her straight,' I said to the helmsman. He held
5 his head rigid, face forward; but his eyes rolled, he kept
on, lifting and setting down his feet gently, his mouth
foamed a little. 'Keep quiet!' I said in a fury. I might
just as well have ordered a tree not to sway in the wind.
I darted out. Below me there was a great scuffle of feet
10 on the iron deck; confused exclamations; a voice
screamed, 'Can you turn back?' I caught sight of a V-
shaped ripple on the water ahead. What? Another snag!
A fusillade burst out under my feet. The pilgrims had
opened with their Winchesters, and were simply squirt-
15 ing lead into that bush. A deuce of a lot of smoke came
up and drove slowly forward. I swore at it. Now I
couldn't see the ripple or the snag either. I stood in the
doorway, peering, and the arrows came in swarms.
They might have been poisoned, but they looked as
20 though they wouldn't kill a cat. The bush began to howl.
Our wood-cutters raised a warlike whoop; the report of
a rifle just at my back deafened me. I glanced over my
shoulder, and the pilot-house was yet full of noise and
smoke when I made a dash at the wheel. The fool-nigger
25 had dropped everything, to throw the shutter open and
let off that Martini-Henry. He stood before the wide

---

9 **scuffle:** Getrappel.
13 **fusillade:** Gewehrsalve.
13 f. **had opened with their Winchesters:** hatten mit ihren Repetier-
gewehren das Feuer eröffnet.
14 f. **to squirt:** spritzen.
18 **to peer:** spähen.
21 **warlike whoop:** Kriegsgeschrei.

opening, glaring, and I yelled at him to come back, while I straightened the sudden twist out of that steamboat. There was no room to turn even if I had wanted to, the snag was somewhere very near ahead in that confounded smoke, there was no time to lose, so I just crowded her into the bank – right into the bank, where I knew the water was deep.

"We tore slowly along the overhanging bushes in a whirl of broken twigs and flying leaves. The fusillade below stopped short, as I had foreseen it would when the squirts got empty. I threw my head back to a glinting whizz that traversed the pilot-house, in at one shutterhole and out at the other. Looking past that mad helmsman, who was shaking the empty rifle and yelling at the shore, I saw vague forms of men running bent double, leaping, gliding, distinct, incomplete, evanescent. Something big appeared in the air before the shutter, the rifle went overboard, and the man stepped back swiftly, looked at me over his shoulder in an extraordinary, profound, familiar manner, and fell upon my feet. The side of his head hit the wheel twice, and the end of what appeared a long cane clattered round and knocked over a little camp-stool. It looked as though after wrenching that thing from somebody ashore he had lost his balance in the effort. The thin

---

6 **to crowd into:** hineinpressen, hineindrängen.
8 **whirl:** Wirbel.
11 **squirt:** Spritze, hier auch: Knarre.
12 **to traverse:** durchqueren.
16 f. **evanescent:** dahinschwindend.
22 **cane:** Stock.
23 **to knock over:** umwerfen.
24 **to wrench:** entwinden.

smoke had blown away, we were clear of the snag, and
looking ahead I could see that in another hundred yards
or so I would be free to sheer off, away from the bank;
but my feet felt so very warm and wet that I had to look
5 down. The man had rolled on his back and stared
straight up at me; both his hands clutched that cane. It
was the shaft of a spear that, either thrown or lunged
through the opening, had caught him in the side just
below the ribs; the blade had gone in out of sight, after
10 making a frightful gash; my shoes were full; a pool of
blood lay very still, gleaming dark-red under the wheel;
his eyes shone with an amazing lustre. The fusillade
burst out again. He looked at me anxiously, gripping
the spear like something precious, with an air of being
15 afraid I would try to take it away from him. I had to
make an effort to free my eyes from his gaze and attend
to the steering. With one hand I felt above my head for
the line of the steam whistle, and jerked out screech
after screech hurriedly. The tumult of angry and warlike
20 yells was checked instantly, and then from the depths of
the woods went out such a tremulous and prolonged
wail of mournful fear and utter despair as may be
imagined to follow the flight of the last hope from the
earth. There was a great commotion in the bush; the

6 **to clutch:** packen.
7 **shaft:** Schaft.
  to lunge: stoßen.
10 **gash:** klaffende Wunde.
  pool: Lache.
12 **lustre:** Glanz.
18 **to jerk:** ruckweise ziehen.
21 **tremulous:** zitternd, bebend.
22 **wail:** Klage.
24 **commotion:** Aufruhr, Tumult.

shower of arrows stopped, a few dropping shots rang
out sharply – then silence, in which the languid beat of
the stern-wheel came plainly to my ears. I put the helm
hard a-starboard at the moment when the pilgrim in
5 pink pyjamas, very hot and agitated, appeared in the
doorway. 'The manager sends me —' he began in an
official tone, and stopped short. 'Good God!' he said,
glaring at the wounded man.

"We two whites stood over him, and his lustrous and
10 inquiring glance enveloped us both. I declare it looked
as though he would presently put to us some question in
an understandable language; but he died without utter-
ing a sound, without moving a limb, without twitching a
muscle. Only in the very last moment, as though in
15 response to some sign we could not see, to some
whisper we could not hear, he frowned heavily, and that
frown gave to his black death-mask an inconceivably
sombre, brooding, and menacing expression. The lustre
of inquiring glance faded swiftly into vacant glassiness.
20 'Can you steer?' I asked the agent eagerly. He looked
very dubious; but I made a grab at his arm, and he
understood at once I meant him to steer whether or no.
To tell you the truth, I was morbidly anxious to change
my shoes and socks. 'He is dead,' murmured the fellow,

1 **dropping shots:** ›tröpfelnde‹, vereinzelte Schüsse.
4 **a-starboard:** nach Steuerbord.
8 **to glare:** starren.
9 **lustrous:** glänzend.
18 **menacing:** drohend.
19 **vacant:** leer.
   glassiness: Starrheit, Glasigkeit.
21 **dubious:** zweifelhaft, ungewiß.
   grab: plötzlicher Griff.
23 **morbidly** (adv.): krankhaft.

immensely impressed. 'No doubt about it,' said I, tugging like mad at the shoe-laces. 'And by the way, I suppose Mr. Kurtz is dead as well by this time.'

"For the moment that was the dominant thought. There
5 was a sense of extreme disappointment, as though I had found out I had been striving after something altogether without a substance. I couldn't have been more disgusted if I had travelled all this way for the sole purpose of talking with Mr. Kurtz. Talking with. . . . I flung one
10 shoe overboard, and became aware that that was exactly what I had been looking forward to – a talk with Kurtz. I made the strange discovery that I had never imagined him as doing, you know, but as discoursing. I didn't say to myself, 'Now I will never see him,' or 'Now
15 I will never shake him by the hand.' but, 'now I will never hear him.' The man presented himself as a voice. Not of course that I did not connect him with some sort of action. Hadn't I been told in all the tones of jealousy and admiration that he had collected, bartered, swin-
20 dled, or stolen more ivory than all the other agents together? That was not the point. The point was in his being a gifted creature, and that of all his gifts the one that stood out pre-eminently, that carried with it a sense of real presence, was his ability to talk, his words – the
25 gift of expression, the bewildering, the illuminating, the

2 **shoe-lace:** Schnürsenkel.
4 **dominant:** vorherrschend.
8 **sole:** alleinig, einzig.
13 **to discourse:** reden, sprechen.
19 **to barter:** eintauschen.
19f. **to swindle:** erschwindeln.
23 **pre-eminently** (adv.): überragend.
25 **bewildering:** verblüffend, verwirrend.
   illuminating: aufschlußreich, erleuchtend.

most exalted and the most contemptible, the pulsating stream of light, or the deceitful flow from the heart of an impenetrable darkness.

"The other shoe went flying unto the devil-god of that river. I thought, By Jove! it's all over. We are too late; he has vanished – the gift has vanished, by means of some spear, arrow, or club. I will never hear that chap speak after all, – and my sorrow had a startling extravagance of emotion, even such as I had noticed in the howling sorrow of these savages in the bush. I couldn't have felt more of lonely desolation somehow, had I been robbed of a belief or had missed my destiny in life. . . . Why do you sigh in this beastly way, somebody? Absurd? Well, absurd. Good Lord! mustn't a man ever — Here, give me some tobacco." . . .

There was a pause of profound stillness, then a match flared, and Marlow's lean face appeared, worn, hollow, with downward folds and dropped eyelids, with an aspect of concentrated attention; and as he took vigorous draws at his pipe, it seemed to retreat and advance out of the night in the regular flicker of the tiny flame. The match went out.

"Absurd!" he cried. "This is the worst of trying to tell. . . . Here you all are, each moored with two good

---

1 **contemptible:** verächtlich.
  pulsating: pulsierend.
2 **deceitful:** trügerisch.
5 **Jove:** Jupiter.
7 **club:** Keule.
12 **destiny:** Schicksal, Bestimmung.
17 **to flare:** flackern.
  worn: erschöpft.
19 **concentrated:** konzentriert.
19f. **vigorous:** kräftig.

addresses, like a hulk with two anchors, a butcher round
one corner, a policeman round another, excellent appe-
tites, and temperature normal – you hear – normal from
year's end to year's end. And you say, Absurd! Absurd
be – exploded! Absurd! My dear boys, what can you
expect from a man who out of sheer nervousness had
just flung overboard a pair of new shoes! Now I think of
it, it is amazing I did not shed tears. I am, upon the
whole, proud of my fortitude. I was cut to the quick at
the idea of having lost the inestimable privilege of
listening to the gifted Kurtz. Of course I was wrong.
The privilege was waiting for me. Oh, yes, I heard more
than enough. And I was right, too. A voice. He was
very little more than a voice. And I heard – him – it –
this voice – other voices – all of them were so little more
than voices – and the memory of that time itself lingers
around me, impalpable, like a dying vibration of one
immense jabber, silly, atrocious, sordid, savage, or
simply mean, without any kind of sense. Voices, voices
– even the girl herself – now —"
He was silent for a long time.
"I laid the ghost of his gifts at last with a lie," he began,
suddenly. "Girl! What? Did I mention a girl? Oh, she is
out of it – completely. They – the women I mean – are
out of it – should be out of it. We must help them to stay
in that beautiful world of their own, lest ours gets

6 **sheer:** rein.
9 **to be cut to the quick:** zutiefst betroffen sein.
10 **inestimable:** unschätzbar.
17 **impalpable:** kaum faßbar.
 vibration: Schwingung, Nachhall.
18 **atrocious:** scheußlich.
22 **to lay a ghost:** einen Geist bannen.

104

worse. Oh, she had to be out of it. You should have heard the disinterred body of Mr. Kurtz saying, 'My Intended.' You would have perceived directly then how completely she was out of it. And the lofty frontal bone
5 of Mr. Kurtz! They say the hair goes on growing sometimes, but this – ah – specimen, was impressively bald. The wilderness had patted him on the head, and, behold, it was like a ball – an ivory ball; it had caressed him, and – lo! – he had withered; it had taken him, loved him,
10 embraced him, got into his veins, consumed his flesh, and sealed his soul to its own by the inconceivable ceremonies of some devilish initiation. He was its spoiled and pampered favourite. Ivory? I should think so. Heaps of it, stacks of it. The old mud shanty was
15 bursting with it. You would think there was not a single tusk left either above or below the ground in the whole country. 'Mostly fossil,' the manager had remarked, disparagingly. It was no more fossil than I am; but they call it fossil when it is dug up. It appears these niggers
20 do bury the tusks sometimes – but evidently they couldn't bury this parcel deep enough to save the gifted Mr. Kurtz from his fate. We filled the steamboat with it, and had to pile a lot on the deck. Thus he could see and

2 **to disinter:** exhumieren, ausgraben.
3 **Intended:** ›Zukünftige‹, Verlobte.
4 **frontal bone:** Stirnbein.
7 **to pat:** klopfen, tätscheln.
9 **to wither:** welken, austrocknen.
11 **to seal:** siegeln.
13 **to pamper:** verwöhnen, verhätscheln.
14 **shanty:** Hütte.
16 **tusk:** Stoßzahn.
17 **fossil:** fossil, versteinert.
18 **disparaging:** verächtlich, geringschätzig.

enjoy as long as he could see, because the appreciation of this favour had remained with him to the last. You should have heard him say, 'My ivory.' Oh yes, I heard him. 'My Intended, my ivory, my station, my river, my—'
5 everything belonged to him. It made me hold my breath in expectation of hearing the wilderness burst into a prodigious peal of laughter that would shake the fixed stars in their places. Everything belonged to him – but that was a trifle. The thing was to know what he
10 belonged to, how many powers of darkness claimed him for their own. That was the reflection that made you creepy all over. It was impossible – it was not good for one either – trying to imagine. He had taken a high seat amongst the devils of the land – I mean literally. You
15 can't understand. How could you? – with solid pavement under your feet, surrounded by kind neighbours ready to cheer you or to fall on you, stepping delicately between the butcher and the policeman, in the holy terror of scandal and gallows and lunatic asylums – how
20 can you imagine what particular region of the first ages a man's untrammelled feet may take him into by the way of solitude – utter solitude without a policeman – by the way of silence – utter silence, where no warning voice of a kind neighbour can be heard whispering of

1 **appreciation:** Würdigung.
7 **prodigious:** ungeheuer.
 peal: Getöse.
7f. **fixed stars:** Fixsterne.
11f. **to make creepy:** erschauern lassen.
14 **literally** (adv.): buchstäblich, wörtlich.
19 **scandal:** Skandal, Klatsch.
 gallows: Galgen.
 lunatic asylum: Irrenanstalt.
21 **untrammeled:** ungehindert.

public opinion? These little things make all the great difference. When they are gone you must fall back upon your own innate strength, upon your own capacity for faithfulness. Of course you may be too much of a fool to go wrong – too dull even to know you are being assaulted by the powers of darkness. I take it, no fool ever made a bargain for his soul with the devil: the fool is too much of a fool, or the devil too much of a devil – I don't know which. Or you may be such a thunderingly exalted creature as to be altogether deaf and blind to anything but heavenly sights and sounds. Then the earth for you is only a standing place – and whether to be like this is your loss or your gain I won't pretend to say. But most of us are neither one nor the other. The earth for us is a place to live in, where we must put up with sights, with sounds, with smells, too, by Jove! – breathe dead hippo, so to speak, and not be contaminated. And there, don't you see? your strength comes in, the faith in your ability for the digging of unostentatious holes to bury the stuff in – your power of devotion, not to yourself, but to an obscure, back-breaking business. And that's difficult enough. Mind, I am not trying to excuse or even explain – I am trying to account to myself for – for – Mr. Kurtz – for the shade of Mr. Kurtz. This initiated wraith from the back of Nowhere honoured me with its amazing confidence before it

---

3 **innate:** angeboren, einer Sache innewohnend.
4 **faithfulness:** Ehrlichkeit, Treue.
6 **to assault:** anfallen, angreifen.
17 **to contaminate:** beschmutzen, vergiften.
19 **unostentatious:** unauffällig.
25 **initiated wraith:** eingeweihtes Geisterwesen (eines gerade Verstorbenen).

vanished altogether. This was because it could speak
English to me. The original Kurtz had been educated
partly in England, and – as he was good enough to say
himself – his sympathies were in the right place. His
mother was half-English, his father was half-French. All
Europe contributed to the making of Kurtz[34]; and by-
and-by I learned that, most appropriately, the Interna-
tional Society for the Suppression of Savage Customs[35]
had intrusted him with the making of a report, for its
future guidance. And he had written it, too. I've seen it.
I've read it. It was eloquent, vibrating with eloquence,
but too high-strung, I think. Seventeen pages of close
writing he had found time for! But this must have been
before his – let us say – nerves, went wrong, and caused
him to preside at certain midnight dances ending with
unspeakable rites, which – as far as I reluctantly
gathered from what I heard at various times – were
offered up to him – do you understand? – to Mr. Kurtz
himself. But it was a beautiful piece of writing. The
opening paragraph, however, in the light of later information, strikes me now as ominous. He began with the
argument that we whites, from the point of development we had arrived at, 'must necessarily appear to
them [savages] in the nature of supernatural beings – we

6f. **by-and-by:** nach und nach.
7 **appropriately** (adv.): angemessen, geeignet.
8 **suppression:** Unterdrückung.
11 **eloquent:** beredt.
   to vibrate: schwingen, vibrieren.
12 **high-strung:** reizbar, überempfindlich.
15 **to preside:** den Vorsitz führen.
16 **rite:** Ritus, feierlicher Brauch.
   reluctantly (adv.): widerstrebend, widerwillig.

approach them with the might as of a deity,' and so on, and so on. 'By the simple exercise of our will we can exert a power for good practically unbounded,' etc. etc. From that point he soared and took me with him. The peroration was magnificent, though difficult to remember, you know. It gave me the notion of an exotic Immensity ruled by an august Benevolence. It made me tingle with enthusiasm. This was the unbounded power of eloquence – of words – of burning noble words. There were no practical hints to interrupt the magic current of phrases, unless a kind of note at the foot of the last page, scrawled evidently much later, in an unsteady hand, may be regarded as the exposition of a method. It was very simple, and at the end of that moving appeal to every altruistic sentiment it blazed at you, luminous and terrifying, like a flash of lightning in a serene sky: 'Exterminate all the brutes!' The curious part was that he had apparently forgotten all about that valuable postscriptum, because, later on, when he in a sense came to himself, he repeatedly entreated me to take good care of 'my pamphlet' (he called it), as it was

1 **deity:** Gottheit.
4 **to soar:** sich emporschwingen.
5 **peroration:** zusammenfassender Schluß einer Rede.
7 **august:** erhaben.
  Benevolence: Güte.
8 **to tingle:** klingeln, kribbeln.
12 **to scrawl:** kritzeln.
13 **exposition:** Darlegung, Ausführung, Ausstellung.
15 **altruistic:** uneigennützig.
17 **serene:** heiter.
  to exterminate: ausrotten, vertilgen.
20 **to entreat:** (dringend) bitten, anflehen.
21 **pamphlet:** Broschüre, Flugschrift.

sure to have in the future a good influence upon his
career. I had full information about all these things,
and, besides, as it turned out, I was to have the care of
his memory. I've done enough for it to give me the
5 indisputable right to lay it, if I choose, for an everlasting
rest in the dust-bin of progress, amongst all the sweepings and, figuratively speaking, all the dead cats of
civilization. But then, you see, I can't choose. He won't
be forgotten. Whatever he was, he was not common.
10 He had the power to charm or frighten rudimentary
souls into an aggravated witch-dance in his honour; he
could also fill the small souls of the pilgrims with bitter
misgivings: he had one devoted friend at least, and he
had conquered one soul in the world that was neither
15 rudimentary nor tainted with self-seeking. No; I can't
forget him, though I am not prepared to affirm the
fellow was exactly worth the life we lost in getting to
him. I missed my late helmsman awfully, – I missed him
even while his body was still lying in the pilot-house.
20 Perhaps you will think it passing strange this regret for a
savage who was no more account than a grain of sand in
a black Sahara. Well, don't you see, he had done
something, he had steered; for months I had him at my
back – a help – an instrument. It was a kind of partner-
25 ship. He steered for me – I had to look after him, I

5 **indisputable:** unbestreitbar.
6 **dust-bin:** Mülleimer.
6f. **sweepings:** Kehrricht.
7 **figuratively** (adv.): bildlich.
10 **rudimentary:** rudimentär, nicht voll entwickelt.
11 **to aggravate:** steigern, übertreiben.
15 **to taint:** verderben, beflecken.

worried about his deficiencies, and thus a subtle bond
had been created, of which I only became aware when it
was suddenly broken. And the intimate profundity of
that look he gave me when he received his hurt remains
to this day in my memory – like a claim of distant
kinship affirmed in a supreme moment.

"Poor fool! If he had only left that shutter alone. He
had no restraint, no restraint – just like Kurtz – a tree
swayed by the wind. As soon as I had put on a dry pair
of slippers, I dragged him out, after first jerking the
spear out of his side, which operation I confess I per-
formed with my eyes shut tight. His heels leaped
together over the little door-step; his shoulders were
pressed to my breast; I hugged him from behind desperately. Oh! he was heavy, heavy; heavier than any man
on earth, I should imagine. Then without more ado I
tipped him overboard. The current snatched him as
though he had been a wisp of grass, and I saw the body
roll over twice before I lost sight of it for ever. All the
pilgrims and the manager were then congregated on the
awning-deck about the pilot-house, chattering at each
other like a flock of excited magpies, and there was a
scandalized murmur at my heartless promptitude. What

---

1 **deficiency:** Mangel, Unzulänglichkeit.
3 **profundity:** Tiefgründigkeit.
14 **to hug:** umarmen.
16 **ado:** Getue, Aufhebens.
18 **wisp:** Büschel.
20 **to congregate:** versammeln.
20 f. **on the awning deck:** an Deck unter dem Sonnensegel.
22 **flock:** Schar.
   magpie: Elster.
23 **to be scandalized at s.th.:** über etwas empört, schockiert sein.

111

they wanted to keep that body hanging about for I can't
guess. Embalm it, maybe. But I had also heard another,
and a very ominous, murmur on the deck below. My
friends the wood-cutters were likewise scandalized, and
5 with a better show of reason – though I admit that the
reason itself was quite inadmissible. Oh, quite! I had
made up my mind that if my late helmsman was to be
eaten, the fishes alone should have him. He had been a
very second-rate helmsman while alive, but now he was
10 dead he might have become a first-class temptation, and
possibly cause some startling trouble. Besides, I was
anxious to take the wheel, the man in pink pyjamas
showing himself a hopeless duffer at the business.

"This I did directly the simple funeral was over. We
15 were going half-speed, keeping right in the middle of
the stream, and I listened to the talk about me. They
had given up Kurtz, they had given up the station; Kurtz
was dead, and the station had been burnt – and so on –
and so on. The red-haired pilgrim was beside himself
20 with the thought that at least this poor Kurtz had been
properly avenged. 'Say! We must have made a glorious
slaughter of them in the bush. Eh? What do you think?
Say?' He positively danced, the bloodthirsty little gingery beggar. And he had nearly fainted when he saw the

2 **to embalm:** einbalsamieren.
6 **inadmissible:** unzulässig.
9 **second-rate:** zweitklassig.
10 **first-class:** erstklassig, erster Klasse.
   temptation: Versuchung.
13 **duffer:** Dummkopf, Stümper.
19 **to be beside o.s.:** außer sich sein.
22 **slaughter:** Schlachten, Gemetzel.
23f. **gingery:** hitzig, reizbar.

112

wounded man! I could not help saying, 'You made a glorious lot of smoke, anyhow.' I had seen, from the way the tops of the bushes rustled and flew, that almost all the shots had gone too high. You can't hit anything
5 unless you take aim and fire from the shoulder; but these chaps fired from the hip with their eyes shut. The retreat, I maintained – and I was right – was caused by the screeching of the steamwhistle. Upon this they forgot Kurtz, and began to howl at me with indignant
10 protests.

"The manager stood by the wheel murmuring confidentially about the necessity of getting well away down the river before dark at all events, when I saw in the distance a clearing on the river-side and the outlines of
15 some sort of building. 'What's this?' I asked. He clapped his hands in wonder. 'The station[36]!' he cried. I edged in at once, still going half-speed.

"Through my glasses I saw the slope of a hill interspersed with rare trees and perfectly free from under-
20 growth. A long decaying building on the summit was half buried in the high grass; the large holes in the peaked roof gaped black from afar; the jungle and the woods made a background. There was no enclosure or fence of any kind; but there had been one apparently,
25 for near the house half-a-dozen slim posts remained in a row, roughly trimmed, and with their upper ends ornamented with round carved balls. The rails, or what-

---

6 **hip:** Hüfte.
9 **indignant:** entrüstet, empört.
18 f. **to intersperse:** einstreuen.
20 **summit:** Gipfel.
22 **peaked roof:** spitzes Dach.
26 **to trim:** stutzen, beschneiden.

ever there had been between, had disappeared. Of
course the forest surrounded all that. The river-bank
was clear, and on the water-side I saw a white man
under a hat like a cart-wheel beckoning persistently
5 with his whole arm. Examining the edge of the forest
above and below, I was almost certain I could see
movements – human forms gliding here and there. I
steamed past prudently, then stopped the engines and
let her drift down. The man on the shore began to
10 shout, urging us to land. 'We have been attacked,'
screamed the manager. 'I know – I know. It's all right,'
yelled back the other, as cheerful as you please. 'Come
along. It's all right. I am glad.'

"His aspect reminded me of something I had seen –
15 something funny I had seen somewhere. As I ma-
nœuvred to get alongside, I was asking myself, 'What
does this fellow look like?' Suddenly I got it. He looked
like a harlequin[37]. His clothes had been made of some
stuff that was brown holland probably, but it was
20 covered with patches all over, with bright patches, blue,
red, and yellow, – patches on the back, patches on the
front, patches on elbows, on knees; coloured binding
around his jacket, scarlet edging at the bottom of his
trousers; and the sunshine made him look extremely gay
25 and wonderfully neat withal, because you could see how
beautifully all this patching had been done. A beardless,
boyish face, very fair, no features to speak of, nose
peeling, little blue eyes, smiles and frowns chasing each

15 f. **to manœuvre:** manövrieren.
18 **harlequin:** Harlekin.
19 **brown holland:** braune, ungebleichte Leinwand.
23 **scarlet:** scharlachrot.
25 **withal:** zugleich, obendrein.

other over that open countenance like sunshine and shadow on a wind-swept plain. 'Look out, captain!' he cried; 'there's a snag lodged in here last night.' What! Another snag? I confess I swore shamefully. I had

5 nearly holed my cripple, to finish off that charming trip. The harlequin on the bank turned his little pug-nose up to me. 'You English?' he asked, all smiles. 'Are you?' I shouted from the wheel. The smiles vanished, and he shook his head as if sorry for my disappointment. Then

10 he brightened up. 'Never mind!' he cried, encouragingly. 'Are we in time?' I asked. 'He is up there,' he replied, with a toss of the head up the hill, and becoming gloomy all of a sudden. His face was like the autumn sky, overcast one moment and bright the next.

15 "When the manager, escorted by the pilgrims, all of them armed to the teeth, had gone to the house this chap came on board. 'I say, I don't like this. These natives are in the bush,' I said. He assured me earnestly it was all right. 'They are simple people,' he added;

20 'well, I am glad you came. It took me all my time to keep them off.' 'But you said it was all right,' I cried. 'Oh, they meant no harm,' he said; and as I stared he corrected himself, 'Not exactly.' Then vivaciously, 'My faith, your pilot-house wants a clean up!' In the next

25 breath he advised me to keep enough steam on the boiler to blow the whistle in case of any trouble. 'One good screech will do more for you than all your rifles. They are simple people,' he repeated. He rattled away

---

5 **to hole:** ein Loch bohren.
6 **pug-nose:** Stupsnase.
12 **a toss of the head:** ein Zurückwerfen des Kopfes.
23 **vivaciously** (adv.): lebhaft.

at such a rate he quite overwhelmed me. He seemed to
be trying to make up for lots of silence, and actually
hinted, laughing, that such was the case. 'Don't you talk
with Mr. Kurtz?' I said. 'You don't talk with that man –
5 you listen to him,' he exclaimed with severe exaltation.
'But now —' He waved his arm, and in the twinkling of
an eye was in the uttermost depths of despondency. In a
moment he came up again with a jump, possessed
himself of both my hands, shook them continuously,
10 while he gabbled: 'Brother sailor . . . honour . . . pleasure . . . delight . . . introduce myself . . . Russian . . .
son of an arch-priest . . . Government of Tambov . . .
What? Tobacco! English tobacco; the excellent English
tobacco! Now, that's brotherly. Smoke? Where's a
15 sailor that does not smoke?'
"The pipe soothed him, and gradually I made out he
had run away from school, had gone to sea in a Russian
ship; ran away again; served some time in English ships;
was now reconciled with the arch-priest. He made a
20 point of that. 'But when one is young one must see
things, gather experience, ideas; enlarge the mind.'
'Here!' I interrupted. 'You can never tell! Here I met
Mr. Kurtz,' he said, youthfully solemn and reproachful.
I held my tongue after that. It appears he had persuaded
25 a Dutch trading-house on the coast to fit him out with

5 **exaltation:** Verzückung.
6f. **in the twinkling of an eye:** im Nu, im Augenblick.
7 **despondency:** Verzweiflung, Mutlosigkeit.
10 **to gabble:** schwatzen, schnattern.
12 **arch-priest:** Erzpriester.
16 **to soothe:** beruhigen, besänftigen.
19 **to reconcile:** versöhnen.
25 **Dutch:** holländisch.

stores and goods, and had started for the interior with a light heart, and no more idea of what would happen to him than a baby. He had been wandering about that river for nearly two years alone, cut off from everybody and everything. 'I am not so young as I look. I am twenty-five,' he said. 'At first old Van Shuyten would tell me to go to the devil,' he narrated with keen enjoyment; 'but I stuck to him, and talked and talked, till at last he got afraid I would talk the hind-leg off his favourite dog, so he gave me some cheap things and a few guns, and told me he hoped he would never see my face again. Good old Dutchman, Van Shuyten. I've sent him one small lot of ivory a year ago, so that he can't call me a little thief when I get back. I hope he got it. And for the rest I don't care. I had some wood stacked for you. That was my old house. Did you see?'

"I gave him Towson's book. He made as though he would kiss me, but restrained himself. 'The only book I had left, and I thought I had lost it,' he said, looking at it ecstatically. 'So many accidents happen to a man going about alone, you know. Canoes get upset sometimes – and sometimes you've got to clear out so quick when the people get angry.' He thumbed the pages. 'You made notes in Russian?' I asked. He nodded. 'I thought they were written in cipher,' I said[38]. He laughed, then became serious. 'I had lots of trouble to keep these people off,' he said. 'Did they want to kill you?' I asked. 'Oh, no!' he cried, and checked himself. 'Why did they attack us?' I pursued. He hesitated, then

---

1 **interior:** Innere(s), Binnenland.
21 **ecstatically** (adv.): verzückt, schwärmerisch, begeistert.

117

said shamefacedly, 'They don't want him to go.' 'Don't they?' I said, curiously. He nodded a nod full of mystery and wisdom. 'I tell you,' he cried, 'this man has enlarged my mind.' He opened his arms wide, staring at me with his little blue eyes that were perfectly round."

III

"I looked at him, lost in astonishment. There he was before me, in motley, as though he had absconded from a troupe of mimes, enthusiastic, fabulous. His very existence was improbable, inexplicable, and altogether bewildering. He was an insoluble problem. It was inconceivable how he had existed, how he had succeeded in getting so far, how he had managed to remain – why he did not instantly disappear. 'I went a little farther,' he said, 'then still a little farther – till I had gone so far that I don't know how I'll ever get back. Never mind. Plenty time. I can manage. You take Kurtz away quick – quick – I tell you.' The glamour of youth enveloped his particoloured rags, his destitution, his loneliness, the essential desolation of his futile wanderings. For months – for years – his life hadn't been worth a day's pur-

---

1 **shamefacedly** (adv.): mit schamerfülltem Gesicht.
8 **motley:** buntscheckig.
  to abscond: davonlaufen.
9 **mime:** Gaukler, Possenreißer.
  fabulous: fabelhaft, ungeheuer.
11 **insoluble:** unlösbar.
11f. **inconceivable:** unbegreiflich.
19 **destitution:** Hilflosigkeit.
20 **desolation:** Trostlosigkeit, Vereinsamung.
  futile: sinnlos, ziellos.

118

chase; and there he was gallantly, thoughtlessly alive, to all appearance indestructible solely by the virtue of his few years and of his unreflecting audacity. I was seduced into something like admiration – like envy. Glamour urged him on, glamour kept him unscathed. He surely wanted nothing from the wilderness but space to breathe in and to push on through. His need was to exist, and to move onwards at the greatest possible risk, and with a maximum of privation. If the absolutely pure, uncalculating, unpractical spirit of adventure had ever ruled a human being, it ruled this be-patched youth. I almost envied him the possession of this modest and clear flame. It seemed to have consumed all thought of self so completely, that even while he was talking to you, you forgot that it was he – the man before your eyes – who had gone through these things. I did not envy him his devotion to Kurtz, though. He had not meditated over it. It came to him, and he accepted it with a sort of eager fatalism. I must say that to me it appeared about the most dangerous thing in every way he had come upon so far.

"They had come together unavoidably, like two ships becalmed near each other, and lay rubbing sides at last.

1 **gallant:** tapfer.
2 **indestructible:** unzerstörbar.
4 **to seduce:** verführen.
5 **unscathed:** unversehrt.
9 **privation:** Entbehrung, Mangel.
11 **be-patched:** flickenbesetzt.
17 **devotion (to):** Verehrung (für), Ergebenheit.
18 **to meditate:** nachdenken.
19 **fatalism:** Fatalismus.
22 **unavoidably** (adv.): unvermeidlich.
23 **to be becalmed:** in eine Flaute geraten sein.

I suppose Kurtz wanted an audience, because on a certain occasion, when encamped in the forest, they had talked all night, or more probably Kurtz had talked. 'We talked of everything,' he said, quite transported at the recollection. 'I forgot there was such a thing as sleep. The night did not seem to last an hour. Everything! Everything! . . . Of love, too.' 'Ah, he talked to you of love!' I said, much amused. 'It isn't what you think,' he cried, almost passionately. 'It was in general. He made me see things – things.'

"He threw his arms up. We were on deck at the time, and the headman of my wood-cutters, lounging near by, turned upon him his heavy and glittering eyes. I looked around, and I don't know why, but I assure you that never, never before, did this land, this river, this jungle, the very arch of this blazing sky, appear to me so hopeless and so dark, so impenetrable to human thought, so pitiless to human weakness. 'And, ever since, you have been with him, of course?' I said.

"On the contrary. It appears their intercourse had been very much broken by various causes. He had, as he informed me proudly, managed to nurse Kurtz through two illnesses (he alluded to it as you would to some risky feat), but as a rule Kurtz wandered alone, far in the depths of the forest. 'Very often coming to this station, I had to wait days and days before he would turn up,' he said. 'Ah, it was worth waiting for! – sometimes.' 'What

2 **to encamp:** lagern.
4 **to be transported:** mitgerissen sein, bewegt sein.
5 **recollection:** Erinnerung.
12 **to lounge:** faulenzen, herumlungern.
20 **intercourse:** Umgang.
24 **feat:** Heldentat, Kunststück.

120

was he doing? exploring or what?' I asked. 'Oh, yes, of course;' he had discovered lots of villages, a lake, too – he did not know exactly in what direction; it was dangerous to inquire too much – but mostly his expeditions had been for ivory. 'But he had no goods to trade with by that time,' I objected. 'There's a good lot of cartridges left even yet,' he answered, looking away. 'To speak plainly, he raided the country,' I said. He nodded. 'Not alone, surely!' He muttered something about the villages round that lake. 'Kurtz got the tribe to follow him, did he?' I suggested. He fidgeted a little. 'They adored him,' he said. The tone of these words was so extraordinary that I looked at him searchingly. It was curious to see his mingled eagerness and reluctance to speak of Kurtz. The man filled his life, occupied his thoughts, swayed his emotions. 'What can you expect?' he burst out; 'he came to them with thunder and lightning, you know – and they had never seen anything like it – and very terrible. He could be very terrible. You can't judge Mr. Kurtz as you would an ordinary man. No, no, no! Now – just to give you an idea – I don't mind telling you, he wanted to shoot me, too, one day – but I don't judge him.' 'Shoot you!' I cried. 'What for?' 'Well, I had a small lot of ivory the chief of that village near my house gave me. You see I used to shoot game for them. Well, he wanted it, and wouldn't hear reason. He declared he would shoot me unless I gave him the ivory and then cleared out of the

---

7 **cartridge:** Patrone.
8 **to raid:** plündern.
12 **to adore:** anbeten, verehren.
16 **to sway:** beherrschen.

country, because he could do so, and had a fancy for it, and there was nothing on earth to prevent him killing whom he jolly well pleased. And it was true, too. I gave him the ivory. What did I care! But I didn't clear out. No,
5 no. I couldn't leave him. I had to be careful, of course, till we got friendly again for a time. He had his second illness then. Afterwards I had to keep out of the way; but I didn't mind. He was living for the most part in those villages on the lake. When he came down to the river,
10 sometimes he would take to me, and sometimes it was better for me to be careful. This man suffered too much. He hated all this, and somehow he couldn't get away. When I had a chance I begged him to try and leave while there was time; I offered to go back with him. And he
15 would say yes, and then he would remain; go off on another ivory hunt; disappear for weeks; forget himself amongst these people – forget himself – you know.' 'Why! he's mad,' I said. He protested indignantly. Mr. Kurtz couldn't be mad. If I had heard him talk, only two
20 days ago, I wouldn't dare hint at such a thing. . . . I had taken up my binoculars while we talked, and was looking at the shore, sweeping the limit of the forest at each side and at the back of the house. The consciousness of there being people in that bush, so silent, so quiet – as silent
25 and quiet as the ruined house on the hill – made me uneasy. There was no sign on the face of nature of this amazing tale that was not so much told as suggested to me in desolate exclamations, completed by shrugs, in

---

18 **indignantly** (adv.): entrüstet, unwillig.
21 **binoculars:** Fernglas.
28 **shrug:** Achselzucken.

interrupted phrases, in hints ending in deep sighs. The woods were unmoved, like a mask – heavy, like the closed door of a prison – they looked with their air of hidden knowledge, of patient expectation, of unapproachable silence. The Russian was explaining to me that it was only lately that Mr. Kurtz had come down to the river, bringing along with him all the fighting men of that lake tribe. He had been absent for several months – getting himself adored, I suppose – and had come down unexpectedly, with the intention to all appearance of making a raid either across the river or down stream. Evidently the appetite for more ivory had got the better of the – what shall I say? – less material aspirations. However he had got much worse suddenly. 'I heard he was lying helpless, and so I came up – took my chance,' said the Russian. 'Oh, he is bad, very bad.' I directed my glass to the house. There were no signs of life, but there was the ruined roof, the long mud wall peeping above the grass, with three little square window-holes, no two of the same size; all this brought within reach of my hand, as it were. And then I made a brusque movement, and one of the remaining posts of that vanished fence leaped up in the field of my glass. You remember I told you I had been struck at the distance by certain attempts at ornamentation, rather remarkable in the ruinous aspect of the place. Now I had suddenly a nearer view, and its first result was to make me throw my head back as if before a blow. Then I went

13 **aspiration:** Streben, Trachten.
21 **brusque:** ruckhaft.
25 **ornamentation:** Verzierung.

carefully from post to post with my glass, and I saw my mistake. These round knobs were not ornamental but symbolic; they were expressive and puzzling, striking and disturbing – food for thought and also for the
5 vultures if there had been any looking down from the sky; but at all events for such ants as were industrious enough to ascend the pole. They would have been even more impressive, those heads on the stakes, if their faces had not been turned to the house. Only one, the
10 first I had made out, was facing my way. I was not so shocked as you may think. The start back I had given was really nothing but a movement of surprise. I had expected to see a knob of wood there, you know. I returned deliberately to the first I had seen – and there
15 it was, black, dried, sunken, with closed eyelids, – a head that seemed to sleep at the top of that pole, and, with the shrunken dry lips showing a narrow white line of the teeth, was smiling, too, smiling continuously at some endless and jocose dream of that eternal
20 slumber.

"I am not disclosing any trade secrets. In fact, the manager said afterwards that Mr. Kurtz's methods had ruined the district. I have no opinion on that point, but I want you clearly to understand that there was nothing exactly
25 profitable in these heads being there. They only showed that Mr. Kurtz lacked restraint in the gratification

2 **knob:** Knopf, Knorren.
5 **vulture:** Geier.
15 **eyelid:** Augenlid.
19 **jocose:** scherzhaft, heiter.
25 **profitable:** vorteilhaft, einträglich.
26 **gratification:** Befriedigung.

of his various lusts, that there was something wanting in him – some small matter which, when the pressing need arose, could not be found under his magnificent eloquence. Whether he knew of this deficiency himself I can't say. I think the knowledge came to him at last – only at the very last. But the wilderness had found him out early, and had taken on him a terrible vengeance for the fantastic invasion. I think it had whispered to him things about himself which he did not know, things of which he had no conception till he took counsel with this great solitude – and the whisper had proved irresistibly fascinating. It echoed loudly within him because he was hollow at the core. . . . I put down the glass, and the head that had appeared near enough to be spoken to seemed at once to have leaped away from me into inaccessible distance.

"The admirer of Mr. Kurtz was a bit crestfallen. In a hurried, indistinct voice he began to assure me he had not dared to take these – say, symbols – down. He was not afraid of the natives; they would not stir till Mr. Kurtz gave the word. His ascendancy was extraordinary. The camps of these people surrounded the place, and the chiefs came every day to see him. They would crawl. . . . 'I don't want to know anything of the ceremonies used when approaching Mr. Kurtz,' I shouted. Curious, this feeling that came over me that such details

 1 **lust:** Lust, Gier.
 4 **eloquence:** Beredsamkeit.
10 **conception:** Vorstellung, Begriff.
13 **at the core:** im Innersten.
17 **crestfallen:** niedergeschlagen.
21 **ascendancy:** Vorherrschaft, Macht.

would be more intolerable than those heads drying on the stakes under Mr. Kurtz's windows. After all, that was only a savage sight, while I seemed at one bound to have been transported into some lightless region of
5 subtle horrors, where pure, uncomplicated savagery was a positive relief, being something that had a right to exist – obviously – in the sunshine. The young man looked at me with surprise. I suppose it did not occur to him that Mr. Kurtz was no idol if mine. He forgot I
10 hadn't heard any of these splendid monologues on, what was it? on love, justice, conduct of life – or what not. If it had come to crawling before Mr. Kurtz, he crawled as much as the veriest savage of them all. I had no idea of the conditions, he said: these heads were the
15 heads of rebels. I shocked him excessively by laughing. Rebels! What would be the next definition I was to hear? There had been enemies, criminals, workers – and these were rebels. Those rebellious heads looked very subdued to me on their sticks. 'You don't know
20 how such a life tries a man like Kurtz,' cried Kurtz's last disciple. 'Well, and you?' I said. 'I! I! I am a simple man. I have no great thoughts. I want nothing from anybody. How can you compare me to? . . .' His feelings were too much for speech, and suddenly he broke
25 down. 'I don't understand,' he groaned. 'I've been doing my best to keep him alive, and that's enough. I had no hand in all this. I have no abilities. There hasn't been a drop of medicine or a mouthful of invalid food for months here. He was shamefully abandoned. A man

10 **monologue:** Monolog.
15 **excessively** (adv.): übermäßig.
28 **invalid food:** Krankenkost.

like this, with such ideas. Shamefully! Shamefully! I –
I – haven't slept for the last ten nights. . . .'

"His voice lost itself in the calm of the evening. The long
shadows of the forest had slipped down hill while we
talked, had gone far beyond the ruined hovel, beyond
the symbolic row of stakes. All this was in the gloom,
while we down there were yet in the sunshine, and the
stretch of the river abreast of the clearing glittered in a
still and dazzling splendour, with a murky and overshadowed bend above and below. Not a living soul was
seen on the shore. The bushes did not rustle.

"Suddenly round the corner of the house a group of men
appeared, as though they had come up from the ground.
They waded waist-deep in the grass, in a compact body,
bearing an improvised stretcher in their midst. Instantly,
in the emptiness of the landscape, a cry arose whose
shrillness pierced the still air like a sharp arrow flying
straight to the very heart of the land; and, as if by
enchantment, streams of human beings – of naked human
beings – with spears in their hands, with bows, with
shields, with wild glances and savage movements, were
poured into the clearing by the darkfaced and pensive
forest. The bushes shook, the grass swayed for a time, and
then everything stood still in attentive immobility.

"'Now, if he does not say the right thing to them we are

---

9 **dazzling splendour:** blendende Pracht.
  murky: dunkel, trübe, düster.
14 **to wade:** waten.
  waist-deep: bis zur Taille.
15 **to improvise:** improvisieren.
  stretcher: Tragbahre.
19 **enchantment:** Bezauberung, Zauber.
22 **pensive:** sinnend, gedankenvoll.

all done for,' said the Russian at my elbow. The knot of
men with the stretcher had stopped, too, halfway to the
steamer, as if petrified. I saw the man on the stretcher
sit up, lank and with an uplifted arm, above the shoul-
5 ders of the bearers. 'Let us hope that the man who can
talk so well of love in general will find some particular
reason to spare us this time,' I said. I resented bitterly
the absurd danger of our situation, as if to be at the
mercy of that atrocious phantom had been a dishonour-
10 ing necessity. I could not hear a sound, but through my
glasses I saw the thin arm extended commandingly, the
lower jaw moving, the eyes of that apparition shining
darkly far in its bony head that nodded with grotesque
jerks. Kurtz – Kurtz – that means short in German –
15 don't it?[39] Well, the name was as true as everything else
in his life – and death. He looked at least seven feet
long. His covering had fallen off, and his body emerged
from it pitiful and appalling as from a winding-sheet. I
could see the cage of his ribs all astir, the bones of his
20 arm waving. It was as though an animated image of
death carved out of old ivory had been shaking its hand
with menaces at a motionless crowd of men made of
dark and glittering bronze. I saw him open his mouth
wide – it gave him a weirdly voracious aspect, as though

3 **to petrify:** versteinern.
7 **to resent:** übelnehmen.
9 **phantom:** Phantom, Gespenst, Trugbild.
12 **apparition:** Erscheinung.
18 **winding-sheet:** Leichentuch.
19 **cage of his ribs:** Brustkorb.
   astir: in Bewegung.
22 **menace:** Drohung.
24 **weirdly** (adv.): unheimlich.
   voracious: unersättlich, gierig.

he had wanted to swallow all the air, all the earth, all the men before him. A deep voice reached me faintly. He must have been shouting. He fell back suddenly. The stretcher shook as the bearers staggered forward again, and almost at the same time I noticed that the crowd of savages was vanishing without any perceptible movement of retreat, as if the forest that had ejected these beings so suddenly had drawn them in again as the breath is drawn in a long aspiration.

"Some of the pilgrims behind the stretcher carried his arms – two shot-guns, a heavy rifle, and a light revolver-carbine – the thunderbolts of that pitiful Jupiter. The manager bent over him murmuring as he walked beside his head. They laid him down in one of the little cabins – just a room for a bedplace and a camp-stool or two, you know. We had brought his belated correspondence, and a lot of torn envelopes and open letters littered his bed. His hand roamed feebly amongst these papers. I was struck by the fire of his eyes and the composed languor of his expression. It was not so much the exhaustion of disease. He did not seem in pain. This shadow looked satiated and calm, as though for the moment it had had its fill of all the emotions.

"He rustled one of the letters, and looking straight in

---

6 **perceptible:** sichtbar, wahrnehmbar.
7 **to eject:** ausstoßen, auswerfen.
9 **aspiration:** Atemzug.
12 **thunderbolt:** Blitzstrahl, Donnerkeil.
16 **belated:** verspätet.
17 **to litter:** in Unordnung bringen.
19 **composed:** gelassen.
   languor: Mattigkeit, Schlaffheit.
22 **to satiate:** sättigen, befriedigen.

my face said, 'I am glad.' Somebody had been writing to him about me. These special recommendations were turning up again. The volume of tone he emitted without effort, almost without the trouble of moving his lips,
5 amazed me. A voice! a voice! It was grave, profound, vibrating, while the man did not seem capable of a whisper. However, he had enough strength in him – factitious no doubt – to very nearly make an end of us, as you shall hear directly.
10 "The manager appeared silently in the doorway; I stepped out at once and he drew the curtain after me. The Russian, eyed curiously by the pilgrims, was staring at the shore. I followed the direction of his glance.

"Dark human shapes could be made out in the dis-
15 tance, flitting indistinctly against the gloomy border of the forest, and near the river two bronze figures, leaning on tall spears, stood in the sunlight under fantastic head-dresses of spotted skins, warlike and still in statuesque repose. And from right to left along the
20 lighted shore moved a wild and gorgeous apparition of a woman.

"She walked with measured steps, draped in striped and fringed cloths, treading the earth proudly, with a slight jingle and flash of barbarous ornaments. She carried her
25 head high; her hair was done in the shape of a helmet;

---

8 **factitious:** künstlich aufgeboten.
15 **to flit:** huschen.
18 **warlike:** kriegerisch.
19 **statuesque:** statuenhaft.
   repose: Ruhe.
20 **gorgeous:** prächtig, großartig.
23 **fringed:** fransenbesetzt.
24 **jingle:** Geklingel.

she had brass leggings to the knee, brass wire gauntlets to the elbow, a crimson spot on her tawny cheek, innumerable necklaces of glass beads on her neck; bizarre things, charms, gifts of witch-men, that hung about her, glittered and trembled at every step. She must have had the value of several elephant tusks upon her. She was savage and superb, wild-eyed and magnificent; there was something ominous and stately in her deliberate progress. And in the hush that had fallen suddenly upon the whole sorrowful land, the immense wilderness, the colossal body of the fecund and mysterious life seemed to look at her, pensive, as though it had been looking at the image of its own tenebrous and passionate soul.

"She came abreast of the steamer, stood still, and faced us. Her long shadow fell to the water's edge. Her face had a tragic and fierce aspect of wild sorrow and of dumb pain mingled with the fear of some struggling, half-shaped resolve. She stood looking at us without a stir, and like the wilderness itself, with an air of brooding over an inscrutable purpose. A whole minute passed, and then she made a step forward. There was a low jingle, a glint of yellow metal, a sway of fringed draperies, and she stopped as if her heart had failed her.

---

1 **brass leggings:** Messinggamaschen.
 gauntlets: Armreifen.
2 **crimson:** karmesinrot.
 tawny: gelbbraun.
3 **necklace:** Halskette.
7 **superb:** prächtig, herrlich.
11 **fecund:** fruchtbar.
13 **tenebrous:** dunkel, finster.
19 **resolve:** Entschluß.
24 **drapery:** Drapierung, Tuchbehang.

The young fellow by my side growled. The pilgrims murmured at my back. She looked at us all as if her life had depended upon the unswerving steadiness of her glance. Suddenly she opened her bared arms and threw
5 them up rigid above her head, as though in an uncontrollable desire to touch the sky, and at the same time the swift shadows darted out on the earth, swept around on the river, gathering the steamer into a shadowy embrace. A formidable silence hung over the scene.

10 "She turned away slowly, walked on, following the bank, and passed into the bushes to the left. Once only her eyes gleamed back at us in the dusk of the thickets before she disappeared.

"'If she had offered to come aboard I really think I
15 would have tried to shoot her,' said the man of patches, nervously. 'I had been risking my life every day for the last fortnight to keep her out of the house. She got in one day and kicked up a row about those miserable rags I picked up in the storeroom to mend my clothes with. I
20 wasn't decent. At least it must have been that, for she talked like a fury to Kurtz for an hour, pointing at me now and then. I don't understand the dialect of this tribe. Luckily for me, I fancy Kurtz felt too ill that day to care, or there would have been mischief. I don't
25 understand. . . . No – it's too much for me. Ah, well, it's all over now.'

---

1 **to growl:** knurren, brummen.
3 **unswerving:** unerschütterlich.
9 **formidable:** furchtbar, schrecklich.
12 **dusk:** Dämmerlicht, Dämmerung.
18 **to kick up a row:** einen Streit anfangen.
20 **decent:** anständig.
21 **fury:** Rasende, Furie.

132

"At this moment I heard Kurtz's deep voice behind the curtain: 'Save me! – save the ivory, you mean. Don't tell me. Save *me!* Why, I've had to save you. You are interrupting my plans now. Sick! Sick! Not so sick as you would like to believe. Never mind. I'll carry my ideas out yet – I will return. I'll show you what can be done. You with your little peddling notions – you are interfering with me. I will return. I. . . .'

"The manager came out. He did me the honour to take me under the arm and lead me aside. 'He is very low, very low,' he said. He considered it necessary to sigh, but neglected to be consistently sorrowful. 'We have done all we could for him – haven't we? But there is no disguising the fact, Mr. Kurtz has done more harm than good to the Company. He did not see the time was not ripe for vigorous action. Cautiously, cautiously – that's my principle. We must be cautious yet. The district is closed to us for a time. Deplorable! Upon the whole, the trade will suffer. I don't deny there is a remarkable quantity of ivory – mostly fossil. We must save it, at all events – but look how precarious the position is – and why? Because the method is unsound.' 'Do you,' said I, looking at the shore, 'call it "unsound method?"' 'Without doubt,' he exclaimed, hotly. 'Don't you?' . . .

'No method at all,' I murmured after a while. 'Exactly,' he exulted. 'I anticipated this. Shows a complete want

---

7 **peddling:** kleinlich, nichtig, kleinkrämerisch.
12 **consistently** (adv.): konsequent.
16 **vigorous:** nachdrücklich, kräftig.
18 **deplorable:** beklagenswert, bedauerlich.
21 **precarious:** unsicher, heikel.
26 **to exult:** frohlocken.
   to anticipate: voraussehen, erwarten.

of judgment. It is my duty to point it out in the proper quarter.' 'Oh,' said I, 'that fellow – what's his name? – the brickmaker, will make a readable report for you.' He appeared confounded for a moment. It seemed to me I had never breathed an atmosphere so vile, and I turned mentally to Kurtz for relief – positively for relief. 'Nevertheless I think Mr. Kurtz is a remarkable man,' I said with emphasis. He started, dropped on me a cold heavy glance, said very quietly, 'he *was*,' and turned his back on me. My hour of favour was over; I found myself lumped along with Kurtz as a partisan of methods for which the time was not ripe: I was unsound! Ah! but it was something to have at least a choice of nightmares.

"I had turned to the wilderness really, not to Mr. Kurtz, who, I was ready to admit, was as good as buried. And for a moment it seemed to me as if I also were buried in a vast grave full of unspeakable secrets. I felt an intolerable weight opressing my breast, the smell of the damp earth, the unseen presence of victorious corruption, the darkness of an impenetrable night. .... The Russian tapped me on the shoulder. I heard him mumbling and stammering something about 'brother seaman – couldn't conceal – knowledge of matters that would affect Mr. Kurtz's reputation.' I waited. For him evidently Mr. Kurtz was not in his grave; I suspect that for him Mr. Kurtz was one of the immortals. 'Well!' said I at last, 'speak out. As it happens, I am Mr. Kurtz's friend – in a way.'

---

5 **vile:** gemein, schlecht.
11 **to lump s.o. along with s.o.:** jdn. mit jdm. in einen Topf werfen.
partisan: Verfechter, Vorkämpfer.

134

"He stated with a good deal of formality that had we not been 'of the same profession,' he would have kept the matter to himself without regard to consequences. 'He suspected there was an active ill will towards him on the
5 part of these white men that —' 'You are right,' I said, remembering a certain conversation I had overheard. 'The manager thinks you ought to be hanged.' He showed a concern at this intelligence which amused me at first. 'I had better get out of the way quietly,' he said,
10 earnestly. 'I can do no more for Kurtz now, and they would soon find some excuse. What's to stop them? There's a military post three hundred miles from here.' 'Well, upon my word,' said I, 'perhaps you had better go if you have any friends amongst the savages near by.'
15 'Plenty,' he said. 'They are simple people – and I want nothing, you know.' He stood biting his lip, then: 'I don't want any harm to happen to these whites here, but of course I was thinking of Mr. Kurtz's reputation – but you are a brother seaman and —' 'All right,' said I, after
20 a time. 'Mr. Kurtz's reputation is safe with me.' I did not know how truly I spoke.
"He informed me, lowering his voice, that it was Kurtz who had ordered the attack to be made on the steamer. 'He hated sometimes the idea of being taken away – and
25 then again. . . . But I don't understand these matters. I am a simple man. He thought it would scare you away – that you would give it up, thinking him dead. I could not stop him. Oh, I had an awful time of it this last month.' 'Very well,' I said. 'He is all right now.' 'Ye-e-es,' he

---

1 **formality:** Förmlichkeit.
8 **intelligence:** Nachricht, Kunde.
26 **to scare away:** verscheuchen.

muttered, not very convinced apparently. 'Thanks,' said
I; 'I shall keep my eyes open.' 'But quiet – eh?' he
urged, anxiously. 'It would be awful for his reputation if
anybody here –' I promised a complete discretion with
great gravity. 'I have a canoe and three black fellows
waiting not very far. I am off. Could you give me a few
Martini-Henry cartridges?' I could, and did, with
proper secrecy. He helped himself, with a wink at me,
to a handful of my tobacco. 'Between sailors – you
know – good English tobacco.' At the door of the pilot-
house he turned round – 'I say, haven't you a pair of
shoes you could spare?' He raised one leg. 'Look.' The
soles were tied with knotted strings sandal-wise under
his bare feet. I rooted out an old pair, at which he
looked with admiration before tucking it under his left
arm. One of his pockets (bright red) was bulging with
cartridges, from the other (dark blue) peeped 'Towson's
Inquiry,' etc., etc. He seemed to think himself excel-
lently well equipped for a renewed encounter with the
wilderness. 'Ah! I'll never, never meet such a man
again. You ought to have heard him recite poetry – his
own, too, it was, he told me. Poetry!' He rolled his eyes
at the recollection of these delights. 'Oh, he enlarged
my mind!' 'Good-bye,' said I. He shook hands and
vanished in the night. Sometimes I ask myself whether I

4 **discretion:** Verschwiegenheit.
5 **gravity:** Ernsthaftigkeit.
13 **sole:** Sohle.
   sandal-wise: wie Sandalen.
14 **to root out:** ausfindig machen.
15 **to tuck:** verstauen.
16 **to bulge:** ausbeulen.
21 **to recite:** vortragen.

had ever really seen him – whether it was possible to meet such a phenomenon! ...

"When I woke up shortly after midnight his warning came to my mind with its hint of danger that seemed, in 5 the starred darkness, real enough to make me get up for the purpose of having a look round. On the hill a big fire burned, illuminating fitfully a crooked corner of the station-house. One of the agents with a picket of a few of our blacks, armed for the purpose, was keeping 10 guard over the ivory; but deep within the forest, red gleams that wavered, that seemed to sink and rise from the ground amongst confused columnar shapes of intense blackness, showed the exact position of the camp where Mr. Kurtz's adorers were keeping their 15 uneasy vigil. The monotonous beating of a big drum filled the air with muffled shocks and a lingering vibration. A steady droning sound of many men chanting each to himself some weird incantation came out from the black, flat wall of the woods as the humming of bees 20 comes out of a hive, and had a strange narcotic effect upon my half-awake senses. I believe I dozed off lean-

---

2 **phenomenon:** Phänomen, Erscheinung.
5 **starred:** gestirnt, sternenbesetzt.
7 **fitful:** ungleichmäßig, stoßweise.
  crooked: krumm, gekrümmt.
8 **picket:** Feldwache.
11 **to waver:** flackern.
12 **columnar:** säulenartig.
15 **vigil:** Nachtwache.
17 **to drone:** summen.
18 **incantation:** Beschwörung, Zauberformel.
20 **hive:** Bienenstock.
  narcotic: betäubend.
21 **to doze off:** einschlummern.

ing over the rail, till an abrupt burst of yells, an overwhelming outbreak of a pent-up and mysterious frenzy,
woke me up in a bewildered wonder. It was cut short all
at once, and the low droning went on with an effect of
5 audible and soothing silence. I glanced casually into the
little cabin. A light was burning within, but Mr. Kurtz
was not there.

"I think I would have raised an outcry if I had believed
my eyes. But I didn't believe them at first – the thing
10 seemed so impossible. The fact is I was completely
unnerved by a sheer blank fright, pure abstract terror,
unconnected with any distinct shape of physical danger.
What made this emotion so overpowering was – how
shall I define it? – the moral shock I received, as if
15 something altogether monstrous, intolerable to thought
and odious to the soul, had been thrust upon me unexpectedly. This lasted of course the merest fraction of a
second, and then the usual sense of commonplace,
deadly danger, the possibility of a sudden onslaught and
20 massacre, or something of the kind, which I saw
impending, was positively welcome and composing. It
pacified me, in fact, so much, that I did not raise an
alarm.

---

1 **abrupt:** plötzlich, unvermittelt.
2 **pent-up:** zurückgehalten, aufgestaut.
11 **unnerved:** entnervt, entmutigt.
   sheer: rein, völlig, gänzlich.
13 **to overpower:** überwältigen.
16 **odious:** verhaßt, widerlich.
17 **fraction:** Bruchteil.
18 **commonplace:** alltäglich, gewöhnlich.
21 **impending:** drohend bevorstehen.
22 **to pacify:** besänftigen.

"There was an agent buttoned up inside an ulster and sleeping on a chair on deck within three feet of me. The yells had not awakened him; he snored very slightly; I left him to his slumbers and leaped ashore. I did not betray Mr. Kurtz – it was ordered I should never betray him – it was written I should be loyal to the nightmare of my choice. I was anxious to deal with this shadow by myself alone, – and to this day I don't know why I was so jealous of sharing with any one the peculiar blackness of that experience.

"As soon as I got on the bank I saw a trail – a broad trail through the grass. I remember the exultation with which I said to myself, 'He can't walk – he is crawling on all-fours – I've got him.' The grass was wet with dew. I strode rapidly with clenched fists. I fancy I had some vague notion of falling upon him and giving him a drubbing. I don't know. I had some imbecile thoughts. The knitting old woman with the cat obtruded herself upon my memory as a most improper person to be sitting at the other end of such an affair. I saw a row of pilgrims squirting lead in the air out of Winchesters held to the hip. I thought I would never get back to the steamer, and imagined myself living alone and unarmed in the woods to an advanced age. Such silly things – you know. And I remember I confounded the beat of the

1 **ulster:** Mantel.
3 **to snore:** schnarchen.
12 **exultation:** Triumph, Jubel.
15 **to clench:** ballen.
17 **drubbing:** Tracht Prügel.
   imbecile: blödsinnig, schwachsinnig.
18 **to obtrude:** sich aufdrängen.
19 **improper:** unschicklich.

drum with the beating of my heart, and was pleased at
its calm regularity.

"I kept to the track though – then stopped to listen. The
night was very clear; a dark blue space, sparkling with
5 dew and starlight, in which black things stood very still.
I thought I could see a kind of motion ahead of me. I
was strangely cocksure of everything that night. I actually left the track and ran in a wide semicircle (I verily
believe chuckling to myself) so as to get in front of that
10 stir, of that motion I had seen – if indeed I had seen
anything. I was circumventing Kurtz as though it had
been a boyish game.

"I came upon him, and, if he had not heard me coming,
I would have fallen over him, too, but he got up in time.
15 He rose, unsteady, long, pale, indistinct, like a vapour
exhaled by the earth, and swayed slightly, misty and
silent before me; while at my back the fires loomed
between the trees, and the murmur of many voices
issued from the forest. I had cut him off cleverly; but
20 when actually confronting him I seemed to come to my
senses, I saw the danger in its right proportion. It was by
no means over yet. Suppose he began to shout? Though
he could hardly stand, there was still plenty of vigour in
his voice. 'Go away – hide yourself,' he said, in that
25 profound tone. It was very awful. I glanced back. We

---

2 **regularity:** Regelmäßigkeit.
7 **cocksure:** todsicher.
8 **semicircle:** Halbkreis, Bogen.
9 **to chuckle:** kichern.
11 **to circumvent:** überlisten.
15 **vapour:** Dunst.
16 **to exhale:** aushauchen, ausdünsten.
17 **to loom:** undeutlich sichtbar werden.

140

were within thirty yards from the nearest fire. A black figure stood up, strode on long black legs, waving long black arms, across the glow. It had horns – antelope horns, I think – on its head. Some sorcerer, some witch-man, no doubt: it looked fiend-like enough. 'Do you know what you are doing?' I whispered. 'Perfectly,' he answered, raising his voice for that single word: it sounded to me far off and yet loud, like a hail through a speaking-trumpet. If he makes a row we are lost, I thought to myself. This clearly was not a case for fisticuffs, even apart from the very natural aversion I had to beat that Shadow – this wandering and tormented thing. 'You will be lost,' I said – 'utterly lost.' One gets sometimes such a flash of inspiration, you know. I did say the right thing, though indeed he could not have been more irretrievably lost than he was at this very moment, when the foundations of our intimacy were being laid – to endure – to endure – even to the end – even beyond.

'"I had immense plans," he muttered irresolutely. 'Yes,' said I; 'but if you try to shout I'll smash your head with —' There was not a stick or a stone near. 'I will throttle

---

3 **antelope:** Antilope.
4 **sorcerer:** Zauberer.
4 f. **witch-man:** Medizinmann.
8 **hail:** Zuruf.
9 **speaking-trumpet:** Sprachtrichter, Megaphon.
11 **fisticuff:** Faustkampf.
 aversion: Abneigung.
12 **to torment:** quälen, foltern, peinigen.
14 **inspiration:** Eingebung, Erleuchtung.
16 **irretrievable:** unwiederbringlich.
17 **intimacy:** Vertrautheit.
19 **irresolutely:** unschlüssig.
21 **to throttle:** die Kehle zudrücken, erdrosseln.

you for good,' I corrected myself. 'I was on the
threshold of great things,' he pleaded, in a voice of
longing, with a wistfulness of tone that made my blood
run cold. 'And now for this stupid scoundrel —' 'Your
success in Europe is assured in any case,' I affirmed,
steadily. I did not want to have the throttling of him,
you understand – and indeed it would have been very
little use for any practical purpose. I tried to break the
spell – the heavy, mute spell of the wilderness – that
seemed to draw him to its pitiless breast by the awaken-
ing of forgotten and brutal instincts, by the memory of
gratified and monstrous passions. This alone, I was
convinced, had driven him out to the edge of the forest,
to the bush, towards the gleam of fires, the throb of
drums, the drone of weird incantations; this alone had
beguiled his unlawful soul beyond the bounds of permitted aspirations. And, don't you see, the terror of the
position was not in being knocked on the head – though
I had a very lively sense of that danger, too – but in this,
that I had to deal with a being to whom I could not
appeal in the name of anything high or low. I had, even
like the niggers, to invoke him – himself – his own exalted
and incredible degradation. There was nothing either
above or below him, and I knew it. He had kicked
himself loose of the earth. Confound the man! he had
kicked the very earth to pieces. He was alone, and I
before him did not know whether I stood on the ground

2 **threshold:** Schwelle.
3 **wistfulness:** Wehmut.
9 **spell:** Zauber.
16 **to beguile:** bezaubern.
22 **to invoke:** anrufen, anflehen.
23 **degradation:** Erniedrigung, Verderbtheit.

142

or floated in the air. I've been telling you what we said –
repeating the phrases we pronounced – but what's the
good? They were common everyday words – the familiar, vague sounds exchanged on every waking day of
5 life. But what of that? They had behind them, to my
mind, the terrific suggestiveness of words heard in
dreams, of phrases spoken in nightmares. Soul! If anybody had ever struggled with a soul, I am the man. And
I wasn't arguing with a lunatic either. Believe me or not,
10 his intelligence was perfectly clear – concentrated, it is
true, upon himself with horrible intensity, yet clear; and
therein was my only chance – barring, of course, the
killing him there and then, which wasn't so good, on
account of unavoidable noise. But his soul was mad.
15 Being alone in the wilderness, it had looked within
itself, and, by heavens! I tell you, it had gone mad. I
had – for my sins, I suppose – to go through the ordeal
of looking into it myself. No eloquence could have
been so withering to one's belief in mankind as his
20 final burst of sincerity. He struggled with himself, too.
I saw it, – I heard it. I saw the inconceivable mystery of
a soul that knew no restraint, no faith, and no fear, yet
struggling blindly with itself. I kept my head pretty well;
but when I had him at last stretched on the couch, I
25 wiped my forehead, while my legs shook under me as
though I had carried half a ton on my back down that
hill. And yet I had only supported him, his bony arm

6 **terrific:** fürchterlich.
 suggestiveness: Bedeutsamkeit.
9 **lunatic:** Wahnsinniger.
17 **ordeal:** schwere Prüfung, Qual.
19 **to wither:** vernichten, zugrunde richten.
20 **sincerity:** Aufrichtigkeit.

clasped round my neck – and he was not much heavier than a child.

"When next day we left at noon, the crowd, of whose presence behind the curtain of trees I had been acutely
5 conscious all the time, flowed out of the woods again, filled the clearing, covered the slope with a mass of naked, breathing, quivering, bronze bodies. I steamed up a bit, then swung downstream, and two thousand eyes followed the evolutions of the splashing, thumping,
10 fierce river-demon beating the water with its terrible tail and breathing black smoke into the air. In front of the first rank, along the river, three men, plastered with bright red earth from head to foot, strutted to and fro restlessly. When we came abreast again, they faced the
15 river, stamped their feet, nodded their horned heads, swayed their scarlet bodies; they shook towards the fierce river-demon a bunch of black feathers, a mangy skin with a pendent tail – something that looked like a dried gourd; they shouted periodically together strings
20 of amazing words that resembled no sounds of human language; and the deep murmurs of the crowd, interrupted suddenly, were like the responses of some satanic litany.

"We had carried Kurtz into the pilot-house: there was

---

4 **acutely** (adv.): scharf, schmerzhaft.
9 **evolution:** Bewegung.
  to thump: poltern.
10 **river-demon:** Flußgeist, -dämon.
12 **to plaster:** tünchen.
13 **to strutt to and fro:** auf und ab schreiten, herumstolzieren.
17 **mangy:** schäbig, schmutzig, räudig.
18 **pendent:** herabhängend.
23 **satanic:** satanisch, teuflisch.
  litany: Litanei.

more air there. Lying on the couch, he stared through the open shutter. There was an eddy in the mass of human bodies, and the woman with helmeted head and tawny cheeks rushed out to the very brink of the stream. She put out her hands, shouted something, and all that wild mob took up the shout in a roaring chorus of articulated, rapid, breathless utterance.

"'Do you understand this?' I asked.

"He kept on looking out past me with fiery, longing eyes, with a mingled expression of wistfulness and hate. He made no answer, but I saw a smile, a smile of indefinable meaning, appear on his colourless lips that a moment after twitched convulsively. 'Do I not?' he said slowly, gasping, as if the words had been torn out of him by a supernatural power.

"I pulled the string of the whistle, and I did this because I saw the pilgrims on deck getting out their rifles with an air of anticipating a jolly lark. At the sudden screech there was a movement of abject terror through that wedged mass of bodies. 'Don't! don't you frighten them away,' cried someone on deck disconsolately. I pulled the string time after time. They broke and ran, they leaped, they crouched, they swerved, they dodged the flying terror of the sound. The three red chaps had fallen flat, face down on the shore, as though they

2 **eddy:** Wirbel.
4 **brink:** Rand, Ufer.
13 **convulsively** (adv.): krampfartig.
18 **jolly lark:** lustiger Streich, Riesenjux.
19 **abject:** verächtlich, gemein, verworfen.
20 **to wedge:** verkeilen.
21 **disconsolately** (adv.): untröstlich.
23 **to dodge:** aus dem Weg gehen.

had been shot dead. Only the barbarous and superb woman did not so much as flinch, and stretched tragically her bare arms after us over the sombre and glittering river.

5 "And then that imbecile crowd down on the deck started their little fun, and I could see nothing more for smoke.

"The brown current ran swiftly out of the heart of darkness, bearing us down towards the sea with twice
10 the speed of our upward progress[40]; and Kurtz's life was running swiftly, too, ebbing, ebbing out of his heart into the sea of inexorable time. The manager was very placid, he had no vital anxieties now, he took us both in with a comprehensive and satisfied glance: the 'affair'
15 had come off as well as could be wished. I saw the time approaching when I would be left alone of the party of 'unsound method.' The pilgrims looked upon me with disfavour. I was, so to speak, numbered with the dead. It is strange how I accepted this unforeseen partnership,
20 this choice of nightmares forced upon me in the tenebrous land invaded by these mean and greedy phantoms.

"Kurtz discoursed. A voice! a voice! It rang deep to the very last. It survived his strength to hide in the magnifi-
25 cent folds of eloquence the barren darkness of his heart. Oh, he struggled! he struggled! The wastes of his weary brain were haunted by shadowy images now – images of

---

2 **to flinch:** wanken, zurückweichen.
11 **to ebb:** verebben.
13 **placid:** ruhig, sanft, gelassen.
14 **comprehensive:** umfassend.
18 **disfavour:** Mißfallen.

wealth and fame revolving obsequiously round his unextinguishable gift of noble and lofty expression. My Intended, my station, my career, my ideas – these were the subjects for the occasional utterances of elevated
5 sentiments. The shade of the original Kurtz frequented the bedside of the hollow sham, whose fate it was to be buried presently in the mould of primeval earth. But both the diabolic love and the unearthly hate of the mysteries it had penetrated fought for the possession of
10 that soul satiated with primitive emotions, avid of lying fame, of sham distinction, of all the appearances of success and power.

"Sometimes he was contemptibly childish. He desired to have kings meet him at railway-stations[41] on his
15 return from some ghastly Nowhere, where he intended to accomplish great things. 'You show them you have in you something that is really profitable, and then there will be no limits to the recognition of your ability,' he would say. 'Of course you must take care of the mo-
20 tives – right motives – always.' The long reaches that were like one and the same reach, monotonous bends that were exactly alike, slipped past the steamer with their multitude of secular trees looking patiently after this grimy fragment of another world, the forerunner of

1 **obsequiously** (adv.): willfährig.
5 **to frequent:** besuchen.
6 **sham:** Scharlatan, Schwindler.
7 **mould:** Moder.
8 **diabolic:** teuflisch.
10 **avid:** begierig.
15 **ghastly:** gräßlich, grausig.
23 **secular:** jahrhundertealt.
24 **grimy:** rußig, schmutzig.
   forerunner: Vorläufer.

change, of conquest, of trade, of massacres, of blessings. I looked ahead – piloting. 'Close the shutter,' said Kurtz suddenly one day; 'I can't bear to look at this.' I did so. There was a silence. 'Oh, but I will wring your heart yet!' he cried at the invisible wilderness.

"We broke down – as I had expected – and had to lie up for repairs at the head of an island. This delay was the first thing that shook Kurtz's confidence. One morning he gave me a packet of papers and a photograph – the lot tied together with a shoe-string. 'Keep this for me,' he said. 'This noxious fool' (meaning the manager) 'is capable of prying into my boxes when I am not looking.' In the afternoon I saw him. He was lying on his back with closed eyes, and I withdrew quietly, but I heard him mutter, 'Live rightly, die, die . . .' I listened. There was nothing more. Was he rehearsing some speech in his sleep, or was it a fragment of a phrase from some newspaper article? He had been writing for the papers and meant to do so again, 'for the furthering of my ideas. It's a duty.'

"His was an impenetrable darkness. I looked at him as you peer down at a man who is lying at the bottom of a precipice where the sun never shines. But I had not much time to give him, because I was helping the engine-driver to take to pieces the leaky cylinders, to straighten a bent connecting-rod, and in other such

---

11 **noxious:** schädlich.
12 **to pry into s.th.:** seine Nase in etwas stecken.
16 **to rehearse:** wiederholen, proben, einstudieren.
19 **furthering:** Förderung.
23 **precipice:** Abgrund.
26 **connecting-rod:** Verbindungsstange.

matters. I lived in an infernal mess of rust, filings, nuts, bolts, spanners, hammers, ratchet-drills – things I abominate, because I don't get on with them. I tended the little forge we fortunately had aboard; I toiled
5 wearily in a wretched scrap-heap – unless I had the shakes too bad to stand.

"One evening coming in with a candle I was startled to hear him say a little tremulously, 'I am lying here in the dark waiting for death.' The light was within a foot of
10 his eyes. I forced myself to murmur, 'Oh, nonsense!' and stood over him as if transfixed.

"Anything approaching the change that came over his features I have never seen before, and hope never to see again. Oh, I wasn't touched. I was fascinated. It was as
15 though a veil had been rent. I saw on that ivory face the expression of sombre pride, of ruthless power, of craven terror – of an intense and hopeless despair. Did he live his life again in every detail of desire, temptation, and surrender during that supreme moment of complete
20 knowledge? He cried in a whisper at some image, at some vision – he cried out twice, a cry that was no more than a breath –

"'The horror! The horror!'

"I blew the candle out and left the cabin. The pilgrims

---

1 **filings:** Feilspäne.
2 **spanner:** Schraubenzieher.
  ratchet-drill: Drillbohrer.
4 **forge:** Schmiede.
5 **scrap-heap:** Schrotthaufen.
8 **tremulously** (adv.): zitternd, bebend.
11 **to transfix:** erstarren lassen, lähmen.
16 **ruthless:** unbarmherzig.
  craven: feige.

were dining in the mess-room, and I took my place
opposite the manager, who lifted his eyes to give me a
questioning glance, which I successfully ignored. He
leaned back, serene, with that peculiar smile of his
5 sealing the unexpressed depths of his meanness. A
continuous shower of small flies streamed upon the
lamp, upon the cloth, upon our hands and faces. Suddenly the manager's boy put his insolent black head in
the doorway, and said in a tone of scathing contempt –
10 " 'Mistah Kurtz – he dead.'
"All the pilgrims rushed out to see. I remained, and
went on with my dinner. I believe I was considered
brutally callous. However, I did not eat much. There
was a lamp in there – light, don't you know – and
15 outside it was so beastly, beastly dark. I went no more
near the remarkable man who had pronounced a judgment upon the adventures of his soul on this earth. The
voice was gone. What else had been there? But I am of
course aware that next day the pilgrims buried some-
20 thing in a muddy hole.
"And then they very nearly buried me.
"However, as you see, I did not go to join Kurtz there
and then. I did not. I remained to dream the nightmare
out to the end, and to show my loyalty to Kurtz once
25 more. Destiny. My destiny! Droll thing life is – that
mysterious arrangement of merciless logic for a futile
purpose. The most you can hope from it is some knowledge of yourself – that comes too late – a crop of

---

5 **meanness:** Gemeinheit, Erbärmlichkeit.
8 **insolent:** frech, unverschämt.
9 **scathing:** schneidend.
13 **callous:** gefühllos, unempfindlich.
24 **loyalty:** Treue, Loyalität.

unextinguishable regrets. I have wrestled with death. It is the most unexciting contest you can imagine. It takes place in an impalpable grayness, with nothing under-foot, with nothing around, without spectators, without clamour, without glory, without the great desire of victory, without the great fear of defeat, in a sickly atmosphere of tepid scepticism, without much belief in your own right, and still less in that of your adversary. If such is the form of ultimate wisdom, then life is a greater riddle than some of us think it to be. I was within a hair's-breadth of the last opportunity for pro-nouncement, and I found with humiliation that prob-ably I would have nothing to say. This is the reason why I affirm that Kurtz was a remarkable man. He had something to say. He said it. Since I had peeped over the edge myself, I understand better the meaning of his stare, that could not see the flame of the candle, but was wide enough to embrace the whole universe, piercing enough to penetrate all the hearts that beat in the darkness. He had summed up – he had judged. 'The horror!' He was a remarkable man. After all, this was the expression of some sort of belief; it had candour, it had conviction, it had a vibrating note of revolt in its whisper, it had the appalling face of a glimpsed truth –

---

1 **unextinguishable:** unauslöschlich.
  to wrestle: ringen.
2 **contest:** Streit, Wettkampf.
3 **impalpable:** ungreifbar, unfühlbar.
7 **tepid:** schal, lau.
  scepticism: Skepsis, Zweifel.
8 **adversary:** Gegner.
12 **humiliation:** Demütigung.
22 **candour:** Aufrichtigkeit, Offenheit.

the strange commingling of desire and hate. And it is not my own extremity I remember best – a vision of grayness without form filled with physical pain, and a careless contempt for the evanescence of all things –
5 even of this pain itself. No! It is his extremity that I seem to have lived through. True, he had made that last stride, he had stepped over the edge, while I had been permitted to draw back my hesitating foot. And perhaps in this is the whole difference; perhaps all the
10 wisdom, and all truth, and all sincerity, are just compressed into that inappreciable moment of time in which we step over the threshold of the invisible. Perhaps! I like to think my summing-up would not have been a word of careless contempt. Better his cry –
15 much better. It was an affirmation, a moral victory paid for by innumerable defeats, by abominable terrors, by abominable satisfactions. But it was a victory! That is why I have remained loyal to Kurtz to the last, and even beyond, when a long time after I heard once more, not
20 his own voice, but the echo of his magnificent eloquence thrown to me from a soul as translucently pure as a cliff of crystal.

"No, they did not bury me, though there is a period of time which I remember mistily, with a shuddering won-
25 der, like a passage through some inconceivable world that had no hope in it and no desire[42]. I found myself back in the sepulchral city resenting the sight of people hurrying through the streets to filch a little money from

---

4 **evanescence:** Vergänglichkeit.
11 **inappreciable:** unschätzbar.
21 **translucently** (adv.): durchscheinend.
28 **to filch:** mausen, stibitzen.

each other, to devour their infamous cookery, to gulp their unwholesome beer, to dream their insignificant and silly dreams. They trespassed upon my thoughts. They were intruders whose knowledge of life was to me an irritating pretence, because I felt so sure they could not possibly know the things I knew. Their bearing, which was simply the bearing of commonplace individuals going about their business in the assurance of perfect safety, was offensive to me like the outrageous flauntings of folly in the face of a danger it is unable to comprehend. I had no particular desire to enlighten them, but I had some difficulty in restraining myself from laughing in their faces, so full of stupid importance. I daresay I was not very well at that time. I tottered about the streets – there were various affairs to settle – grinning bitterly at perfectly respectable persons. I admit my behaviour was inexcusable, but then my temperature was seldom normal in these days. My dear aunt's endeavours to 'nurse up my strength' seemed altogether beside the mark. It was not my strength that wanted nursing, it was my imagination that wanted soothing. I kept the bundle of papers given me by Kurtz, not knowing exactly what to do with it. His mother had died lately, watched over, as I was told, by his Intended. A clean-shaved man, with an official manner and wearing gold-rimmed spectacles, called on

---

1 **to devour:** verschlingen.
   to gulp: gierig schlucken.
3 **to trespass:** unbefugt eindringen in.
9f. **flaunting:** Zurschaustellung.
15 **to totter:** wanken, wackeln.
17 **inexcusable:** unentschuldbar.

me one day and made inquiries, at first circuitous,
afterwards suavely pressing, about what he was pleased
to denominate certain 'documents.' I was not surprised,
because I had had two rows with the manager on the
5 subject out there. I had refused to give up the smallest
scrap out of that package, and I took the same attitude
with the spectacled man. He became darkly menacing at
last, and with much heat argued that the Company had
the right to every bit of information about its 'ter-
10 ritories.' And said he, 'Mr. Kurtz's knowledge of unex-
plored regions must have been necessarily extensive and
peculiar – owing to his great abilities and to the deplorable circumstances in which he had been placed: therefore —' I assured him Mr. Kurtz's knowledge, however
15 extensive, did not bear upon the problems of commerce
or administration. He invoked then the name of science. 'It would be an incalculable loss if,' etc., etc. I
offered him the report on the 'Suppression of Savage
Customs,' with the postscriptum torn off. He took it up
20 eagerly, but ended by sniffing at it with an air of
contempt. 'This is not what we had a right to expect,' he
remarked. 'Expect nothing else,' I said. 'There are only
private letters.' He withdrew upon some threat of legal
proceedings, and I saw him no more; but another
25 fellow, calling himself Kurtz's cousin, appeared two
days later, and was anxious to hear all the details about
his dear relative's last moments. Incidentally he gave

1 **circuitous:** weitschweifig, indirekt.
2 **suavely** (adv.): höflich, verbindlich.
3 **to denominate:** benennen.
17 **incalculable:** unberechenbar, unschätzbar.
20 **to sniff:** schnüffeln.
27 **incidentally** (adv.): zufällig, beiläufig.

154

me to understand that Kurtz had been essentially a great musician. 'There was the making of an immense success,' said the man, who was an organist, I believe, with lank gray hair flowing over a greasy coat-collar. I had no reason to doubt his statement; and to this day I am unable to say what was Kurtz's profession, whether he ever had any – which was the greatest of his talents. I had taken him for a painter who wrote for the papers, or else for a journalist who could paint – but even the cousin (who took snuff during the interview) could not tell me what he had been – exactly. He was a universal genius – on that point I agreed with the old chap, who thereupon blew his nose noisily into a large cotton handkerchief and withdrew in senile agitation, bearing off some family letters and memoranda without importance. Ultimately a journalist anxious to know something of the fate of his 'dear colleague' turned up. This visitor informed me Kurtz's proper sphere ought to have been politics 'on the popular side.' He had furry straight eyebrows, bristly hair cropped short, an eyeglass on a broad ribbon, and, becoming expansive, confessed his opinion that Kurtz really couldn't write a bit – 'but heavens! how that man could talk. He electrified large meetings. He had faith – don't you see? – he had the faith. He could get himself to believe anything – anything. He would have been a splendid leader

---

4 **greasy:** fettig, schmierig.
10 **snuff:** Schnupftabak.
14 **senile:** greisenhaft, altersschwach.
15 **memoranda** (pl.): Memorandum.
19 **furry:** buschig.
20 **bristly:** borstig.
23 f. **to electrify:** elektrisieren.

of an extreme party.' 'What party?' I asked. 'Any party,' answered the other. 'He was an – an – extremist.' Did I not think so? I assented. Did I know, he asked, with a sudden flash of curiosity, 'what it was that had induced him to go out there?' 'Yes,' said I, and forthwith handed him the famous Report for publication, if he thought fit. He glanced through it hurriedly, mumbling all the time, judged 'it would do,' and took himself off with this plunder.

"Thus I was left at last with a slim packet of letters and the girl's portrait. She struck me as beautiful – I mean she had a beautiful expression. I know that the sunlight can be made to lie, too, yet one felt that no manipulation of light and pose could have conveyed the delicate shade of truthfulness upon those features. She seemed ready to listen without mental reservation, without suspicion, without a thought for herself. I concluded I would go and give her back her portrait and those letters myself. Curiosity? Yes; and also some other feeling perhaps. All that had been Kurtz's had passed out of my hands: his soul, his body, his station, his plans, his ivory, his career. There remained only his memory and his Intended – and I wanted to give that up, too, to the past, in a way – to surrender personally all that remained of him with me to that oblivion which is the last word of our common fate. I don't defend

---

3 **to assent:** zustimmen, bejahen.
9 **plunder:** Beute, Raub.
13f. **manipulation:** künstliche Gestaltung.
14 **pose:** Haltung, Stellung.
16 **reservation:** Vorbehalt.
25 **oblivion:** Vergessenheit.

myself. I had no clear perception of what it was I really wanted. Perhaps it was an impulse of unconscious loyalty, or the fulfilment of one of these ironic necessities that lurk in the facts of human existence. I don't know. I can't tell. But I went.

"I thought his memory was like the other memories of the dead that accumulate in every man's life – a vague impress on the brain of shadows that had fallen on it in their swift and final passage; but before the high and ponderous door, between the tall houses of a street as still and decorous as a well-kept alley in a cemetery, I had a vision of him on the stretcher, opening his mouth voraciously, as if to devour all the earth with all its mankind. He lived then before me; he lived as much as he had ever lived – a shadow insatiable of splendid appearances, of frightful realities; a shadow darker than the shadow of the night, and draped nobly in the folds of a gorgeous eloquence. The vision seemed to enter the house with me – the stretcher, the phantom-bearers, the wild crowd of obedient worshippers, the gloom of the forests, the glitter of the reach between the murky bends, the beat of the drum, regular and muffled like the beating of a heart – the heart of a conquering darkness. It was a moment of triumph for the wilderness, an invading and vengeful rush which, it seemed to

---

1 **perception:** Wahrnehmung, Empfindung, Vorstellung.
7 **to accumulate:** anhäufen.
11 **decorous:** anständig, gesittet.
   alley: Allee, Gang.
   cemetery: Friedhof.
15 **insatiable:** unersättlich.
25 **vengeful:** rachsüchtig.

me, I would have to keep back alone for the salvation of
another soul. And the memory of what I had heard him
say afar there, with the horned shapes stirring at my
back, in the glow of fires, within the patient woods,
5 those broken phrases came back to me, were heard
again in their ominous and terrifying simplicity. I
remembered his abject pleading, his abject threats, the
colossal scale of his vile desires, the meanness, the
torment, the tempestuous anguish of his soul. And later
10 on I seemed to see his collected languid manner, when
he said one day, 'This lot of ivory now is really mine.
The Company did not pay for it. I collected it myself at
a very great personal risk. I am afraid they will try to
claim it as theirs though. H'm. It is a difficult case. What
15 do you think I ought to do – resist? Eh? I want no more
than justice.' . . . He wanted no more than justice – no
more than justice. I rang the bell before a mahogany
door on the first floor, and while I waited he seemed to
stare at me out of the glassy panel – stare with that wide
20 and immense stare embracing, condemning, loathing all
the universe. I seemed to hear the whispered cry, 'The
horror! The horror!'
"The dusk was falling. I had to wait in a lofty drawing-
room with three long windows from floor to ceiling that
25 were like three luminous and bedraped columns. The
bent gilt legs and backs of the furniture shone in indis-

---

  1 **salvation:** Rettung.
  9 **tempestuous:** stürmisch, ungestüm.
    anguish: Pein, Angst, Schmerz.
 17 **mahogany:** Mahagoni(holz).
 20 **to loathe:** verschmähen, verachten, verabscheuen.
 26 **to gild:** vergolden.

tinct curves. The tall marble fireplace had a cold and monumental whiteness. A grand piano stood massively in a corner; with dark gleams on the flat surfaces like a sombre and polished sarcophagus. A high door opened – closed. I rose.

"She came forward, all in black, with a pale head, floating towards me in the dusk. She was in mourning. It was more than a year since his death, more than a year since the news came; she seemed as though she would remember and mourn for ever. She took both my hands in hers and murmured, 'I had heard you were coming.' I noticed she was not very young – I mean not girlish. She had a mature capacity for fidelity, for belief, for suffering. The room seemed to have grown darker, as if all the sad light of the cloudy evening had taken refuge on her forehead. This fair hair, this pale visage, this pure brow, seemed surrounded by an ashy halo from which the dark eyes looked out at me. Their glance was guileless, profound, confident, and trustful. She carried her sorrowful head as though she were proud of that sorrow, as though she would say, I – I alone know how to mourn for him as he deserves. But while we were still shaking hands, such a look of awful desolation came upon her face that I perceived she was one of those creatures that are not the playthings of Time. For her he had died only yesterday. And, by

---

1 **marble:** Marmor.
4 **sarcophagus:** Sarkophag, Sarg, Steinsarg.
7 **mourning:** in Trauer, Trauerkleidung.
13 **fidelity:** Treue.
19 **guileless:** arglos.
25 **plaything:** Spielzeug.

Jove! the impression was so powerful that for me, too, he seemed to have died only yesterday – nay, this very minute. I saw her and him in the same instant of time – his death and her sorrow – I saw her sorrow in the very moment of his death. Do you understand? I saw them together – I heard them together. She had said, with a deep catch of the breath, 'I have survived' while my strained ears seemed to hear distinctly, mingled with her tone of despairing regret, the summing up whisper of his eternal condemnation. I asked myself what I was doing there, with a sensation of panic in my heart as though I had blundered into a place of cruel and absurd mysteries not fit for a human being to behold. She motioned me to a chair. We sat down, I laid the packet gently on the little table, and she put her hand over it. . . . 'You knew him well,' she murmured, after a moment of mourning silence.

" 'Intimacy grows quickly out there,' I said. 'I knew him as well as it is possible for one man to know another.'

" 'And you admired him,' she said. 'It was impossible to know him and not to admire him. Was it?'

" 'He was a remarkable man,' I said, unsteadily. Then before the appealing fixity of her gaze, that seemed to watch for more words on my lips, I went on, 'It was impossible not to —'

" 'Love him,' she finished eagerly, silencing me into an appalled dumbness. 'How true! how true! But when you think that no one knew him so well as I! I had all his noble confidence. I knew him best.'

23 **unsteadily** (adv.): schwankend, unbeständig, unstet.
24 **fixity:** Starrheit.

160

"'You knew him best,' I repeated. And perhaps she did. But with every word spoken the room was growing darker, and only her forehead, smooth and white, remained illumined by the unextinguishable light of belief and love.

"'You were his friend,' she went on. 'His friend,' she repeated, a little louder. 'You must have been, if he had given you this, and sent you to me. I feel I can speak to you – and oh! I must speak. I want you – you who have heard his last words – to know I have been worthy of him. . . . It is not pride. . . . Yes! I am proud to know I understood him better than any one on earth – he told me so himself. And since his mother died I have had no one – no one – to – to —'

"I listened. The darkness deepened. I was not even sure whether he had given me the right bundle. I rather suspect he wanted me to take care of another batch of his papers which, after his death, I saw the manager examining under the lamp. And the girl talked, easing her pain in the certitude of my sympathy; she talked as thirsty men drink. I had heard that her engagement with Kurtz had been disapproved by her people. He wasn't rich enough or something. And indeed I don't know whether he had not been a pauper all his life. He had given me some reason to infer that it was his impatience of comparative poverty that drove him out there.

"'. . . Who was not his friend who had heard him speak

4 **to illumine:** erleuchten.
17 **batch:** Stapel, Packen.
20 **certitude:** Gewißheit.
22 **to disapprove:** mißbilligen.
24 **pauper:** Armer, Mittelloser.
25 **to infer:** folgern, schließen.

once?' she was saying. 'He drew men towards him by what was best in them.' She looked at me with intensity. 'It is the gift of the great,' she went on, and the sound of her low voice seemed to have the accompaniment of all
5 the other sounds, full of mystery, desolation, and sorrow, I had ever heard – the ripple of the river, the soughing of the trees swayed by the wind, the murmurs of the crowds, the faint ring of incomprehensible words cried from afar, the whisper of a voice speaking from
10 beyond the threshold of an eternal darkness. 'But you have heard him! You know!' she cried.

" 'Yes, I know,' I said with something like despair in my heart, but bowing my head before the faith that was in her, before that great and saving illusion that shone with
15 an unearthly glow in the darkness, in the triumphant darkness from which I could not have defended her – from which I could not even defend myself.

" 'What a loss to me – to us!' – she corrected herself with beautiful generosity; then added in a murmur, 'To the
20 world.' By the last gleams of twilight I could see the glitter of her eyes, full of tears – of tears that would not fall.

" 'I have been very happy – very fortunate – very proud,' she went on. 'Too fortunate. Too happy for a
25 little while. And now I am unhappy for – for life.'

"She stood up; her fair hair seemed to catch all the remaining light in a glimmer of gold. I rose, too.

" 'And of all this,' she went on, mournfully, 'of all his

---

2 **intensity:** Stärke, Heftigkeit, Intensität.
7 **soughing:** Sausen, Pfeifen.
20 **twilight:** Zwielicht, Dämmerung.
27 **glimmer:** Schimmer.

promise, and of all his greatness, of his generous mind, of his noble heart, nothing remains – nothing but a memory. You and I —'

" 'We shall always remember him,' I said, hastily.

" 'No!' she cried. 'It is impossible that all this should be lost – that such a life should be sacrificed to leave nothing – but sorrow. You know what vast plans he had. I knew of them, too – I could not perhaps understand – but others knew of them. Something must remain. His words, at least, have not died.'

" 'His words will remain,' I said.

" 'And his example,' she whispered to herself. 'Men looked up to him – his goodness shone in every act. His example —'

" 'True,' I said; 'his example, too. Yes, his example. I forgot that.'

" 'But I do not. I cannot – I cannot believe – not yet. I cannot believe that I shall never see him again, that nobody will see him again, never, never, never.'

"She put out her arms as if after a retreating figure, stretching them black and with clasped pale hands across the fading and narrow sheen of the window. Never see him! I saw him clearly enough then. I shall see this eloquent phantom as long as I live, and I shall see her, too, a tragic and familiar Shade, resembling in this gesture another one, tragic also, and bedecked with powerless charms, stretching bare brown arms over the glitter of the infernal stream, the stream of darkness. She said suddenly very low, 'He died as he lived.'

22 **sheen:** Schein, Glanz.
26 **gesture:** Gebärde.
    to bedeck: schmücken, zieren.

" 'His end,' said I, with dull anger stirring in me, 'was in every way worthy of his life.'

" 'And I was not with him,' she murmured. My anger subsided before a feeling of infinite pity.

5 " 'Everything that could be done —' I mumbled.

" 'Ah, but I believed in him more than any one on earth – more than his own mother, more than – himself. He needed me! Me! I would have treasured every sigh, every word, every sign, every glance.'

10 "I felt like a chill grip on my chest. 'Don't,' I said, in a muffled voice.

" 'Forgive me. I – I – have mourned so long in silence – in silence. . . . You were with him – to the last? I think of his loneliness. Nobody near to understand him as I would

15 have understood. Perhaps no one to hear. . . .'

" 'To the very end,' I said, shakily. 'I heard his very last words. . . .' I stopped in a fright.

" 'Repeat them,' she murmured in a heart-broken tone. 'I want – I want – something – something – to – to live

20 with.'

"I was on the point of crying at her, 'Don't you hear them?' The dusk was repeating them in a persistent whisper all around us, in a whisper that seemed to swell menacingly like the first whisper of a rising wind. 'The

25 horror! the horror!'

" 'His last word – to live with,' she insisted. 'Don't you understand I loved him – I loved him – I loved him!'

"I pulled myself together and spoke slowly.

30 " 'The last word he pronounced was – your name.'

---

4 **to subside:** sich legen, nachlassen.
29 **to pull o.s. together:** sich zusammenreißen.

"I heard a light sigh and then my heart stood still, stopped dead short by an exulting and terrible cry, by the cry of inconceivable triumph and of unspeakable pain. 'I knew it – I was sure!' . . . She knew. She was
5 sure. I heard her weeping; she had hidden her face in her hands. It seemed to me that the house would collapse before I could escape, that the heavens would fall upon my head. But nothing happened. The heavens do not fall for such a trifle. Would they have fallen, I
10 wonder, if I had rendered Kurtz that justice which was his due? Hadn't he said he wanted only justice? But I couldn't. I could not tell her. It would have been too dark – too dark altogether. . . ."
Marlow ceased, and sat apart, indistinct and silent, in
15 the pose of a meditating Buddha. Nobody moved for a time. "We have lost the first of the ebb," said the Director, suddenly. I raised my head. The offing was barred by a black bank of clouds, and the tranquil waterway leading to the uttermost ends of the earth
20 flowed sombre under an overcast sky – seemed to lead into the heart of an immense darkness.

---

2 **to exult:** frohlocken.
20 **overcast:** bedeckt, bewölkt

Editorische Notiz

Der englische Text folgt der Ausgabe: Joseph Conrad, *Youth, A Narrative, and Two Other Stories*, London: The Gresham Publishing Company, 1925. Das Glossar erklärt in der Regel alle Wörter, die über die Wertigkeitsstufe 4 des *Englischen Arbeitswörterbuches* von Alfred Haase (Frankfurt a. M.: Moritz Diesterweg, ⁷1979) hinausgehen. Im Zweifelsfall wurde großzügig verfahren, d. h. eher eine Vokabel mehr aufgenommen als dort vorgesehen.

Im Glossar verwendete Abkürzungen

adv.	adverb
fig.	figuratively (übertragen)
frz.	französisch
ital.	italienisch
lat.	lateinisch
o.s.	oneself
pl.	plural
s.o.	someone
s.th.	something

Anmerkungen

1 Nach seiner Rückkehr vom Kongo und seiner Genesung unternahm Conrad mehrere Segelausflüge mit seinem Freund G. F. Hope auf dessen Yacht »Nellie«. Die Erinnerung an diese Ausflüge liegt der Gestaltung der Rahmensituation zugrunde. Hope war ein »Director of Companies«, und zwischen ihm und Conrad gab es »the bond of the sea«, da beide auf der »Duke of Sutherland« zur See gefahren waren.

2 Bei Gravesend weitet sich die Themsemündung. Aus den Landschaftsbeschreibungen läßt sich rekonstruieren, daß die »Nellie« auf der Höhe von Lower Hope Point, am Beginn des »sea-reach of the Thames«, geankert haben muß.

3 Sir Francis Drake (um 1540–96) kämpfte als Freibeuter gegen die Spanier. Zwischen 1577 und 1580 umsegelte er auf der »Golden Hind« als erster Engländer die Welt. 1581 wurde Drake an Bord seines Schiffes von Elizabeth I. geadelt, die damit seine Seeräuberei öffentlich billigte. Als Vizeadmiral nahm Drake 1588 vor Cadiz und im Ärmelkanal am Kampf gegen die Armada teil. Mit den materiellen Beweggründen Drakes kontrastiert Marlow die Expedition Sir John Franklins (1786–1847), der 1845 mit den Schiffen »Erebus« und »Terror« zur Erforschung der Nordwestpassage aufbrach. Zwischen September 1846 und April 1848 lagen Franklins Schiffe im Eis vor King-Williams-Land fest. In dieser Zeit starben Franklin und 24 Männer; die 125 Überlebenden verhungerten oder erfroren bei dem Versuch, die Hudson Bai zu erreichen. »Erebus« (lat., ›die Finsternis‹) verweist zudem auf Conrads Titel und Thema. Es ist das dunkle Land, wo Hades und das Reich der Kimmerier liegen. In der Theogonie des Hesiod ist Erebus der Sohn des Chaos und Bruder und Gatte der Nacht.

4 Deptford, Greenwich und Erith, allesamt am Südufer der Themse gelegen und heute Stadtteile Groß-Londons, waren traditionelle Ankerplätze.

5 Die East India Company wurde 1600 gegründet und war Wegbereiter der britischen Herrschaft in Indien und im Pazifik. Sie verfügte über eine große, gut ausgerüstete Handelsflotte.

6 Die römische Besetzung Großbritanniens begann 55 und 54 v. Chr. durch Cäsars Feldzüge. 43 n. Chr. wurde Südengland unter Claudius dauerhaft erobert. Den Vergleich zwischen dem vorrömischen England und dem barbarischen Afrika hatte Stanley, der Erforscher des Kongogebiets, bereits in einer von der *Times* am 4. Oktober 1892 gedruckten Rede gezogen.

7 Vgl. Cäsar, *Bellum Gallicum*, Buch IV und V. Soweit man die zur Überfahrt benötigten Schiffe nicht von den gallischen und germanischen Küstenvölkern requirieren konnte, wurden sie an Ort und Stelle gebaut.

8 Feuriger, heller Wein aus Falerno in Kampanien, galt in der Antike (Horaz) als bester Wein Italiens.

9 Ravenna an der Adria war in der römischen Kaiserzeit neben Misenum der bedeutendste Kriegshafen.

10 Zur Bedeutung der Buddha-Vergleiche s. Nachwort.

11 Marlows Angaben enthalten autobiographische Bezüge. Auch Conrad war vor seiner Reise zum Kongo ungefähr sechs Jahre zur See gefahren. Marlow ist jedoch trotz aller Parallelen kein »alter ego« Conrads, sondern eine autonome Erzählerfigur, deren Erlebnisse sich gerade in dem für *Heart of Darkness* entscheidenden Erzählzusammenhang, der Annäherung an und Begegnung mit Kurtz, mit Conrads Biographie nicht mehr gleichsetzen lassen.

12 Zur Entstehungszeit von *Heart of Darkness* war der Nordpol zwar noch nicht erreicht worden, aber zahlreiche Expeditionen hatten in der 2. Hälfte des 19. Jh.s das Polargebiet systematisch erforscht.

13 Den Kontakt zu Albert Thys, damals Direktor der Kongo-Gesellschaft, hatte Conrads in Brüssel lebende Tante M. Poradowska vermittelt.

14 Ein Däne namens Freiesleben war tatsächlich unter den von Marlow geschilderten Umständen ums Leben gekom-

men, und Conrads Vertrag sah vor, daß er dessen Schiff übernehmen sollte. Vgl. Norman Sherry, *Conrad's Western World,* Cambridge 1971, S. 15–22.

15 Marlows Reisestationen sind mit denen Conrads identisch. Conrad verließ am 10. Mai 1890 Bordeaux auf der »Ville de Maceio« und erreichte Boma, den Überseehafen an der Kongomündung, am 12. Juni.

16 Neben Grand Bassam (Elfenbeinküste) und Grand Popo (Dahomé) wohl Banana an der Kongomündung.

17 Boma.

18 Matadi. 1890 lebten hier 170 Weiße. Es gab vier Fabriken, und mit dem Bau der Eisenbahn, die den Transport entlang des wegen der Stromschnellen nicht schiffbaren Teils des Kongo ermöglichen sollte, war bereits begonnen worden.

19 In Dantes *Divina Commedia* fällt der Höllentrichter des »Inferno« in neun Kreisen zum Sitz Luzifers im Erdmittelpunkt ab.

20 Zur Frage, inwieweit Conrad das Schicksal des Handelsagenten Hodister für Kurtz als Vorlage nahm, vgl. Sherry, S. 92–118. Den Namen Kurtz übernahm Conrad von einem anderen Handelsagenten namens Klein, der während Conrads Rückreise von Stanley Falls an Bord der »Roi des Belges« starb. Bei der Überarbeitung des Manuskripts änderte Conrad »Klein« in »Kurtz«. Daß Conrad die Fakten zweier Schicksale in der Figur von Kurtz verschmolz, unterstreicht die ästhetisch autonome Konzeption dieses Charakters.

21 Marlows Vergleich ist keineswegs willkürlich. In Deal landeten 55 v. Chr. Cäsars Legionen, und über Canterbury führte eine von den Römern gebaute Straße nach London, deren Verlauf die heutige A 2 noch auf weiten Strecken folgt.

22 Die Sultane von Sansibar unterhielten Handelsbeziehungen bis ins Kongobecken und waren als Sklavenjäger und -händler berüchtigt. Daß die Kongo-Gesellschaft Araber aus Sansibar als Soldaten verpflichtete, charakterisiert ihre Haltung gegenüber den Eingeborenen.

23 Kinshasa, heute die Hauptstadt Zaïres.

24 Als Conrad Kinshasa erreichte, mußte er erfahren, daß sein Kommando, die »Florida«, auf Grund gelaufen war und erst geborgen werden mußte.

25 Matrose, vgl. dt. »Teerjacke« für »Seemann«. Conrads Verhältnis zu Cammille Delcommune, dem Manager der Zentralstation, war von Beginn an gespannt und bestärkte Conrad in seinem Entschluß, den Dienst bei der Kongo-Gesellschaft zu quittieren.

26 Eine Expedition in das Katangagebiet verließ während Conrads Aufenthalt die Zentralstation. Sie wurde von Alexandre Delcommune, dem Bruder des ›Managers‹, angeführt.

27 Vorbild für Kurtz' Station war Stanley Falls, eine Niederlassung der Gesellschaft, zu der Conrad am 4. August 1890 mit der »Roi des Belges« aufbrach. Conrad war jedoch während der Hinreise nur Passagier, »second in command«, denn im Gegensatz zu Marlow war es ihm nicht gelungen, sein Kommando aus dem Fluß zu bergen. Und während Marlow in seinem Bericht die Einsamkeit der Flußfahrt herausstellt, läßt sich aus zeitgenössischen Quellen erschließen, daß auf dem Kongo bereits reger Schiffsverkehr herrschte.

28 Wahrscheinlich waren hier die Eingeborenen vom Stamm der Bangala Vorbild, die, obwohl Kannibalen, wegen ihrer Kenntnis des Flußlaufs gern angeworben wurden.

29 Das für die Kessel der Flußdampfer notwendige Feuerholz wurde gewöhnlich von der farbigen Crew während der nächtlichen Rast geschlagen.

30 Der Titel ist bislang nicht identifiziert, doch gab es einen Verfasser von Segelhandbüchern namens John Thomas Towson, dessen Werke um 1850 erschienen waren.

31 Amerikanisches Repetiergewehr mit einem 15 Patronen fassenden Magazin. Die Repetiergewehre, besonders das von Marlow ebenfalls erwähnte Martini-Henry-Gewehr, waren wegen ihres harten Rückstoßes berüchtigt, und dies erhellt Marlows abfälligen Kommentar (S. 113) über die ungezielt aus der Hüfte schießenden »pilgrims«.

32 Messingdraht war am Kongo akzeptiertes Zahlungsmittel. Er wurde in 60 Pfund schweren Rollen geliefert, dann in »Normstücke« von ungefähr zwei englischen Fuß zerschnitten, die wiederum in Kinshasa einen Tauschwert von etwa 1½ englischen Pennies hatten.

33 Kassava- oder Maniokbrei, der aus dem Mehl der zerstampften Wurzel angerührt, gepreßt und für den Transport in Bananenblätter gewickelt wurde.

34 Kurtz ist nicht nur durch seine Herkunft Erbe des kolonialen Gedankens. Der »Beitrag ganz Europas« ist wörtlich zu nehmen, denn auf der von Bismarck 1884 veranlaßten Kongo-Konferenz in Berlin einigten sich die Vertreter der europäischen Mächte und auch der USA auf das Prinzip der Handelsfreiheit und der Freiheit der Schiffahrt für das Kongogebiet. Mit der gemeinsam unterzeichneten Generalakte von 1885 schufen sie die völkerrechtliche Grundlage für die Tätigkeit der Kongo-Gesellschaft.

35 Eine Gesellschaft dieses Namens ist nicht belegbar, doch gab es in zahlreichen europäischen Staaten Gesellschaften, die sich für die Abschaffung und Bekämpfung der Sklaverei einsetzten und humanitäre Programme für die Kolonialgebiete verfochten. Im Kongogebiet hatte die Berliner Konferenz die Sklaverei verboten, woran sich auch die Kongo-Gesellschaft de jure hielt. De facto wurden aber, wie Marlows Bericht zeigt, die wegen geringfügiger Vergehen als »Kriminelle« verurteilten Schwarzen wie Sklaven behandelt. Vor dem Hintergrund realer Vorkommnisse ist auch die Kurtz zugeschriebene Ausrottungspolitik glaubhaft, mit der er sich seinen Elfenbeinschatz verschafft.

36 Zwischen Marlows Beschreibung und der weiträumig ausgebauten Niederlassung, die Conrad vorfand, gibt es keine Parallelen.

37 Für ein mögliches Vorbild des ›Harlekin‹ vgl. Sherry, S. 114–117.

38 Marlows Annahme, bei den kyrillischen Buchstaben handele es sich um einen Code, kann als Indiz gewertet werden, daß Conrad, dem das Russische wohlvertraut war,

keine Identifikation von Autor und Erzähler bewirken wollte.

39 Vgl. Anm. 20.

40 Flußaufwärts hatte die »Roi des Belges« 27 Tage benötigt, die Rückreise erfolgte in 18 Tagen, während der Conrad kurzfristig das Kommando für den erkrankten Kapitän Koch übernahm.

41 Möglicherweise die Herrscher der Signatarstaaten des Kongo-Vertrags.

42 Auf der Rückreise von Kinshasa nach Boma, die Conrad im Oktober 1890 antrat, litt er unter schweren Anfällen von Fieber und Dysenterie. Nicht anders als Marlows Gefährte auf dem Hinmarsch mußte er über weite Strecken getragen werden.

Literaturhinweise

Die zwischen 1895 und 1966 veröffentlichten Studien zu Conrad erfassen Bruce E. Teets und Helmut E. Gerber, *Joseph Conrad. An Annotated Bibliography*, De Kalb (Ill.) 1971. Einen systematischen Forschungsüberblick bis zur Mitte der siebziger Jahre gibt Ferdinand Schunck, *Joseph Conrad*, Darmstadt 1979. Verwiesen sei auf die Jahresbibliographien in *Conradiana* sowie auf Todd Kay Bender, *A Concordance to Conrad's »Heart of Darkness«*, New York 1979. Eine umfassende biographische Studie bietet Frederick R. Karl, *Joseph Conrad. The Three Lives*, New York 1979.

Bredella, L., »Hinweise zu einer Unterrichtseinheit über Joseph Conrad ›Heart of Darkness‹ und Rudyard Kipling ›The Man who would be King‹«, in: L. B., *Ästhetische Erfahrung und soziales Handeln*, Frankfurt/Berlin/München 1975.

Conrad, J., *Congo Diary and other uncollected pieces*, hrsg. von Z. Naider, Garden City (N.Y.) 1978.

Dean, L. F. (Hrsg.), *Joseph Conrad's »Heart of Darkness«: Backgrounds and Criticisms*, Englewood Cliffs (N.J.) 1960.

Dowden, W., *Joseph Conrad: The Imaged Style*, Nashville (Tenn.) 1970.

Erzgräber, W., »Joseph Conrad: *Lord Jim*«, in: *Der englische Roman im 19. Jahrhundert. Interpretationen*, hrsg. von P. Goetsch, H. Kosok und K. Otten, Berlin 1973.

Evans, R., »Conrad's Underworld«, in: *Modern Fiction Studies* 2 (1956) S. 56–62.

Feder, L., »Marlow's Descent into Hell«, in: *Nineteenth Century Fiction* 9 (1955) S. 280–292.

Goetsch, P., *Die Romankonzeption in England 1880–1910*, Heidelberg 1967.

Guerard, A., *Conrad the Novelist*, Cambridge (Mass.) 1958.

Harkness, B. (Hrsg.), *Conrad's ›Heart of Darkness‹ and the Critics*, San Francisco (Calif.) 1960.

Karl, F. R. (Hrsg.), *Joseph Conrad: A Collection of Criticism*, New York 1975.

– »Introduction to the ›danse macabre‹: Conrad's *Heart of Darkness*«, in: *Modern Fiction Studies* 14 (1968) S. 143–156.

Lincoln, K., »Comic Light in *Heart of Darkness*«, in: *Modern Fiction Studies* 18 (1972) S. 183–197.

Nicolaisen, P., »Die Darstellung der Wildnis in Joseph Conrads *Heart of Darkness*«, in: *Die Neueren Sprachen* 67 (1968) S. 265–281.

Ramsey, R., »The Available and the Unavailable ›I‹: Conrad and James«, in: *English Literature in Transition* 14 (1971) S. 137–145.

Reitz, B., »›I've never seen anything so unreal in my life‹ – Unwirklichkeit als Darstellungsproblem in Coppolas *Apocalypse Now* und Conrads *Heart of Darkness*«, in: *anglistik & englischunterricht* 16 (1982) S. 119–144.

Roussel, R., *The Metaphysics of Darkness: A Study in the Unity and Development of Conrad's Fiction*, Baltimore (Md.) 1971.

Sherry, N., *Conrad's Western World*, Cambridge 1971.

– (Hrsg.), *Conrad: The Critical Heritage*, London/Boston 1973.

Stallman, R. W. (Hrsg.), *The Art of Joseph Conrad: A Critical Symposion*, East Lansing (Mich.) 1960.

Stein, W. B., »Buddhism and *Heart of Darkness*«, in: *Western Humanities Review* 11 (1957) S. 281–285.

– »*The Heart of Darkness*: Bodhisattva Scenario«, in: *Orient/West* 9 (1964) S. 37–46.

Uehlein, F., »Joseph Conrad: Heart of Darkness«, in: *Die englische Kurzgeschichte*, hrsg. von K. H. Göller und G. Hoffmann, Düsseldorf 1973.

Weiand, H. J., *Joseph Conrad. Werk und Leben*, Düsseldorf 1979.

Wilcox, S., »Conrad's ›Complicated Presentations‹ of Symbolic Imagery in *Heart of Darkness*«, in: *Philological Quarterly* 39 (1960) S. 1–17.

Wilkening, V., *Die Erzählsituation der Ich-Form im Werke Joseph Conrads*, Diss. Berlin 1960.

Nachwort

Thomas Mann bewunderte Joseph Conrad. In ihm sah er den »ersten Erzähler der Epoche«, an dem das eigene Schaffen nicht zu messen war. Und als der Kritiker F. R. Leavis in den vierziger Jahren daranging, die Entwicklungslinien des englischen Romans fortzuschreiben, begann er mit dem apodiktischen Satz, »The great English novelists are Jane Austen, George Eliot, Henry James and Joseph Conrad –«.[1] Conrads Beitrag zur englischen Erzähltradition, den die Wahlheimat mit der allerdings ausgeschlagenen Erhebung in den Adelsstand ehren wollte, entstand jedoch erst in der zweiten Lebenshälfte des naturalisierten Briten. Denn nicht als englischer Staatsbürger, sondern als Pole, dessen voller Name Józef Teodor Conrad Korzeniowski lautete, wurde Joseph Conrad 1857 in Berdyczów geboren. Dem wegen antirussischer Agitation verurteilten Vater folgte Conrad mit der Mutter in die Verbannung, und nach dem frühen Tod der Eltern übernahm 1869 Conrads Onkel Thaddeus Bobrowski die Erziehungsverantwortung.

Der heranwachsende Joseph Conrad sperrte sich allerdings gegen den vom Onkel für ihn vorgesehenen großbürgerlichen Bildungsgang. 1874 setzte er seinen Willen durch, zur See zu gehen, und nach Lehrjahren auf französischen Schiffen faßte er den Entschluß, das Kapitänspatent der englischen Handelsmarine zu erwerben. Es war dies zugleich der Entscheid für einen Lebensentwurf. Denn das seemännische Ethos, der Pflichtbegriff und das Festhalten an einer selbstgewählten Verantwortung auch dort noch, wo jede Ordnung sich auflöst und jeder Lebenssinn fraglich wird, sollte in seinen Romanen und Erzählungen immer wieder zur letzten gesicherten existentiellen Basis seiner Erzähler und Protagonisten werden. Auch in *Heart of Darkness* sucht Marlow seine Integrität durch die Konzentration auf seine Arbeit und seine Pflicht zu behaup-

1 F. R. Leavis, *The Great Tradition*, Harmondsworth ²1967 (1. Aufl. London 1948), S. 9.

ten, und angesichts der Auflösung aller Werte um ihn erscheint ihm das Seemannshandbuch des Harlekin, das er im Dschungel findet, als mehr denn nur ein Dokument praktischer Vernunft, »luminous with another than a professional light« (S. 82).

Um sein Ziel zu erreichen, lernte Conrad Englisch im Selbststudium, heuerte als Matrose auf einem englischen Schiff an, verfolgte nun energisch seine seemännische Karriere und erwarb 1886, im gleichen Jahr, in dem er auch sein Kapitänspatent erhielt, die englische Staatsangehörigkeit. Die Schiffsreisen jener wie der folgenden Jahre führten ihn in den Fernen Osten und in die malaiische Inselwelt. Hier lernte er die Schauplätze und auch die Menschen kennen, die er später darstellen sollte. 1890, nach einem längeren Urlaub in Polen und in Brüssel, übernahm Conrad jedoch spontan ein Süßwasserkommando: er heuerte als Kapitän eines Flußdampfers der belgischen Kongo-Gesellschaft an.

Wenn Marlow in *Heart of Darkness* das Kongogebiet als »a white patch for a boy to dream gloriously over« (S. 14) bezeichnet und damit die Neugier auf einen noch weitgehend unerforschten Flecken der Erdkarte als wichtigsten Anstoß für das Kongoabenteuer bezeichnet, benennt er auch das für Conrad selbst ausschlaggebende Motiv. Doch der Aufenthalt am Kongo, der auch den Hintergrund für die Erzählung »An Outpost of Progress« (1896) abgibt, sollte für Conrad fatale Folgen haben. Nicht anders als sein Erzähler Marlow erwies er sich den Tropenkrankheiten nicht gewachsen und mußte bereits im Januar 1891 schwerkrank über Brüssel nach London zurückkehren. Zwar übernahm er nach einer langwierigen Genesung noch zwei weitere Kommandos, doch mußte er einsehen, daß seine angegriffene Gesundheit den Anforderungen des Seemannsberufs nicht länger gewachsen war. 1894 heuerte Conrad endgültig ab.

Zu dem Entschluß, nach den Jahren auf See eine zweite Karriere als Schriftsteller zu beginnen, trug sicherlich bei, daß der bereits 1889 begonnene Roman *Almayer's Folly* nahezu fertiggestellt war. In Fisher Unwin fand Conrad zudem einen engagierten Verlag, und nach dem erfolgreichen Start veröffentlichte Conrad in dichter Folge bis 1907 (*The Secret Agent*) seine berühmtesten Romane und Erzählungen. Nach einer längeren Pause folgte 1911 *Under Western Eyes*, ein Roman, der wie schon *The Secret Agent* im Milieu der Anarchisten und Revolutionäre spielt und mit dem Conrad eine weitere Korrektur seiner Festlegung als Autor von Seeromanen bewirkte. Mit *Chance* erzielte er 1913 einen Publikumserfolg, und mit dem Spätwerk von *Victory* (1915) bis *The Rover* (1923) vermochte er zwar sein Ansehen weiter zu festigen, erreichte aber nicht mehr die darstellerische Intensität und Komplexität der Texte aus dem Jahrzehnt um die Jahrhundertwende. Von einem schweren Rheumaleiden geschwächt und in seiner Schaffenskraft behindert, erlag Conrad im Sommer 1924 einem Herzanfall.

Verglichen mit *An Outcast of the Islands* (1896), *Lord Jim* (1900) oder gar *Nostromo* (1904) ist *Heart of Darkness*, 1898 bereits fertiggestellt, aber 1902 erst veröffentlicht, ein eher schmales Bändchen, kürzer noch als *The Nigger of the ›Narcissus‹* von 1898. Aber wie *The Secret Agent*, dessen differenzierte Zeitstruktur sich nur dem aufmerksamen Leser erschließt, kompensiert auch *Heart of Darkness* den Verzicht auf epische Breite durch eine poetisch dichte und bildhafte Sprache und durch eine komplexe Erzählstruktur. Hinter dem scheinbar geradlinigen Nachvollzug von Marlows Erlebnissen am Kongo werden im Prozeß des Erzählens zudem grundlegende moralische und existentielle Fragestellungen evoziert, die *Heart of Darkness* als einen wichtigen Text der modernen Erzählliteratur ausweisen.

Dieser Dimension war sich offenbar T. S. Eliot bewußt, als er der ersten Fassung seiner für die Moderne richtungweisenden Dichtung *The Waste Land* (1922) Marlows Fragen und Kommentar zu dessen letzter Begegnung mit Kurtz voranstellte:

»Did he live his life again in every detail of desire, temptation, and surrender during that supreme moment of complete knowledge? He cried in a whisper at some image, at some vision – he cried out twice, a cry that was no more than a breath – ›The horror! The horror!‹« (S. 149)

Eliot schrieb *The Waste Land* vor dem Hintergrund der Erfahrungen des Ersten Weltkriegs. Aber er erkannte offensichtlich, daß das für die Moderne charakteristische Gefühl der Illusionslosigkeit, des Ausgeliefertseins an ein Leben ohne Sinn und des Verlusts von Idealen, Werten und Ordnungen, die dem Menschen Halt geben können, von Conrad bereits thematisiert worden war.

Im Schicksal von Kurtz als dem Berührungspunkt zwischen dem Dichter Eliot und dem Erzähler Conrad wird deutlich, daß eine Interpretation von *Heart of Darkness*, die allein um den Aspekt der Kolonialismuskritik kreist, dem Inhalt wie der Form des erzählerischen Anliegens nicht gerecht wird. Auch der amerikanische Regisseur Francis Ford Coppola hatte diesen über die Kolonialismusproblematik hinausweisenden Ansatz Conrads vor Augen, als er 1979 in seinem Vietnam-Film *Apocalypse Now* unter Beibehaltung der Erzählstruktur die Handlung von *Heart of Darkness* in die Gegenwart transponierte.[2]

Über die Bedeutung der Kolonialismuskritik hinaus der umfassenderen moralischen Fragestellung nachzugehen, heißt nicht, den zeitkritischen Ansatz Conrads zugunsten eines zeitübergreifenden zu verwerfen. Marlow macht aus seiner Abscheu vor der kolonialen Praxis, die er am Kongo vorfindet, keinen Hehl, und auf der Ebene der Kolonialismus- bzw. Gesellschaftskritik läßt sich die Begegnung mit Kurtz durchaus als intendierte Steigerung der Exzesse kolonialistischen Gebarens verstehen. Die Diskrepanz zwischen dem idealistischen humanitären Anspruch und der entmenschlichten oder vielleicht besser allzu menschlichen Wirklichkeit mußte zudem Conrads Zeitgenossen besonders bewußt werden, da ihnen die vorgeblich rein altruistischen Zielsetzungen der Kongo-Gesellschaft noch geläufig waren, die der belgische König Leopold II. 1879 bei der Gründung der »Association Internationale du Congo« so beredt herausgestellt hatte und in den nachfolgenden Jahren

---

2 Vgl. Bernhard Reitz, »›I've never seen anything so unreal in my life‹ – Unwirklichkeit als Darstellungsproblem in Coppolas *Apocalypse Now* und Conrads *Heart of Darkness*«, in: *a & e* 16 (1982) S. 119–144.

unermüdlich propagierte. Und auch für Henry M. Stanleys enthusiastische Schilderung *The Congo and the Founding of its Free State* (1885) war Conrads illusionslose Darstellung eine einschneidende Korrektur.

Marlow enthüllt sich die schäbige Wirklichkeit der Kolonialherrschaft schrittweise. Als er nach der beschwerlichen und desillusionierenden Anreise die Zentralstation erreicht, kommentiert er das Gebaren der »jolly pioneers of progress« so:

> »They wandered here and there with their absurd long staves in their hands, like a lot of faithless pilgrims bewitched inside a rotten fence. The word ›ivory‹ rang in the air, was whispered, was sighed. You would think they were praying to it. A taint of imbecile rapacity blew through it all, like a whiff from some corpse. By Jove! I've never seen anything so unreal in my life.« (S. 49)

Gegenüber der grenzenlosen Habgier, der abgestumpften Unmenschlichkeit, der eitlen Selbstgefälligkeit und der kleinlichen Eifersucht der Handelsagenten vermag Marlow jedoch seine Integrität zu behaupten. Der Abstand, den er im Umgang mit ihnen aufrechterhält, die Überlegenheit, mit der er sich ihren Intrigen verweigert, und die Gleichgültigkeit, mit der er ihren Vertraulichkeiten wie ihrem Mißtrauen begegnet, bezeugen eine innere Distanz, die auch durch seine sarkastischen, oftmals sogar zynischen Urteile bestätigt wird. »Imbecile rapacity« und »rapacious folly« charakterisieren zwar die Welt, in die er ahnungslos hineingestolpert ist, aber in ihrer Primitivität stellen sie für ihn keine existentielle Herausforderung dar.

Mit dieser Herausforderung wird Marlow erst im Herzen der Finsternis konfrontiert, im Zusammentreffen mit Kurtz, dessen zunächst geheimnisvolle und von Gerüchten umhüllte Existenz zu einer Wirklichkeit wird, die nicht nur Marlows Selbstgewißheit und Selbstkontrolle, sondern auch das moralische Ordnungssystem in Frage stellt, an das Marlows fiktive Zuhörer an Bord der »Nellie«, »each moored with two good addresses«, so unerschütterlich glauben. Allerdings, und daran läßt Conrad keinen Zweifel, können Marlows Zuhörer dessen

Erfahrungen und dessen Erkenntnisprozeß trotz Marlows erzählerischem Bemühen nicht wirklich nachvollziehen. Einer von ihnen weist Marlows Darstellungs- und Deutungsversuch ausdrücklich als »absurd« zurück (S. 103), und der Rahmenerzähler, der eingangs mit der Bemerkung »between us there was [...] the bond of the sea« (S. 4) das die Teilnehmer der Segelpartie Verbindende herausgestellt hatte, erklärt am Schluß, »Marlow [...] sat apart, indistinct and silent« (S. 165).

Unübersehbar hat aber auch Marlow selbst Schwierigkeiten, sich mit zunehmender Annäherung an Kurtz mitzuteilen. Während er die »pilgrims« an Bord weiter mit bissigen Kommentaren bedenkt, flüchtet er dort, wo er von Kurtz spricht, immer wieder in Beschreibungen und Bilder, und wie bei der nebelverhangenen Flußlandschaft verschwimmen auch bei seinen Aussagen die Konturen. Insofern sind in den Reaktionen der fiktiven Zuhörer die Rezeptionsschwierigkeiten, die Marlows »inconclusive experience« auch für den Leser birgt, bereits vorweggenommen. Der Wandel in Marlows Erzählweise, der mit einer wachsenden persönlichen Betroffenheit einhergeht, ist aber auch Indiz dafür, daß Conrads erzählerisches Anliegen über die ansonsten klar formulierte Kolonialismuskritik hinauszielt. Hierfür hat Conrad seinen Lesern eine Orientierungshilfe gegeben. Denn noch bevor in *Heart of Darkness* Marlow selbst das Wort ergreift, weist der Rahmenerzähler darauf hin, daß Marlow niemals ein Seemannsgarn herkömmlicher Machart spinne:

>»The yarns of seamen have a direct simplicity, the whole meaning of which lies within the shell of a cracked nut. But Marlow was not typical (if his propensity to spin yarns be excepted), and to him the meaning of an episode was not inside like a kernel but outside, enveloping the tale which brought it out only as glow brings out a haze, in the likeness of one of these misty halos that sometimes are made visible by the spectral illumination of moonshine.« (S. 9)

Innerhalb des fiktiven Kontexts wird hier Marlow bereits jenes Differenzierungsvermögen und Reflektionsniveau zugebilligt, das er auch als dominierender Erzähler in *Lord Jim* unter

Beweis stellen sollte.[3] Wenn aber Marlows Geschichte keinen
»soliden« Kern hat, keine fertige Moral für den Alltagsge-
brauch präsentiert, sondern Sinn, Bedeutung und Aussage sich
wie ein Schleier und ein Abglanz um das Erzählte legen, dann
müssen Zuhörer und Leser neben der Faktizität der *story* und
der konkreten Kritik vor allem das Wie des Erzählens, den
Erzählvorgang selbst im Blick behalten. Und wenn es der
»spectral illumination of moonshine« bedarf, damit die Bedeutung von Marlows Geschichte überhaupt sichtbar wird, dann
kommt der Atmosphäre der Unwirklichkeit in *Heart of Darkness*, die Marlow immer wieder zu beschwören versucht, offensichtlich konstitutive Bedeutung für das Textverständnis
zu.

Anders als etwa das berühmte Vorwort zu *The Nigger of the
›Narcissus‹* wird in *Heart of Darkness* die erzähltheoretische
Einführung des Rahmenerzählers jedoch eher beiläufig voran-
gestellt, und dies hat dazu beigetragen, daß sie von den Kriti-
kern lange Zeit unberücksichtigt blieb. Bei aller Bewunderung
für Conrad kritisierte etwa Leavis an *Heart of Darkness* gerade
jene von Marlow beschworene Atmosphäre der Unbestimmt-
heit und Unwirklichkeit:

> »Conrad must here stand convicted of borrowing the arts of
> the magazine-writer [. . .] in order to impose on his readers
> and on himself, for thrilled response, a ›significance‹ that is
> merely an emotional insistence on the presence of what he
> can't produce. The insistence betrays the absence, the willed
> ›intensity‹ the nullity [. . .]. If he cannot through the concrete
> presentment of incident, setting and image invest the words
> with the terrific something that, by themselves, they fail to
> convey, then no amount of adjectival and ejaculatory em-
> phasis will do it.«[4]

Leavis vermag in der von Marlow vergegenwärtigten Unwirklichkeit seiner Erlebnisse nichts anderes als die vordergründige

---

3 Vgl. Willi Erzgräber, »Joseph Conrad: *Lord Jim*«, in: *Der englische Roman
im 19. Jahrhundert*, hrsg. von Paul Goetsch, Heinz Kosok und Kurt Otten,
Berlin 1973, S. 288–306.
4 Leavis, S. 199–200.

Exotik der Unterhaltungsliteratur zu erkennen. Seine Argumentation offenbart jedoch, wie sein Urteil noch von traditionsgebundenen Vorstellungen über den realistischen Roman geprägt ist. Er fordert die objektivierende Wirklichkeitsdarstellung, während Conrads erzählerischer Neuansatz darauf abzielt, an dem Protagonisten und Erzähler Marlow die subjektive Brechung der Wirklichkeitserfahrung deutlich zu machen. Sie findet in erzähltechnischen Steigerungen von Marlows Gefühl der Unwirklichkeit seiner Erlebnisse ihren Ausdruck.

Bereits die Rahmensituation, das nächtliche Warten auf den Gezeitenwechsel, enthält ein Element des Unwirklichen. Sie bereitet ebenso wie der von Marlow zunächst gezogene Vergleich zwischen dem barbarischen England der Römerzeit und dem unerforschten Afrika, zwischen den »dunklen« Strömen Themse und Kongo, auf die unwirkliche Atmosphäre des Kongoabenteuers vor. Marlow steigert in seinem Bericht diesen Eindruck dann sukkzessiv. Brüssel erscheint ihm als »whited sepulchre« und das Gebaren der Angestellten der Kongo-Gesellschaft rätselhaft. Aber nicht nur die Düsternis und das Ominöse, die über dem wahren Tun der Kongo-Gesellschaft liegen, und die Düsternis des Dschungels, der seine wahre Natur nicht preisgibt, tragen zum Eindruck der Unwirklichkeit bei. Zur Unwirklichkeit des von Marlow Erlebten gehört auch die »sordid farce acted in front of a sinister back-cloth« (S. 26), in die sich Marlow schon während der Anreise versetzt fühlt und die im Gebaren der Handelsagenten ihren Höhepunkt erreicht. In der Menge der Akteure sind zwar einzelne Figuren wie der pompös auftretende, aber zugleich verunsicherte Leiter der Zentralstation oder der »papier-maché-Mephistopheles« schärfer konturiert, doch alle sind von dem »flabby, pretending, weak-eyed devil of a rapacious and pitiless folly« besessen (S. 33 f.). Auch die Commedia-dell'arte-Figur des Harlekin ist durch diese Farce geprägt, und selbst Kurtz, dessen tragische Dimension Marlow als einziger zu erkennen vermag, ist davon gezeichnet und wird während der Rückreise von Marlow als »pitiful Jupiter« und als »sometimes [...] contemptibly childish« (S. 147) beschrieben. »All Europe contributed to the making of Kurtz« (S. 108), kommentiert Marlow, und daß auch Kurtz in die schmutzige Farce von humanitärer Prätention und kolonialer Wirklichkeit eingebunden ist, zeigt, daß das Lächerliche und Absurde – etwa der Versuch, den brennenden Schuppen mit durchlöcherten Eimern zu löschen – niemals nur komisch ist, sondern einem krankhaften Verhalten entspringt. Als den Ursprung dieses Verhaltens begreift Marlow die grenzenlose Gier nach Bereicherung durch Elfenbein, aber er muß in der Begegnung mit Kurtz auch erkennen, daß bei diesem eine Persönlichkeitsveränderung eingetreten ist, die an der primitiven Habsucht der »pilgrims« nicht mehr gemessen werden kann.

Mit dem Aufbruch zur Suche nach Kurtz erfährt die Unwirklichkeit von Marlows Situation eine weitere Steigerung. »The reality, the reality – I tell you – fades« (S. 73), versucht er, wenngleich vergeblich, seinen Zuhörern klar zu machen. Ihn erfaßt zunächst das Gefühl der Unwirklichkeit des Märchens:

> »The approach to this Kurtz grubbing for ivory in the wretched bush was beset by as many dangers as though he had been an enchanted princess sleeping in a fabulous castle.« (S. 92 f.)

Die Vorstellung von einer Märchenreise durch den dunklen, gefahrvollen Wald verharmlost jedoch, was Marlow wirklich erwartet. In Kurtz' Station am Oberlauf des Kongo wird er weder ein verwunschenes Schloß noch eine verzauberte Prinzessin finden, und die schwarze »Prinzessin«, die Kurtz sich auserkoren hat und die er zurücklassen muß, ist allenfalls eine tragische Travestie des Märchenmotivs. Für Marlow steigert sich nach der Abreise die Unwirklichkeit der Farce zur Unwirklichkeit des Traums, der auch im Nachvollzug noch Alptraum bleibt. Daß er einen Traum zu erzählen versucht, darauf hat Marlow seine Zuhörer ausdrücklich hingewiesen:

> »Do you see him [Kurtz]? Do you see the story? Do you see anything? It seems to me I am trying to tell you a dream – making a vain attempt, because no relation of a dream can convey the dream-sensation, that commingling of absurdity,

surprise, and bewilderment in a terror of struggling revolt,
that notion of being captured by the incredible, which is the
very essence of dreams . . .
He was silent for a while.
. . . No, it is impossible; it is impossible to convey the life-
sensation of any given epoch of one's existence – that which
makes its truth, its meaning – its subtle and penetrating
essence. It is impossible. We live, as we dream – alone . . .«
(S. 58)

Es gehört zu Marlows »inconclusive experience«, daß er das
Unmögliche trotzdem versucht. Sein Kommentar läßt aber
auch seine eigentliche Intention erkennen. Denn Marlow
erzählt, im Wissen, daß seine Zuhörer ihm nicht werden folgen
können, nicht nur um etwas oder sich mitzuteilen, sondern der
Akt des Erzählens ist, und darin liegt seine Bedeutung für den
Erzähler selbst, der Akt der Bewältigung einer extremen Erfahrung.

Daß Marlows Reise zu Kurtz für ihn die Unwirklichkeit eines
Traums hat, belegt seine Schilderung mannigfaltig, und »that
commingling of absurdity, surprise, and bewilderment« wird in
den Episoden auf dem nebelverhangenen Fluß eindringlich
beschworen. Für Marlow wird die Flußfahrt zum Alptraum,
der seinen »precarious grip on existence« ständig bedroht, und
dieser Alptraum erreicht seinen Höhepunkt, als Marlow in
dem »Schatten« Kurtz »the nightmare of my choice« erkennt
(S. 139). Während er bei der von den Handelsagenten aufge-
führten Farce nur distanzierter Zuschauer war, ist er nun in
dem Alptraum selbst betroffen, gefährdet und herausgefor-
dert. Farce und Alptraum sind beides Zerrbilder der Wirklichkeit und machen dadurch deren Unwirklichkeit stärker
bewußt, sie schaffen aber auch, und hierin liegt der Sinn von
Conrads Abkehr von einer traditionell realistischen Darstellung, die Voraussetzung für ein tieferes Verstehen dieser
Wirklichkeit.

Diese Befähigung zu einem tieferen Verstehen unterscheidet
Marlow sowohl von seinen fiktiven Zuhörern wie von den
»pilgrims«, die über das Scheitern und den Tod eines lästigen

Konkurrenten wie Kurtz nur Genugtuung empfinden können. Marlow dagegen begreift, daß Kurtz als Repräsentant des kolonialen und imperialen Gedankens nicht nur die dunkle Seite des als »the white man's burden« formulierten ideologischen Postulats bis zum Exzeß getrieben hat. Der Kurtz, den er vorfindet und den er aus dem Dschungel zum Schiff zurückschleppt, hat sich nicht nur einer grenzenlosen materiellen Gier anheimgegeben, sondern hat auch alle moralischen Bindungen abgestreift und sich als Hohepriester unbeschreiblicher Rituale zum Gott erhoben:

> »He had taken a high seat amongst the devils of the land – I mean literally. [. . .] I had, even like the niggers, to invoke him – himself – his own exalted and incredible degradation. There was nothing either above or below him, and I knew it. He had kicked himself loose of the earth.« (S. 106, 142)

Aus dem einstigen »emissary of pity, and science, and progress« (S. 54), als der Kurtz nach Afrika gegangen ist, ist die Inkarnation des Bösen selbst geworden, und Marlow erkennt zugleich erschrocken und fasziniert, daß Kurtz, anders als die in ihrer stumpfen materiellen Gier befangenen »pilgrims«, diesen Schritt willentlich und wissentlich vollzogen hat. Das Potential idealistischer Größe, an das Kurtz' Verlobte noch immer glaubt, hat sich in der Wildnis, wo die Kontrolle üblicher zivilisatorischer Verhaltensweisen nicht mehr gegeben ist, zur Befähigung uneingeschränkt amoralischen Handelns gewandelt, und anders als seine Zuhörer, die auf die stabilisierende Kraft ihrer »two good addresses« vertrauen, begreift Marlow in der unwirklichen Situation seiner Erlebnisse am Kongo, wie brüchig und gefährdet die scheinbar geordnete Wirklichkeit tatsächlich ist. Daß er seine Zuhörer hiervon nicht überzeugen kann, wirft ein erhellendes und zugleich ironisches Licht auf sein Verhalten gegenüber der Verlobten von Kurtz. Auch sie lebt als Gefangene einer Illusion, und auch sie hätte er von der Wahrheit kaum überzeugen können. Wo die Wahrheit nicht mehr ausrichten kann als die Lüge, wird auch das moralische Versagen relativiert, als das Marlow sein Verhalten gegenüber der Verlobten empfindet.

Marlows Einsicht, daß er seine Erfahrungen nicht wirklich mitteilen kann, und die vom Rahmenerzähler hervorgehobene wachsende Distanz zu seinen Zuhörern verweisen über die erzählerische Steigerung des Elements der Unwirklichkeit hinaus auf ein weiteres Strukturprinzip des Romans. In der Forschung ist Marlows Kongofahrt immer wieder symbolhaft gedeutet worden, als Gralssuche und als Hadesreise nach dem Vorbild der *Aeneis*, oder auch als eine Dantes »Inferno« vergleichbare Reise durch die Hölle.[5] Als Analogien, die das Textverständnis erleichtern, können solche Interpretationen hilfreich sein; sie bergen aber auch die Gefahr, dem Text eine vom Autor nicht intendierte Struktur aufzuzwingen. Was *Heart of Darkness* betrifft, so bedarf es derartiger analoger Deutungen eigentlich auch nicht, denn Conrads Text zeigt bei näherem Hinsehen eine eigenständige symbolische Strukturierung. Die entscheidenden Hinweise hierfür kommen wiederum vom Rahmenerzähler, der nicht nur Marlows Geschichte einleitet, sondern auch alle Unterbrechungen kommentiert. Bereits eingangs sagt er über Marlow,

>»[He] sat cross-legged right aft, leaning against the mizzen-mast. He had sunken cheeks, a yellow complexion, a straight back, an ascetic aspect, and, with his arms dropped, the palms of his hands outwards, resembled an idol.« (S. 4 f.)

Daß Marlow die Pose des meditierenden Buddha eingenommen hat, wird wenige Seiten später ausdrücklich bestätigt: »with his legs folded before him, he had the pose of a Buddha preaching in European clothes and without a lotus-flower« (S. 11). Und noch einmal, am Schluß, bekräftigt der Rahmenerzähler diesen Eindruck: »Marlow ceased, and sat apart, indistinct and silent, in the pose of a meditating Buddha« (S. 165).

Man kann sich darauf beschränken, in diesen Textstellen nichts anderes als eine Bekräftigung von Marlows meditativer Konzentration und Selbstversenkung zu sehen. Dann aber wären die Buddha-Vergleiche, anders als der ausdrückliche

---

5 Vgl. Bernhard Reitz, »The Meaning of the Buddha-Comparisons in Joseph Conrad's *Heart of Darkness*«, in: *Fu Jen Studies* 13 (1980) S. 41–53.

Hinweis des Rahmenerzählers auf Marlows besondere Art des Erzählens, für ein tieferes Verstehen von Marlows Geschichte ohne Bedeutung, und es bliebe die Frage, weshalb Conrad gleich dreimal die Parallelen zwischen Marlow und Buddha hervorhebt. Conrad war durch seine Asienreisen mit der Geschichte Buddhas zweifellos vertraut, und vor dem Hintergrund dieser Geschichte läßt sich ein Zusammenhang zwischen den Buddha-Vergleichen und dem Aufbau von *Heart of Darkness* durchaus erkennen.

Nach der Überlieferung gelangte der Prinz Siddhartha zur Erleuchtung, d. h., er wurde zum Buddha, nachdem er, der im väterlichen Palast von der Wirklichkeit abgeschirmt aufgewachsen war, auf drei Ausfahrten erkannte, daß der Mensch dem Alter, der Krankheit und dem Tod preisgegeben ist. Denn auf diesen Ausfahrten begegnete er einem alten Mann, einem Pestkranken und einem Leichenzug. Durch diese Erfahrungen gereift, wanderte er umher, bis er sich unter einem Baum niederließ und in einer Nacht des Ringens mit Mara, dem Prinzip des Bösen, erkannte, daß Durst, d. h. die Begierde, die Ursache allen Leidens ist und Befreiung nur durch Überwindung der Begierde erreicht werden kann.

Nicht anders als der unerfahrene Siddhartha wird in *Heart of Darkness* der erlebende Marlow von dem erzählenden Marlow als unreif und neugierig, als »silly little bird« bezeichnet. Und wie in der Buddha-Überlieferung, in der Siddharthas Vater die Stadt vor der Ausfahrt frisch weißen läßt, damit der Sohn den Schmutz und das Elend nicht sehe, wird in dem »whited sepulchre« Brüssel die unangenehme Wahrheit übertüncht. Marlows Aufenthalt in Brüssel läßt sich aber auch analog zu Siddharthas erster Ausfahrt sehen, denn in den ältlichen Sekretärinnen und dem »old doctor« im Verwaltungsgebäude der Kongo-Gesellschaft begegnet auch er dem Alter. Analog zu Siddharthas zweiter Ausfahrt dominieren dann im nächsten Abschnitt von Marlows Reise, vom Verlassen Brüssels bis zur Ankunft in der Zentralstation, Bilder der Krankheit und des Verfalls. »Insanity« manifestiert sich in dem sinnlosen Bombardement des Dschungels bereits während der Anreise, von

Krankheit und Begierde sind die Menschen gekennzeichnet, denen Marlow begegnet, und selbst das mühselig herangeschaffte Material wird dem Verrotten preisgegeben. Im dritten Abschnitt von Marlows Reise schließlich, der Flußfahrt zu Kurtz, werden die Todesbilder bestimmend. Erschüttert erlebt Marlow den Tod seines Steuermanns, erblickt die Schädel, mit denen Kurtz seine Station geschmückt hat, wird Zeuge von Kurtz' letzten Stunden und erliegt beinahe selbst einer tropischen Erkrankung.

Sowohl für Siddhartha als auch für Marlow folgen auf diese Erfahrungen, die sie reifen lassen, Jahre des Umherwanderns. Ausdrücklich sagt der Rahmenerzähler von Marlow, »He was a seaman, but he was a wanderer too« (S. 8). Während jedoch für seine Zuhörer der nächtliche Aufenthalt auf der Themse nur durch die Gezeiten erzwungen ist, hat Marlow den Abschluß seiner Entwicklung nun erreicht. Die Nacht auf der »Nellie«, die er, an den Mastbaum gelehnt, meditierend und erzählend verbringt, wird für ihn zur Nacht der Erkenntnis. In seinem Ringen um Worte, in der auch physischen Anstrengung, die das Erzählen für ihn bedeutet, begreift er das Prinzip des Bösen und kämpft wie Siddhartha mit ihm: »If anybody had ever struggled with a soul, I am the man« (S. 143). Aber im Gegensatz zu Siddhartha bleibt er »a Buddha [. . .] without a lotus flower«, dem Symbol der entstehenden Erde. Marlow, der seine Erkenntnis nicht mitteilen kann, kann auch keine Erneuerung bewirken.

Inhalt

Fremdsprachentexte

IN RECLAMS UNIVERSAL-BIBLIOTHEK

Philipp Reclam jun. Stuttgart

Englische Romane

IN RECLAMS UNIVERSAL-BIBLIOTHEK

Philipp Reclam jun. Stuttgart